DOMINIC NOLAN

AFTER
DARK

HEADLINE

First published in 2020 by
HEADLINE PUBLISHING GROUP

1

Cataloguing in Publication Data is available from the British Library

Hardback ISBN 978 1 4722 5470 2
Trade paperback ISBN 978 1 4722 5469 6

Typeset in 11/15.25 pt Adobe Garamond Pro by Jouve (UK), Milton Keynes

Printed and bound in Great Britain by Clays Ltd, Elcograf S.p.A.

HEADLINE PUBLISHING GROUP
An Hachette UK Company
Carmelite House
50 Victoria Embankment
London EC4Y 0DZ

www.headline.co.uk
www.hachette.co.uk

For Keir

my big little brother

Truth, in the end, can never be spoken aloud,
For the future is always unpredictable.
But so is the past

Robert Penn Warren

PROLOGUE

Five years ago

The hunters walked with their pieces broken open over the crooks of their arms. Rough shooters, they ambled through the private woodland, dogs out ahead of them. Leaving behind a small clearing where a spring rose up, they followed the narrow brook it fed, cleaving gently down a jawbone hollow and guttering into a chain of duck ponds where occasionally there was good fishing. The dogs bounded away, disappearing into the bushy growth around the ponds, their barks echoing across the water.

Hanley Moss wore an olive paddock jacket and a dark fedora. A pipe was clamped between his teeth and its stale odour carried on the air. He walked with a slight hitch from a worsening arthritic hip that he was ignoring until he got used to the idea of being cut on. His companion, Teddy Blackborne, the last of an old name, sported a beige gilet with a tweed cap. When they had dressed that morning, neither had known it would be the final time they would select their wardrobe.

The woods were mostly oaks and ancient hornbeams, grey and twisted as if formed from wax drippings. Some showed signs of former pollarding, thick upper limbs obscuring the sun. Leaning against one such tree, Moss studied his pipe. He made a clicking sound with his mouth and searched his pockets for his tobacco pouch. Closing the break in his gun, he stood it against the tree and tapped the pipe out in his palm, peering at the burnt makings as if through some botanomancy he might read augurs, before dropping them to the ground. Looking up, he watched Teddy stride away after the dogs.

When he began carefully packing the bowl of his pipe once more, Boone stepped away from the tree where she'd been hiding. Moving easily upon him from behind, she snatched up his shotgun and retreated a few yards from him. She had a pistol of her own, a Browning Hi-Power holstered on her hip, but didn't think she'd need it.

'This is private property,' Moss said, unable to conceive of the temerity. 'Hand me back that gun.'

Boone must have been an odd sight. The hood of her oversized cagoule was drawn up, black running tights below that and trainers with the soles of a larger pair fixed underneath them. Moss frowned. She gave him a moment, seeing the realisation dawn across his face. Unhurried, she broke open his gun and loaded a single cartridge from her own pocket, a bespoke six-pellet LG shot she had made for the occasion. It would guarantee the desired outcome, and later, when the police came to the hunting lodge near the main house, they would find capping and roll turnover tools and all the ingredients for the home-made ammunition, tying a neat bow around the tragic event.

'Sit,' she said, indicating with the barrel of the gun to a spot between the thighs of the tree roots.

Moss looked down but didn't move.

'It's all the same to me if you die standing or sitting.'

Confused, he lowered himself down against the tree. Boone pulled her hood tight around her face and sat on her haunches before him. Dilated capillaries mapped his cheeks, the whites of his eyes feathered with red veins. He was still clutching his pipe, so she held her hand out and he gave it to her. Remarkable how compliant people could be even in the most perilous of circumstances, perhaps hoping cooperation would afford them just a little more time.

'You remember me,' she said, not a question.

He nodded.

'Good. Open your mouth.'

He did as he was told and she slid the barrel of the shotgun between his teeth, angling it up slightly. Just as he tried to say, 'Wait,' around the metal, she pulled the trigger.

Birds exploded from the trees.

The top of his head emptied out, leaving a shroud of skin resembling a face mask pulled loosely over shattered bones. His great flapping ears hung there still.

Teddy was calling and the dogs barked excitedly.

'Hanley? Hanley? Did you take a shot?'

Boone hid behind the thick hornbeam with Moss's shotgun. As she waited, she sprayed WD-40 inside the barrels from a small can in her pocket and produced a brush fitted with a bore guide she'd made from an emptied shell. Giving both barrels a good brushing to remove any blood, she also wiped down the outside with a cloth. As she loaded another home-made shot into the unused barrel, she heard footsteps approaching.

'Hanley, what *are* you doing? Hanley . . .'

The footsteps slowed. Boone could feel Teddy staring at her friend. Swinging round the tree, she levelled the shotgun at the woman. Teddy Blackborne recognised her immediately, and for a fraction of a second her face slipped before she regained that haughty composure.

It had been almost a year since Teddy had seen her, but for Boone the older woman had been a familiar sight. First had come the healing, and then the intelligence. Knowing your quarry, learning the routines they slipped into, the follies that made them vulnerable. Boone had come to know all about Teddy Blackborne.

'What have you done?' Teddy said. 'What is this about?'

What was it about? Boone barely knew where to begin – even the beginning wasn't the beginning. Two years ago, waking up hurt and confused in a strange room, her memory obliterated, her life robbed from her. Battling to get out of the flat, away from the men who had held her for four days, barely escaping with her life. Weeks in the hospital healed her body, but months in the clinic did nothing for the amnesia. Nothing to allow her to remember her friends and family, her time as a detective sergeant with Kent Police.

But this went back further than that day.

It went back years.

This was about Jack, a husband she didn't remember falling for, or marrying, or living with. This was about Quin, a son she didn't remember carrying, or birthing, or nurturing.

This was about a girl called Sarah Still, born of sexual abuse and herself subjected to horrors for years before her eventual murder, body wrapped in a sheet and buried beneath an abandoned fruit farm. A girl who, in her past life, Detective Sergeant Abigail Boone had been looking for when she was herself abducted.

This was about uncovering the sexual predations of late industrialist Sir Alex Blackborne, father both to Sarah and to Sarah's child, taken from her at birth and never found.

This was about former MP and peer of the realm Hanley Moss, who used his position for decades to hide his and Blackborne's abuse of countless children, many of whom never made it out alive.

This was about Blackborne's widow, Lady Theodora, the real power behind the family company, complicit in covering for her husband and Moss.

This was about Teddy murdering her own son when he learned the truth, staging it as a hunting accident, and escaping justice for that and all her past crimes.

And this was about Roo. Trafficked into a life of misery, escaping from the flat that day with Boone, only to be lost again to the same men who had tried to kill them before.

Most of all, this was about Roo.

Boone would have done anything to swap places with her, would have gleefully given her own life in exchange so the world could hear Roo's voice once more. She had stoked within Boone feelings she couldn't remember having, feelings she thought had been lost for ever with her memories.

'This is about the dead whore, isn't it?' Teddy said.

She must have caught a flicker of something in Boone's face, because she smiled. Boone took a step closer, shotgun aimed at Teddy's chest. The dogs gambolled about them, not realising the kind of hunt it had become.

'Oh look at yourself,' Teddy said. 'Here in the woods with a gun, and still no real idea how you got here. Would you like me to tell you? Would you like me to tell you what I told you two years ago when you first came here? Before your accident? When I told you—'

Boone fired, nearly cutting Teddy in half.

She was thrown back in a heap, making low moaning sounds, barely audible. The shot hit in a tight cluster just under her chest, riding up her gilet with the impact. Boone leaned over to examine Teddy's gun and, satisfied it was unloaded, left it where it had fallen. Kneeling beside the woman, she slipped a handful of the shells she'd made into the pocket of the shredded and bloodied gilet.

Returning her attention to Moss, she took a dozen or so cartridges and carefully put them in his jacket, trying not to disturb it too much. His pipe, which had been safe from spatter in Boone's pocket, she also slid in there. Briefly inserting the ends of the barrels into what remained of Moss's mouth, she let the shotgun fall into his dead lap.

Behind her, the hounds moiled around their mistress's lifeless body, already a feast for flies. A rabbit hung slack between the jaws of one. Not finding Teddy accommodating to their ministrations, they turned instead to their prey, the bunny torn apart amid the in-fighting.

When they were done, one of them approached the old man, nosing at his boots and hand, licking his ruined head. Another returned to his mistress's corpse. It started to rain. Walking through the mulched leaves to the treeline above, Boone debouched onto a quiet lane to the sound of the dogs lapping at gunshot wounds.

PART ONE

IN THE FUTURE
PERFECT

I

Present day

This was home.

A carelessly flung corner of land on an island clinging to the skirts of Europe, charmed by ocean currents that favoured the planting of vineyards at latitudes where other nations watched for polar bears. At various times an occupied territory inhabited by grubby and roadless pagans, and a seat of great empire holding Christian sway over the farthest reaches of heathenry.

Barb's feet were cold inside her wellies. She had the wrong socks on again.

'So where exactly were you when you saw her?'

'Like I said, Constable, up there.' The man pointed. 'On the ridge, just the other side of the fence.'

Three times already she'd explained she was a detective inspector, but what did it really matter? The lane was cut low into the land between shallow ditches, little more than damp ruts really. Banks rose on either side to the surrounding fields, so the tops of the fences bordering them were above head height if you were standing in the road, as they were.

'She was down there,' he said, pointing to the ditch on the other side of the road, a nearly grassed-over depression. 'She was lying there curled up in a ball.'

His name was Cameron, and though he didn't sound as if he'd spent a day of his life in Scotland, the first thing he'd worked into conversation was that he owned a lochside cabin in the Trossachs ('I was out walking, you see. I enjoy walking. Take a break every summer to my place on the shore of . . .').

'And you didn't see which direction she came from?' Barb asked.

He shrugged.

'So a barely clothed child turns up on the side of a country lane, miles from anywhere, and you didn't see anything until you tripped over her?'

'It was more like the foetal position,' he said, upon reflection.

'Right.'

'Of course, she was on the other side of the road, you understand, Constable.'

'And?'

'I walk inside the fences so I can look out over the fields and not see roads. Not see anything man-made.'

'There's a barn right there,' Barb said, pointing a few fields over. 'And I can see a water tower in the distance.'

'They're a long way off.'

She pinched the bridge of her nose.

'I put my coat over her, see. She flinched when I touched her shoulder, but she let me do that, with the coat. Didn't feel right, just leaving her there like that. You know?'

'Boss.'

Detective Constable Barry Tayleforth walked over. The once rising star of Kent Police, his career progression had come to a shuddering halt following a formal reprimand for engaging in a reckless pursuit that conjoined his unmarked vehicle with a cherry tree. Blown radiator blessing the scene like an aspergillum, pink blossoms mottling the roof and crumpled bonnet.

'Will I be here long, sir?' Cameron asked Barry.

'Yes, will Mr Cameron be here long, sir?' said Barb, smiling sweetly.

Barry waited.

'If you could excuse us for a moment, Mr Cameron,' Barb said, leading Barry aside. 'I'm not going through this again with dickbeans over here. Sir, he calls you. Fucking sir.'

'Search hasn't found much,' Barry said. 'There hasn't been any rain for a couple of weeks, so there are no footprints.'

'Mean to tell me you can't trace her movements by way of broken twig and upturned leaf?'

Barry was the sort who always carried on like witty repartee wasn't happening.

'Uniforms have conducted a line search of the immediate fields and come up with nothing,' he said. 'We're pushing it out further.'

'She was only wearing a slip. Barefoot. Cuts and scrapes. Must have left some trace. I mean, how far had she come? There's not much out here.'

'I'll get a few bodies and go back over the perimeter of the fields. They're hedged, but it's cut away in a few places. If she came across the fields, she could only have come through those gaps. We'll take a closer look. I've sent a car off in either direction to check the properties they come to. If she walked the road, there are only so many places she could have started.'

'This Cameron man is useless. Little girl, you'd think she magically sprouted out of the ground the way he tells it.' She scanned the scene for the other coppers. 'Who's got the log going?'

'Mackintosh.'

A water carrier, but he always got the paperwork right and didn't need telling the basics. Barry followed her thoughts.

'He can handle the searches too. I'll get uniforms to take Cameron back to the Shed. Tell him we need a formal statement, best to give it when fresh in the mind. Nice cup of tea, bit of time to settle. He might remember more.'

'Okay, yeah. Good. Thanks, Barry.'

She gripped the lapel of his jacket between finger and thumb momentarily before releasing it. The spectacular grounding of his career was going to be the making of him as a copper, pruning the political ambition and turning him back to the job for the foreseeable. She thought of a few others in desperate need of a car crash.

Crossing the ditch near where the girl had been discovered, she scrambled up the bank to the edge of the rapeseed field above. A patchwork quilt of yellows and greens stretched out for miles around, seamed with hedges and the odd copse.

Behind her, she heard Cameron putting up futile resistance to going to the nick, Barry easing him into the back of his car and pushing the door shut. Heard his boots trotting back toward her. He joined her on higher ground and handed her a pair of binoculars.

'Just happened to have them with you?'

'In the boot.'

'Do I want to know why?'

'You never know.'

Barb looked out over the fields. 'Any ideas where she might have come from?'

He pointed to a short horizon. 'Nearest village is over a mile if you have wings, longer by any reasonable route you might walk. Few houses a way off. What looks like an old farm.'

'Checking them?'

He nodded. 'Knocked on the houses. They saw nothing. The farm looks like it's been abandoned for years. We're trying to trace the owner now. Couple of uniforms standing by.'

'Tell them to have a butcher's round the outside,' Barb said. 'Discreet, mind. Windows and doors only. Don't want the owners turning out to be real citizens and getting all upset.'

'I reckon she must have been dropped off.'

'Her feet were in a bit of a state.'

'A lot of her was, but it wasn't any walk that did it.'

'Yeah.'

'You going back to talk to Cameron?' he said.

Barb shook her head. 'Anyone can deal with him. Make sure everyone knows what's what with the search, checking the surrounding properties, so forth. Then you're with me. We'll go see the girl.'

He bounded down the slope, easing to a more practised walk on the flat of the road. Barb ran the glasses over the land again, looking at nothing in particular. Somewhere church bells pealed, and the time was the same as it always was.

This was the hour the dog returned to its vomit.

This was the end of the world.

2

A looming Victorian pile, the hospital in Margate had grown several shinier new wings connected by gleaming glass and chrome walkways. Barry pulled Barb's Audi into the car park and instinctively went to reach for the log to put in the windscreen.

'Shit,' he said.

Barb shook her head. 'Every time.'

He spread his hands out, the lack of a police book triggering some existential parking dilemma.

'I'll get a ticket,' she said.

She hated driving. The hum of the engine lulled her into something approximating thoughtfulness, wherein she only wanted to watch the scenery glide by rather than look out for traffic and head-on collisions and likely death. She liked keeping Barry close at hand for driving duties.

She also hated faffing about for one of the diminishing stock of squad cars, so had taken on the crushing paperwork required to clear her own vehicle for force use. What that really meant was her own seat covers, her own bags of fruit pastilles and her own CDs. She'd put on Julianna Barwick for the drive. Wasn't even sure how she felt about it, music not being something she had ever had a particularly strong reaction to, but she thought it wouldn't be mocked or criticised by younger ears, so that would do.

Returning with a two-hour ticket, she slid it down inside the windscreen.

'Only three quid,' she said cheerfully. 'All goes to the hospital.'

Barry gave her the same look he might an old bag lady showing her arse in the street.

'Come on,' Barb said.

The children's ward was pretty much the most awful place, Barb was certain, and rubber-footed plods filling the corridors weren't going to improve anyone's day. She arranged for a PC outside both entrances to the ward and a couple more down in the cafeteria to relieve them later.

She recognised the woman from child social services sitting on a modern-looking leather sofa outside an observation room. Two sofas were angled in the corner, a low coffee table with magazines between them.

'Hey, Beth.'

Beth Chapel noticed Barb and Barry and stood.

'Inspector.'

'You know DC Tayleforth?'

Beth nodded to Barry.

'You're taking the case?' she said.

'Until we know what it is,' Barb said.

'There's an officer from the child sexual exploitation team here.'

Barb nodded. 'We're happy to be hands-off with the girl. You guys and CSE know the best way of handling that. But since we don't have suspects, or even a crime scene yet, Serious Crime is going to set up an incident room.'

The three of them looked through the blinds into the private room. The girl was sedated, tubes running to her arms and nostrils. Malnourished, she was that tiny Barb felt she'd fit in her hand.

'Christ,' Barry said.

We don't have punishment enough for this, Barb thought. She turned to Beth. 'Has she said anything? Given her name?'

'We haven't got anything coherent out of her.'

'What have the doctors said?'

Beth took a deep breath. 'Well, there was a bit of a fuss.'

They took seats, Barb and Barry on one sofa, Beth on the other. An expensive leather jacket was draped over the back beside her.

'Yours?' Barb asked.

'No. That's what I was saying, there's someone here from CSE. I've worked with her before. She's great, but—'

She fell silent as footsteps clacked down the hall. A woman approached with a steaming machine coffee. She moved with purposeful elegance, not gliding but prowling, like a big cat. Placing the cup on the table, she sat next to Beth.

'Smells something like coffee, so I'm going to leave it there and inhale the fumes, but don't let it fool you.'

Barb and Barry glanced at one another. She was tall and lithe, this woman, in dark tailored trousers and a ribbed cream turtleneck. Perfectly white hair cropped short pixie style with wispy bangs on one side, looking soft as down even though it was spiky on top. In tandem with her glacially blue eyes, it left a striking impression. Barb would have guessed early forties, but from her hands she was probably past fifty.

A passing nurse recognised the woman.

'Doctor,' she said.

The woman smiled before turning back to Barb.

'DC Storm Mathijsen,' she said, pronouncing it like Mike Tyson.

'DI Bowen,' Barb said, taking Storm's hand. 'This is DC Tayleforth.'

'Barry,' said Barry, shaking.

'Bowen?' Storm said. 'Barbara Bowen?'

'I—' Barb hesitated, foolishly feeling the impulse to deny who she was. 'Yes?'

Storm nodded, half a smile.

'I won't ask who you've been talking to,' Barb said.

'I've heard about you only in glowing terms. And from someone who generally doesn't have a good word for anybody.'

'And you're a doctor?' Barb said, interrogation her best tool to rebalance things. 'I thought you were CSE?'

'I'm both. I was a clinical psychologist before I joined the police.'

'Detective constable doesn't seem like an upgrade from there.'

'Depends what you want to do.'

'Storm's a hell of a name.'

'My mother read English at Somerville and was quite mad.'

Barb nodded, as if that cleared everything up. 'I was just telling Beth, Serious Crime is setting up an incident room. I don't want to step on any CSE toes, though.'

'We're happy with that,' Storm said. 'We don't even know what we're dealing with yet.'

'Have you spoken to the girl?'

'She was conscious when she came in but didn't respond to verbal communication. She's severely malnourished and was dehydrated. Do you have a name for her?'

'No. She was found on a roadside out in the middle of nowhere. Didn't speak to anyone at the scene. We haven't been able to match her to any missing children reports, but we weren't sure how old she was, so it's difficult.'

'She weighs less than fifty pounds,' Storm said. 'From her size, you might think she was seven or eight. But accounting for the fact that she's unhealthily underweight, I think ten or eleven might be more accurate.'

'Good God,' Barb said, standing to look at the girl.

'She hasn't uttered a word. A few grunts and some screaming, but nothing comprehensible.'

Barb shook her head. 'Have you ever seen anything like this?'

'Once,' Storm said, not elaborating.

'Her injuries?' Barry said.

'Almost too many to count, and many of them are historic. The fresh cuts and scrapes look like they're from being outside within the last twenty-four or thirty-six hours, but there is bruising on top of bruising. There's also evidence of broken bones, some of which didn't set properly.'

'Sexual abuse?' Barb said.

'Almost certainly. She hasn't been fully examined yet. A nurse tried, but she became wild, began attacking herself.'

'They sedated her then?' Barb said.

'Yes. But there was something else before that.'

'Beth said there was a fuss?'

Storm nodded. 'Dr John entered the room. He's a consultant paediatrician. He's around here somewhere. When she saw him, her behaviour changed radically. He was the first male who saw her in here. She pulled up her gown and began . . . well . . . it was almost Pavlovian.'

'Christ,' said Barb.

'What's the score now, in terms of protecting her?' said Barry.

'We've applied for a court order,' Beth said. 'Even if we find a legal guardian, state she's in she would be removed into care. She'll be kept here for the time being. She needs to be fully assessed, fed and hydrated properly.'

'DNA?' Barb said. 'How do we deal with consent?'

'Depends on what the court says, but I imagine we'll be able to take samples later today,' said Beth.

'Here he is,' Storm said, standing.

Tall, dark-skinned, with a mane of treacle-black hair streaked with silver, Dr John wore a corduroy sport coat and carried a well-garnished burger in one hand.

'Ravi,' Storm said. They kissed on both cheeks. 'Dr Ravi John, this is Detective Inspector Bowen and Detective Constable Tayleforth.'

'Excuse the beef,' Ravi said. 'I was here on call all night, and then they brought the girl in. First chance I've had to stave off the fainting. Do we know anything more about her?'

'Nothing,' said Barb. 'Like she fell out of the sky.'

'More likely she climbed out of a hole,' he said.

'How's that?'

'This is, without doubt, the worst case of abuse I've ever seen. Aside from the obvious malnourishment, she has other, serious health problems. Her joints are in bad condition, like she's never used them, and her ribcage is undersized. She doesn't seem capable of focusing on anything more than a metre away. It's like she's been kept in a dark, confined space for a very long time. Years, I would say.'

'Storm said she hasn't spoken,' Barb said.

'No, and her reactions to both verbal and non-verbal stimuli were not promising. Could be shock, some form of dissociation. Hard to tell until she comes round again.'

He turned to Storm. 'I'm glad you're here. We have to be very careful how we handle her. She is incredibly damaged.' He smiled at Barb. 'Storm and I used to work together. I have a clinic near Canterbury for traumatised children and adolescents. Nobody's better. Then she ran off to solve crimes in London.'

'Purely so I have some idea of timescale, when do you suppose we might be able to speak with her?' Barb said.

Ravi shook his head. 'Even if I thought she would be capable of having such a conversation, my sole concern right now is her well-being. We'll take it day by day, hour by hour even, but I cannot allow anything to upset her. I understand that this isn't the result of an accident. Someone has done this to her, and that someone needs to be held to account. But immediately, right now, trying to acclimatise her to new surroundings is the priority.'

He excused himself to spend some alone time with his burger, and Barb turned back to the observation window. The girl hadn't stirred.

'She was incredibly clean,' Storm said.

'Clean?' said Barb, puzzled.

'For someone who appears to have been kept in confined quarters, other than the dirt on her feet and hands from being outside, she was very clean. Freshly bathed, even. Her hair was soft and shiny. I mention it only because I thought it so incongruent to her general condition.'

'Doesn't feel right, not having a name for her,' Beth said.

'I'll try to speak with her,' Storm said. 'When she comes round. I won't question her, but I'll try to make a connection, get her talking.'

'You're staying here?' Barb said.

Storm nodded. 'I'll discuss it with Ravi, but I'd like to be available to her whenever she wakes up. Someone should be here around the clock anyway.'

'Okay, good,' said Barb. 'You're based out of HQ in Maidstone?'

Storm nodded.

Barb fetched a card out of her jacket pocket and handed it to her. 'We're in the Shed, so we're neighbours anyway, but anything happens, whenever it happens, you can call me on this mobile.'

Storm studied the card, flashed that half-smile again.

'All right, Detective Inspector Barbara Bowen.'

'What do you make of Storm?' Barb said, stretched out with her seat pushed right back as Barry drove them to Maidstone.

'I've heard about her.'

'Ooh, gossip. Spill.'

'She joined the Met's detective recruitment drive. No time on the streets. Transferred to Kent after a couple of years.'

'Okay, I buy that. Previous experience as a psychologist gives her a sought-after skill set.'

Barry said nothing.

'Don't tell me; she can't be a real copper,' Barb said.

'It's not that. I mean, there will be loads that'll say that. I don't see how it can be bad getting people with her qualifications into the force, though.'

'We select detectives from a small and brackish pool. What is it then?'

'Well, she was a clinical psychologist. That must have taken years. You don't do that unless you're completely into it. And I bet she was well compensated. Now she's on a DC's salary and putting up with all the shit that comes with it?'

'Doesn't seem the type would give a single baked fuck what anyone said about her.'

'No shit. What about that hair?'

'You'd give at least two toes to have hair like that, Barry.'

'In fact, I would.'

Serious Crime was housed in a new-build tucked in behind headquarters in Maidstone on what had been a bowling green. As was fitting for its award-winning ecologically friendly design and vaguely Scandinavian all-wood exterior, it was known by all as the Shed.

The main work space, the bullpen, was open plan, with Barb's small office to one side. Mackintosh was perched on the edge of his desk, flipping through a file, waiting for them with a practised nonchalance.

'Anything from our Mr Cameron?' Barb said.

'He was useless in terms of information about the girl. Out for a walk, there she was. Couldn't give me any more than that.'

'Believe him?' Barry said.

Mackintosh nodded. 'I was minded to anyway, and then I noticed he has one of those fitness bands on his wrist. He let us download the data, and it shows his whereabouts for the last week.'

'Or the band's whereabouts,' Barb said.

'Aye, but it matches what he told us,' Mackintosh said. 'And he has a wife who says he was home all night and confirmed what time he went out for a walk this morning. If he was messing around with that girl, I dunno when he's supposed to have been doing it.'

'You let him go?' Barb said.

'Thought I'd wait for the nod from you.'

Barb nodded.

'I'll find someone to drop him home,' Mackintosh said.

'Doesn't feel like our man,' Barb said, when he'd gone.

Barry shrugged. 'Sometimes you can't tell. Keep an eye?'

'Oh yes. Beady little ones.'

3

It was dark when Barb got in. She lived a ten-minute drive from the Shed in a small village east of town. She'd bought the flat when she made sergeant, her father helping out with a substantial deposit. It was a two-bed set out over two floors in what had been a coal merchant's shop. An entrance hall led to a large living space with a kitchen just off, one bedroom downstairs and the master up. Light and airy, with high ceilings, she loved it. She usually did anyway.

Barb saw living alone as a perk. Eat what you like, when you like. Don't have to share the TV, or get dressed at the weekend, or clean up if you don't feel like it (but if you do, things are still tidy the next day). Some days, though, the place seemed to echo with loneliness.

She flicked the lights on and drew the curtains, using a rod to pull the blinds on the angled skylights. Turning the news on, she found a report recorded earlier in the day, a correspondent standing on the roadside behind the police cordon, a few hundred yards from where the girl was found.

'—side of this quiet lane in the Kent countryside. Police haven't named the girl, or even confirmed if they have identified her at this stage. What we do know—'

She changed the channel, finding another piece on the girl, this time live from a reporter outside the hospital.

'Christ,' she said, switching the television off. Fiddling with her phone, she sent a message.

You awake?

Took it with her upstairs to the master bedroom, putting it on the bedside cabinet as she undressed. The vibration when the reply arrived dragged the handset close to the edge.

Yep. You okay?

She ran through a couple of replies, trying for funny before deciding on plain old honest.

Come over?

He was online and read it immediately.

20 mins.

Cool.

She showered and washed her hair, then found clean pyjamas. Baggy elasticated bottoms and a long-sleeved top. He was exactly twenty minutes, and she opened the door before he knocked.

'Hey,' Barry said.

'Hey.'

She led him down the hall to the living room and hovered about the entrance to the kitchen as if about to prepare something. Without saying anything, he wrapped his arms round her and she nuzzled into his shoulder.

'Shit day,' he said.

'Shit day.'

'How were the brass?'

Barb had endured a late briefing of the behatted ranks after Barry left the office.

'No matches to missing persons, and they were rightly sceptical about a child apparently materialising out of nowhere. Court granted the care order, though, so I think there will be samples ready for the morning.'

'I'll pick them up first thing and run them back to be rapid-tested.'

'What do you reckon the chances are?'

'State she was in, I doubt the parents are law-abiding subjects of the realm. Familial match would not be a surprise.'

'You see the news?'

'We knew that was going to be a circus, especially with how little information was in our statement.'

She peered up from beneath his arm. 'You want wine or anything?'

'Nope. I want you to sleep, because tomorrow will be longer than today, and probably even shitter once we get a full report from the doctors.'

'Ugh.'

Barb trudged upstairs as Barry turned the lights out. She sat on the bed waiting for him to undress, not wanting to get under the cool covers without him.

'Cameron?' she said.

'Uniforms dropped him home. He owns the house. Another car is sitting outside.'

'Discreetly.'

'Discreetly. Bowman and Hiller wanted the overtime.'

'Good.'

'Five hours,' Barry said, setting the alarm on his phone.

'Yippee.'

Tucked up with her head on his chest, Barb felt tiny and protected. It was exactly that feeling that had worried her about getting involved in the first place – she was the boss when they were at large. The dynamic had never felt weird, though. He had been the high-flyer, expected to be fast-tracked to inspector, but her career had leapt ahead of his, largely on the back of a few big cases, one in particular. The uncovering of a network of cannabis grow-houses and the arrest of the ringleaders of the Vietnamese gang that operated them. Nothing had happened between them until after that, and Barry had been completely different to how she'd imagined. They'd never really dated, but it had never felt casual either. From the off they'd been close and comfortable, and the idea now of being with someone else was unthinkable.

The Vietnamese case had been big news at the time: drugs, people-trafficking and mobile phone footage of Barb tackling one of them when he tried to flee the scene on foot. It had earned her a lot of currency in the force. It had been more fortune than anything, though. An anonymous tip had handed her a gold mine, but she'd closed it out effectively and sent down the major players on long tariffs. They'd never identified any well-organised rivals to the operation, and Barb had always suspected someone on the inside sold them out.

This new case, though, this girl, the television already had it and it would be splashed over the morning's front pages, exploding it nationally. She needed movement, anything to show progress. Currency depreciated quickly with the brass.

4

The day waved green as the trees and grass yielded to the morning breeze. It was before eight and Barb was in her wellies again, standing in a field in front of what used to be a dairy farm. A more modern cottage, 1960s probably, stood near it. Both were empty.

'It's apparently owned by a Constance Bobb,' Mackintosh said, reading off his phone.

'Constance Bobb. Good old Connie Bobb.'

'You know her?'

'No.'

'Nor does anyone else. Checked with the neighbours, such as they are, and nobody had heard of her or knew anything about what goes on here. One bloke reckoned there might have been some building carried out about four or five years ago. He remembered a digger being brought in. But he also said that might have been a different place as he, quote, ain't one to be keeping records of other folks' affairs.'

'No other trace of her?'

'Checking tax and social, but nothing yet.'

'Probably a ghost.'

Barb surveyed the plot of land. She knew nothing about acres or hectares or any of that stuff, but reckoned it to be about three football pitches' worth. Could have been five or six, though. From what she could make out through the windows of the cottage, the place hadn't been lived in for a while. The other building, the one locals referred to as the dairy, was harder to peek into. The windows were higher and covered in filth, some papered over from the inside. It was a sprawling structure, fifty yards at its widest, including an old barn, and at least half that deep. The cottage was much smaller, four rooms from what they could tell.

Crime took the colour grey in her mind. The walls and skies of Gillingham and Swale and Ramsgate and Dartford. Stabbings, pub fights, rapes, murders. Its smells were synthetic, man-made. The scent of the free land seemed to Barb to come in cycles with the sun and the moon, conducting some kind of order. Yet for all that, at the last house she'd called on in the middle of nowhere she had found her friend Boone lying broken and mutilated, and went on to excavate the remains of eight bodies. Eight who had reached personhood, anyway. Countless others that hadn't amid the waste of a ghastly backroom surgery.

Land was never what it appeared.

Thick woods hid the buildings from the lane a couple of hundred yards away. The unmarked entrance sported a rotting wooden gate, and the drive curved through the trees so nobody could look down it. A small team of SOCOs were examining the mouth, which they were treating as public highway, for tyre marks, but it seemed to be a popular spot to pull over and let cars pass on the narrow lane.

On two other sides, dense rows of junipers provided cover, with an unbroken hedge on the fourth. It was a woodland arena, almost completely obscured from prying eyes. Ideal place for funny business. Barb felt that familiar, gathering sense of purpose that grew within her when a case started to gain its own momentum. This place, Barry off fetching samples taken from the girl at the hospital; they were on the brink of something, she knew it.

'They're not finding anything at the gate,' Mackintosh said. 'You want me to draw up a Section 8, apply for a warrant?'

'Be very specific,' Barb said. 'We're not going to get permission for a fishing expedition. Not practicable to communicate with any person entitled to grant entry, so forth. Make it clear we're only looking for evidence of the girl's presence, given there's fuck all else around here.'

Mackintosh was furious with the taking of notes.

'Keep on trying to track down this Constance Bobb,' Barb said, 'and leave a couple of uniforms here. I don't want anyone coming in without us knowing about it. I've spoken to the farmer who owns the fields to the east and south, and he's happy for us to walk them, so tell the uniforms to keep a constant eye out round the back too. Not just on the gate.'

Mackintosh nodded. His phone rang and he stepped away to answer it.

'Your phone, boss?'

Barb fished it out of her pocket. 'Left it on silent.' Three missed calls from Barry. 'That himself now?'

Mackintosh nodded, at the same time listening to his phone.

'Okay, yeah. Hold on.' Then, to Barb, 'Boss, we staying here or you want to go to the hospital? Barry wants to meet up.'

Barb looked about. 'You get on the warrant,' she said. 'We get it, you look after the breach and the search. Keep it all in hand. I don't want a case going to shit because we overstepped. Tell Barry to head for the hospital and I'll meet him there.'

Storm Mathijsen was wearing the same clothes as the day before, and from the way her jacket was folded up like a pillow on one of the sofas outside the girl's room, Barb supposed that was where she'd slept. Still looked better than Barb would after the greatest night's kip of her life. It was times like this that she really needed another woman on her team, someone to talk to about other people behind their backs.

'DI Bowen.'

That half-smile. Did everyone get that, Barb wondered, or was she especially amusing? 'Storm.'

They shook hands.

'And it's Barb,' Barb said.

'Barb it is. No bagman today?'

'Meeting Barry here. Had to drive myself, for heaven's sake.' She looked through the window at the girl in her bed. 'Still asleep.'

'Only just asleep. We had a hectic night.'

'Get anything from her?'

'Learned a lot about her, but not what you would call pertinent details. She's completely non-verbal. Her cognitive skills appear to be those of an infant, at best. It was impossible to make even basic instructions clear to her.'

'Retarded?' Barb said, immediately regretting the word. 'Or whatever.'

'No, I don't think so. The problems with her faculties are symptoms, not a cause. I believe she has lived a life utterly without stimuli. If I had to make an educated guess, I'd say she's been kept in a confined space since birth by someone whose only interactions with her constituted the vilest abuse and occasional feeding. For all intents and purposes, she's feral.'

'She's been kept in isolation for her whole life? How is that even possible?'

'I don't know. The effort and discipline it would take to do that to someone is terrifying.'

'And it's not just that she can't talk – she can't understand either?'

Storm shook her head. 'Look, it's very early. We don't know what she has experienced exactly, and perhaps this could be a post-traumatic reaction.'

'But you think otherwise.'

'From what I've seen, I don't think she has ever acquired language.'

'Will she learn? Is that possible at her age?'

'I really don't know. I've seen children who have suffered terrible things, but never anything quite like this. The world as we know it, in terms of our daily experiences and social activities, is heavily reliant on the language habits of our group. The way we learn about things, the way we comprehend or tell others what we know, these things are to a large extent predisposed by our common tongue. It isn't as simple as there being a monolithic, objective world that people interact with in different languages. Those languages make their own worlds. And she has no language. No method of forming ideas. I can't even begin to imagine what world she lives in.'

'She could be like this for ever then.'

'This is the beginning. It's going to be a long process. It could be we make very little progress, or it could be she picks things up quickly. At this point I wouldn't like to hazard a guess.'

'But in terms of getting information from her about who did this . . .'

Storm pursed her lips. 'Certainly not in the short term. And even if she does develop communication skills, who's to say what she will be able to tell us about her past, the things that happened to her before she had such skills? It could be like us trying to recall what happened when we were nine months old.'

'And physically – has she been fully examined now?'

'The good news is there's no identifiable brain damage. The malnutrition and dehydration are easily treatable. Her bones and joints, we just don't know. Her muscles will build up with use, coupled with a proper diet. But her bones are very weak and misshapen or undersized in places. She may have long-term or permanent difficulties with mobility.'

'What about other stuff?'

'There is extensive physical evidence of historical abuse. Sexual.'

'Forensics? You said yesterday she was surprisingly clean.'

'Yes. There were no usable biological samples.'

'Someone fastidious about removing trace evidence?'

'Could be. Her hair was shampooed and conditioned, though. Combed.'

'Someone keeping her pretty?'

Storm raised her brows.

Barb moved closer to the glass, watching the sleeping child. 'She's holding something.'

Storm smiled. 'My sock.'

Barb frowned.

'I had fresh socks in my bag, anticipating possibly staying overnight. When I wasn't getting very far with her, I decided to use one as a puppet. It was the only reaction I got. Wouldn't say it was a smile, but it was something. She took it from me. It isn't much, but a sense of possession is better than nothing, so I left it with her. Or it would be more accurate to say she hasn't let go of it since and threw a tantrum when a nurse tried to take it when changing her.'

'There was a toy at the scene. She was found with a stuffed dog or something. It's with Forensics.'

'That's interesting. Given to her as a distraction probably, but it suggests she has previously had some notion of ownership, even on an instinctual level.'

'When the guys and gals at the lab are done with it, I can get it back for her.'

Storm considered this. 'It might give some indication of her memory and recall. Might also remind her of what happened when she had it, which mightn't be helpful. We can ask Ravi what he thinks, see how it goes. We have to be careful with her.'

'You said tantrum?'

'She lashes out, much as an irritated or scared animal might.'

Barb nodded. 'She had on some kind of nappy when we found her.'

'Yes. We've had to maintain that. Her incontinence is severe, both when awake and asleep.'

'The result of physical trauma, or . . .'

'I don't think so. It's more like she's never been shown how. Never been shown how to do anything, as far as I can see. She can't even chew. We tried small pieces of fruit, but she sat there with it in her mouth and then spat it out. She'll only take soft food, baby food. Given the state she's in, it wouldn't surprise me if that's all she's ever had, and barely enough of it.'

'Jesus,' Barb said. 'What is going to become of her?'

'She'll be here for a few more days at least. Make sure her cuts and bruises are okay. It can be hard to diagnose problems when the patient can't communicate. They've done a few X-rays, but Ravi would like more. She wasn't terribly cooperative, though. After that, we're having discussions with safeguarding and local authorities. If we can't identify her or find a responsible family member or carer, I've spoken to Beth Chapel about the LA placing her at Ravi's clinic. They have a residential wing and can care for her there.'

'And study her.'

'The two aren't mutually exclusive. The more we can learn about her, the more we can help her. I suspect she would progress a lot faster in a properly supervised environment than she would going home with people who don't have the resources at the clinic's disposal. I used to work there, Barb. It's a fantastic place.'

'Not going to be a happy ending, though, is there?'

'It'll be better than how it was, I can promise that.'

'Listen, I've spoken to your DI. We're running the case out of Serious Crime, but I want someone with more experience of cases like this. If you're interested, I'd like to second you for the investigation, put you to work out of the Shed.'

'Definitely.'

'Yeah? Good. I don't know what your workload looks like right now, but speak to your DI and take the rest of the day to smooth things out. I'll see you in the Shed tomorrow morning.'

'I appreciate that, Barb. I'd like to see this one through.' Storm's eyes moved past Barb. 'DC Tayleforth is here.'

Barry was at the entrance to the ward in conversation with the constable on duty there. He had a file with him and carried himself with the demeanour of someone orchestrating crucial affairs.

'He's found something,' Barb said as he walked towards them.

Holding the file out to Barb, he greeted Storm.

Storm smiled. 'He was a verray, parfit, gentil knyght.'

'I don't—?'

'Don't worry about her,' Barb said. 'She's weird and clever and on her way back to HQ.'

'Maybe a shower first,' Storm said, making her excuses and leaving.

'Now, what have you got?' Barb asked Barry.

'We got a DNA hit on the missing persons database.'

'You could have called with that.'

'I could have, but you never would have believed me, and I wanted to see your face.'

'Why wouldn't I believe you?'

He handed Barb the file and she flipped it open, scanning the report. She frowned. She looked up at him.

'This has to be bollocks.'

He shook his head. 'We had two samples. I ran both of them. It's right. There's a full array going to the lab just in case, but think about it. It would be too much of a coincidence to be a mistake.'

'Mary's fanny. You know what this means?'

'Yep. You can go. I'm not.'

'Fucking hell,' Barb said. 'I hate prisons.'

5

Barb drove alone to Sheppey. She made a call to the governor of HMP Brabazon explaining the situation, and arrangements were made for her visit. Giving them a couple of hours to get sorted, she decided to make a stop along the way.

Years since she'd been out on the headland; didn't look like much had changed. The charred remains of the caravan still sat in a black scorch in its field. A little lower than she remembered, perhaps, the final standing side collapsed now and the rains having pounded the whole thing into the ground again and again over the years.

A quarter-mile further along, she turned into the winding drive lined with mature trees and parked outside the cottage. A Mercedes sat along the side, wheel-less and up on bricks. An American-style double-cab pickup, only slightly smaller than a Chieftain tank, sat beside it. The smell hit Barb as soon as she opened her door. Something rotten catching the wind so that it was there and it was gone and it was back again like you might be losing your mind.

She saw Tess through the kitchen window, sitting at the table with her back to her, and rapped on the door with two knuckles. Tess turned and considered her for a moment impassively. Barb wondered if she didn't know who she was, but she got up and opened the door.

'DS Bowen. What brings you out here?'

'It's Detective Inspector now, but that's by the by. How are you, Tess?'

Tess smiled obscurely. 'Coffee?' she said, going to the counter and pouring a cup anyway.

'Sure.'

Out the other window, Barb could see Mickey Box. Cannabis kingpin and mobster of the Kentish marshlands. Or used to be. She was taken aback at the sight of him. In the few encounters they'd had, he'd always seemed remarkably virile, despite his calm exterior, a raw energy simmering just beneath, suggesting nothing was capable of stopping his progress. The man she saw now was a husk. Pale and wizened, he sat slumped in a deckchair on the patio, staring out over the creek that ebbed back into the Medway. He wore the look of a man who'd surrendered, who could cut the white flag from his own hide. A reminder of the dreadful sloth that overtakes all haste eventually.

Tess caught her looking. 'Sits out there for hours sometimes.'

A couple of hundred yards at its widest, the creek was once busy with traffic when a shipyard operated at its foot. Now all it did was separate Mickey Box's headland from the pumping station and sewage works that squatted behind the saltings on the peninsula across the way, whose effluence had once foamed the water.

'Nice view, I suppose.'

'Not really,' Tess said, dropping a coaster on the table and setting down Barb's coffee. 'I don't know what it is he looks at.'

Barb eased into the chair across from her.

'Thanks.' She blew on the steaming mug and sipped. If nothing else, Mickey Box always taught his people how to make proper coffee.

There it was again, that smell. Tess noticed Barb's reaction, a slight movement of her head or quiver of the nostril perhaps.

'It's the pile.'

'The pile?'

'Mick doesn't run the scrapyard any more. Started a refuse collection service, taking away the sort of stuff you can't put in the bins or be bothered to take to the tip. So much of it, it just piled up.'

She ducked down low, looking through the window into the sky and pointing.

'See that?'

Barb followed her finger, finding a dark wisp rising and fading away in the clouds.

'The smoke?'

'That's the pile. Usually it's on fire in at least one place. Smouldering, Mick calls it, on account you can't actually see the flames because they're inside the pile somewhere.'

'On the laundry list of fucked-up shit your dad gets up to, I'm sure this only reaches the middle, but all the same. How the hell is that allowed?'

'I've asked him to sort it out. It's not good for Jim, and it'll only get worse. I even called the council once. Without telling him, obviously. Think someone came and had a look. Nothing happened. We were in Sevenoaks, I'm sure the fire brigade and the SAS would have been dispatched.'

As though aware he had been talked about, a young boy charged into the room wearing a pirate's hat and brandishing a plastic cutlass.

'Hello,' he said.

'You must be Jim,' said Barb.

'What have I said about talking to strangers and the police?' Tess said.

Barb gave her a look. The boy clenched his teeth and stood en garde with his sword held flat beside his head, blade pointed at Barb.

'Attaboy,' Tess said.

'Can I do a treasure hunt?' Jim said.

'Pop Pop's outside. He'll help you.'

The boy flew outside and snuck up on his grandfather, Mickey Box feigning fright as Jim challenged him with his cutlass.

'My God, how old is he now?' Barb said.

'Coming up six. Unless you meant Mick.'

'Can always look him up.'

Climbing out of his chair, Mickey Box chased the boy around the garden, waving an obviously home-made cutlass of his own and crabbing along as if struggling with a wooden leg. The child squealed with delight as he evaded his grandfather's clutches. Barb smiled, watching him gallivanting around. The boy would have no idea who he was, just his grandfather to him. How old was Tess when she knew who Mickey Box really was?

'Best friends,' Tess said, also watching the two of them. 'Fighting sea monsters and fending off scurvy knaves. Serious business that. There's maps and buried treasure and ooh arrs. He's different with Jim.'

'Hmm.'

Barb noticed, draped over the back of a chair, a navy tunic top with white trim.

'You're back working?'

'Few years now. Not full-time, just a few shifts a week. Nights mostly.'

Barb nodded. 'I don't see the other one around.'

Tess frowned as if she wasn't sure who Barb meant. 'Fitz?'

'Yeah. Always thought I'd end up nicking him.'

'Fitz was—I thought you knew. He was shot. Hunting accident.'

A vague memory caught in Barb's mind. Before she could apologise, Tess said, 'You're not here about any of that, though.'

'No.'

'Have you seen her?'

Barb shook her head. 'Not for years. Since before the trial. When they arrested her, I couldn't get involved after that.'

Tess nodded.

'You seen her?'

'I went there once. Early on. Then there was the thing with the fight and she was on restriction for a while. After that – I don't know. It's strange. She's what, fifteen miles away? Not even. She must be due out soon.'

'Couple of weeks.'

'That what this is about? Coming round to see the lie of the land?'

'No. Sad to say, but I don't think I would even have thought about her at all. Something came up, though. I was hoping maybe you'd seen her, so I could gauge what sort of reception I might get. I'm on my way there now.'

'Probably she'll tell you to fuck off.'

'Yeah. Has Mick seen her?'

'If he has, he didn't tell me. Wouldn't surprise me, though. Those two were always . . . it's hard to explain. Friends is the wrong word. It's like two animals who come across each other in the wild and recognise that they're the same. There was an accord between them. He probably feels he owes her something.'

'For what? Keeping shtum? About what?'

Tess smiled. 'Come on now, Inspector.'

Barb got to her feet. 'I'm due there shortly.'

'When you see her, tell her . . .'

'Yeah?'

'I dunno. Tell her something pretty.'

6

HMP Brabazon was the newest addition to the Sheppey prison cluster, named for the first Briton to fly without the aid of a cliff. Privately built, privately run, publicly funded, it was the state of the nation in microcosm. Its bright, faux-antiseptic aesthetic was like a school or hospital stripped of the instruments of learning or healing.

Barb was led to a long hall. Down the centre stretched a row of tables bolted to the floor, with plastic bucket seats, two one side and one the other. She sat in one of the pair at the first table. They were green, the solitary seat across from them yellow. Colour-coded in case anyone forgot the order of things. She was left alone with her thoughts for a few minutes, until the door at the far end of the hall opened.

A guard escorted Boone. Didn't so much as blink when she saw Barb, just walked the length of the hall and sat across from her, no discernible emotion on her face. She looked thin, though her arms were muscled, veins cording round them. She wore no make-up, the pale flesh of her scar standing out on her cheek where it hooked down from the outside of her eye to the edge of her nose. There was other damage to her face, more recent. A nick over the other eye, a fat lip. She looked different, something around the mouth. Barb couldn't quite explain it.

Boone placed her hands flat on the table between them, fingers spread out. Barb saw the missing one, ring finger on the left hand. Just a nubbin remained. She'd read about it, of course, but hadn't seen it before.

She swallowed.

'Abigail Boone, last of the great rustlers.'

Boone stared at her, said nothing.

'Need a favour,' Barb said.

Boone leaned back. 'Knew it. First time I see you in years. Hey, Boone. How you doing, Boone? Time going well? How's work? What about your love life? How about a fucking favour, Boone?'

Barb figured out what was wrong with her friend's mouth. Her front teeth, and a good few others, were missing, leaving a hollow mien and an alien quality to her voice.

She looked to the guard. 'It's okay, you can leave us.'

The guard hesitated.

'She'll be fine,' Barb said.

The guard smirked. 'Wasn't her I was worried about.'

Barb looked at Boone, who looked at the guard.

'Don't know that she'll ever be fine, but she's in no danger from me,' Boone said.

The guard shrugged. 'It's your neck. I'll be outside those doors. I'll get here as fast as I can if I hear you screaming.'

They sat silently as the guard trudged down the hall, rubber-soled boots squeaking on the hard floor. When the door closed behind her, Boone slouched in the chair, elbows on the table. She was working hard at appearing casual.

'Bring me any treats?'

Barb looked around the hall. There was a row of vending machines beside the door she'd come in through.

'Got change for the machines,' she said, picking up her bag.

'Need tokens for them. Four quid for a bottle of water. Three quid for a piss-weak tea. Two-fifty for a Yorkie. That sort of thing.'

'I don't have tokens.'

'Then what use are you?'

Barb closed her bag slowly and deliberately, placing it on the floor beside her. She gathered her hands in her lap, shoulders drooped. Like a forlorn child, her emotions plain in her posture.

'I couldn't,' she said.

'What's that?'

'I couldn't come and see you.'

'Couldn't?'

'For fuck's sake, Boone. You and I both know this could have turned out a lot worse. The blood in the truck? Someone got hurt and you did fuck all to cooperate. How would it have looked, me getting involved?'

'I didn't do the hurting in that business,' Boone said. 'I was one of those who got hurt.'

'Well, let's put it another way. Is there anyone who would still be alive today if it wasn't for you?'

Boone stretched her spine over the back of the chair, letting her head fall back.

'This isn't as much fun as I thought it'd be.'

'It's about to be even less fun.'

Boone straightened up. 'Something's happened? Tess? Quin?'

'No, it's nothing like that. It's about a case.'

'Mick?'

'No. At least I don't think so. I hope not.'

Boone shook her head, confused.

'We found a young girl. Around ten or eleven years old. She was on a country lane, middle of nowhere. You should have seen the state of her. It was . . . I don't even have a point of comparison. The doctors, they think she'd been raised in captivity. Never had any human contact, other than the kind no child should suffer.'

'Who is she? This a misper case I'm supposed to have worked on the force?'

'No. She didn't match any descriptions of missing children. We didn't have anything to go on until we ran her DNA and got a hit.'

'Yeah?'

'Familial match. Maternal. To Sarah Still.'

A laugh escaped Boone's mouth. 'Jesus fucking Christ. It really never ends, does it?'

Sarah Still. The girl Boone had been searching for when she got herself abducted and held in a flat for four days. Got herself thrown off a balcony. Got herself so forgetful that everything in her life previous to waking up in that flat was lost to her for ever. By the time she went back to looking for Sarah, the girl was already dead and buried beneath an abandoned farm, though they wouldn't find that out for weeks. Found out some other things too, such as Sarah having had a child that was taken away from her at birth, seemingly lost for ever. Until now.

Barb leaned over the table. 'I don't know why – I mean, there's no reason you should know anything about this. But given who she is, and what happened previously, I just thought I had to come and see you.'

'Where was she found exactly?' Boone said.

'On the Downs. Maybe a third of the way between Ashford and Canterbury. Nearest village is a place called Elsham Green.'

Boone stared at her. 'Near the old dairy?'

Barb narrowed her eyes. 'Yeah.'

'Shit.'

'Boone, what the fuck do you know about this?'

'You need to get me out of here.'

'Yeah, no worries. Slip you in my bag and we'll be off.'

'I'm serious. You need to speak to someone, pull some strings. Get me out on Special Purpose or something.'

'You're out in a fortnight, I thought?'

'You see this?' Boone tongued her swollen lip out. 'And this?' She pointed to the cut above her eye. 'I don't have a fortnight. I couldn't figure it out, why people were coming for me now. Just because I was getting out maybe? But it's more than that. It's no coincidence that this all starts happening just as I'm due out. This girl turning up, these attacks on me. Somebody's trimming loose ends.'

'You tell me what you have, and I can arrange protective custody.'

'On restriction?' Boone laughed. 'No fucking way. You think that'll stop it? They'll find me hanging in my cell.'

'Boone, I can't just—'

'Sally. That's who had the girl. You're looking for Sally. You need to get me out of here so I can help you.'

'Sally? Who the fuck is Sally?'

But Boone was already on her feet, heading back to the door.

'Get me out. I don't say another word until I'm outside this place.'

PART TWO

THE GATHERING PAST

7

Four years ago

Cold like only 3 a.m. can be. A callous hour, before birdsong or bright, sat in a car with no heat as the engine couldn't be on. Boone stretched out across the back seat, keeping an eye through the rear window. Wearing gloves, hands pressed into her pockets, she could still feel the chill bone-deep.

'Supposed to be summer.'

'Seasons are out the window,' said Fitz.

Sat shotgun, chair reclined all the way back, he was methodically eating sunflower seeds, stacking the empty shells into a small cairn on his belly. Monty was beside him, a kid Fitz had found on an estate somewhere. Strictly wheel duty, hadn't embarrassed himself yet and didn't say much. He was okay with Boone.

'Can feel you watching me,' Fitz said.

'That's your conscience, Fitzgerald. It's saying, why are your manners honed only for the expression of uncouthness?'

'Why does my conscience sound like Emily Post?'

Boone didn't know who that was so let it slide. Fitz's knowledge was surprising and unspeakably arbitrary. He'd once told her he spoke four languages – French, Spanish, Italian, and it had taken an embarrassing minute for her to realise the fourth was English.

Hours they'd been there, watching the large detached house on the corner. Boone had scouted the place, knew the points of entry and egress. Front door solid wood; back door fully glazed PVC; first-floor window at the back opening onto the extension's flat roof. Six-foot wooden fencing around three sides, the front open, with a gate on the corner leading to the rear garden, which was overgrown and strewn with old furniture and God knows what.

Weeks to get to this point. Weeks of living in her van, following dealers to identify couriers, following couriers to identify the grow-houses, and sitting on those houses to identify middle management. Fitz had trailed the players to other grow-houses and to their laundering locations – cash businesses, three nail salons and a launderette. They'd mapped everything out, noted everything down, looking for patterns in schedules and habits. What they needed now was to shake the tree, see how they reacted under pressure. See if they could force the jefe to break cover.

A four-bed in a commuter town, the house looked like a refurbishment that had stalled. Windows boarded up, scaffolding on the side. The neighbours had no idea that a twelve-year-old Vietnamese boy was living inside, never allowed out for any reason. He slept on a sofa in an upstairs hallway. Every room was stripped out and filled with fast-flowering skunk plants growing under LED panels. No heat signature, no crazy utility bills, no chance of remote detection. He watered the plants and monitored the electrics, keeping the lighting going.

Every couple of weeks, a man came round to check on things. If neighbours asked, he said he was the owner, looking in on his empty property. He'd bring a supply of frozen microwave meals for the boy and leave with black bin bags of weed, the managed growth of the plants maintaining a constant yield. Neighbours thought he was carting away rubbish.

Tonight, that all ended.

Fitz was fidgety, drumming his fingers on the dash. Got that way when he was hungry. They'd done more all-nighters than Boone could count, and she knew his tells. Only way to get to know someone, to really know the mess and the marrow of them, was to allow them to be themselves. Easiest way that happened was to be bored shitless in each other's company. Like, for instance, on endless nights of stake-outs. Reaching into a rucksack on the floor, she pulled out a sandwich packet and handed it to him.

'You've had this the whole time?'

'Uh huh.'

'And you're just giving it to me now?'

'If you knew, you'd have eaten it hours ago, and you'd be hungry and irritable again now but I'd have nothing to give you.'

He thought about this. 'When was the last time you showered?'

'Fuck off,' she said softly.

Boone and Fitz were accomplices, but lately it felt like things would inevitably deteriorate into friendship. Her experience with people was that they usually got close to one another by some mistake or mis-understanding, and the time the two parties spent together waiting for the true nature of that to come to light was what was commonly known as being mates. That sort of thing could take years, lifetimes even, to sort out.

Surreptitiously, she sniffed herself. On the road too long, too many consecutive nights sleeping in her van, for sure.

A squelching sound, three times. Boone lifted the walkie-talkie from the seat under her legs and returned the signal.

'Hey,' said Fitz, as she took a half-eaten sandwich from him and slotted it back into its packaging.

'Can have it back later,' she said, wrapping it in a carrier bag and tucking it into the rucksack. 'We're on.'

Somewhere else, on a night-quiet high street where foxes' eyes borrowed an alien shine from street lights as they foraged in bin bags, another group were waiting in a van. Boone didn't know them – Mickey Box had arranged them through an intermediary. Just thugs, street faces brought in as vandals. They'd hook chains from their van to the shutters on one of the nail salons and rip them from their housing. The place would be destroyed inside. Basins would be smashed, tiles would be torn from the walls, the floor would be pulled up. One of the vandals would defecate on the seating. It would be over in minutes and they would be gone.

Fitz had a stick of dark face paint and applied a band from ear to ear, across his eyes. Pulling on a balaclava, only his whites were visible. A valance of blonde was attached to the hem, making it look like his own hair poking out. From the glove compartment he stuffed half a dozen cable ties into his pocket along with a centre punch.

He handed the stick to Boone, who did her face likewise. Pulling her hair back tightly, she tied it into a bun and slipped a woolly cap over it. She strapped on a half-face pollution mask, the kind cyclists wore, and between the high collar of her biker's jacket and the cap tugged down, there was nothing of her to see. From the rucksack on the floor she took a smaller drawstring pack, her job bag, which contained an eighteen-inch rounders bat with rubber grip and a few other bits and bobs.

Slipping out of the car, they silently shut the doors and approached the house at pace from the corner. Boone took a knee beside the fence, Fitz boosting himself to the top off her thigh and quickly pulling her up after him. They carefully lowered themselves down the other side, the long grass littered with obstacles.

At the glazed back door, Fitz pressed the centre punch against the glass and Boone drew the bat from her bag like a sword. The glass shattered, hanging like a spider's web in winter, and Boone cleared it away with the bat so they could walk right on in.

Two at a time Fitz took the stairs, the kid sleeping through it with a phone lying on his chest, mouth wide open with terror when he was dragged off the couch. His wrists were zipped together behind his back before he even knew that he didn't know what was happening.

Every room was filled with plants, except the downstairs bathroom. The kitchen and the family bathroom upstairs had been gutted to accommodate more weed. A sprawling network of vents and electric wiring covered walls and slithered through holes punched in ceilings and floors. In a nook under the stairs stood a fridge freezer and a table with a microwave, a bin bag beneath it with boxes from the ready meals.

Boone took the bag and emptied it in one of the front rooms, soaking the cardboard packages in lighter fluid. She squirted the place up and down with the stuff, all the ground-floor rooms, as Fitz carried the boy downstairs and out the back. He lay silently on the ground, fear the best gag of all. Fitz tossed Boone the lad's phone. There was a messaging app with one number stored, a history of video calls to it on a very regular schedule.

Boone called the number, switching to the phone's rear camera when it was answered. Ignoring the voice on the other end, she walked between the rooms, showing them the house, and at the back door lit a match and tossed it inside. Flames went off like a domino display, racing through the house. Someone was shouting on the other end of the call, but Boone terminated it and dropped the phone in the grass.

Fitz unbolted the gate and they walked out with the boy. The house was on the edge of an estate, a brook across the road separating them from farmland. A two-post road sign was concreted into the ground there, and Fitz bound the boy to it with cable ties.

Monty had the car idling and they got in, rolling off down the road away from the town and out onto country B roads. No eyes, no cameras, no need to rush. Being a getaway driver wasn't about speed; it was about getting away. The rest of the job was someone else's responsibility. Mickey Box had eyes on the Vietnamese middle management, watching their reaction, hoping to follow them somewhere crucial.

Boone handed Fitz a tub of wet wipes, and he worked away at the paint on his face. They pootled through hedge-lined lanes and none of them said a word until Monty pointed to a sign.

'Litton.'

'East side,' Boone said. 'Right here, and then first left over the stone bridge.'

They were in coal country, and on the outskirts of the village of Litton was a disused railway station, once servicing the old Ashford to Lark line, chopped by the Beeching axe. The stretch of track running through it had been repurposed for the colliery railway until the mines too were shut down. Since then, the station had housed various businesses, most recently a builders' merchant that had gone belly-up a few months prior, windows now boarded, its cameras vandalised. The service lane that had doubled as a car park remained easily accessible despite its isolated location. A safe place to leave the Transit.

'Leave the car clean,' she said, opening the rear door.

Fitz gave her some side-eye.

'Don't look at me like that.' Reaching down to the floor beneath his seat, she came up with a sunflower shell and dropped it in his lap. As she walked towards the van, Fitz was all eyes front but giving her the finger as they passed, disappearing off into the night.

Windowless, nobody would give the Transit a second glance. Boone slid open the side door and threw in her rucksack. Panelled out and crudely insulated, she had fitted a small water tank and basin with an outflow, a few storage units, and a bench seat that folded down into a bed. There was also an electric system including two 115Ah batteries housed beneath the bench feeding some 240v outputs. It was practical, if inelegant, with no bespoke finishing or carpeted walls.

Stripping off, she gathered up her job clothes and mask and put them in a black bin bag along with the rucksack and anything else she'd had with her. Stop at a high street and dump them in a wheelie bin, somewhere with regular collections for commercial refuse.

Inside the rear doors, at the end of the bench, was a portable ten-litre commode. She sat and did her toilet, realising she'd been holding it for a while. Adrenaline. In the course of her work for Mickey Box, she'd seen men piss themselves without even knowing. The loo paper was cheap and thin, all the commode could handle. Pouring water into the basin, she washed her hands and scrubbed the paint from her face with cold cream, giving the rest of herself a quick going-over with wet wipes. Rummaging through strewn clothes, she picked out a pair of dark cargos and a tee. Sniffed them – laundry needed doing. She sprayed antiperspirant before dressing, then some more over the clothes.

Firing up the van, she rolled out of the station. No going home tonight; she'd keep herself to herself until the next day in case anything went sideways in the meantime. Back roads took her back to the Medway, avoiding motorways and even A roads when she could. Caution wasn't an afterthought, it was a discipline that kept you safe. Fastidiousness was always preferable to incarceration.

An open box of Pop Tarts lay on the seat beside her and she tore the foil off one with her teeth. Only food she ever kept in the van. Lasted for ever and tasted the same stale or fresh. End-of-days food.

She listened to Bobbie Gentry as she drove. Boone had been thinking about her mother a lot recently. She knew her father had died when she was nine, but her mother had left for Canada shortly after she was born, so she never had any memories of her to lose. She felt that now made her closer in some strange way. Other similarities struck her. Jack had told her she had always harboured anger at her mother for leaving. You leave twice, was what she used to tell him. You leave as a wife and you leave as a mother. Her old self setting it up for her new self to knock right down.

After she'd moved out of the family home, Jack had dropped round some of her belongings, including a couple of boxes of her father's stuff. Among those she'd found a handful of C60 cassettes, one of them labelled *Sandra Lucey's Road Tape*. At some point, the Lucey had been scribbled out and replaced with Kelly. Her mother's, from around the time she met Boone's father. She'd found a picture of her wearing headphones sitting beside a metal-faced hi-fi with great needle dials and twisty knobs.

Boone had bought a second-hand cassette deck and gone through the tape, which had no track listing, figuring out the songs before setting about collecting the albums for herself. Along with Bobbie there was Janis Joplin, Carole King, Dusty, Joni, Nico, Linda Ronstadt, Fleetwood Mac, Astrud Gilberto, Patti Smith, and countless others. Holding out for some psychic connection across the years, she'd felt a childish yearning in her chest.

'He Made a Woman Out of Me' came on and she mumbled along to the chorus, mouth full of Pop Tart.

In a residential neighbourhood in Gillingham she found a quiet-but-not-too-quiet street and parked close to a corner, the van along the windowless side of a house where it wouldn't be in view. Across the road were playing fields, the grass silver beneath the fat moon. Climbing into the back, she pulled across the blackout curtain. A book rack, the kind you saw on boats, was fixed to one wall, but she was too done in to read.

She folded down the bed. Though shattered, her body remained intoxicated with the thrill of the job, as it always did. Waiting for sleep, she masturbated to an ongoing fantasy she'd been working on since watching *Night Train to Munich* and *The Wicked Lady*, about being alone with Margaret Lockwood in a bomb shelter during the Blitz.

8

School traffic woke her. Cars rattling by and the squawk of mothers and prams. She waited for it all to die down before getting on the move again. Nipped into Tesco for a few bits: loo roll (cheap and thin), shampoo and smellies, half a dozen boxes of Pop Tarts. Cash, yes I'll take a bag, no I don't have a Clubcard, thanks.

Back home, there were two launderettes in town. Dorothy's offered an over-the-counter service and had a few machines. The one that just said *Laundry* over the door was completely self-service and employed someone only to watch for children and dogs climbing into the drums. Boone visited the latter, machines being less disposed to conversation. From her rack she'd taken Leonora Carrington's *Down Below*, a gift from a friend, and read it straight through while she waited for her washing.

Weeks since she'd been at the caravan, she found it as she'd left it. The step on the decking she'd been meaning to fix still creaked underfoot. Condensation still clung inside the glazing of the sliding door, encouraging the growth of a grassy rind along the rubber seals. The green waters of the creek still slid imperceptibly to and fro behind the bulge of a long-grounded barge on the shore, its skyward hull drooping where its weight sank in on itself like rotted fruit. Damp and moss-furred, a dormant beast.

She took her time beneath a hot shower, washing until her skin was red and tingly. Drying off, she applied make-up to her scarred face and even dabbed a little perfume. She drove the van the short distance to the cottage, parking up beside the septic. The Mercedes wasn't there, but she could see Mickey Box sitting at the kitchen table.

It had been almost a decade since Boone, still a uniformed constable, had nicked him for a brawl in a Canterbury pub in which Mickey Box had settled an old score and left a young man with irreparable damage. He'd served half of a six-year sentence, but during his time had had cause to ask Boone to help Tess, who'd been trafficked by a small-time pimp and dealer. Boone had found Tess, earned her way out of uniform and begun her strange association with Mickey Box. Of course she remembered none of that, and their relationship no longer straddled the thin blue line. Now they stole horses together.

'Smells fresh,' she said, poking her head through the door.

'Wondered when you'd surface,' he said.

She poured herself a coffee and joined him.

'Talk to Fitz?'

He nodded. 'Anyone keeping a careful eye on the news over the next few months will no doubt read about the misfortunes of one Vincent Tran.'

'The jefe?'

'Unassuming businessman, he'd say. Owner of an import/export enterprise. Arrested at his home near Canterbury just after dawn in possession of a large cache of weapons and several young teenagers whose immigration status was sketchy at best. Nine others arrested with him. Called your mate on the force, like you said. She turned up with that shine and a shower of others, got the collar. Should do well out of it, I'd say. Tran was plugged into the Honourable Dead.'

'He had a covers band?'

'Gang with ties to the Red Scorpions in Vancouver. They move serious weight wholesale to street gangs in London. "Better to die with honour than live in shame." All have little tattoos right here on their shoulders. Fuck knows how validating yourselves for anyone to see makes sense, but there's no accounting for cultural heterogeneity with our slope friends.'

'And we got away clean? No complications with the urchins you used on the shop?'

'Nah. In and out. Empty packet of Marlboros was left. Smuggled in, Albanian warning on the box. Tran was having trouble with Tirana. This won't improve relations.'

'And he doesn't even know you exist.'

'Might catch a whiff of my musk when we start filling holes in the supply chain. But that's just capitalism for you.' He stood up, moving to the Welsh dresser. 'Something else. You had a visitor.'

'Here?'

'Knocked at the caravan first, they said. Then came here to ask if I knew you. Obviously I denied it. Reputation to think of. Standing in the community.'

'Who were they?'

'She left a number.' He fetched a scrap of notepaper from a shelf in the dresser and dropped it on the table.

'She?'

'As in a woman. Well dressed. About my age, I suppose. Not as good-looking.'

'No name?'

'Didn't leave one, or any indication what she wanted.'

They drank their coffees in silence. Boone watched him, looking out the window, picking lint from his trousers, scratching his face.

'Say it.'

'Just that I hope we don't make a habit of perfect strangers turning up and asking for you by name at places where you shouldn't be widely known.'

'If hopes were giraffes we'd all be eating neck.'

The Mercedes pulled up outside and Fitz climbed out. Strapped into the baby seat in the back was Jim, Mickey Box's grandson. And, unbeknownst to both boy and grandfather, Fitz's son. A fleeting indiscretion between him and Tess, and now a secret Mickey Box could never learn of if Fitz valued breathing and the like. Boone watched the boy lifted out in the arms of the father he'd in all likelihood never know as such.

'Playgroup,' Mickey Box said.

He went outside, returning shortly in hot pursuit of Jim, who came giggling and tumbling into the cottage. He'd started walking a few months earlier and nothing was going to stop him now. Had armed himself with a handful of words, too.

Charging over to Boone, little legs churning, he gawped up at her, fists clenching and unclenching at his sides. Some part of him was always on the move, forever restless.

'Boo,' he said, no respecter of syllables or full and given names.

She spread out her hands like she was coming for him, and he gurgled delightedly before running and burying his face in his grandfather's leg.

'Need to use the septic,' Boone said.

'You know how,' said Mickey Box, taking his seat again and lifting Jim onto his lap. The boy pulled the man's ear and wiped his nose on his shoulder.

Fitz was back behind the wheel of the Merc, window open.

'You good?' she said.

'Copasetic.'

'Off again?'

'Picking up Monty. Taking me on a tour of Afghanistan and Baghdad. See the sights. Meet the mans.'

'Try not to get yourself killed. You can be a bit . . .'

'White?'

'. . . of a twat.'

'Bear it in mind,' he said, pulling off.

Afghanistan. The Angell Town estate in Brixton, where Fitz had found Monty. A roadman since his pre-teens, on spare couches through the day, on his toes through the night. Roving from block to block, he ran traps and steered fiends for a street operator who bought from a man who bought from Fitz. Until by chance Fitz met him and saw he was smarter than what he was doing, work any kid with shoes could do. Replaceable where he was, he could be effective elsewhere. His father hadn't been in the streets but had driven artics, been on the road through the boy's life. Those times he was back, though, he'd shown his son his trade. Years away from being able to claim a licence, Monty could drive twelve-speed split sticks and turn sixteen metres of truck and trailer. Adroit spotter of talent was Fitzy.

Boone backed up the Transit to the cover of the septic tank. She unlocked the rear doors and removed the commode, emptying it into the tank and hosing it off. As she was fitting it back into the van, a small car she didn't recognise chuntered up the drive. Tess got out with a couple of friends Boone half knew by sight. She'd started picking up a few shifts with an agency, care worker at residential homes, and was meeting people her own age again.

Jim staggered out of the cottage like a drunk old man, initially seeking his mother but finding the open side door of Boone's van a more tempting prospect. He peered inside, gave Boone a quick glance and then started climbing up. Boone crouched behind him like a wicketkeeper, but the step was extended and he managed by himself.

'You think you might find something in there?' she said.

Tunnelling in beneath a pile of freshly laundered clothes, he came up with a brassiere.

'Precocious, this one,' Boone said as Tess wandered over.

'Hey, old man. You're here.' Tess was wearing a leather moto jacket with a slanted zip.

'In the flesh.'

She looked back at the others, holding bags from a Thai takeout. 'We just knocked off the early shift. Picked up some food, but . . .'

'I've got plans.'

Boone retrieved her unmentionables from Jim and lifted him down from the van.

'Boo,' he said again.

At that age when it was like a puppy learning to talk. Don't do it, pal. No good can come from words.

He had in his hand a rubber ball, ping-pong-sized. It flashed when it bounced.

'Can I see?' Boone said, holding a hand out. He placed it in her palm and she threw it.

'Fetch.'

Giggling like a machine gun, he chased after it. Could almost hear him panting. Picking it up proved a challenge as he kept kicking it before he could snag it in his hand, the flashing eliciting further laughter.

'Looks good,' Boone said, nodding at Tess's jacket.

'Yeah, it's a perfect fit.' She ran her hands round her waist.

'Good,' Boone said.

With no rent to pay, and not being burdened by any intentions to tell the taxman, Boone didn't have to do many jobs for Mickey Box to feel like she earned hilarious amounts of money. Tess spent most of the money her few shifts brought in on Jim, and Mickey Box was funny about giving her cash. Boone would see her flicking through catalogues, looking at certain things, and sometimes she'd buy them without telling her, have them arrive with her name on them.

Convinced happiness would be wasted on herself, Boone acted vicariously through Tess. Things were better between them, but still not what they once had been. Maybe they never would be. Roo's death had broken something.

She was aware of the other couple watching them, Tess's scarred and amnesiac friend a source of some interest.

'Have you gifts for us all?' the man said, in an oops-did-she-hear-me voice. The woman whacked his arm with the back of her hand. The man grinned and waved, as if Boone was in on the joke.

'They think there's something going on,' Tess said. 'With me and you. Buying me things. He thinks he's being funny. He doesn't mean anything by it.'

'Didn't realise I was getting shorted on the deal,' Boone said.

Tess looked at her sideways. 'You can join us, you know. There's plenty of food really. Donal has a movie, something with Julie Christie. Remember we saw *Petulia*? I told him we love her, she's something else. It's a Western he's got, I think. I dunno.'

'I do have stuff to do,' Boone said. 'Besides, he might be funny again and really mean it this time.'

'Okay, Boone.'

She ran the Transit back to the caravan. There wasn't anything in the world she wanted more than a movie and takeout with Tess, but, as she found with most things in life, other people were an unwanted complication. She missed her friend. The nature of what she did with Mickey Box kept her from building any real bridges with Barb, and the thought that Fitz was the person she talked to the most was too much to countenance.

There was maybe someone else, though, and having lied about having plans, she now felt compelled to actually make some, for reasons of both aesthetics and loneliness. She composed a text.

Eight words.

Took her almost ten minutes.

You free? Fancy coming round for your tea?

The reply was instant.

My dinner. Give me an hour.

9

Way the light hit the glazing of the caravan's sliding doors, you could sit behind them and nobody outside could see you until their nose was pressed against the glass. Boone watched the Volvo crunch along the gravel and roll to a stop. The driver's door opened and Storm's legs swung out. In her heels, she walked on the uneven ground like someone finding their way in the dark. Boone got up and slid the door open.

'Dr Mathijsen.'

'Abigail,' Storm said, stepping up onto the decking.

'I made coffee.'

'I brought wine.'

'Nowhere to be later?'

'The evening is mine entirely. As is the morrow.'

'Grape it is then. Food's ready.'

'Great. I considered gnawing on the steering wheel on the way over.'

The small table was laid with a damask cloth and faux-leather mats. A black calla lily stood with a cerise carnation in a slim vase.

'Okay,' Storm said. 'What's going on? First *you* call *me*, which is weird enough. But now there are flowers.'

'Shut up,' Boone said, bringing out two immaculately presented plates with some kind of breaded burgers in freshly baked rolls.

'Cod katsu burger, panko-breaded, with home-made slaw and a sweet chilli mayo made with aquafaba.'

'That's a posh fish finger sandwich.'

'And is there anything more magnificent than a fish finger sandwich?'

'A posh one, apparently.'

They sat and Storm poured the wine. 'When did you get back?'

'This afto.' Boone lifted her burger in both hands and took a huge bite.

'And the first thing you did was call me?'

Boone shrugged. 'Tipped the commode in the septic first.'

'The delights of the adventuring life. The gadabout. The wayfarer. The road agent.'

Boone took another bite.

'Would you tell me what you did, if I asked?'

'Are you asking?'

'No.'

Storm cut her sandwich in half with a knife and pecked at it delicately. 'This is good. Why is this so good?'

'Fried. The best fish fingers are fried fish fingers.'

Boone had polished hers off already and Storm caught her smiling at her little nibbles.

'You eat like a man,' she said.

'You eat like a teenage girl.'

'I want to tell you something.'

'Okay.'

'I'm selling up.'

'What do you mean?'

'The clinic. Ravi and the others are buying me out.'

'Fuckers.'

'Oh, they're not forcing me to go. I raised the idea of leaving, and they made an offer.'

'Why? What will you do?'

'I have a few ideas. I'm still deciding how crazy they are.'

'I'm your gal for crazy. Fancy being a gadabout? A wayfarer? A road agent? Room for two in the old Transit. I can offer rudimentary washing facilities and a change of clothes at least once a week. Fortnight.'

'Well, that's probably the most ghastly proposal I've ever received.'

'I read the book.'

'Oh? What did you think?'

'I like what she said about how being hospitalised made her realise the importance of physical health in avoiding disasters of the mind. Having spent some time in a clinic, I get that.'

'I got you something else. I saw it and it reminded me of you.'

'Ooh, where is it?'

'I left it on the side there.'

Boone got up and ripped the paper bag from around the book. *Astragal*. Albertine Sarrazin.'

'It's about an outlaw woman with a gimpy leg.'

Boone stared at her. 'You think you're funny.'

'Many people think I'm funny. I'm known far and wide for my witty rejoinders.'

Boone leaned with her hip against the kitchen counter and laid down the book. 'Well I'm not laughing.'

Storm got up and came over.

'This gadabouting of yours. Was it dangerous this time?'

'No more than usual.'

'Did you have to run for your life?'

'I sauntered away. There were drugs and fire and the threat of violence, but little actual hazard. No stitches required this time.'

When they'd first met, in the hospital, Boone's face was heavily bandaged from a knife wound. Way she told it to Storm, the eighty-three stitches became a hundred and ten, because no matter how bad things were, they could always be worse.

Storm moved closer. 'You smell nice.'

'Right? I've been living in a van for three weeks, so I spruced up.'

'Uh huh.'

'It has been a very long three weeks.'

'And what have you been thinking about during that time?'

'Mostly Margaret Lockwood.'

They were very close now. 'Oh yeah?'

'Yeah.'

'Margaret Lockwood can't do this, though, can she?' Storm said. 'Or this.'

IO

Boone awoke suddenly. She thought a noise had stirred her and tried to reconstruct it to work out if it had been real or she had dreamt it. Storm pressed against her back and gently shook her shoulder.

'You awake?'

'Mmm.'

'There was knocking.'

Boone looked over her shoulder. 'At the door?'

On cue, there was a rat-a-tat against the glass of the sliding door.

Boone stared at the narrow hall outside the bedroom.

'Aren't you going to get that?' Storm said.

'Nobody ever knocks.'

'What?'

'You always tell me in advance if you're coming. Mick would wait until I came to him. Fitz lurks outside and ambushes me. And Tess just wanders in.'

'It isn't locked?' Storm said.

Boone shrugged. 'From who? Nobody comes here.'

The knocking didn't abate.

'Abigail, seriously.'

'All right, all right.'

She got up and hurriedly pulled on a robe, tying it loosely at the waist. Fishing her bridge out of its glass of solution, she shook it off and slid it into her mouth, making a face. She looked round the room.

'If someone shoots me, climb out the window and run for the cottage a couple of fields over.'

'Don't say things like that,' she heard Storm call down the hall after her. 'You know I can't tell when you're joking.'

Boone pulled back the drapes from the doors and found herself looking at a woman's lean face, dark and expensively gathered curls hanging about her shoulders. If there was any openness to her face, it led only to the gently disguised miseries of her life. Eyes lined, neck slightly craped, she looked like a French actress who'd seen it all. Boone pictured her with tighter skin, eyes not so sad, but doubted she'd be any more beautiful.

She slid the door open. 'Hello?'

'I'm looking for Abigail Boone,' the woman said. 'Or just Boone.'

'I'm just Boone.'

'My name is Kate Porter. I've been trying to reach you for a couple of weeks.'

Boone frowned, remembering the note Mickey Box had given her with a telephone number.

'Away on business,' she said.

'I was hoping I could talk to you about my son, Noah.'

'Your son?'

'He went missing, you see.'

'Police are your best bet, Mrs Porter.'

'The police cannot help me. I need something else.'

'Mrs Porter, I don't know how you came to find me, but I don't do that sort of—'

'I saw your name in the news last year. The stories about that girl, Sarah Still. I understand it was connected to other crimes. Historical crimes. That house out near Kearswood, they said they found bodies that had been there since the eighties. You see, Noah went missing almost thirty years ago.'

And there it was. Like a flare luring her back to the surface.

'Why don't you come in?' Boone said. 'It's chilly this morning.'

Kate moved easily, as if gravity weakened around her. She wore clothes that were made for her, clothes you might see in magazines, in subtle, earthy tones. Lowering herself carefully onto the edge of the sofa, she clutched her hands in her lap.

'You mind if I just throw something more respectable on?' Boone said, looking down at her robe.

Kate arranged her mouth into a thin line that might have been a smile. 'Of course.'

Like the granting of fucking permissions, Boone thought. Paying deference in your own home now, on top of having your lie-in cut short and probably any chance of late-morning how's-your-father with it.

She opened the bedroom door and put her finger to her lips to hush Storm.

'What's happening?' Storm mouthed.

Boone shrugged. She dropped the robe and pulled on the previous day's jeans and jumper, skipping underwear.

'Missing son?'

Boone pointed at the glass of denture solution. 'Tip it out and hold the glass to the door, you'll hear better,' she whispered.

Storm glared, eyes like a strangling. 'Go talk to her. Listen to what she has to say.'

'You okay here?'

'Yeah. Go.'

'Sorry about that,' Boone said, striding back into the living room. 'Can I get you a coffee or a tea? I need a coffee.'

'I'm fine, thank you.'

'You're local?' Boone said, wanting to keep the chat light while she was making her drink.

'Yes. No. Lark. We live just outside the town.'

'We?'

'My husband and I. Do you know the old waterworks? It was built in the Queen Anne style, large enough to accommodate two beam engines. The idea appealed to my husband. You see, when I married him, oh, twenty years ago now, he ran a small refuse collection firm. After a few years he started getting contracts from local authorities, put together a fleet of trucks. Now he's the biggest name in recycling in the south. Works in six counties and across the capital. Says he'll recycle anything, even buildings. Of course we bought the place fully refurbished.'

Boone sat in the armchair, legs crossed ankle-over-knee, and blew on her mug. 'How did you find me, Mrs Porter?'

'It's Kate, please.'

'Okay, Kate. I'm not a particularly easy person to just stumble across.'

'I've thought about how best to go through all of this. Would you mind – could I start at the beginning?'

'Sure.'

'I wasn't always Kate Porter. I didn't come from money. Neither did my husband. We built the company up to what it is, made a fortune from nothing. But for all that, what I really owe my husband is giving me the strength to help myself. I was an addict. From my early teens and for many years after that. I got clean a few times but always fell back into old habits. It wasn't until I met my husband that I straightened myself out for good. It had taken its toll by then, though.

'I was fifteen when I gave birth to Noah. I was Kate Maxwell back then. Dad was long gone and Mum, bless her, couldn't handle me, let alone a small child on top. It was a struggle from the off. When he was eight, he was removed from my care. I can't argue with it. I was using heavily, wasn't feeding him or getting him to school. He'd run off repeatedly. Just for a few days, here and there. Always came back on his own. He started to steal. Food and clothes, things I couldn't provide.'

She halted momentarily, and a tear cut down her cheek. She didn't move to wipe it away, didn't worry what she looked like to Boone.

'He was eight and he was stealing to live. They put him in a local place, Eastry House. On the sea, south of Lark. He hated it there. He changed. He'd always been such a lively boy, even with the life I gave him. Chatty, curious, forever on the go. He simply . . . shrank. Withdrew into himself. He ran away constantly, coming back to me. I'd been warned that if I didn't notify the home to come and collect him, they'd remove him from me permanently. So each time, I had to wait with him until someone came to fetch him. He never cried. Not once. He looked at me, through me really. I waited three days before telling them he was with me once, and the social worker told me the police would be involved the next time. That I could be charged with abduction. My own child.

'The last time he ran away, he didn't come to me. The social worker turned up at my door, aggressive, throwing around threats, but I didn't have him. The police were brought in, but nothing serious was done for days. His history of running, they said he'd come back when he was hungry. But he never did. He was never seen again. He was ten and he was lost for ever.'

She held her knees together, hands folded so she didn't wring them. One foot was going. Boone noticed her nails, each one chewed down to the quick, incongruous with the rest of her appearance. She could still have been a user, but her green eyes that had once been greener bore no signs of a current habit. The battle for her was probably hard and without end.

'I could use a cigarette,' she said.

'We'll sit on the deck,' Boone said.

Outside, Kate leaned against the wooden balustrade on her elbow and lit her cigarette.

'I know my son is dead, Boone. I'm not a fool. Missing that long, with not a single trace of him. A few years ago I engaged a private detective to look into the matter. Even just to confirm what I thought would have been something. He found absolutely nothing. He said it was possible Noah had changed his name, accounting for the lack of a credit record or any public information. But he was ten when he went missing. How do you do things like that when you're ten?'

'Forgive me, Kate, but if you're certain your son is dead, then—'

'I thought I had made peace with that. My husband doesn't like me dwelling on it. We never had children. I had a procedure when I was twenty-five, before I met him, and there were complications. He had a big enough task looking after me, to be honest, and then we had the company and everything that came with that. He prefers the past to stay in the past. The thing is, it's only ever other people's past that is actually past, isn't it? Your own past is a festering thing.'

Boone didn't bite on that.

'As I said, I saw you in the newspapers. When they said they had found remains at that house, it gave me unexpected hope. Sounds remarkable to confess to having hoped your own child's body would be found. It's the kind of hope that runs you through like a lance. For weeks I found myself expecting the police to knock on the door. The first detective I hired, he arranged for DNA samples to be put on a database, you see. None of that existed at the time Noah disappeared.'

'They didn't knock?'

'No. But the whole thing had woken something up inside me. I kept it from my husband, but I hired a new firm to start a fresh investigation. I thought I could live with knowing he was gone, but I can't. I need to know what happened. Maybe even where he ended up. Whatever's left of him.'

'Thirty years is a long time. The chances of finding anything now are almost non-existent.'

'That's what the firm said. But I told them that you'd found stuff about children who'd been missing that long. One of them said, why don't you hire her then? He was joking, of course, but I tasked them with finding you. When they did, I paid them off. And here we are.'

'Did they tell you what happened to me?'

'They told me you had been a detective, and that you were hurt in the line of duty. That after you had recovered, you investigated the case yourself and uncovered that ghastly house and everything that was hidden there.'

'Did they tell you what I lost?'

'They said you were no longer with your family.'

'Did they tell you I suffered total retrograde amnesia? Two years ago, I woke up in a grubby little flat in east London, and I have no recollection of anything that happened before that day. I don't remember my childhood. I don't remember my marriage. I don't remember giving birth to or raising my son. Nothing. Complete obliteration. That was why I investigated the things I did. Not to work a case, or to catch criminals. I did it to find out who I was. Who exactly Abigail Boone had been.'

'And did you?'

'No. Not in any meaningful way. What I did find out, something your detectives couldn't possibly tell you, is what it feels like to lose someone I cared for deeply because of my own recklessness. A dear friend of mine was killed by the men I had been looking for. A loss that cost me more than any answers could ever be worth.'

'You caught them, though, the men responsible?'

'No. They got away. After nearly killing me again.'

'You know who they were?'

'Not really.'

'So you don't think you solved it?'

'There is no solving crimes, Kate. They're not puzzles. They're not mathematical problems. There is no formula you can apply or working out you can do to bring about a definitive solution. Crimes are like stories. They never end, they linger. Even if you manage to assign guilt to someone, that doesn't change what happened. Sometimes you can do everything right, do everything that is humanly possible, and still not get the answers you're looking for. If you don't think you can live with that, my advice is to not start asking questions to begin with.'

'I have to try something.'

'I'm not a detective any more, Kate.'

'Detectives haven't been of much use to me so far. Maybe what I need is whatever you are.'

'I'm sorry.'

'I can pay. I know it sounds obscene, but you use whatever is at your disposal, and I am a very wealthy woman.'

'It's not a matter of money.'

Kate nodded. 'Will you look at one thing?' She opened her bag and retrieved a photograph. An old Kodak 35mm print, the kind you sent away the little reel and got the pictures back in the post. It was Kate, decades earlier, standing with her hands on the shoulders of a young boy in front of her. She looked strung out, eyes an intense red where her dilated pupils caught the flash. The corner of the picture flared red and purple.

Boone took it from her and just about had a heart attack.

'This is your son? This is Noah?'

Kate nodded.

Boone remained silent, trying not to show any outward sign of the chaos in her mind. This boy, this Noah, she knew his face. She'd seen it before.

His hair.

His button nose.

His chin, split down the centre with a white scar.

She had seen it in a Polaroid she'd found at the house where Roo died, along with similar pictures of other children. All burned up and gone to ash now, along with all the other evidence. Now here he was, some kind of spectre come back from that place.

'That was his birthday,' Kate said. 'The last one he had. It was taken at Eastry, the care home. Either he ran away and perished on the streets, or—or someone took him and killed him. Either way, some-one somewhere must know something.'

'Three decades, Kate. I'm not even sure where to begin. If someone did take him, there's a good chance that person is dead by now anyway.'

'I have stuff. Paperwork from the local authority, and from the police when he was reported missing. And letters Noah sent me from the home.'

Boone knew her resistance had slipped. The inevitable was going to happen.

'If I do this, I make no promises. Set your expectations somewhere around zero.'

'I understand.'

'Do you?'

'I have the stuff in folders.' Kate pointed to the black SUV parked behind Storm's Volvo.

'All right,' Boone said. 'Let me keep it a few days, read through it all. That'll give me a clearer idea of where to start. Of whether there even is a place to start.'

Kate fetched three large ring binders from the back seat and handed them over. She wrote the number of her personal mobile on the cover of the top one.

'There's also these,' she said, presenting a set of keys. 'They're for Eastry.'

'The care home?'

Kate nodded. 'I bought it a few years ago. It had been closed down and the council eventually decided to sell it to developers. My husband knows people, through the council contracts we have with the firm. I didn't let him develop it, though. It's just sitting there. I don't know why, exactly. I couldn't let it be pulled down before anyone had been able to tell me about my son. It's been derelict for ages. I don't know if there's anything there that'll be of use.'

'I'll take a look. Call you in a couple of days,' Boone said.

She remained on the decking, holding the folders, as the SUV drove away.

'What the fuck are you doing?' she muttered to herself.

Quicksand, she thought. She'd put her foot in and she would never be free. The more she fought it, the deeper she sank.

II

'That poor woman,' Storm said.

'Yeah, it's a tale of woe.'

'Surprises me.'

'People hold onto things their whole lives,' Boone said. 'Hard to account for which random moment they'll choose to act on them.'

'No. I meant you. Agreeing to look into it. I thought you'd left all that behind, looking for missing people. Women and children.'

'You don't think I should get involved?'

'I think you should do whatever you think is right. If you're going to be taking risks anyway, this is maybe a better reason than most.'

'Taking risks?' Boone smiled. 'I thought ignorance was bliss as far as how I filled my days?'

'I tried ignorance on and didn't find it a good fit.'

Boone sat beside Storm. Opening one of the folders, she found a photocopy of the picture Kate had shown her of Noah. 'Noah Maxwell. I've seen him before.'

'You've seen the boy? How? He'd be almost the same age you are, so you'd have been a child when he disappeared.'

'Not in the flesh. A photo of him. One of the ones that burned in the fire.'

'How certain are you?'

'Ninety per cent?'

'You saw the picture once, under stressful conditions.'

'Storm, there is nothing I have forgotten about that house. Absolutely nothing. The second Kate showed me the picture, I was back there. It was his face I saw. Her son's face.'

'So the men you found at the house, you think they took Noah?'

'No. This dates back before them. Back to when the man who owned the house was using it for his sick little gatherings. He and his friends, the children who were brought there for them.'

They were getting into ground she'd never covered with Storm, the side of the story the police hadn't been too enthusiastic to look into.

'A man called Blackborne owned the house,' she explained. 'He'd bought it through a company owned by a company, in a way you never would have been able to connect him to it on paper. He was wealthy, an industrialist, and a serial predator. He bought the house in the early eighties and used it to host parties for men who shared his tastes. Not the least of whom was Hanley Moss.'

'Moss? The MP who killed himself?'

'That's him.'

'There was a woman, too. Murder-suicide.'

'That was Blackborne's widow.'

'My God. That was all to do with you?'

Boone nodded.

'You think he was afraid of his past coming out, so he . . .' Storm put handgun fingers to her head.

'I suspect it had something to do with them dying,' Boone said. 'There were photos dating back to the eighties in the house, along with videos made more recently by the two monsters I was chasing. I don't know when Blackborne started employing them exactly. Probably at some point he could no longer act with brazen impunity. Rich and famous men openly doing what they wanted with children became slightly more conspicuous, and he sought the services of someone who could provide him with what he wanted. They used a taxi service as cover, finding girls and trafficking them. But the picture of Noah dated back before all that. Back to the parties Blackborne and Moss held.'

'Blackborne and Moss are dead, though.'

'I know,' Boone said. 'But I doubt they found the children themselves. There had to be someone facilitating it.' She looked at the stack of folders. 'Look, probably I'll run into nothing but dead ends with all this, but I couldn't just brush her off. Least I can do is look through this stuff. See if anything comes up.'

'Are you going to tell her that you recognised her son?'

'I don't know. I want to, but if there's nowhere we can go with it, I don't know what good it will do.'

Storm stood up. 'Right, then. You'd better get to it.'

'Now? Why? Are you going?'

'I'm going to fix us both brunch, and then I'll help you sort through this stuff.'

'*Brunch?*'

Storm glanced at her watch. 'What would you call it?'

'Not *brunch*.'

She opened the fridge. 'Got any hollandaise?'

'Who the hell keeps hollandaise on hand?'

Storm was bent over, rummaging about.

'Smoked salmon. I don't think I've ever looked in your fridge before. And you have chives.'

Her head popped up above the door. 'You can cook and you keep a reasonably well-stocked fridge. I'm learning a lot about you here.'

'Think I lived on pizzas and Pop Tarts alone?'

'I had wondered.'

'When I'm back from a job, I like to cook for myself. Feels like something real people do.'

'You have muffins. Excellent. Salmon, muffins, and eggs royale.'

'Eggs royale?'

'You don't like? That's okay, you don't have hollandaise, so there won't be any Benediction. Really it'll just be poached eggs.'

'No,' Boone said. 'It sounds lovely.'

Storm got about it in the kitchen, and Boone opened the folders on the coffee table. They were only roughly ordered, so she unbound the papers and sorted them into piles. Noah's childhood artwork, which would be of the most value to Kate but useless to Boone, was pushed to one side. Then she gathered together all the photos into one heap, all the official-looking documents into another, and a final small pile for the letters Noah sent Kate after he was taken into care.

The photographs were mostly of Noah, either alone or with Kate. A few featured men, three different ones, each of them only appearing once. Boone hadn't thought to ask about Noah's father. She kept those pictures separate to ask Kate to identify the men.

There were three letters from Noah to Kate. They were brief, undated, and contained mostly a generic level of detail. He did mention a few other children at the home, though, and Boone jotted down their names. Might be a chance of locating them, getting some first-hand accounts of the place and of Noah whilst he was there.

The paperwork included court documents and letters from the local authorities, as well as reports from social workers and letters Kate had written. They painted a bleak picture of her life at the time. A single mother, out of work and struggling with addiction. She hadn't been capable of looking after herself, let alone a young boy. After Noah got in trouble a few times, shoplifting and fights at school, the council starting monitoring the situation. He was removed from her care shortly after his eighth birthday, following a fire at the council flat he and Kate lived in.

Life at the home didn't agree with Noah. Notes from the care workers there suggested behavioural changes, and there were multiple reports of fights and incidents of him running away. Each time they found him back with his mother. Each time until the last time, after which nobody saw him again. Police investigated it, and a few searches were organised, but no trace of the boy was ever found. Run away to London was the general consensus. Kate fell deeper into her addiction, a balm for the despair, Noah existing only in the corners of her memory. Twenty-five years later, living a different life, she was flush with guilty resolve.

As hopeless a cause as Boone could imagine.

Storm brought over their breakfast, perfectly poached eggs sitting atop piping hot muffins and curls of smoked salmon. Whereas Storm sliced though her yolk, letting it run over the rest, Boone carefully cut away the white until she was left with a chalky pocket of yellow that she deposited whole into her mouth and allowed to dissolve on her tongue in a moment of ecstasy. She opened her eyes to find Storm smiling, shaking her head.

'Is good,' Boone said.

Storm lent her professional eye to a combing of Noah's letters, and flicked through reports from doctors and social workers, seeing if she might pick anything up. A grunt signalled something of note.

'What have you got?' Boone asked.

'I know one of the social workers. Knew him, I should say. These situations are hard enough as it is, and he wouldn't have made it any easier.'

'Why?'

'There was a lot of talk about him. Let's say he was quick to take some kids into care, especially from vulnerable young mothers. Single, working class, often records for drugs or solicitation. Girls who had nobody to fight their corner. There were other rumours about him too, he was a strange man.'

'Nothing ever substantiated?'

Storm shook her head. 'Maybe six or seven years ago it looked like he was going to be investigated. A woman accused him of sexually abusing her when she was younger, said he removed her from her mother and raped her over the course of several years when she was in care. He died soon after, though, and it was one of those things that never gained any traction.'

'What was his name?' Boone said, scooting along the couch nearer Storm to get a look at the file she was holding.

'Jerry Killock,' Storm said.

'Christ.'

'Heard of him?'

Boone nodded. 'He was Sarah Still's case worker. That's a hell of a coincidence. A second one, on top of Noah's picture having been at Blackborne's house.'

'Did you look into Killock?'

'I didn't think much of it at the time. I spoke to someone at social services and they told me he was dead and they couldn't talk to me about his cases. Fair enough. I left it at that. I mean, he was a social worker. His name must be in the files of hundreds of kids who were abused. Maybe even others who ran away and went missing. But you said yourself there were whispers about him. Who's in a better position to prey on vulnerable children than a social worker?'

12

'You calling me, I don't have to guess whether it's business or pleasure,' Barb said by way of answering the phone, already figuring she was being tapped for something.

'Could be both,' Boone said.

Barb muttered some incoherent profanity beneath her breath.

'Besides, who cancelled on who the last few times?' Boone added.

Barb had arranged and then shied off several lunch dates at short notice over the previous few months. She blamed work, but Boone knew it was more than that. The stuff she got up to with Mickey Box, Barb had her suspicions and it didn't sit well with her. Neither did the way the Sarah Still business had finished up, with Barb finding Boone in a smashed heap outside a burning house and Roo dying in hospital. Coupled with Boone's increasingly asocial attitude, both of them were only making the barest gestures toward maintaining their friendship.

'I'm in Lark,' Barb said. 'Might be able to get away for a bit, but it'll have to be local and it can't be for long.'

Boone had a two-birds-with-one-stone kind of idea. 'We'll make it a picnic. I'll bring food and text you the place.'

Eastry House for Boys and Girls was derelict. Drive a mile south of Lark, past the camping park, and it stood alone on the shore as if it had dragged itself from the sea and come to rest at the first convenient spot. A once grand building, now in ruins, its windows put in by stones, walls annotated with graffiti.

Barb was waiting, parked up in the mouth of the drive, the gates padlocked. Boone pulled in behind her.

''Kin' hell, Boone. What's this place about?'

Boone held up a carrier bag. 'I have harissa chicken with couscous salad, or a roasted vegetable one with pomegranate tabbouleh. Look, it has squash and everything.'

'Who the fuck are you and what have you done with Boone?'

Barb took the chicken salad and rooted about in it with the plastic fork Boone gave her like she expected to find wall plugs buried in there.

'I tried eating a pomegranate once,' Boone said. 'Like you'd eat a normal bit of fruit. Didn't work out as well as I'd hoped. But I like it when other people put it in stuff.'

'I wanted a burger,' Barb said miserably, spearing three bits of chicken onto her fork and eating them at once. 'Not bloody Waitrose.'

'Courgette?' Boone offered a bit.

Barb glared as if she'd interfered with her pet. 'That other thing you asked about, a while back. Your mother.'

'I thought you said you couldn't—'

'Yeah, well. I did. You said she sent a postcard?'

'I'm getting this third hand off myself via my dead father and my ex-husband. Jack told me that I said my father told me that he received a postcard when she reached Canada. I don't know if I ever saw it or not.'

'Passport and visa records from back then are usually a bitch to confirm. But this was easy, because she never had a passport, so there are no records.'

'Never had one at all?'

'That name, that date of birth, never one issued. Tried her maiden name too.'

'So my father lied.'

'Unless she got documents in another name. Easier to do that back then. It would have been weird, though. I mean, why would she?'

'So my father couldn't find out where she went?'

'Seems extreme.'

'Maybe making up a story was easier for him. Meant I wouldn't go looking for her too.'

'You know what else it means.'

'She could be alive and here in Britain.'

'Could be. I found no social security records of any kind either, though. No benefits, no pension. And nothing comes up on a credit search.'

'Maybe the idea of her using another name isn't so unlikely then.'

'Maybe your dad killed her and she's under the patio at your child-hood home.'

'I've seen pictures. There wasn't a patio. There was a shed. Could be under that.'

'It's strange, her just disappearing. You find anything in those boxes of yours?'

'Nothing that helps find out what happened to her. She's given me a new appreciation of Judee Sill and Vashti Bunyan, though.'

'Sometimes I fear you'll sound like a student the rest of your life.'

'Well, technically I'm not even three years old, so that puts me ahead of the curve.'

Barb picked the last of the chicken out of her salad and snapped the plastic container shut with the fork inside, sitting it on the bonnet of her car. 'What did you call me out here for?'

'Kate Porter.'

'Kate Porter,' Barb repeated, as if scouring her memory.

'Thirty-odd years ago, she was Kate Maxwell. Her ten-year-old son, Noah, went missing. Never found. I met her this morning. Husband is big in recycling.'

'Porter? Like on the side of all the dustbin trucks?'

'That's them. Owns this place too.'

A low stone wall topped with wrought-iron palisades surrounded it, but boarding had been put up over the railings so the building could only be seen through the gates. Barb looked through them at the now overgrown plot, the house sitting forlornly at the centre.

'Old children's home.'

'Her son was taken here when he was removed from her. This was way back in the day, before she was married and a millionaire. She had him when she was fifteen, and that was about as good as it got. She was a user, street worker, your basic fairy-tale stuff. The kid ran away a few times. Last time, didn't come back.'

'Jesus, Boone. If you're looking for a kid missing three decades, I can tell you now how this one ends.'

'She knows he's dead. She thinks finding out what happened to him will put old ghosts to rest.'

'You disabuse her of that notion?'

'What are you going to tell someone who lost a child?'

'You got a lead then? That why you called me?'

'Maybe. Thing of it is, I've seen the boy before.'

'How's that now?'

'He was one of the children in the photos at Blackborne's house that burned down.'

Barb stared at her.

'And,' Boone went on, 'one of the social workers who dealt with the boy also worked with Sarah Still. That's two connections to the worst child predators nobody will ever know about.'

'Never going to let that go, are you?'

Blackborne and Hanley Moss were dead, but with the evidence destroyed by fire, the police never investigated their involvement in child trafficking and abuse, their public reputations tarnished only by the nature of the deaths of Moss and Blackborne's widow, Teddy.

'I'm going to need details,' Barb said.

Boone handed her a hand-written sheet from a spiral notepad.

'Gimme a sec.' Barb stepped away with her phone.

While Barb was busy, Boone unlocked the padlock on the gates to Eastry House. The wall only ran along the front of the property, the house standing in a large, perfectly square plot of land that was boxed in on the other three side by trees, bounded by a low rail fence that had fallen away in places. Tiling was missing from the roof of the house and the guttering had been torn away. Brickwork on one side was streaked black, evidence of a small fire. Strands of dead ivy clung desperately to the front, crisp brown trails hanging loose in places. The grass surrounding the house was waist high and seethed in the wind.

'Place has been empty years,' Barb said, approaching from behind.

'She bought it so they couldn't knock it down. I think she wanted me to see it. God knows why.'

'Some new psychic investigative technique? Picking up any vibrations?'

Boone ignored her and made for the house, the long grass kneeling underfoot. The double front doors were splintered around the lock and swung open with a shrill whine. The hall was large, matching flights of stairs climbing opposite walls and meeting in a mezzanine above them. Both had been shorn of their balustrade, as had the balcony between them. Peeling paint hung from the wall in great fronds.

'So?' Boone said.

'This Jerry Killock, we knew about him.'

'I heard there were rumours. So?'

'So what? He's a bit dead. There were accusations against him, but it was difficult to get movement on. Victims were reluctant to come forward, and then he went and died. Social services had no paperwork on Sarah Still.'

'How is that possible?'

'Well, if Killock was up to his tits in this like you think he was, I suspect he had probably grown adept at covering his tracks. Look, we can't speak to Killock, and we can't speak to Noah, so I'm not sure what you want us to do.'

'That's it? Another child predator goes uncovered.'

'I can tell you this – I'm growing a little tired of your insinuations. And what's more, I'm going to give you some unsolicited advice. Send that nice woman on her way so she can find some way of making peace with this tragedy. Your track record on this sort of thing isn't pretty reading, and nobody comes out of it better than they went in.'

'All right, take it easy.'

'I found you fucked up and bloody on the ground beside an inferno. Your friend lying not five yards away in a dramatically worse state than you. I thought we'd got past this sort of shit, Boone, I really did. Whatever you get up to now, I don't ask any questions. But it's better than the previous.' She tossed her salad container onto a heap of folded and mouldering carpets.

'Well, who else is going to help this woman?'

'You don't think I want to be able to tell her something about her son? You don't think my heart breaks for her? Unless we have new evidence, Boone, my hands are tied. There's a difference between knowing things happened and being able to prove them. But you will go round raking up old shit, no doubt getting yourself in a world of trouble, and people will say, oh why is it the brave and wonderful Abigail Boone can find this stuff out when she's but a lone woman, and the police can't do squat? But the fact is, we do know. Only we have to be able to take the thing to court.'

'Police didn't know shit last time. Sarah Still. Blackborne.'

'Actually, point of fact, we did know. We had a very capable detective sergeant who knew quite a lot. Unfortunately, she declined to share with her colleagues, so when she walked into a situation all alone, it lasted four days in a shithole flat in east London and ended with one dead body, two escaped murderers, a blazing fire, and her getting tipped off a balcony and smashed to bits. You think you're a different person to the Boone from before then, but everything still seems to end with dead girls, house fires and long falls with you.'

'Oh fuck off.'

'There is zero appetite to open up a can of these kind of worms, and we don't have the manpower to do it when I have what looks like some kind of Vietnamese gang conflict going off involving people-traffickers and weed suppliers. Unless your employer has some kind of professional insight he can offer on the latter.'

Boone snorted.

'Exactly. Thanks for the lunch. Go fuck yourself.'

Barb strode off, cutting a faint line through the grass and vanishing between the trees. Boone let her go. Variations of the row had happened before and would no doubt happen again.

Back in the Transit, Boone dialled a number she had searched out earlier.

'Hi, I'd like to speak to Harry Eustace if possible. Yep, I'll hold.'

Eating another mouth of cold squash, she considered that she really should have picked up burgers.

'Hello, Mr Eustace? My name is Abigail Boone. I'm sure you don't remember me but . . . Uh, yeah, that's right. Sarah Still. Listen, I know you can't really speak to me, but I represent a woman called Kate Porter. Her son, Noah Maxwell, was in the system some time ago, in the eighties. I was . . . No, I'm in the Lark area right now . . . Yeah, I know where that is. Fifteen minutes? Sure. Thanks. See you then.'

She hung up, somewhat baffled. Harry Eustace had worked with Jerry Killock and taken over a lot of his cases, but when Boone had asked him the previous year about Sarah Still, he had given her short shrift. Now he was being more than accommodating, clearing time for her to come in and see him. Still, gift horses and mouths.

Harry Eustace had never met a door he couldn't hold open for someone. If Boone had imagined a social worker, he was exactly what she might have conjured up. Probably her age, forty at most, with a full beard but thinning on top. Brushed-cotton trousers with a midnight-blue puppytooth waistcoat over an unironed shirt.

A woman in a small window in the wall didn't look up as she greeted Eustace, buzzing him through a door to a suite of offices on the fourth floor. Lark District Council was housed inside a grey monstrosity that seemed to block out the sun from any angle.

His office was the last on the left in a thin corridor that stank of cheap cleaning products. It was small – anything more than the desk and two chairs would be too tight – and had a solitary window. Boone noticed an empty lunch box on the sill behind the desk, debris on the floor below. The window had no view to speak of, a crack of sea between the surrounding buildings, but she could picture Eustace sitting there for his lunch. Even a yard from the desk making it feel like a break.

'I was surprised you agreed to see me,' she said.

Eustace held his hands up, surrendering.

'Confession upfront. I can't tell you anything about Noah Maxwell. Though if you've spoken to his mother, I suspect you know about as much as I do anyway. The police had his file and I understand they showed it to her.'

'They did.'

'I saw you in the papers. When was that, a year ago?'

'Thereabouts.'

'Remembered you from when you called. Everyone here knows what you did.'

Boone could hear the blood in her ears. For a moment she imagined she would have to fight to get out of there alive. She had no blade on her, had allowed herself to get soft. Pen caddy on the desk. One sharpened HB pencil, a lidless biro, and what looked like a staple remover that could be put to good use.

'The things they found at that house,' Eustace said. 'You're a hero to some of us. Did they ever catch the men?'

Boone relaxed. 'No. Never did. Fled the country, they think. Between me and you, though, I managed to hurt one of them, so he might not have got that far.'

Eustace grinned. 'When you said you were in the area, well, I know it's a bit cheeky, but I sort of wanted to meet you. Explain face to face why I brushed you off before, with Sarah Still. Information on people like that, it's just not something I can give out, no matter how much I want to. Police don't do a damnable thing about some of these kids, and nobody hears about us unless we act too early or too late. It's fine lines.'

'I wouldn't like to be making the calls. My experience has all been on the too-late end of the spectrum.'

Eustace's face turned grave. 'With Jerry. That was a hell of a thing. Worked with the man for years and he always seemed perfectly normal. No, that's not true. He was better than normal, one of the best. I just couldn't believe it when the stories started.'

'You believe them now?'

Eustace blew his lips. 'I don't know. I don't want to, I know that much. I don't want to believe that anyone who worked here was capable of taking advantage of the kind of vulnerable people we come into contact with.'

'None of it went anywhere when he was alive.'

'No. This was before Savile, mind. It was a cause that hadn't found its moment yet. You don't want to know the breadth of institutional abuse in this country through the seventies and eighties. My God. And there were countless convictions, but the story just never seemed to take off in any wider sense.'

'The police said Killock had no files on Sarah Still.'

'That's the other thing I wanted to tell you. I can't give you files, but I figure telling you about the absence of files is a grey area. One of the coppers, he said he thought Jerry had been grooming girls. Maybe even effectively running cases, making home visits and the like, but never officially opening files. I looked through the stuff we had on Noah Maxwell too.'

He faltered, and Boone thought he seemed visibly shaken.

'That boy was failed in more ways than I can count. What might have become of him, it doesn't even bear thinking about.'

'His mother has come to terms with the idea that her son is probably dead. What she wants is to find out the circumstances. See if we can find any trace of him after his time at Eastry.'

'Christ, that place.'

'Bad?'

'Bad enough it was closed down. Looks lovely, down there on the seafront. Loads of land around, the water right there. You know, I'm not supposed to say things like this, but when you look into it, in the years after the war when the welfare state grew and local authorities opened these homes, they were all run by women. So many widows, I guess. Most of them lived in the homes with the children. I'm not saying they weren't strict, the matrons and what have you, but you never had the likes of what happened later. Men started taking the jobs; they had become better paid, I suppose. Sixties and seventies and everything started changing.'

'Killock have much to do with Eastry then?'

'It was closed before my time, but his name crops up in connection quite a lot. Can't say more than that now, but quite a lot.'

'I understand.'

'With young Noah, though, like I said, I read his file. I think it was pruned. There's nothing essential missing, nothing where you'd say, oh, where's the court paperwork or the form for this or that. But it just felt slight. Like it had been kept to a minimum so you couldn't learn much from it.' He shook his head. 'I knew the man. What does it say about me that this sort of thing went unnoticed?'

'Nobody knows what goes on in the heads of others.'

'Listen, if anything crops up, new evidence and the like, if you get the police involved, then I can help you out, no sweat. People here are absolutely sick about Jerry and will pull up trees to help in any way. But we need authorisation, court orders and whatever. We have that, and we're in business.'

'I appreciate that, Harry.'

'Here, take one of these.' Eustace handed Boone his card. 'Mobile's scribbled on the back there, so you can get straight through to me.'

'Thanks.'

'I know it means less than nothing now, but please offer Mrs Porter my sympathies. It can't have been easy for her back then, single mother struggling. I hope she finds what she's looking for.'

13

The harbour at Lark was home now to a smattering of small boats that weekenders pottered about in, and a couple of larger yachts that looked like they'd got lost trying to find Poole. Boone left the Transit in the car park out near the harbour arm and walked back to the foot of a now pedestrianised street that curved up a gentle slope to the crown of the hill overlooking the seafront.

Once the town's high street, many of the shops were closed now, and those that weren't were eateries or estate agents. A café shared the ground floor of a grand Victorian building with a small supermarket. It sported gothic finials and had been recently dressed in terracotta. Half a dozen tables sat outside on the broad pavement, and Kate Porter was already there, with an empty coffee cup before her. It was after five and still bright, but a chill was coming in off the water.

'Kate, hey. Thanks for meeting me.'

She stood up. 'No problem. Got me out. I can spend days rattling round that old mausoleum. Did you have a read of the stuff?'

'I did.'

Boone wanted to tell her there was little chance of discovering what had happened to Noah and she'd be better off trying to come to terms with things some other way. Eustace had said he hoped Kate found what she was looking for, but Boone doubted the woman even knew what that was. She figured the kindest thing to do would be to hunt down what little there was to go on and let things take their natural course. She ordered coffee for them both and pulled out a thin folder with some of the papers Kate had given her.

'Someone knows what happened to my boy,' Kate said, clutching her coffee in both hands. 'He can't just be lost.'

'These photos you gave me.' Boone fanned them out on the table. 'There are three different men who appear with you and Noah. Who are they?'

'That's my brother.' Kate pointed to a smiling, sandy-haired chap. 'Matty. He lives in Tenby. Don't see him much. He and my husband don't get on. Noah didn't remember him when he came to visit that time as Matty hadn't seen him since he was in nappies.'

She slid the picture aside and picked up the next one.

'Col McGregor. Knocked around with him for a bit till he joined the army. He was in Ireland when Noah was taken into care. Never saw him again. He was killed by a sniper in Andersonstown the year before Noah went missing.'

She dropped his picture and tapped the last one.

'Racked my brains trying to remember him, but I've no idea. Truth told, he probably was someone I scored with. Look at Noah there, though. Can't have been more than six, so it was years before he disappeared.'

Boone collected the pictures and put them away. 'We never spoke about the father.'

'Not much to say. I didn't know who he was. I was young and a bit of a one. Didn't even know I was pregnant until the fifth month. Or didn't want to know.'

'Any chief suspects? Someone who could have put it together themselves later on?'

'Faces came and went in my life back then. It could have been one of . . . God, I'd be embarrassed to even try and put a number on it. Whoever he was, he never knew.'

'Okay.'

'This isn't helping, is it?'

'Ruling stuff out is good at this point. What about the kids Noah mentioned in his letters? Did you ever meet them? He talks about a Gary and a Sean.'

'Maybe, when I visited him. I didn't really know the boys. It's the girl I mostly remember. She'd chat with me and play with Noah when I was there.'

'This would be Lilly?' Boone scanned through one of the letters.

Kate smiled. 'Noah called her that, but she'd tell adults it was Lillian, as if it was more grown-up.'

'Any idea on her surname?'

'Bancroft,' Kate said, surprisingly fast.

'That stuck in your mind.'

'I loved Anne Bancroft. My mother took me to see *The Turning Point* at the pictures. We used to go a lot, but not after Noah came. Do you think you can find her?'

'Maybe. Now, something else. The paperwork from the local authorities, a lot of it was drawn up by the same social worker. He would have made home visits, written reports. The file is pretty thin, but he would have been instrumental in Noah being taken into care. Jerry Killock his name was. Ring any bells?

Kate nodded. 'I wouldn't have been able to name him before, but the private investigators I hired told me about him, and I vaguely remember a man calling himself Jerry. I can't fill in any details, though. You have to remember, I was using heavily back then. I was in no state to remember. That's why they took Noah away.'

'Thing is, I've heard of Killock before.'

'That sounds ominous.'

'What I told you, about what happened to my memory. About the men who killed my friend. The whole thing was connected to a grooming gang who had operated for years in the area. I think Jerry Killock was involved with them.'

Kate's face stiffened but didn't give.

'The reason I'm telling you this is because if we press ahead and by some miracle do find something . . . the chances are it isn't going to be particularly pleasant news.'

Kate went quiet, and Boone willed her not to cry. She had a horror of ministering to the tearful.

'I've imagined all the things that might have happened to my son. Imagined them endlessly and vividly. I expect the truth, whatever it might be, won't be nearly so bad.'

'Okay. I want you to look at something.' Boone slid a picture across the table, a headshot cropped from a larger photograph. 'Do you think that could be Lilly? She'd be eighteen or nineteen here, so older than when you knew her.'

'Lord, it was almost thirty years ago. I doubt I'd even recognise Noah now, if he was still alive, let alone his little mates.' She squinted at the picture. 'My God. Yes, that could be her. Around the eyes, and that smile.'

Boone had searched social media for mentions of Eastry House, hoping to track down people who'd been there in the eighties. A Lilly Bancroft had tweeted about the fire there the previous year. Reading back through her posts, Boone discovered she had done some modelling in the nineties, and found some of her work on an online forum.

'That woman's name is Lilly Bancroft, so I'm pretty certain it's the same person.' She showed Kate another photo. 'This is her now.'

'Big lass,' Kate said.

It was a recent picture, taken from Twitter, Lilly standing outside the shop she worked in, wearing the green fleece jacket all the staff had.

'Wait,' Kate said, turning in her seat to look behind her. 'That's here. That's the supermarket.'

'Eyes forward, lady.'

'Is that her at the till?'

'Kate, we're not stalking the shop assistant. We're just out of a late afternoon, having coffee and a natter.'

Excited by this new glimmer of hope, Kate pushed her sunglasses up onto her head and then slid them back down again. She chewed at a snagged nail. She drank her coffee in about three gulps. She talked nervously.

'I don't really do this. I don't have many friends that I can just call and meet for a coffee. My husband and I go to a lot of events through his work, but that's an extension of the business. I spend most of my free time in the garden looking after the hydrangeas. My old friends were all users, which means they're not really friends at all. And since then—'

'Do what I do. Pretend you're playing a human.'

'The other day, you told me you had a son.'

Boone nodded. 'Quin.'

'How old?'

'He'll be sixteen now.'

'You see much of him?'

'No. Things I did, I gave him reason to be afraid of me. And I put him in danger. That age, there's so much going on with them anyway.'

Kate nodded. 'You don't remember his childhood?'

'No. Not a thing.'

'When something like that happens, when you lose your memory, what do they do for you? Hypnosis or something?'

'I was in a clinic for nine months. I don't remember all of that, but I know they tried everything. Including hypnosis.'

'Is it better?'

'What do you mean?'

'Not being able to remember. Is that better?'

Nobody had ever asked Boone that before. 'I forgot all the good stuff. The bad stuff has all happened since. So no.'

Behind Kate, a broad whey-faced woman stepped out of the shop. She wore a green fleece and a look of existential distress. She lit a cigarette, stuffing the box back into a brown satchel bag slung over one shoulder, and hurried purposefully up the cobbled street, head down as if she was scouring the ground for dropped change.

'Here we go,' Boone said.

'We're just going to go up to her?'

'Hopefully. I've been known to tell a few fibs, so just go with it.'

They had to climb the steep road at a gallop to catch up with her.

'Excuse me, Lilly?' Boone said.

She turned, eyeing them warily. A piercing in the side of her nose, a small gold seahorse, glinted with the odd errant sunbeam.

'It is Lilly, isn't it?'

'Who are you?'

'My name's Boone. I was wondering if I could talk to you for a minute. It's about Eastry House.'

'Eastry—I'm sorry, who are you? Who told you to speak to me?'

'If we could go somewhere, buy you a coffee or something, I can explain.'

'Are you press? I don't want to talk about that place. Leave me alone.'

She started to walk off, and Boone said, 'It's about Noah Maxwell.'

Lilly stopped but didn't turn back towards them.

'I'm not press. I'm not police. I'm looking for Noah and wanted to speak to someone who was at Eastry with him.'

'I don't know anything about that,' Lilly said, her voice low. 'I'm going. Don't follow me.'

'We played skittles once,' Kate said, stepping forward. 'Noah had a set at Eastry, plastic in a net bag. He was rubbish at it. He was never much cop with throwing or kicking things. But you fetched two brooms and showed him how to hold them together so he could roll the ball down the groove between them, aiming it at the skittles.'

Lilly looked at her, mouth open.

'It's me – Kate. Noah's mum.'

'It's just a quiet word,' Boone said. She held out a pair of twenties between her fingers. 'Information is all we're after.'

Lilly looked up the street. She threw her cigarette, still half of it left, into the narrow gutter by the kerb, and it floated away haphazardly on a trickle of water, collecting with others of its kind on the grating over a drain.

'Usually I get a drink after my shift.'

'Lead on,' Boone said.

Kingsgate had been a historical street destroyed by shelling during the war. Though the road no longer existed, the junction at the top of the hill where new streets met was commonly known as the Kingsgate, and the expensive hotel there still bore the name.

The Ship was tucked away round a corner from the main drag, with a mock-Tudor facade and tiny windows thicker than bottle glass. It was a pub like they used to be except emptied of its smoke and punters. Fruit machines hid in nooks and crannies as if in shame of their wares, and a refrigerated display promising pies and pasties was stripped bare, unplugged and unloved.

Lilly ordered two large whiskies and left Boone to pay as she carried them to a table.

'I remember you, you know,' she told Kate. 'Didn't nobody visit me, so I liked it when other parents came. Some of them, anyways. They never found him then, Noah?'

Kate shook her head.

'And you're looking for him now?'

'I'd like to know what happened.'

'I was ten, not sure what help I can be. Things that happen, you can't know if they was exactly like you remember. They change in your mind.'

Boone pulled up a stool across from her. 'What do you remember from the time Noah went missing?'

'Well, he ran, didn't he? Did it a few times before and all.'

'He always used to run home, to me,' Kate said. 'They'd come and get him. That last time, though, I never saw him.'

'I don't remember it being no different. At the back of Eastry there was a flat roof, and you could get on it from the window in the hallway above. It was open in the morning when we found him gone, so everyone reckoned he did what he always did.'

'Lilly, do you remember a man called Jerry Killock?' Boone said.

Lilly sized her up. 'Still fuzzy on who you are.'

'She's a friend,' said Kate. 'Helping me look into things.'

'He was a social worker,' Boone said.

'He was a lot of things, that one,' Lilly said.

Boone glanced at Kate. 'We heard there were rumours about him.'

'Weren't no rumours. Whatever you heard, he probably did it.'

'Did he take you anywhere?' Boone said. 'Away from Eastry?'

'The seaside house, you mean?'

'Seaside house?' Boone said.

'That's what they called it. Big house by the sea. Not his home, like, but another place.'

'He took you there?'

'Killock was one for the boys, him. He'd buy them things. Toys or games.' She looked at Kate. 'That skittle set.'

'The skittles,' Kate said. 'So he took Noah?'

'Took a lot of boys. Noah was small for his age. He liked them small.'

Kate gripped the banquette seating either side of her. She breathed deeply. Boone reached out below the corner of the table and touched her hand lightly.

'You don't know where this was?' Boone said.

Lilly shook her head. 'Only heard tell. I remember Noah telling me he thought he woke up underground.'

'Like a cellar?' said Boone.

Lilly shrugged. She drained one of her glasses in quick little sips, licking her lips in between.

'I did some modelling, you know,' she said. 'I did Page Three.'

'That right?' Boone said.

'In the *Sunday Sport*. Pages nine and seventeen too. Bit of acting. Played a tart in *The Bill*. Went back to the glamour stuff after that. And a few other things. Won't seem it now, all gone to seed, but I was a looker back in the day. Though I always looked fat, even when I wasn't. Around the face and that. Sometimes I think maybe I was born to be fat. That's silly, though. Nobody's born to be anything, except maybe kings and queens.'

Legs crossed, one foot bouncing up and down at a rate, she fooled around with her second drink, turning the glass on the table.

'I had to throw up for *The Bill*. In the scene, I mean. The character had to. It was what they call off-screen, and they made me make the noise, like I was coughing or choking. I said to them you don't really make that sort of noise when you're heaving because your throat's full of vomit. You only hear the splash. I even told them I could do it for real. Just get me some water and an apple. Cut it into little chunks, no problem. I did these other films, see, where I had to throw up, and that's how they did it. But *The Bill* didn't want the real thing. Just the noises.'

'Lilly?' Boone said.

'Yeah?'

'This is difficult, what we're asking you to remember. I know that. Did Killock ever take kids somewhere else? Not near the sea, but in the country somewhere. Maybe to see other people.'

'Treats, he called them. Trips out for children who behaved themselves. He'd give us drinks, remember the things with the ice? They'd put the bright syrup on the crush. Do they still have that? I guess he laced them with something. Everything was like you were just falling asleep after that. Sometimes I had to be carried out of the car. Sometimes I think maybe I was dreaming.'

'I thought he only liked boys?' Boone said.

'He used to like Lego.'

'Who? Killock?' said Boone.

'She means Noah,' Kate said.

'I remember he had Lego. Though it was mostly just the little people, not any blocks or anything. I used to pluck off their heads, leave them in a row on the windowsill as a warning to other little Lego men. He didn't like that.'

'Lilly, you said Killock took you somewhere. Was this to a big house out in the country?'

'It was big. But it was a farm or something. They called it the dairy. Christ, Killock knew some evil people, but Sally was something else.'

'Sally?' Boone said.

'And that other one.' Lilly ran a hand across her face, down her jaw to her chin. 'With the face. Something wrong with him.' She looked quickly at Boone. 'Not like you, with the . . .' She pointed at Boone's scar. 'His whole face was misshapen, like he was deformed. He had no mouth, it looked like. It was horrible. We called him the goblin. He was nothing compared to Sally, though.'

'Who's Sally, Lilly?' Boone asked.

Lilly let her second whisky slide down her neck in one. 'Look, ta for the drink and that, but I have to be off.'

'Lilly, please,' Kate said.

'I told you that sometimes it feels like it was all a dream. That's not true. There were things that happened that are more real than anything else in my life. I'm forty years old and sometimes those things fill every year I've been alive, and I could believe they were the only things that ever happened to me.

'Whatever you're doing, looking for Noah or what might have happened to him, if you start rooting around in all of that, Sally and the old dairy, nothing good will come of it. You don't want any part of those people. Nobody walks away from Sally the same. I'll not have it on me that you got tangled up in all that.'

She stood, pulling on her green fleece.

'Lilly, please wait,' Boone said.

'Don't come to the shop again. Don't try to contact me. I can't help. I ever see either of you again, I'll up sticks and go. You'll never find me.'

A few earwiggers had picked up on the tension, watching them closely after Lilly left. Kate nodded toward the door. Boone agreed and they left their drinks and hurried out.

'Sally mean anything to you?' Kate said.

Boone shook her head. 'Hasn't come up before.'

'Who do you suppose she was? Another social worker, like Killock? Someone who worked at Eastry?'

'No idea,' Boone said. 'But I know someone who might.'

14

Boone told Kate she'd let her know if anything new cropped up. On the drive home, she called Harry Eustace, who picked up almost immediately.

'Harry, it's Boone.'

'Blimey, thought it'd be longer than a few hours before I heard from you again.'

'I just spoke to a woman who was at Eastry with Noah.'

'That must have been a pleasant chat.'

'It was a bad place, Harry.'

'I'd say it left its mark on people.'

'A name cropped up. I know you can't tell me much, but I think this person might have been staff at Eastry, or a social worker perhaps.'

'Might be I could look at some records, and if I were to cough, who could say what that meant?'

'Thanks, Harry. I've only got a first name. Sally.'

'Sally. Sally. Nobody called Sally ever worked at Social as long as I've been here. Give me a sec to look at the system. How did you find this woman so quickly?'

'Social media. Loudest, most dramatic cry for help in history.'

'Ha. I had a look, though, and didn't find you online.'

'Different kind of help I need.'

'Only showing two Sallys working for Kent social services during the time, and both of them were strictly admin. Doesn't match any of the staff at Eastry. Of course, there could have been volunteers and what have you, people who helped out casually. It was a different time, safety checks weren't what they are now.'

'Yeah, okay. It was a long shot anyway.'

'Is Jerry tying in to any of this?'

'Woman I spoke to, Lilly Bancroft, she says Killock was her case worker. She had strong views on the man.'

'Okay. I'll run it up the pole to my superiors. Might be, if they feel there's enough to look at it again formally, they'll contact the police.'

'Yeah, all right. Cheers for that, Harry.'

'No worries. Keep in touch.'

Boone promised she would and ended the call. By the time she got back to the caravan, the sun was down and she had listened to The Slits' first album twice. She poured herself a glass of white from an open bottle in the fridge and drank it at the kitchen counter, looking out over the fields. There were lights on at the cottage.

Putting on her boots, she took the pathway along the creek, ignoring the sententious bleating of the Calvinist sheep in the next field, and came up behind the cottage. The back door was unlocked, so she kicked her boots off in the porch and went in. Nobody was in the kitchen, the smells of dinner lingering, but she heard voices in the lounge.

'Hey,' she said.

Mickey Box grunted from his armchair. Tess, sprawled on the sofa, neither said anything nor moved to make room for Boone. Fitz was sat cross-legged on the floor helping Jim slot wooden shapes into their matching holes in a box. On the television Gene Hackman's private eye was showing Jennifer Warren a move on a travel chess set.

'Love this film,' Boone said.

She watched Fitz with the boy, an unlikely sight and yet the most natural thing in the world. He showed Jim a triangular piece of wood and demonstrated how it fitted into a triangular slot. Jim held out a tiny hand, as if in eagerness to show he understood, and when Fitz handed him the wooden triangle he threw it clear across the room and grinned when it clattered against the sideboard. Nobody could so completely misunderstand a child as its parent.

'Generous of the boy to work on your yorker with you, Fitzy,' Boone said.

Out of the corner of his eye, Mickey Box surveyed the scene for damage but made no comment. Boone caught a look from Tess and wished she hadn't said anything. Mickey Box didn't know the boy was Fitz's son and Boone got the feeling everyone was more settled in that ignorance when she wasn't there. She wished she didn't know, then perhaps others wouldn't worry when she was around.

Self-conscious, Fitz said he should be going and made to get up.

'No,' Boone said. 'I'm interrupting. You stay where you are.'

Placing a hand on his shoulder, she eased him back down. Jim climbed onto unsteady feet and plonked himself down in Fitz's lap, drumming his shin with the rectangular wooden block.

'I, uh, really only came for coffee,' Boone lied. 'Forgot to pick any up. Wondered if I could steal a few beans.'

'Know where it is,' Mickey Box said, not taking his eyes away from the television. He was watching Hackman, who was watching all the splendours of the Gulf sliding beneath a glass-bottomed boat.

Boone returned to the kitchen feeling stupid. She took a small baggie of coffee beans from the cupboard and walked back to the caravan, tossing the coffee in the bin. Fetching her own ground coffee from an airtight canister on a shelf, she fixed up a brew in the cafetière and sat down in front of the television with a mug. *The Go-Between* had just started and she stayed with it until it finished. Julie Christie really was something else.

She showered, leaving her hair until the morning, and got into bed. Night draped around her, dark as the days gone before and those yet to come. She fell into fitful sleep and dreamed of a mother she never knew, in this life or the last, recognising her face without ever seeing it in any way that made sense. She pressed on, deeper into the dream's maw, believing it to be a pure kind of blackness she imagined, close and suffocating and pouring down her throat, filling her lungs like deep seawater. But it wasn't that at all.

It was smoke, and the caravan was aflame.

15

Boone lay awake and still for a moment, sifting through her mind for the noise that had disturbed her. She coughed. The sound had been unfamiliar and perhaps hadn't been real at all. The coughing turned into a fit, good Lord, and she had to sit up and fumble about for the glass of water, don't grab the one with the dental bridge by mistake. Her eyes stung. Suddenly alert, she swiped at the smoke she was choking on and rolled off the bed onto the floor, keeping low.

A hue of fire at the door rim, heat leaping off it before she even got close. Reaching up to her bedside cabinet, she spilled the glass of solution but closed her fingers around her bridge. Holding it in her fist, she scrambled round the bed on her hands and knees and raised the window, batting away the bug screen. She looked back with thoughts of saving things, but black smoke was rolling up from beneath the door now, mushrooming under the ceiling, and with it came the petrochemical stench of an accelerant.

She clambered out of the window head first and tumbled to the ground below. The dewy grass was cold beside the fire's heat. Staggering a few steps away, she vomited in the grass and dropped to her knees, retching. Her eyes teared, blinded by the smoke. Her ears hummed with sounds that had no natural origins until through the clamour she made out her name. She searched her mind for reasons someone might be in her home but found none. Then Tess appeared round the corner of the caravan.

'Jesus, Boone,' she said, running over. 'I thought you were inside.'

Boone coughed and spat up black phlegm.

'Window,' she managed, pointing.

'I saw the flames from the kitchen,' Tess said.

Fire engulfed one side of the caravan and curled wickedly onto the roof. Boone was barefoot in shorts and a tee, her arms and legs streaked black. She slipped her bridge into a pocket and they walked away from the caravan and towards the cottage.

'Gas,' Boone said suddenly, turning and dashing back.

Next to the decking round the front was a shed with two sections, one for Boone's bike and the other housing the gas cylinders. She pulled open the hinged door and disconnected the gas, heaving the cylinders out and dragging them a safe distance from the fire.

'Fuck,' she said, as if remembering something else.

Tess yelled at her to stop, but she leapt up onto the decking and tried to open the door. The metal handle burned her, so she grabbed it through her T-shirt and slid the door back. Smoke churned out everywhere, like culprits fleeing the scene and, pulling her shirt up over her mouth and nostrils, Boone disappeared into the darkness beyond.

She re-emerged what felt like hours later clutching two photo frames, coughing violently, her hair smouldering. Tess pulled her away to the fence at the edge of the caravan's plot and patted down her hair.

'What the hell were you doing?'

Still coughing, Boone handed her the pictures. One was of Roo, spinning and laughing in a summery dress; the other was of Sarah Still as a child, before she went missing, before she was killed and buried beneath a lonely field.

'Jesus fucking Christ, we've got pictures on digital, Boone. Can just print new ones out.' She dropped the frames on the soft ground.

'Not that one,' Boone said, pointing to the one of Sarah Still.

Tess shoved her hard. Then struck her on the arm with the heel of her hand, turning into little fists hammering at her chest and shoulders.

'What the hell were you doing?' she screamed.

Boone went down on one knee, spluttering and being knocked about and wondering which one of them was loopier. Mickey Box appeared holding a fire extinguisher. He looked at the fire and put the green can down. Things had gone a bit past that. Eyes blacker than slag in the dark, his edges blurred in the warp of heat. There was nothing left to do but stand and watch.

'Where's Jim?' Tess said.

'In his cot, wondering what the fuss is about,' Mickey Box said.

Boone stood, cradling her burned hand. Tess collected the photo frames from where she'd dropped them and, without a word, turned and marched back to the cottage. Suddenly feeling exposed in her nightwear, Boone hurried after her, hopping gingerly through the field unshod.

In the kitchen, Tess took hold of her hand, turning it this way and that, tutting and sighing.

'Wrap it round a cold rum and Coke and the pain will go away,' Boone said.

Tess didn't laugh. She pressed Boone down into a chair at the table and ran a bowl of cool water, having her soak her hand. It wasn't so bad. She applied a soothing antibiotic ointment to the livid skin and loosely bandaged it. The frames were on the table. The back of Roo's was fire-damaged and there was some scorching to the edge of the photograph. Tess spun it round to face her and smiled, but her face cracked a little and she brought her hand to her mouth.

'I thought you were stuck.'

'I'm fine.'

'You always say that.'

'Tess, really. I'm—'

'Why did you go back inside?' She quickly stood up, turning herself away, but Boone caught her hand, holding it over her shoulder as Tess stood behind her.

'Fuck.' Tess mashed a fist into a damp eye. 'You're an idiot, you know that? And you're insane.'

'Not completely. Just a borderline case.'

Tess fell upon her like a blanket, arms round her tight.

'Bad enough people keep setting fire to places with you in them. Please don't run back into them when you've got out.'

'That was my first time. Can't say I cared for it.'

Fire consumed the caravan in under half an hour. The roof and decking collapsed and only one corner remained standing on the metal base as the flames subsided to a low lick. The night was still and the smoke stood thin and unwavering in the grey moonlight.

Boone slept for a few hours on the sofa, Tess folded up beside her. The smell of coffee woke them both. Tess found her a robe and woolly socks from her room and the pair padded through to the kitchen, where Mickey Box was dishing up a full English. They ate quietly and contentedly.

'These are all the clothes I own,' Boone said, looking down at herself. 'And the robe and the socks aren't mine.'

'Most of your stuff has needed torching for a while,' Tess said. 'Ooh, we can go shopping. There's a boutique in Tunbridge Wells I've always wanted to spend someone else's money in.'

Boone couldn't believe this was happening to her.

'You two friends again then?' Mickey Box said.

They went quiet, stealing little glances at each other.

'See?' he said to Boone. 'Should have burned that thing down ages ago.'

His phone went and he stepped away from the table, it being Fitz as everyone else who had the number was sitting there. Tess sized Boone up with narrowed eyes.

'Ask yourself this,' Boone said. 'If I burned the place down, would I leave my music in there?'

'Fair point.'

Tess looked round to find her father and, seeing he had wandered off down the hall to the living room, pushed the door closed.

'Is this something to do with Mick?' she said.

'I don't see how.'

'Whatever job you just did for him. Something coming back on you?'

'That went down clean. Nobody traced us back here. And if it was about Mick, they'd have come for the cottage. I think it's about something else.'

Boone explained about Kate Porter and Noah and what she'd found out over the past few days.

'So, who are you thinking? This Lilly?'

'I don't know. How she's grown up having to fend for herself, she's slyer than she lets on. Honestly, she could have followed us back from the pub. I wasn't looking for her, so might not have noticed.'

'Were you drinking?'

'I was not.'

'Because a couple of jars and you're not as sharp as you'd like to think. And a couple of jars is becoming a regular habit.'

'Keeping tabs now?'

'Never stopped.'

'Shit,' Boone said, standing suddenly. 'Whoever it was, they might have gone for Kate too. I need to call her. My phone was in the fire.'

'We have tons of phones. Mick keeps loads of them for as and when.'

'I don't know any numbers.' Boone thought about Storm and Barb and even Jack. 'Fuck.'

'I got you on that front. As often as you lose the fucking thing, it got annoying finding all the numbers again. It backs you up online.'

'You backed the phone up? Tess—'

'Your personal phone. Not your out-on-the-rob phones.'

'And the numbers are all . . .' Boone waved her fingers upwards, 'up in the sky somewhere?'

'Yes. They're all up in the sky in the cosmic drives where all data goes to die.'

'I might have forgotten a good many things, but not how to dish out a sound thrashing.'

'Try it, old man.'

Boone sat down. 'I don't even have any clothes I'd feel good about starting a fight in.'

'Come on,' Tess said.

In her bedroom, she rooted out some clothes for Boone and then scavenged about in drawers until she found an old phone handset. As Boone dressed, she reset the device and logged Boone in, retrieving her numbers.

'There.'

Boone looked at it suspiciously, always certain there was some angle she was missing with technology, something that would hang her out by her own petard eventually. She called Kate, who reported that the waterworks had not been burned to the ground but insisted on coming to the cottage. She said she wanted to check on Boone, but Boone thought she was afraid and didn't want to be home alone, and who could blame her for that?

By the time she arrived, Boone had inherited a pair of wellies from Tess, as all her shoes were a couple of sizes too small, and from Mickey

Box an old parka whose pockets were ripped through to the lining, and she had the general appearance of a Guy on Bonfire Night.

Turned out Kate wasn't as afraid as Boone had thought.

'I think it was Lilly,' she said, walking over to the caravan with Boone and Tess.

'Why?' said Boone.

'I dropped in at the shop before I came. The girl at the counter said she hadn't shown up this morning to open and the manager was furious. Had been trying to call her but had no luck.'

'Jesus, Kate. If it was her and she had been there—'

'She wasn't going to do anything in front of people buying their morning papers.'

The metal base frame of the double-wide was charred black and hung with globs of melted plastic. The fridge and oven could be made out, heeled in the cinder dust, but there was nothing to be salvaged. The pale smoke of the dying fire ascended as though through rents in the earth and ravelled into the blue above.

Boone tallied the cost in her head. Quite apart from the quotidian – clothes, food, books, television and a hard drive of illicitly downloaded films – the few things of meaning she had assembled in her life were also gone. The iPod, a final gift from her son. The boxes of her father's possessions. Her mother's mixtapes. All the pictures she had of her parents.

It was a second erasure of her life, and although on a much smaller level than the first, which took her memory from her, the fact that she remembered the things she'd lost this time stung in a different way.

At the cottage, Tess made coffee and they confabbed round the kitchen table. Mickey Box sat in on things, the arsoning of property he owned not a quarter-mile from his home being grounds enough to command his full attention.

'If some mad cunt is trying to cook you, and they knew about the caravan, then they just as like know about this place, which means I'll be needing to give them the short talk.'

'It doesn't make sense,' Boone said. 'I can't see why Lilly would do it.'

'She's done a runner, though,' Kate said.

'And that I understand,' said Boone. 'All of this getting stirred up again, I can see her just packing up and hauling out. I can maybe even see her deciding to follow me, see who I am. But why torch the caravan? If she's leaving anyway, what does she get by putting the frighteners on me?'

'Looked more than a warning,' Mickey Box said. 'Lit the place up proper, no regard for who or what was inside.'

'Well, exactly. That makes even less sense.'

'Who else could it have been, though?' Kate said.

'To consider the number of people who want this one dead is to conjure at the infinity of space,' Fitz said, appearing at the back door.

'Smell his hands for petrol,' said Boone.

'What if it wasn't Lilly?' Kate said.

'Parties unknown,' Mickey Box said. 'A development that comforts me no end.'

'She talked about a place called the dairy,' Boone said. 'Linked it to some woman called Sally. We don't know what their relationship is. There's no accounting for how that sort of thing works. She might still be in contact with her. Told her that someone was sniffing around historical abuse at Eastry. Jerry Killock. Whatever.'

'And Sally sets fire to the caravan,' Kate said.

'What fucking Sally?' Mickey Box said.

Boone told him what Lilly had said about the dairy, about her fear of the place and a woman called Sally. Mickey Box laughed.

'Happens more than you'd think,' Boone said. 'A woman like that.'

Mickey Box shook his head.

'Sally isn't a woman,' he said. 'And if he's who I think he is, we're good and fucked.'

PART THREE

THE FUTURE TENSE OF JOY

16

Present day

She'd almost dozed off again, but the hum of the electric shower in the en suite stirred her. Sweat painted her fringe to her forehead and a light patina glazed most of the rest of her. She could feel the sheets sticking to her. The shower turned off.

Barb didn't want to move.

'I don't want to move.'

Barry's voice was muffled by a towel. 'You're the boss. You have to.'

Pouting, she fingered sweaty sigils in the fine down across her belly. He'd nipped downstairs before his shower to peel her an orange, which was in a bowl nestled on the duvet beside her. As he kissed her before he got under the water, she'd smelt the rind beneath his nails when he touched her cheek. She pressed a segment into her mouth and it burst like a tardy, epiphanic orgasm, though anything could seem transcendent after triumphant shagging.

'This was your big idea,' Barry said, turning the shower on again to warm up for her.

'Pfft,' Barb said. 'Loopy tart basically extorted me. We're nowhere with the girl, and my only hope is colander brains because she's somehow hooked into half the crime that goes down in this county.'

'Know what I think? I think you'll be happy to see her.'

'Will not,' Barb said, resolving not to be.

Showered and dressed, she ran Barry back to his place in Canterbury. They sat in the Audi round the corner from his flat.

'What do you want me to do?' he asked.

Barb shrugged. 'Christ knows what she's got. Or how she'll choose to dole it out. She knew the old dairy, so we have to assume she's going to give us that. Do a Section 8 and I'll send across her statement as soon as I get it, so we can get a warrant. I gave Forensics a heads-up about the site, so they should have drawn up plans. Tell them to be ready to go the minute we've got the warrant. Storm Mathijsen will be joining us today too. She's smart, capable. Not just with the kids' stuff. Use her.'

'What time are they releasing the other one?'

'Now. Ish. They do it before they let everyone out for the day. There will be a shitstorm of paperwork, though, her being out on Special Purpose Leave technically.'

'That's not a case of technically, Barbara.'

'Yeah, I know.'

'Do you? I get that she's a mate—'

Barb snorted.

'—or whatever she is. But she's a criminal too, one who is attracted to violence like moths are to flames. She needs to understand that you are responsible for her until the SPL is up and she goes on licence. That's legally, technically, and every-ally. She fucks up, and you're in it up to your neck.'

'You're right.'

'I know.'

'And magnificently humble.'

He opened the door to get out and she grabbed his arm, kissed him.

'I know how I can be with jobs like this. Having you, even if I'm—'

'I don't put up with you, Bowen. You know that, right?'

She kissed him again. 'I liked this morning very much. It's good when we're both—you know.'

'That's easy to arrange,' he said, stepping out of the car. 'Tell me when you're—you know. Because I always am.'

17

Boone awoke from an alien sleep, barely worthy of the name, and her pyjamas felt strange on her skin. She dressed hurriedly. It was cold, so she put on her sweater. She'd gathered all her belongings together the night before, arranging them in a neat pile on the table. It was early, an hour till they'd come for her, so she sat and tried to read, a Joan Murray collection a friend had sent, but she could do no more than dip in and pick at the odd line like a pigeon.

There was an otherness to prison, a permanent sense of displacement. Coughs and hacking from other cells. Lonely but never alone. You awoke in a bed that wasn't yours, washed in borrowed water, and sat at hard furniture to eat barbarous food concocted solely to provoke offence. It was almost as ghastly as going on holiday.

She had assumed that when the time came to be released there would be some euphoric feeling of homecoming. She had been wrong. Her memories of the world were cracked and paltry things, leaving her with an intermittent impression of what she was returning to. Returning was the wrong word – more than half the life she could remember had been spent in a cell. Her release felt less like the restoration of a previous state than a liminal difficulty to be endured along the way to some new phase of existence, one no doubt replete with fresh variations of the humiliations and indignities that life seemed to accrue like moss the longer it lasted.

She was hungry. Opening her breakfast pack, she picked at the roll, ate the cereal dry like crisps. Hadn't had a coffee since she came in. Sometimes she imagined she could smell it.

Fifteen minutes before the cells were usually unlocked, her door opened. The guard tossed a plastic tub onto her bed for her bits, and Boone transferred her neat piles into it. A few items of clothes, a couple of unread books, and her photographs. Tess and Jim smiling in the sun, though he'd be a lot bigger now. Another of Roo, in a dress of Boone's, the edges of that one blackened by fire. She'd had other clothes, more books, a television and dynamo-powered radio, but had arranged for them to go to fellow inmates.

The guard led her down to reception, where she was left alone in a locked room for half an hour. A different member of staff peered through the window in the door as if at the reptile enclosure, went away for a few minutes, and then returned with purpose. She tipped out the contents of the box, rifling through the items thoroughly before depositing them back. She instructed Boone to undress for a physical search. Boone couldn't imagine any smuggling operation aiming to remove contraband from prison, let alone one heinous enough to warrant such inconveniences.

There followed a great epoch of paperwork that began sometime in the Middle Ages and came to an end mid-morning, when she was finally shown to the public waiting area of reception. There she saw Barb sitting in a plastic chair, her face darkened with a peevishness that promised so much.

Barb took to her feet when she saw her. 'She all done? Paperwork and all that?'

The equally querulous-looking old duck sitting behind the front desk, with its shatter-resistant Perspex, nodded and gestured for

Boone to accompany the detective out of her otherwise peaceful reception.

'You've got a room set aside for me. DI Bowen. I arranged it with your governor.'

The woman checked her monitor. She stood up in instalments and shuffled out through a locked door beside her desk. They followed her down the hall, where she unlocked another door and went back the way she'd come without so much as a word.

It was a large room with a range of curved tables that fitted together into something approximating a teardrop. Metal chairs upholstered in bright blue were scattered around it. Barb put her case on the table and motioned for Boone to sit.

'Water?'

'Thanks.'

Barb skidded a bottle over.

'I'm going to question you and we're going to put your answers into a statement that one of my officers will then use to support a request for a warrant on the dairy premises near Elsham Green. The broader you can be in terms of linking the premises to criminal enterprise, the better. Gives me more scope on the search.'

'Okay. I need something first, though.'

'I don't think you're getting how this works.'

'It's important. And it's not really for me, per se.'

'Go on.'

'If I was being targeted because my release was coming up, the fights and everything, then other people might be in danger too.'

'Tess?'

'No. She's with Mick. He'll take precautions. Quin. And Jack.'

'You want officers with them?'

'They have a police alarm button, after what happened before. I think it's still active.'

'I'll have someone check. You want to go round and talk to them?'

Boone hadn't seen her son and ex-husband for over five years. She wondered at the welcome she'd receive with news of another potential threat to them.

'No. Maybe have someone call them or drop by. Explain that I'm helping with an investigation and there's a slim possibility it might blow back.'

'Okay. Fine. Ready to get on with the questions now, or is there anything else I can do for you?'

'I think that's it.'

'Good. Let's start with this mysterious Sally, then. Who is she? Full name would be nice.'

'No idea.'

'What do you mean?'

'Didn't get a surname. Just Sally. Wasn't like we were formally introduced.'

'You didn't get a fucking—' Barb stopped. She'd promised herself she wouldn't get angry, which was her knee-jerk reaction to most things Boone said and did. 'Well, what do you know about her?'

'I know that he's not a her. And he'll probably be about seventy now.'

'A fella? How's that work?'

'I'm only guessing here, but I'd say it wasn't his real name. Probably to protect his actual identity, he uses a pseudonym or a sobriquet. A *nom de guerre*, if you like.'

'I can leave you here. I don't have to take you with me when I go. Put you back on the wing with whoever it was gave your face a few new dents, probably find some reason to keep you in a spell longer for good measure.'

'What I went down for—'

'Theft, aggravated, and animal cruelty.'

'The night of, I was at the dairy you're asking about. That was where I met the man I only knew as Sally. He bankrolled the job and was going to sell the meat. I think he operated some butcher's or abattoir or something like that. A legit front.'

'He owned the dairy?'

'That's the impression I got.'

'Who else was there?'

'There was another man, who I understood to be Sally's son. He called him Ferg. Again, I don't think that was his real name.'

'And who else?'

'I don't recall the names of the other parties.'

'Yeah, really? And did one of these parties unknown bleed all over the inside of the truck you set fire to?'

'I don't recall.'

'Was there anyone else at the premises who hadn't been on the job with you?'

'There was another man. I never got his name. He was—I don't know if simple is the right word. He was disfigured, like he had no jaw. He couldn't speak.'

'And what was he?'

'I don't know. Some kind of caretaker for the place. Weird little goblin.'

'And at any point did you see anyone else at the dairy?'

Boone hesitated.

'Boone?'

'Not *see*, no.'

'But?'

'I heard something. Someone. Sally tried passing it off as an animal. He kept dogs for fighting, had at least one there that I saw. But this wasn't a dog. There was a locked door and there was a person behind it. I never saw who.'

'You didn't try to help them?'

'There were exigent circumstances.'

'And this wasn't worth mentioning to the police later?'

'I didn't know what the situation was.'

'We've searched the premises. Not only did we find no trace of the girl having been there, but it looked as if nobody at all had been there in years.'

'I imagine they cleared out when I was arrested. I wasn't ever supposed to leave that place. Not alive.'

'I have to tell you, Boone, this is disappointing. You've basically told me nothing, except that Sally is a bloke. People were already thinking I'd lost my mind securing your release from here, and this is going to confirm that for them.'

'Search the dairy—'

'We have searched the dairy.'

'Not with me you haven't.'

'I'm so mad right now I can't even think of anything profane to say.'

'Barb, the girl was there. I'll show you. Get a warrant that lets you tear the place apart. Full forensic analysis. I promise you, there will be enough there to keep you busy for a lifetime.'

18

Boone waited on a plastic seat in reception as Barb made phone calls and emailed across the statement.

'It'll take a few hours to sort the paperwork on the warrant and corral everyone together. Told them I'd meet them at the site at midday. Gives us, what? Just over two hours. Conditions of your release, I need to see your accommodation. Why I let you arrange somewhere, I do not know. Should have found you a Travelodge.'

'Could have stayed with you.'

'Get your box. Let's go.'

They pushed through the double doors out into sunlight, freedom, an inevitable reintroduction to the taxation system. The marshes of southern Sheppey stretched out before them, the hills of the Downs in the distance. Somewhere in between, out of sight, flowed the Swale.

'Blinding brightness and an empty road,' Boone said.

'That's the happy ending you get on screen. Violent-piece-of-shit convicts who blackmail old friends and lawfully warranted police inspectors into securing their early release don't get that. They get me watching their every move. And I've been sitting in a room filling out paperwork on you for fucking hours because apparently there are seven thousand forms need completing before I get the pleasure of your company.'

'There was a surprising amount of paperwork,' Boone agreed.

She dumped her box on the back seat of the Audi and clutched the leather interior almost indecorously as Barb pulled away with unnecessary haste.

'What's it like, then?' Barb said.

'Freedom?'

'I know what freedom's like. Prison. What's prison like?'

Boone gazed out the window at the passing hay field, which rose sharply to a near horizon.

'It's like Basingstoke. Full of people asking themselves, how did it come to this?'

'Provided with a cell of your own, though. Television and so forth.'

Boone was a criminal, guilty of what she considered the trifling crimes she had been convicted of and incarcerated for, and also of rather more serious ones she had not. Being criminally minded, she felt she had a broader, more panoramic view of the human tapestry than someone who had never experienced prison. That is to say, she wasn't offended by the idea of prisoners being human, and she was expert at deflecting petty provocations that in prison could escalate swiftly into aggro.

'The magnanimity of our prison service would be the pride of any forward-thinking society.'

'I was assured you had digs lined up in a safe and lawful environment. I resisted the urge to laugh. Where we headed then? The cottage?'

Boone shook her head and showed Barb a slip of paper.

'Here.'

'Lark. Don't recognise the street.'

'That thing'll know.' Boone pointed at Barb's phone in its dashboard cradle.

Barb looked at her watch. 'In and out. Drop your things off and then we're moving again.'

'Understood.'

'Your time is not your own – I'm responsible for everything you do. So you do nothing without my knowing about it first.'

'Crystal clear, Detective Inspector Bowen.'

'Better be.'

'Need to make a stop first, though.'

'No stops.'

'Need to pick up keys to the new place.'

'Fuck's sake. Where?'

'Know the caravan parks on the north of the island?'

'Uh huh.'

'Shop on the main road there.'

By shop, Boone meant amusement arcade. Coinland was the size of a large supermarket, stretching half the length of a road that ended in views of the North Sea. They parked in a pay-and-display and walked round. Bright signs in the windows cried that the place was open *10 TO 10 EVERY DAY, EVERY WEEK, EVERY YEAR*. A man was opening up the folding doors onto the street and brushing the previous night's detritus from the pavement. He nodded when he saw Boone.

'Best you stay here,' she told Barb. 'They'll smell your kind a mile off.'

Already there were a couple of sly-eyed boys in there, attached to machines by their hips, keeping track of who came and who went. A woman sat behind a caged window in the wall with the same perm she'd had for thirty years. She watched Boone all the way from the door to her window.

'You're Mick's one.'

'Yep.'

The woman nodded. She slid an A4 envelope through the cash tray beneath the cage.

'Thanks,' Boone said.

She stopped among the amusement machines and opened the package. Two sets of keys, her driving licence and passport, three wads of cash (tens, twenties and fifties) and a cylindrical plastic container. She unscrewed the cap, carefully as it contained liquid, and pulled out a dental bridge. Fitting it in her mouth, she tongued it, opening and closing her jaw until it was comfortable.

Outside, she flashed Barb a new grin.

'Lovely.' Barb squinted into the murk of the arcade. 'Been out for, what, half an hour? Should I guess how many laws have been violated already?'

'You broke me out of prison and you're asking that?'

'Uh huh.'

'There's a grocery place. Just pick a few bits up.'

'Uh huh.'

The minimart was across the other side of one of the large caravan parks. It was a local chain shop, four aisles and two tills. Boone grabbed a basket and began to fill it with essentials, like foot lotion, moisturiser, and an almond and linseed shampoo. She opened a tube of something and put a little on her hands, rubbing and then smelling them.

'Mmm. I miss toiletries that don't smell like hospitals.'

There was a small fresh produce section and she put all sorts in the basket – peppers and apples and cucumber and lettuce and a mango and apricots and broccoli and grapes.

'Nothing but noodles for four years, I don't even want to imagine what this much real food is going to do to my guts.'

She threw bags of posh crisps in on top.

'Who's paying for all this?' Barb said.

'You know how much you lot gave me this morning?'

'How much?'

'Well, if I add the nothing to the zero and carry the nought and the square root of absolutely sweet fuck all . . . Apparently I'm not actually discharged yet, so I wasn't eligible for the generous forty-six-quid stipend that would have had to last me until I got a job or the six weeks until the Universal kicked in.'

'So I'm paying?'

'Don't be daft. I have an advance on my new job.'

'Job?' Barb snorted. 'Should I even ask?'

'I will be driving.'

'For whom?'

'Medway Logistic Solutions Limited.'

'Mickey Bollocks Box Limited, more like. And what are you going to be driving? Meals on wheels? Aid packages for the needy?'

'You know what I really fancy? Fish and chips. Good fish and chips. Light but crispy batter and chips with genuine crunch.'

'Less than an hour from prison and she's in on the fucking chips already. This isn't a holiday. Let's hurry this up.'

'Never want to see any of them again as long as I live,' Boone said as they passed the instant noodles.

When she placed two bottles of Sauvignon Blanc in the basket, Barb grabbed them back out and replaced them on the shelf.

'What? Why?'

'Uh, against the rules?'

'I can't drink on licence? But I'm on licence for years. That's bullshit.'

'You're not on licence. They wouldn't move your release date, so your noble and munificent governor is authorising back-to-back Special Purpose Leaves. And whilst on SPL, you may not partake in alcohol.'

'Is this the law, or just your doing?'

'One's the same as the other as far as you're concerned.'

Boone peeled off a fifty from her roll to pay at the till.

'Shitting Christ, Boone. How am I supposed to explain that?'

'Probably best to pretend it's not happening.'

She collected her bags, receiving no help from Barb, and they set off again, walking round the caravan park on the sea side. There was a children's playground on the front, a few future chimneysweeps loitering. Boone stopped at a bench and sat down.

'What are you doing? We've only got to go over there. Few hundred yards.'

'Yeah, all right. Give me a sec.'

Barb sat next to her. She squeezed Boone's bicep. 'Nothing wrong there. What happened? You miss leg day?'

'I dunno.'

'Boone, you haven't walked further than the canteen in four years. This happens to everyone when they get out.'

'So I'm not dying?'

'I'd say you're never more than a day or two from some potentially life-ending mayhem, so it's hard to tell.'

'Freedom is less fun then I remember.'

'It's not supposed to be fun. I'm trying to find out who exactly it was did horrifying things to this poor girl. Raising her in a box, can't speak or think or do anything for herself, endured Christ knows what for the entirety of her miserable existence, probably will never be able to enjoy a normal life. And you're supposed to be helping me with that, which is why I got you out of clink early and saved you from the many beatings to come, because you promised you had information. But all we have so far is honey-glazed beetroot and parsnip crisps.'

'How is she? The girl?'

'I don't know. I don't even know if she passes as a person. The doctors are saying she has the cognitive skills of a pre-lingual infant, and they're not sure what progress she'll make.'

'I'm not having you on, Barb. I know this fucker. He's evil. And he had the girl at the dairy. I was there. I'm sure of it. We'll drop this stuff at the new place, and then go there, and you'll see.'

She closed her eyes and smelled the sea. The salt surprised her still. Less than three miles from the small room she'd been locked in for the past four years, but it might as well have been the moon.

19

'This can't be right,' Barb said.

'It's right.'

The drive to Lark had been uneventful. Boone munched crisps, and Barb sat in quiet restraint, silently suffering the torment of someone dropping crumbs in her car. It was as if they were ashamed of conversation.

The satnav on Barb's phone directed them past the old harbour and the long-closed tidal pool and down a narrow street not far from the front. They sat in the Audi and looked up at a mechanic's garage on a walled-in plot with a padlocked gate. Jumping out, Boone unfastened the padlock with one of the keys she'd picked up at the arcade and slid the gate aside. Barb rolled the Audi onto a forecourt in front of the fifteen-foot rolling steel service door. There was a normal door beside it, which Boone opened.

A narrow hallway led to a steep staircase. Before the steps was a door on either side, one leading into the large workshop and the other to an office with other rooms behind it. Boone turned the handle on the one on the left and went through onto the shop floor. It was a large hall, sixty feet long and half that across. A skylight roof pitched twenty feet above the front half of the space, the ceiling only half as high at the rear where the floor above spanned the workshop.

Standing in the middle of this space was the Transit, looking every bit the shitheap it always had, but with brand-new tyres. Boone opened her arms and hugged it.

'These aren't getting any lighter,' said Barb, who had fetched the shopping bags from the car.

Boone took them off her and they went upstairs. The space on the first floor was divided in two. The rooms directly over the workshop had been used for storage, weathered boxes of automotive parts and rusty old tools stacked up in them. On the other side, above the offices, walls had been knocked through to open up a large living space, its bare bricks painted white. A kitchenette had been fitted at the far end, but it had little counter space and looked like someone had given up after completing half the job.

At the centre of the large room, two second-hand sofas faced off across a low coffee table. The front wall was constructed almost entirely from six-inch waved glass blocks, with two wide windows built in among them. Along the wall at the other end to the kitchen, shelves had been fashioned from cinder blocks and planks. A few books were scattered on them. An ersatz wooden floor had been laid, cold and bare.

At the rear were two rooms – a cheaply fitted bathroom, and a sparse bedroom with a double bed and a clothes rail along one wall. Nothing hung from it. French doors in the bedroom led to an unguarded flat roof overlooking a yard behind the garage. High walls surrounded it on all sides. The sea could be smelled but not seen.

'Balcony views,' Boone said.

'Normal people just get a flat.'

'This is a flat.'

'You know what I mean.'

'Nobody will come here. Nobody will find me here.'

Barb shook her head. 'You think your grief and loneliness won't fatten if you never allow them to be seen, in the same way those men believe never seeing the quack is a cast-iron guarantee of continued good health.'

Boone put milk, chicken, veg and fish in the fridge, placing the remaining groceries into cupboard units on the wall. Someone had left a cafetière, grinder and a bag of coffee beans on the side.

Barb still couldn't get over the place.

'Boone, you can't leave prison and move into—*this*. Is it allowed? Has anyone else looked at it?'

'Looked at it? Barb, they shove people out the gates at Brabazon and hand them tents. Actual tents. Nobody gives a shit. Number of girls who break licence first week out just so they can get sent back in is staggering. And I'm not talking about those who bring balloons full of pills back in. I'm talking about girls who think a bed and being fed three times a day, no matter what sort of slop it is, is a better shake than they have on the outside. Is it allowed? This is palatial fucking estates, this is.'

Barb sat on a sofa. 'Earlier, when I was being an idiot. Televisions in the cells and what not.'

'I know.'

'How bad is it?'

'Let me see. Last year there were three consecutive days on my wing, that's about a hundred and thirty women, three days in a row when there wasn't an instance of self-harm. Only time that happened when I was there. You'd be surprised what you can make ligatures from when you've nothing else to think about.'

'Did you ever?'

'There are different ways to hurt yourself.'

Barb's mobile rang.

'Bowen . . . Yep. Okay, we'll be right there.' She pocketed the phone. 'That was Barry. We got the warrant. We have to go.'

Groceries away, Boone offered a hand and hauled Barb out of the sofa.

'Did you check for anything buried?' Boone said.

'What?'

'At the farm. Graves. Did you look for graves?'

'Nothing beyond a surface search. Previous warrant was only given on the grounds that it wasn't practicable to speak with anyone who could grant access, so we could only look for signs the girl had been there. There were none.'

'Might want to tell them to ready themselves.'

20

The dairy was deep in the Downs between Ashford and Canterbury. They drove narrow lanes cutting between fields left to green. Nothing larger than a field mouse ranged across them, perhaps the occasional fox, though the skies above were busier. A skein of geese passed overhead in formation, their shadow selves rippling across the grass.

You'd scarcely notice the turning, set back as it was. A single-track lane wound through trees to a clearing in a large saucer-like depression, the surrounding high ground heavily wooded. Boone surveyed the land. She knew it was the place, recognised the cottage and the dairy building at the centre of the space. Felt different, though. Variety of reasons that might be, she considered.

Daylight.

Presence of police.

Heart not pounding in terror of impending death.

Three generators stood outside the dairy, their hum filling the air. Barry, all done up in white Tyvek coveralls, was waiting for them with uniforms and a forensics team. He and Boone nodded their acknowledgements, no handshake, and he led them inside the back of the truck housing the mobile command. A ten-metre Scania rig, the side extended out on hydraulics, steps dropping down to provide access.

Inside, an array of screens and consoles glittered, and down the far end was a comfy nook with built-in sofas and a kitchenette.

'Ready to roll?' Barb said.

'Just waiting on you,' said Barry.

Barb unbagged a set of coveralls and stepped into them.

'I'd love a set of those,' Boone said.

'You're staying here,' Barry said.

'Then how will you know how to find stuff?'

Barry shook his head.

'Abigail?' a voice said behind them.

Boone turned to find Storm standing at the door. 'What the fuck?'

'*Abigail?*' Barb laughed.

'Shut up,' said Boone.

'*You're* the source of the information for the warrant?' Storm said.

'Why'd you say it like that? And hold on. Let's back up a little to the bit where you're a bloody copper. You're a bloody copper?'

'You two know each other?' Barb said.

'In a previous life,' Storm said.

Boone was beside herself. 'I don't even—and what do you mean, *you're* the source? Why wouldn't I know stuff you lot don't? I only unmasked one of the country's worst child predator rings. And before that I was—'

'Abigail.'

'I mean, it's not fucking fantastic to think that I might be of some use, especially given how you lot were looking for a woman this whole time and—'

'Abigail.'

'What?'

'It's good to see you.'

Storm glided over. Boone was unsure what was expected. Something as simple as kissing an old friend hello was not so straightforward in

practice, complicated as it was by surprising career changes and four
years in prison. It had been so long. Aiming to be Continental, peck
on each cheek, her nose smudged against Storm's and her lips caught
the corner of her mouth.

'Oh,' Storm said, pulling back.

Boone murmured an apology. She was sure the sheer horror of it
would revisit her again and again in the middle of nights for the rest
of her life.

'I'll just shake,' Barb said.

There wasn't anyone in the world Boone didn't hate right then.

'You all right to stay here and babysit?' Barb asked Storm. 'I can get
someone else.'

'No. It's fine.'

'You,' Barb told Boone, 'I want you to write down everything you
remember about the buildings. The cottage and the dairy.'

'I was never in the cottage,' Boone said.

'The dairy then. What rooms you remember, what was in them.'
She looked to Storm. 'Make sure she . . .'

'She will.'

'I was in there on the first search, and there was nothing like you
described,' Barry said. 'A room off another room? I was in all of them
and didn't see that.'

'Did you measure them?'

Barry stared at her. He looked out of the truck's small window at the
building, maybe thinking about the layout, the strangeness of the place.

'Shit.'

'Did you find a wet room in there?' Boone asked him.

'Wet room?'

'Tiled out, like a bathroom, shower on the wall.'

'No shower. There's a room that looks like it used to be tiled, though.
Smashed bits on the floor, bond still on the walls.'

'I'd start there if I were you.'

Barry and Barb left, heading for the dairy building with others in coveralls and face masks, looking like they were going to fumigate the place.

'Pad and pen on the table,' Storm said.

Boone sat and got to work, recording what she could remember of the building from her brief time there.

'Coffee?' Storm said. 'It's filter.'

'Sure.'

Storm brought her a cup and stopped short, noticing Boone's finger for the first time. Boone made a fist, hiding it, and Storm didn't comment.

'Thanks,' she said, taking a sip.

As she wrote, Storm busied herself around the truck, talking on the two-way and checking site maps. They exchanged only pleasantries. Barb returned an hour later, plaster dust on her face. She threw a set of coveralls at Boone.

'Come on.'

Boone put them on hurriedly and jogged after her. The dairy's large double doors were wide open, and they entered the old milking parlour. A scaffold of pipes still ran down the centre of the hall, but the stalls had been torn out. Boone toed a pipe end hanging loose above the elbow joint it had been snapped free from.

'Found some DNA in here,' Barb said. 'Several different samples. Lab is separating them. Cow, most likely.'

Maybe some Boone too, thought Boone.

The beam of a flashlight cut the darkness from a corridor behind one of two doors at the end of the hall.

'She should have a look at this,' Barry said.

'Cat's mother here too?' Boone said.

Barry and his flashlight vanished back down the hall.

'Twat,' Boone said.

'Just go and see what he wants,' Barb said.

Boone followed the corridor round several sharp turns to a long stretch with eight doors off it in quick succession.

'You know what these were?' Barry said.

The rooms were empty, wallpaper and carpets stripped out, holes in the plasterboard walls so you could see through to the next bare little chamber.

'This is what it was all about.'

'How's that?'

'Used to be carpets and a bed in each one. Some other furniture. What they came here for.'

Barry nodded. 'We found evidence of cabling in the ceiling.'

'They forgot to take it out?'

'Well, not the actual cables, but there was trenching up high, in the walls above the drop ceilings, and some sockets left. Coaxial.'

'They had cameras installed?'

'That'd be my guess.'

He started off further down the corridor. 'We found what you spoke about.'

Walking the corridors in a circle, they looped back round to the other side of the building. Boone didn't recognise much. Floodlights had been set up as many of the halls and rooms were windowless, their wires trailing back to the generators outside. In the light the place was different. They came to a larger room, lit only from a hatch in its ceiling. The walls were rough with adhesive, and a scree of broken tiles had accumulated at their foot. Units of aluminium shelving had been pulled away from one wall, in which a large hole had been cut with power tools to reveal a door hidden behind.

'That's it,' Boone said.

Barry opened the door. The room behind was bare – concrete walls and a concrete floor, with an opaque corrugated ceiling, the dirt and bird muck of years collected in its troughs. Two bolt holes in the wall like empty eyes.

'Nothing,' Barry said. 'Place has been thoroughly sluiced out with bleach, the SOCOs reckon. Hydrogen peroxide. Years ago, probably. There's no usable evidence here.'

'If there were cameras, there's evidence somewhere.'

'Good luck with that,' Barry said.

Barb was fuming. She stalked through the place in silent rage, examining every stripped and empty room, every dark hallway, every nook and cranny. Boone kept out of her way. She saw in her future a swift return to her cell.

'Barbara,' Storm called out from the double doors at the front.

Maintaining a cautious distance, Boone followed Barb back to the milking parlour.

'Pathologist wants you out here,' Storm said.

Barb turned to Boone and beckoned her outside with one finger. A helicopter passed overhead. Forensic bods were out in the field staking out little plots, planting red markers in the turf. The pathologist, a man called Middlewitch, brought a tablet over to show Barb the relevant data. Barb liked him. She had requested him specifically because of his experience in the Middle East with mass graves.

'We have light detection and ranging capabilities from the air,' Middlewitch said. 'We can 3D-map the land and identify abnormalities in the topography. We're doing this plot and the surrounding fields. We also requested satellite imagery. Infrared can show up increased levels of nitrogen, which can indicate burial sites.'

'Long story short,' Barb said. 'The areas you're taping off?'

Four-foot metal rods were being hammered into the earth, crime-scene tape wound between them to section off three distinct areas. The heads of two dozen red flags poked up amid the grass.

'Where we're about to begin excavation,' Middlewitch said.

'And the little red flags?'

'Where we believe something has been buried.'

'Fucking hell,' Barb said, looking about.

'We're starting in this area because it's unusually large,' Middle-witch said, pointing at a rectangle about the size of a penalty box that had been marked off.

'They had a digger,' Boone said. 'JCB-type thing with a big shovel at the front and a scoopy arm at the back.'

Middlewitch considered the area again. 'Certainly more likely to have been dug out mechanically than manually.'

Barb took Boone by the arm and dragged her roughly away from the others.

'Hey,' Boone complained.

'Hey yourself. What the fuck are we going to find here, Boone?'

'I don't know.'

'Bullshit. *Bullshit*. You told me to get ready to dig, and now there are red flags all over the goddam place. Who's down there?'

'Barb, I—'

'Don't you lie to me. I went out on a limb for you. I got you out of prison, saved you, at the very least, from a beating. Probably worse. And so far your spirit of reciprocity has extended to handing me a shit sandwich and telling me to smile while I eat it. A building with nothing in it. And now a field lousy with dead bodies. You were supposed to give me Sally.'

'This was the last place I saw him. Only place I saw him.'

'I'm going to need a hell of a lot more than that. We don't even know if this is where the girl was kept.'

'She was found, what, a few hundred yards from here? A place belonging to a criminal and probable predator. What's that, coincidence? Might not be able to prove it yet, but we *know* she was here.'

'Must be nice. To be able to stake everything on gut feelings rather than evidence. On what you know rather than what you can prove. Must be nice not to be shackled by police procedure, or the conventions of justice, or, you know, the laws of the fucking land.'

She walked off, but turned quickly back.

'And another thing. Why did you never mention this place? Back then, when they took you in? If you thought they were keeping a girl here, locked up like that, why on earth would you keep that to yourself?'

'I didn't know that, Barb.'

'You couldn't *prove* it, but you *knew* it.'

'Jesus Christ. I was here once, I knew there was something going on, but I had to . . .'

'Had to what?'

Had to try to save Fitz, she wanted to say.

Had to try to get them out of there before they both died and were left under the soft earth for someone to mark out with a little red flag one day.

If I'd known, I'd have left him there, she wanted to say.

I'd have killed them all with my bare hands and broken down the door.

'Who else was here with you?' Barb said.

'I said I'd help you find a man who did unthinkable things to a child. I never said I'd add colour to crimes I've already served my time for.'

'And what about the ones you haven't answered for?'

Boone covered a sharp stab of panic, believing for a second that Barb knew about things she couldn't possibly. Knew about Teddy Blackborne and Hanley Moss in the woods. But she was gazing out over the field at the little red flags fluttering like fresh blooms, holding Boone to account for whatever horrors had transpired there.

*

Over the course of a long afternoon, Boone realised she had been harbouring foolish thoughts of her and Barb working together on the
case. Instead, she was sat with Storm in the command truck and
made to go over everything she remembered about the place with
scrupulous precision. Over and over again, with the hope that the
act of repetition would add new layers, find some new detail in her
memories.

Outside, the SOCOs had brought in their own digger and were
carefully excavating shallow strata from the main dig site. In other
locations, men and women on their hands and knees scraped away the
topsoil by hand.

It was from one of these small digs that the first stirrings grew,
people crowding the perimeter as a find was made. The place was
alive with the excitement that horror brought. By nature, people were
vultures of misfortune, and this would be one to savour. They would
relish it, sharing the details with friends and loved ones, turning it
over in their mouths like it offered sustenance. Boone had nobody to
tell, though. And even if she had, she wouldn't have breathed a word.
She was too ashamed of the price her silence had come at to break
it now.

She stood at Barb's shoulder and saw the pit teeming with thin
bones. Mahogany red, there was a grace to the way they lay in perfect
order, each with its legs pulled up beside its spine, three of them with
the promise of more.

'Canine,' Middlewitch said.

'They bred fighting dogs,' Boone said. 'Probably you'll find more of
them.'

Food was found, supermarket sandwiches, and Boone was glad to
be in the truck as an evening chill passed over. Storm came and went,
popping off to relay Boone's recollections to Barb and returning with
new lines of questioning. Boone had remembered that there had been

a car parked in the barn attached to one side of the dairy. They tried to identify make and model from her memory alone, narrowing it down with the use of googled pictures until they all agreed it had been a Morris Marina.

As darkness descended, large floods were set up spilling thousands of lumens across the crime scene. Boone was taken to the main dig site and stood at the edge of the hole looking down on the unearthed Marina. No longer mustard as she recalled, it was now colourless. Or rather, it had taken on the hue of the chalky loam in which it had been buried. The boot was open, and inside, the bones of the long dead lay in a clutter. Boone could see arms and legs and countless smithereens no untrained mind could name. Divested of the sloppy taint of life, they gleamed in the artificial light with a simple photonic purity. A skull cackled up at the onlookers, and the dark tousle of hair still clinging to it was an obscenity.

Barb showed Boone back to the truck and told everyone except Barry to leave. She spoke quietly. 'Two men. One skull is intact. The other has been decimated by a gunshot to the rear that blew the upper face out. There are other signs of violence. For example, one of them appears to be missing his entire complement of fingers.'

Boone covered one hand with the other, concealing her own abridgement.

'These are men who are going to have people somewhere. Families who haven't seen them in years and who wonder still what became of them. It would be something if we could let them know. Give them some closure.'

Boone said nothing.

'Let me put it another way. If you had to guess, just a pie-in-the-sky pull-it-out-of-your-arse long shot that would neither prejudice nor incriminate your fine self, then what might you say?'

'Barb, I can't—'

'Yes you can. Yes you fucking can. Look, I'll stipulate here and now that you're a snout giving an opinion on people you might have heard worked with Sally. On the grapevine. Rumour and hearsay. Nothing more.'

'And if you catch Sally and begin to mount a case against him and are in need of explaining how you know what you know to the good people of a jury, what then?'

'Boone, I need to know who these people are. I need to know just what went on here, because it's starting to look a lot like the inner circles of hell. It's the fucking Somme. They're pulling bones out of every divot they make, and I'm still having a hard time comprehending why you would keep all of this to yourself. When it was just a bit of rustling and you didn't want to implicate your accomplices, then fine. I get that. You went down and did your time like a good little soldier. But this is a different kind of fucking battlefield out there. It's war. And you need to start talking.'

'I can't, because I don't know.'

'That's bollocks,' Barry chimed in. 'And fuck your time served. Everything we're seeing here, it wouldn't take much to lay new charges on you. This is some dark shit and you kept quiet on all of it. No jury would believe you didn't know. A woman who went sheep rustling? Who killed over a hundred animals and burned their carcasses? Let's say a woman like that doesn't elicit much sympathy.'

'Let's say you don't know what the fuck you're talking about,' Boone said. 'Let's say a child was missing. Missing for years because the police did their usual piss-poor job of finding him, and in all probability dead. And let's say Sally was involved in that, so a job was arranged to lure him out. Let's say all of that and agree that you're a prick to boot.'

'This was about Noah Maxwell?' Barb said.

'Yeah.'

'Is he going to be in that field, Boone? Are we going to find children?'

'I honestly don't know. Things didn't exactly go according to plan.'

'When do they ever with you?' Barry said.

Boone smiled. 'You were a sergeant last time I saw you.'

'All right, cut it out,' Barb said. 'Back then, you were thinking Noah Maxwell had been taken here?'

'Thought it was a possibility.'

'Why?'

'Jerry Killock.'

'Fuck me,' Barb said.

'Who's Jerry Killock?' said Barry.

'Social worker, and in all probability a wrong 'un,' Barb said. 'He died before any investigation really got going, and it was pretty much left alone after that. It was thought he was grooming vulnerable kids, falsifying cases to remove them into care and then exploiting them.'

'I spoke to one of his victims,' Boone said. 'They were brought here. Killock facilitated it.'

'He knew Sally?' Barb said.

Boone nodded. 'Why I ended up here.'

Storm knocked on the door and looked in.

'Tents are up. Might be some rain. Pathologist is having the bones taken back to the lab. They're going to resume digging in the morning.'

'Okay, good. You've arranged for there to be someone here through the night?'

Storm nodded.

'Send everyone else home. Back at seven a.m., eyes and tails. Barry, get some people to dig into this Killock business back at the Shed. Keep it low key for the moment – we don't need it getting into the press.' She turned to Boone. 'I'll get someone to drop you back to Lark.'

Barry hung back when the other two left.

'It's all on her, what happens with you. If this works out badly for her, you need to know I'll do everything I can to fuck you.'

'Nice chat, Barry. Cheers.'

He shook his head and left. Boone half thought everything might go easier if she just lay down with the dogs in the ravening dirt.

21

The site wound down. Boone hoped to cadge a lift from Storm, maybe get some time to talk alone, but she had made herself scarce. Barb got a constable Boone didn't know to drop her back to Lark, with only the scantest conversation. Boone was a peculiarity to the force – a hunter of predators but also herself an outlaw. Something to be kept at arm's length so the accepted order of things wasn't upset.

She entered the garage like she was breaking in, opening the door soundlessly, walking on light feet. She made coffee and took the mug onto the flat roof outside the bedroom. It wasn't the decking of her caravan, but it'd do. It looked out over the high-walled yard at the back, street lamps on the road behind lending the space a dull amber glow, the waxing moon pressing back the shadows.

Brushing her cheek, she found wet there.

'Fuck's sake.'

It wasn't new. Couple of times in her cell, she'd found herself crying for no apparent reason, tears sneaking up on her. She wiped them away and decided she was hungry.

The routine of prison meals was out the window and her body protested the change. Usually, locked in her cell by now, she'd suppress her appetite or, if desperate, have a handful of cereal from her breakfast pack. This was the free world, though, and the possibilities were endless. Marmite on toast. Peanut butter and an apple. Posh crisps. A racy infusion of the three. The chicken and fresh vegetables in the fridge sat untouched and never to be called into action, like an exercise bike bought off the telly, or the hopes and dreams of youth.

Crisps had the advantage of requiring zero preparation, and she sat on a sofa and munched. The living space was large and the lights very bright, shining harshly off the painted brickwork. Too large. Too bright. She took the bag of crisps to the bedroom, but something wasn't right there either. It didn't smell like home. Didn't even smell like someone else's home.

She grabbed her keys and went out, looking for a supermarket or off-licence. She found the latter on the nearest main road, old-fashioned-looking place obviously run by a father and son. She smiled when she saw cloudy lemonade. One of the girls in Brabazon would buy it at extortionate rates from the commissary, and they'd drink it with vodka brought in through the kitchen. Gaolhouse gimlets, they called them. She picked up a bottle of each and went back to the flat, mixing them in equal measures in a pint glass.

Grabbing her crisps, she went downstairs to the workshop, where the Transit stood. She unlocked the side door and slid it back. Same as it ever was. Faint chemical scent of the commode mixed with new oil. Old blankets folded and piled beneath the bench. Her dog-eared road books, the only ones that had survived the fire, still on the shelf – Joanna Russ and Jean-Patrick Manchette, Bette Howland and Albertine Sarrazin. A brand-new unopened box of Pop Tarts kept them company.

Boone pulled the door closed and folded the seat down into a bed. Polishing the gimlet off, she shook a blanket out over herself. This felt more like home. For as long as she could remember, with the tyranny of habit, she had replaced one cell with another, continually smaller in size. The beach house, to the caravan, to Her Majesty's pleasure, to the

Transit. This constriction of life was, she believed, a plan for defeating time, drawn up as a consequence of her forgotten past. Even now, after years locked away, she had emerged less than she had been before, in all senses, and the passage of time eluded her still, creeping past in the dark.

Other people her age had survived four decades of life, only to complain it had gone by too quickly. If they lived average lives, which so many liked to believe they did, then more days had gone than they could expect still to come. In the blink of an eye, Boone's past had been stacked up behind her with terrifying asymmetry, and stemming the flow with ever-shrinking cells had proved a fruitless strategy. Perhaps she'd been going about it all wrong. Perhaps time needed to be freed into space for it to be vanquished. Perhaps life needed to be opened up.

The thought scared her. Entering prison, she had made a very simple decision – she could trust nobody, not even herself. She didn't know what she had done in her past life as a police officer, and she was being confined in a place with other women she might have put there. She didn't know who she'd met, how she might have exposed herself. Paranoia became the tradecraft by which she lived, by which she told herself she would survive. That kind of thinking couldn't be turned off with the flick of a switch.

There had been long hours in which she had wondered whether surviving would be enough. She had long suspected there would never be any more than that for her, which really only left one other option. With all the time in the world to think about such matters, she had formulated plans. Leave nothing traceable. For reasons inexplicable even to herself, the thought of her remains, of people finding and handling them, was unacceptable. She'd thought about fire, but you'd have to be gone first, otherwise it'd be the worst of ways to die, and then trust the fire to do its job after you were gone. She didn't trust. Plus, it would leave a mess for someone to clear up. The sea was what she kept coming back to.

On the other hand, tomorrow was another day. Working with Barb would keep her busy for a spell, and keeping busy was good. The more time she had on her hands, the heavier it weighed upon her. Spend some time outdoors. Get used to feeling free air in her lungs again. Get reacquainted with time and space.

Barb was right about one thing. That place was a battlefield, and this was most certainly a war. The enemy was Sally, and while Barb and her teams of investigators and forensic officers sought to collect evidence and build a case for the courts, Boone had other plans for him altogether.

22

Boone barely slept, feeling dreadful when she got up. It was still dark. Liberating oneself from routine was a wearying exercise. She ran a bath and lounged in it, enjoying the water and the perfume and the pruning of her fingertips, mulishly remaining in the tub through its lukewarmth. At seven, she was ready and waiting outside when Storm pulled up in an unmarked Skoda.

'This is where you're living?'

'Better than prison.'

'Thought you'd be at the cottage.'

Boone wondered if Mickey Box had cleared away the charred debris of the caravan, or if it lay there still like a shed skin. The thought of visiting the cottage terrified her only slightly less than being burned alive, so she suppressed it.

'Thought you were avoiding me,' she said.

'I was. Then Barb told me to come and get you. We're meeting her at the clinic.'

'What clinic?'

'They've discharged the girl from hospital and the local authority have placed her in Ravi's care.'

'What about the dairy?'

'They found remains, beneath the dog bones. Human. Small.'

The silence in the car was ringing. Storm checked her mirrors a lot. Boone thought about turning some music on, but worried it was a bit familiar.

'Weird,' she said eventually. 'You being police.'

'No weirder than you being a livestock rustler. One minute I'm visiting the caravan, and the next it had burned down and you were living in a van, and then you were under arrest and I don't know what to think.'

'They allow visitors now. It's all very civilised. You could have come and asked.'

'No, I couldn't.'

'No, you couldn't. That would have been unseemly.'

'How am I the villain here? Sheep rustling, Abigail? Shots fired? God knows what else.'

'You knew what I was.'

'I didn't know you were *that*.'

'I'm not *that*. But you had a fair idea.'

'I knew you were a bit screwy, but what happened there was beyond the pale.'

'A bit screwy? That a professional diagnosis, Dr Mathijsen?'

'Abigail Boone. Guerrilla in the streets, vanilla in the sheets.'

'Oh. Right. Wow.'

'I didn't mean that.'

'It sounded heartfelt.'

'It was harsh. I'm sorry.'

'No, don't walk it back now. Tell me what you really think. It's fine. Hey, remember those heady times when we were . . . what were we? Friends? Lovers? Fuck buddies? You gave me books and I was a shit shag. Halcyon days.'

'I had it saved up for a long time and it was too much to resist.'

'If you've got any more zingers you've been working on, let them fly. Now's the time.'

'It wasn't true, Abigail. It was designed to hurt. I was mad at you for quite some time.'

'You were mad at me? I never saw you. Never heard a thing. I was in prison and alone and it was as if you never even existed.'

'You were a criminal, for God's sake.'

'I was a criminal long before that.'

'And a killer of sheep? What was I supposed to do? The papers said there was a shootout and that you torched a truck to destroy evidence.'

Boone swatted the accusations away from her face like a fly. 'Half of what you see and none of what you hear. You don't know anything about what happened at that place.'

'So tell me.'

'What would be the point?'

'For me to understand. Tell me what I don't know.'

'Oh, okay, *Constable*. Besides, I've been in prison. Things I could tell you that you don't know. Vanilla my arse. Bet I could teach you a few tricks now.'

'Locked up with the gay-for-the-stay girls?'

'And the bull dykes bossing the wings. It was like a dime-store novel in there.'

'Was it really?'

'No. A woman called Pamela had the run of the place and it was filled with young woman trying to harm themselves. You want me to tell you something you don't know? The guards all carried pocket knives. Not as weapons or for defence, but because they had to cut ligatures that often.'

'I did think about contacting you. I was worried that you might— you know.'

'No. Not in there. I'd wait until I was out just to spite the world.'

Storm glanced at her. 'How are you doing? With being out.'

'It's been twenty-four hours. I really don't know anything about anything.'

'You should talk to someone.'

'Ha.'

'Not me. Someone. Just turning your thoughts into words, getting them out into the world, can make a difference.'

'Maybe.'

They turned off the Dover road onto a winding tree-lined lane leading to the Redfearn Institute, the private clinic where Sarah Still's child was now being cared for. It had been the estate of a once-great hall that had succumbed firstly to the decline of its seated family and then more terminally to fire. The clinic itself was a new-build, overlooking a splendid lake and sheltered from the A2 by newly planted woodland. A short walk round the water provided views of the black ruins of the grand old house.

'There is something I need to talk to you about, though,' Storm said. 'Just to get it out there. You see—'

'You're married.'

'I—yes. How did you know?'

'I deduced it.'

'You *deduced* it?'

'I am a deducer. It was something about the way you carried yourself. Your voice. You have the voice of a married person.'

'That's—I don't—'

'And your walk. When I saw you walk yesterday. It's like when you get a bad back. You have the gait of someone carrying two souls now.'

'I see. You're having fun with me.'

'I read an article about you in the local wotsit. *Kentish Bugle* or something.'

'Regular reading in Brabazon was it, the *Bugle*?'

'I googled you one day. Mildly embarrassing, but there you are. Locked away from everything, I felt the need to check in. It wasn't long after I went away.'

'No. We'd known each other a while.'

'I thought there might have been someone else.'

'Not like that. I mean, we had been before, but not when I was with you. We got back together afterwards. Probably because of you, if I'm being truthful. I didn't want there to be any confusion now.'

'I'm seldom anything less than confused. Don't believe others who say they're not, either. Who is she? The article was mostly about your work at the clinic. Didn't mention you joining the police.'

'I hadn't joined yet. I'd applied, but I didn't tell the journalist that.'

'She's a professional, though, your wife? Not a doctor. A lawyer?'

Storm drew in her cheeks. 'Architect.'

'That's splendid. People must absolutely adore the pair of you. I bet you get invited to just about everything.'

'How is it you can start describing a life you know nothing about, and I start hating myself?'

'Don't listen to a word I say. Loopy nine-fingered ex-con whose entire life would fit in a carrier bag. I wish I was married to a no doubt flawlessly beautiful architect.'

'Damn right you do.'

From behind the reflective glass of the reception area, Barb watched them get out of the Skoda. Seemed to be chatting freely enough, which was good. Old loyalties died hard, though, and she wasn't sure how willing Storm would be to break confidences. Time was fast approaching when she would try pretty much anything to get more information from Boone. The dairy site had produced old bones but no new leads towards finding Sally. Getting Boone out of prison early had been a calculated gamble on Barb's part, but one that could raise questions among the upstairs brass if it didn't pan out.

A television in a high corner had the news on mute. A local correspondent with their fifteen minutes in the national spotlight stood outside Maidstone nick with a scrum of other reporters. No information about Jerry Killock or the mysterious Sally had been released, and the absence of any new information was being interpreted across all channels and front pages as the police not having a sodding clue what they were doing. The impending press conference about the human remains found at the dairy was not going to convince anyone otherwise.

'You look like you got a good forty-five minutes' kip,' Barb said, as Boone pushed through the front doors.

'Cheers, pal. You look great too.'

'Want to mix yourself up a Berocca and get your head back in the game, lady.'

Dr Ravi John appeared at the top of a curving open-flight staircase.

'Oh here we go,' said Barb, attacking the stairs like she was crushing grapes.

'My understanding,' Boone said to Storm, 'is that if I kill her, they'll give me my own cell on a pretty much permanent basis, right?'

'She got you out. You don't want her regretting that.'

The upper floors were laid out in suites more closely resembling a five-star hotel than a hospital. Through a floor-to-ceiling observation window, they watched a woman trying to coax the girl into playing with different-shaped bricks. The girl wasn't for playing, though, and took a pyramidal block and added it to a pile of random items she'd hoarded in one corner. Her gait was awkward and stilted. She walked as if the floor was covered with Lego, each step a new trial in pain.

'I'm not sure she was ever given the freedom to move more than a few paces in any direction,' Ravi said. 'We took her out for a walk this morning but had to resort to a wheelchair after twenty yards.'

'The woman called her Molly,' Boone said.

'We and the local authority agreed she should have a name,' Ravi said. 'I saw in a file that that was her grandmother's name. The LA are working on making it official.'

'Great-grandmother,' Boone said. 'Might be a relief she didn't live to witness this. Everything she went through with her daughter and granddaughter, this would have been too much. It would be too much under any circumstances.'

'You don't approve?' Ravi said.

'No, I like it,' Boone said. 'I don't suppose she'll ever fully understand where she came from anyway.'

'How is it going, though?' Barb asked. 'Can she communicate?'

'Verbally, not at all,' Ravi said. 'She can't speak and shows little sign of comprehension. Her reaction to cues is instinctive at best.'

'Still taking stuff,' Storm said, indicating the girl's hoard in the corner.

'Doesn't seem to be any pattern to it,' Ravi said. 'Something catches her eye, she has it off you and in the pile, and God help anyone who tries to get it back.'

'In the hospital, you said she was like an infant,' Barb said.

'In terms of cognitive function, in normal human terms, yes. But she doesn't adhere to normal human terms. She has a decade of experience of the worst abuse imaginable. Absent any knowledge of language, some instinctual defences have built up. She can lash out. Spit. Scream. But there are also very basic things she can't do. Chewing food, for instance. We have to feed her softs. She has used a potty, but remains incontinent during both the day and night.'

'Is it too late for her to acquire language?' Barb said.

'I don't know,' said Ravi. 'This is new territory. I've never seen anything like it. I've spoken with other psychiatrists across the world, and there have only ever been one or two other cases that remotely resemble

Molly's situation. You have to understand, this is the first week, and any degree of recovery is going to be a process that takes years. It'll take us weeks, months maybe, to even draw up a fundamental strategy for her. Right now, she'll be cared for night and day and engaged with as much as possible. My instinct is to pursue rudimentary sign language with her, try to build it up in sophistication as we go. But that's just an idea.'

'Poor little mite,' Barb said.

'In terms of her physical condition,' Ravi said. 'They were thorough at the hospital, but we've drawn up a comprehensive report that will be useful for you from a criminal evidence standpoint. We took photographs and did an array of scans. We treat a lot of victims of serious sexual assault and many of our staff specialise in the area. I can have someone go through it with you.'

'Yes,' Barb said. 'Thanks.'

Ravi set them up in a comfy room with tea and biscuits, and a short man called Gerald who would take them impassively through the unpleasant details.

'I'll wait outside,' Boone said.

'Not likely,' Barb said. 'You'll hear this.'

She watched Boone closely as everything was laid out before them. A week ago, if anyone had asked whether she thought Boone would knowingly leave a child imprisoned like that, she'd have said no way. Not a chance. In fact, knowing things Boone had done in the past, she'd have said it was more likely she'd die trying to free the girl. She tended towards believing Boone's story that the rustling job was a plan to trap Sally that went wrong, and that she didn't know exactly what was going on at the dairy. But she knew more than she was letting on, and Barb couldn't work out why she was still keeping secrets. Perhaps provocation might loosen her lips.

Afterwards, outside, she lit a cigarette.

'When'd you start back up with them?' Boone said.

'Whenever we have a horror case that goes nowhere.'

'Something will shake loose.'

'Yeah? You ready to offer something then?'

'I've told you what I know about Sally, Barb.'

'Then what use are you? Why am I keeping you out here?'

Boone glanced at Storm, looking for help, but she was keeping out of it, gazing away over the lake somewhere.

'What about the Killock connection?' Boone said. 'That might be something.'

'It's being looked at.'

'Look, there might be something else. There might be someone I can speak to who knows stuff.'

'Mighty vague there.'

'Well, they won't talk to you. And they won't talk to me if I'm with you.'

'So I'm supposed to let you off the leash on a lick and a prayer?'

'Where am I going to go that I couldn't already have gone last night?'

'How much time are we talking about for you to see this mystery person?'

'Track them down and visit. Couple of days, maybe.'

'You keep in contact at all times, you hear me? Regular updates. And if I call, you answer. Otherwise I'm putting warrants out on you.'

'You're the boss.'

'Fucking believe it.'

Barb drove alone back to the Shed, the other two following. She called Barry.

'It's me. We're headed your way.'

'Anything?'

'Maybe. I threatened to put her back inside. I want to push her further, though.'

'Sounds like you have a plan.'

'I do have a plan. And you're a major part of it.'

Barb explained what she wanted and hung up. Pleased with herself, she put a Phoebe Bridgers album on and drummed her fingers along to it on the wheel.

23

Television news crews bivouacked on the grass verge of the A274, jock-eying for position to frame the police headquarters in shot. Boone pulled up her hood and hid her face as they turned in, cameras flashing up against the windows. Uniformed officers prevented the reporters and photographers from following their cars onto the grounds and Storm sped up the access road to the car parks behind the main building.

'Three bodies,' Barry said when they entered the Shed.

'Come again?' said Barb.

'Middlewitch reckons the bones they excavated are three people. All adolescent or younger. Bones are at the lab, but they're still digging. The car's in the warehouse with a team going over it, but it looks to be the same old story.'

'Nothing usable?'

He shook his head.

'Bollocks.'

'We've started looking into missing persons cases with any connection to Eastry House or Jerry Killock. There's surprisingly little on file.'

'In here,' Barb said, ushering them all into her office and drawing the blinds.

'Surely people would have noticed reports of missing kids before,' Storm said.

'I'm saying there's hardly any crime on file,' Barry said. 'Burglary, vandalism, aggro. These places usually come with files as thick as your arm, but there's nothing.'

'Maybe Killock had ways of keeping it under control,' Boone said. She leaned against the edge of Barb's desk.

Barry carried on as if nobody had spoken. 'I've been in touch with social services. We're trying to get access to files of cases involving Killock. The problem is specificity. We can't go on a fishing expedition in files like that, and we have a lack of compelling evidence. If anything, we're probably looking at two investigations here. What happened to the girl—'

'Molly,' Boone said.

'What happened to the girl, which we think is an investigation into who Sally is. Even then we're not sure, since we have nothing concrete linking Molly to the dairy other than a vague statement by one witness who, frankly, could have heard dogs.'

'Dick,' Boone hissed under her breath.

'And then any crimes that occurred at Eastry House, committed by Jerry Killock or other parties. If we were looking at these objectively, I'm not sure we'd run them as a single investigation. There's too much to cover and not enough proven ties between them.'

'Killock was Sarah Still's case worker,' Boone said. 'There's a pattern of behaviour established by the initial work of the investigation that was shuttered after his death. And we have a witness who was at Eastry who connects him to Sally.'

'No we don't,' Barry said.

'He's right,' said Barb. 'You spoke to her, not us.'

'I told you her name in my statement.'

'We can find no trace of this Lillian Bancroft,' Barry said. 'She was reported missing from home four years ago by her boss at the shop where she worked. She hadn't turned up for five days and wasn't responding to calls or texts. Didn't have any family and didn't seem to have too many concerned friends. Constables went to her flat. Landlord let them in and they found the place cleaned out. No clothes, no toiletries. Landlord said he hadn't touched the place, liked her as a tenant as she always paid the rent on time. Bank account was slightly overdrawn, but nothing unusual. General feeling was she wasn't endangered, so it went to the bottom of the pile.'

'Any activity on the bank account since?' Barb said.

'No. Nothing. No tax, nothing on the social. No new credit history. Couple of loans went unpaid, and the debt collectors couldn't trace her either.'

'So she's probably dead,' Barb said.

'Either way,' Barry said, 'unless someone is more forthcoming with information, there's not much to go on.'

'Boone has an idea,' Barb said. 'She's going to have a word with someone.'

'*Someone?*' Barry said.

'Won't tell me who it is,' Barb said. 'Someone not receptive to any police approach.'

Barry shook his head. 'This is a massively shit idea.'

'You got any better ones?' Boone said.

When she spoke, he acted as if she wasn't there. Barb could see it getting Boone's heckles up.

'She's out on Special Purpose, which means she should be anchored to you,' Barry told Barb. 'She should be in the presence of a police officer at all times. I can't even believe you let her roam wild at night.'

'Who's this *she* you keep talking about?' Boone asked.

'She's a snout,' Barry said. 'And now the snout's going to have a snout?'

Barb held her palms up, playing mediator. 'We expect Boone to provide information. That's what I got her out for. And to do that, she's going to need to cosy up to people who wouldn't let us through the door. She gets a couple of days to see what pans out, and she keeps in contact with me at all times. Meanwhile, we go back and have a closer look at Jerry Killock. His personal life, people he knew. Have a look at the original investigation, root and branch. See if there was anything that wasn't run down the first time.'

'Do we have to rake up the past?' Barry said. 'Examine previous instances in which she ran off on her own in cases like this? Either she gets hurt, or she gets someone else hurt, or everyone gets hurt and people die.'

Boone said, 'Well, if Kent Police did their jobs like—'

'Kent Police are in the habit of building robust criminal cases to present to the courts, not the scorched-earth policy you seem to favour,' he said sharply, addressing her directly for the first time. 'I was there after that house burned down. Watched them shovelling out all the useless evidence, bags of ash. Then I watched them dig up the bodies. And for what? Nobody was held to account.'

'I should have just waited there for you idiots to find the place? Let them carry on torturing Roo? I needed to move immediately.'

'How'd that work out? Because I was also at the hospital when Barb informed her family she was dead. Don't remember you sticking around for that, hero.'

Boone was up from her perch on Barb's desk quicker than anyone else could move. Barry appeared ready for her, but she slipped his attempt at a wristlock and clipped him above the eye with a hook, kicking the inside of his knee as he lunged forward at her and sending him sprawling across the floor.

Storm grabbed her from behind and turned her away, and Barb jumped in between everyone.

'All right, all right,' she said. 'Take her to the lav.'

Storm led Boone out, and Barry picked himself up gingerly. Barb sat him on the edge of her desk and tilted his head back to get a look. The cut was little more than a nick, but blood had run down his face onto his shirt.

'Turns out you're pretty good at winding her up,' she said.

'She's going back in for this.'

'Calm down. That would defeat the point of the plan in the first place.'

'Getting her upset so she gives us information is one thing, Barb. Punching me in the face is another. It's assault of a police officer. It's revoking her licence and tacking on another six months for good measure.'

'You want to go to court and tell everyone she beat you up? Are you going to mention that your SIO told you to deliberately provoke her while you're at it?'

'I'm bleeding.'

'I know. And I'll fix it.' She peered at the cut. 'She got you a good one, though. See the way she escaped your grip and then nailed you when you were floundering about? That was impressive.'

'I was not floundering.'

'There was some flounder. How's your knee?'

'It smarts.'

'You were very brave not mentioning it, though.'

'Barb, she's unhinged.'

'Yeah. But we know that. Admittedly, she went zero to sixty a little quicker than I had anticipated. Note for future – using Roo against her is a no-no. She doesn't take that well.'

'Who do you think this person she's going to speak to is?'

'Boxall, probably. It always comes down to Mickey bloody Box.' She dabbed at his eye with a tissue. 'Hold that there. And don't move.

Can't have people seeing you spurting blood everywhere. You got another shirt in your locker?'

'Yeah.'

'Combo?'

He hesitated. 'I'll fetch it.'

'No you won't. Point of me going is so nobody notices the blood on your shirt. Come on, you can change the number afterwards if you want. Or is there something in there I can't see?'

'It's not that.'

'Stash of nudie mags?'

'It's not 1985, Barb. I have the internet for that.'

'So . . .'

'Your birthday. Day and month.'

She smiled. 'You'll be mocked and rewarded for that in equal measure.'

'Yeah.'

In the ladies' toilets, Boone hadn't yet contained her fury, but had limited it to pacing back and forth like a sore bear and angrily pointing at the door, rather than actual words.

'I know,' Storm said. 'He was out of line with the Roo stuff.'

'Just with the Roo stuff?'

'His broader point, I think, was that we're not here to help you with a case. You're here to help us. That means we gather intelligence, sift out the pertinents, and build an evidenced narrative. We can't just wade in with fire and chaos.'

'He talks to me like that again and I'll hurt him in ways he won't walk away from the same.'

'I don't doubt it. And I'm sure it'll provide fleeting pleasure. And the next thing that'll happen is you'll be back in Brabazon serving the remainder of your original sentence. What's that? Forty-odd months?

And more on top of that for assaulting a police officer. As much as they can throw at you, because you'll be an ex-cop two-time shite-hawk. Then you're nearly fifty and all you know is prison, so it's all you ever will know.'

Boone stared at herself in the mirror. Weighing it up, life outside didn't seem a vast improvement on prison routine so far.

'From what I hear, you used to give it to him pretty good when you were both job,' Storm said. 'Probably he sees his chance to return some in your direction. Just rein it in. Ignore him, or laugh at him. Nothing a man fears more than a woman laughing at him. Let's not go with the punches to the face any more, yeah?'

Boone nodded and turned away quickly. She could sense her eyes filling, something inside sneaking up unawares. Her own body ambushing her. She took a few paces, leaning with both hands flat against the tiled wall as if shaking off the anger, and blinked away the tears. Need to get a fucking grip here, Boone. Can't be falling apart at the slightest provocation.

Barb came in. She looked at Storm, who made a face she couldn't read. Either everything's okay, or she's probably going to find and kill Barry in his sleep.

'You calm?' Barb said.

'Yes.'

'Can't hear you. Look at me.'

'Want a salute, too?' Boone said, turning round.

'That back there, I can't be having that.'

'I know.'

'Do you? You twatted one of my officers. If anyone else had seen that, how do I not arrest you? Who even does that? How worried do I need to be about you?'

'Momentary lapse.'

'A momentary lapse that would cost anyone else in the world at least six months of their life. Hell, if Barry decides to press it, it'll cost you a hell of a lot longer.'

'I know, Storm's already made the point.'

'Forgive me for assuming not clumping cops might be a point worth making twice.'

'Barb—'

'Look, let's just put a lid on it. You have a few days to sort out what you need to sort out. Find us something to work with. You and Barry don't see each other, everyone gets time to settle down.'

'Sure.'

'But you keep in contact. Don't think I won't get them out to slap a tag on your ankle. I need to hear from you throughout the day.'

'I get it.'

'Can you give her a ride home?'

Storm nodded.

Barb fetched a shirt from Barry's locker and returned to her office. She had plasters in her bag and gently affixed one over the cut. With a wet wipe, she cleaned away the errant blood.

'No need for the needle and thread.'

'If I'm going to be taking punches, we better get something to show for it.'

'Should probably enrol you in some classes, too. Or maybe Boone can just show you a few moves.'

'She's going to turn out to be more trouble than she's worth,' Barry said, not seeing the funny side.

24

Storm had moved on from her Volvo to a sleek black SUV.

'This the marriage-mobile?'

'This is all mine,' Storm said.

'Mid-life crisis?'

'Not exactly.'

'Slightly-later-than-mid-life crisis?'

'Watch it.'

They stopped at lights and Boone pretended not to notice as Storm studied her.

'How are you doing?' Storm said. 'Really?'

'I have absolutely no idea.'

'You and Barry . . .'

'I don't know what happened there.'

'Felt like he was pushing you deliberately and you fell for it.'

'Pair of them not letting you in on their plans?'

'I guess not.'

Boone looked about the car, opening the glove compartment and lifting the armrest between them to examine the storage beneath.

'You used to keep sweets.'

'Now I keep trim.'

She was right, but Boone didn't comment. Instead, she said, 'I slept in the van.'

'You—what?'

'Mick kept the Transit. It's in the garage. I couldn't sleep in the bedroom, so I went down and got in the back of the van.'

'Can I say a few things?'

'Asking permission. I must come across worse than I thought.'

'The circumstances of your return to life aren't exactly ideal. It was rushed, there's a threat hanging over you, Barb wants results. You need to reach out to someone, Abigail.'

'Join Facebook maybe. Connect.'

'You think steeling yourself against the world will protect you, but it doesn't. Life only flourishes when you disarm yourself. Expose yourself. Make yourself vulnerable.'

'The meek shall inherit the earth?'

Storm turned the SUV through the open gates of the garage and pulled up outside the rolling door. 'Ask yourself who wears armour. People going to war, people in tanks. They're people who don't expect to live, Abigail.'

'I've proved pretty adept at surviving so far.'

'Surviving isn't living. I know you get lonely. I saw it before, and it'll only be worse now. Here. Keeping yourself away from everything.'

'Everyone gets lonely. Better than the alternative, though. One of those cure's-worse-than-the-affliction type of situations.'

'Oh, don't talk wet. Have you spoken with Tess? That girl thinks more of you than just about anyone in her life, other than that lad of hers. And I might not understand how you and Mickey Box work as a pair, but I understand enough to know you're important to each other. And you've a son of your own out there.'

'He doesn't want to see me.'

'How do you know what he wants? It's been five years since you've spoken to him. He was a boy. You don't know what's changed. You're his mother. Who doesn't want their mother to walk back into their life? What are you going to do, Abigail, live on the hems of society for ever? The kooky old maid whose eccentricities include sleeping in vans, worrying sheep, and the occasional spot of diabolical violence? Three centuries ago they'd have dunked you in a river to see if you floated.'

'All right, all right.'

'Nobody's saying you have to join a book club. Or talk to the neighbours. But there are comforts to be taken from life if you allow yourself.'

'There are many fine and wonderful things in the world,' Boone said. 'Freshly baked bread. Good foot massages. Winners at Wembley. Slim novels that change your life. Other people's misfortune.'

They sat quietly for a while, Boone staring up at the flat above the garage.

'I should go,' she said. 'Local witch things to do. Mixing nostrums. Casting runes. Things of that nature.'

'Invite me up for one of your coffees.'

'Really?'

'I know the first thing you did was get a press and some beans. And I have something for you. Housewarming gift.'

'Ooh, exciting. Is it a pony?'

'Yes. It's a pony. You'll have to help me get her out of the back.'

Storm opened up the back of the SUV, where two cardboard boxes sat.

'Grab the other one,' she said, lifting the smaller of the two.

'Why do I get the big one?'

'Because when I bravely dragged you away from giving my colleague a fearful beating earlier, I happened to notice you'd obviously been at the iron while you were inside.'

Boone let them in and they hauled the boxes upstairs.

'Very . . . minimal,' Storm observed.

'Gaolhouse chic. Helps with the transition. Can I open my present now?'

'Knock yourself out.'

Boone pulled open the flaps on the box she'd carried up, finding a stack of books inside. Titles she used to have in the caravan, dozens of them, and more in the second box.

'Storm, thank you.'

'Your library went up in smoke and I figured you wouldn't have got around to replacing it yet. I see a few on the shelf there, though.'

'Mick left some.'

'Yeah, I can't imagine why you would want to make contact with people who know you so well. Horrible thought.'

'Shut up.'

Boone made them coffee and they sat on the sofas across from one another.

'Actually, I can very well imagine why you haven't spoken to anyone,' Storm said. 'You're afraid. Of yourself.'

'You saw me with Barry earlier. I used to get angry before, but now it's a perpetual state of rage. I'm not sure I can control it.'

'Humans are born, but people are made.'

'What does that mean?'

'It means, what kind of person you are doesn't matter as much as what kind of world you live in. You were born in a small flat amid violence and hatred. Powerful crucibles. Living normally after that was difficult enough without spending four years in prison. Two thirds of the life you've known has been lived behind bars. That can have a profound effect.' She hesitated, looking at Boone funnily. 'Abigail?'

'Yeah?'

Storm pointed to her own face, and Boone ran a hand across hers, finding wet there again.

'Aw, Christ.'

Storm got up and sat beside her. 'That happened before?'

'It's like they just leak.'

'And you're not sleeping?'

'Used to be I fought sleep because I was afraid I'd wake up mad. That's how it felt, coming around in that flat, not knowing anything. Felt like I'd lost my mind. Now I'd give anything for a good night's kip, no matter how I woke up.'

Storm took her hand and held it in her palm. She ran a finger down the back of it and along to the tip of the nubbin that was once a ring finger.

'Truncated,' Boone said. 'Curtailed. Pruned. Reduced.'

'Abigail Boone, the *Reader's Digest* edition.'

Boone laughed and sniffled. 'That's good. I'm taking that and I'll tell people I thought it up myself.'

'What on earth were you doing, Abigail?'

'Doesn't matter now.'

'Doesn't it? See, Barb believes she's using you to find out who did those things to Molly. But I think she's being used and doesn't realise it. I think you're helping the investigation to get close to Sally so you can deal with matters yourself.'

Boone said nothing.

'You've lost so much, Abigail. Do you want to lose more by going back to prison? For a much longer spell this time.'

'I can never get back what's gone.'

Storm shook her head sadly. 'I mean, honestly. Rustling? Didn't that go out with the cowboys?'

'They still have cowboys. And rustling, apparently.'

'Abigail, how does one lose a finger whilst rustling?'

'Will you stop saying rustling?'

'I can't. It's very satisfying. I want to tell everyone I meet that I know a real-life rustler.'

'You fuck one goat . . .'

'Abigail.'

'I didn't lose it. It wasn't that I was careless and misplaced the damned thing.'

Tears ran freely now. Storm found a tissue in her bag and wiped Boone's cheeks, dabbing beneath her eyes. She placed a cushion on her lap and pulled Boone's head down. She scraped her hair out of her face.

'Abigail, how exactly does one lose a finger whilst rustling?' she asked again.

And so, sparing her a few of the finer details, Boone told her, and when she'd finished, they remained as they were, Storm holding her in silence until she fell asleep.

PART FOUR

THE DARK DECAYED

25

Four years earlier

'He's a mythical beast,' Mickey Box said.

They all sat round the kitchen table, Boone, Tess, Kate Porter and Fitz. Even little Jim in his highchair was rapt, his grandfather's voice an anodyne.

'Most people don't even know Sally exists. Those that do, half of them don't believe it. Like he's a bogeyman, some tall tale faces tell each other. The rural fixer, the man at the heart of everything, taking a slice from each pie.'

'Always sounded like bollocks to me,' said Fitz.

'That's because it is,' Mickey Box said. 'That's part of the genius, I suppose. People dismiss it. He's just a crook like the rest of us, but tells a better story. Superior PR. He was ahead of his time. Spread absurd falsehoods, deny the truth, make it so nobody can tell fact from fiction. You get to run great nations that way these days, and he's been doing it for more than thirty years.'

'So who is he?' Kate said.

'Fucked if I know,' said Mickey Box. 'Never met him, or worked on anything he was connected to. Just heard the stories.'

'The whole calling-himself-Sally thing?' Boone said.

'Someone once told me he was the son of a Russian émigré, a man

who fought the Nazis and came here after the war. Salemov or something. Almost certainly bullshit. I suspect it's some cunt called Brian
who thought an unusual name would ring out better.'

'So he's just an operator with a flair for the dramatic?' Boone said.

'He's a little more,' Mickey Box said. 'He's violent. I don't mean in
a get-the-job-done kind of way. I mean he's a psychopath. I know a
fella who's done jobs for him, and he's legitimately terrified of Sally.
Says he enjoys hurting people. Killing them. Has a taste for it.'

'And possibly for children too,' Boone said.

'Now that is one of the few things I do believe about him,' Mickey
Box said. 'Same person, who generally won't say a dicky bird about
him, said he has a prodigious appetite in that regard. That's not something someone would put around about themselves. Has a whiff of
truthiness about it, especially given how afraid this person is of Sally.'

'You have any idea where he runs out of?' Boone said.

Mickey Box shook his head. 'Don't especially want to know. Either
he's a mad bastard headcase, or an entitled twat wanting a cut of everyone else's hard work, or the lethal combination of the two. I don't need
to involve myself in that.'

'Who is this person, the one that worked with Sally?' Boone said.

'You know him. Good mate of Fitzy's here. Bit too friendly with
our furry friends.'

'Roper?' Fitz said, surprised.

Mickey Box nodded.

'Never said shit to me about Sally,' Fitz said.

'Like I said. Petrified.'

'You think he'd talk to us?' Boone said.

'About Sally?' Mickey Box shook his head. 'Nah. Aside from the
fact he thinks he's a nutter, Sally's a good payer. Roper does country
jobs with him, lot of livestock. Gets good money by weight. I had to
guess, I'd say this Sally was a butcher of some sort. Cuts the animals

himself and sells the meat. Restaurants, butchers, farm shops, whoever. Probably your best way in, if you wanted to use Roper.'

'How'd you mean?' Boone said.

'Find a job. Scout it. Bring it to Roper. If he's interested, he'll probably take it to Sally himself. He'll think it's his idea.'

'This explains a lot about my upbringing,' Tess said, slipping her hands over Jim's ears.

'He'll be running schemes before he has hair on himself, this one,' Mickey Box said.

'Now all we need is a job,' Boone said.

26

The patrol car rolled up in the afternoon. Fitz spotted it out the window, watched it park by the remains of the caravan, a uniformed copper getting out and having a shufti. He knocked on the window to alert Boone, who was hanging washing from a line stretched between the Transit and the side of the cottage. She saw it and nodded.

'Take Jim for a walk up the headland, past the scrapyard,' she said. 'Tell everyone else to keep out of sight. I'll deal with him.'

Fitz nodded and vanished from the window.

'What's going on?' Storm said, face appearing at the side door of the Transit.

Fitz had grabbed the cottage's spare room after the caravan fire, drafted in as security until they knew the exact nature of the threat. Mickey Box told Boone to park up the Transit and kip in there. She'd called Storm to tell her what had happened, hoping for and receiving a sympathy visit.

'Police,' Boone said. 'Let me do the talking.'

The patrol car turned up the cottage drive, cutting a line of dust with it. The officer wore Aviators and a thin smile, taking his time looking about the place before he said anything.

'Fall asleep with a fag between your fingers?' he said. 'Or one of them gas cylinders? Gas set-ups can be a fiddle.'

'Can I help you with something, Constable?'

'Sergeant, actually.'

'To what do I owe the honour?'

'You're Abigail Boone. You live in that caravan.'

'Not any longer, Sergeant . . . ?'

'Fuller. Roy Fuller.'

'We know each other, Sergeant Roy Fuller?'

'Not really. We met on scene a couple of times before you left the force.'

'Nice of you to pop round and check on my welfare.'

'We received a call. Local resident, little nervous about a raging fire here last night. I checked with the fire brigade and they said they hadn't been called out. Thought I'd come and check for myself.'

'Burned itself out. No harm done, other than the obvious.'

'Still should have called someone. Never know if these things are going to get out of control.'

'Consider me admonished.'

'Way it burned, doesn't look like an accident.'

'I woke up and it was on fire. Didn't hang around to examine the scorch patterns.'

'Take my word for it. Looks like arson. Any reason someone would want to do that?'

Boone shrugged her chin.

'No?' Fuller said. 'Track record you have, sticking your nose into things and almost getting it cut off. I hear stuff. Ex-copper still thinks she's job. Digging up old news. Seeing if she can't make clowns out of Kent Police.'

'Kent Police does a fine enough job itself without my help.'

'It's not looked upon favourably. Not by anyone. Upstairs or on the streets. This kind of shocking event, maybe it's an opportunity for a fresh start. Somewhere other than here.'

'I'm comfortable where I am, thank you, Sergeant. And I'll look into whatever matters I see fit.'

'We don't like people stepping on our toes. And active investigations aren't something civilians should be meddling with.'

'Active? Cases don't age like fine whiskies. The boy's been missing thirty years. Police did nothing back then, and they're certainly doing nothing now.'

Fuller took a couple of quick strides, giving himself an angle through the side door of the Transit. Storm was lying on the bed, sheets up around her.

'Do apologise,' Fuller said, smirking. 'Didn't realise you had a friend over.'

Boone slid the door shut.

'Anything else you need, Sergeant?'

'You must have a lot of friends. Whoever lives in this cottage, for example. Kind of them to let you park up and sleep here. You and your friend.'

'Neighbours being neighbourly. I realise your sort doesn't believe in society, so it might be hard to accept.'

'These neighbours about?'

'No, don't believe they are.'

'Got a name for them?'

'You wanting me to do Kent Police's work again?'

'Caravan sits on land owned by a company. Had some difficulty tracing it back to its ultimate owner. What can you tell me about that?'

'I can tell you I'm getting a little tired of this, Sergeant. I can tell you I think you should leave and, unless you have a warrant, not come back.'

'Maybe I'll do that,' Fuller said. 'Maybe I'll look into getting me a warrant.'

He removed his cap as he got back into his car. The window slid down.

'Tell your friend goodbye from me,' he said.

Boone watched him leave before she opened the Transit door again.

'You all right?' she said.

Storm nodded. 'What was that about?'

'Establishing of diplomatic relations with the local constabulary. I'm not massively popular with the force. Barb looking into a few things for me must have raised an alarm somewhere.'

'You don't think they were responsible for the fire?'

'I doubt it,' Boone said, not entirely convincingly. 'Just taking advantage. Look, it might be better if you steer clear of here for a bit. I don't want you getting caught up in all this if Fuller decides to take it further.'

'He better fucking not,' Mickey Box said, standing in the back door of the cottage.

'How much did you hear?' Boone said.

'Enough,' he said. 'Enough.'

27

The marshes were still. Strung out along the horizon, wind turbines stood like a band of lost creatures awaiting assurance, motionless blades aloft in celebration or despair. Behind them, the chain of pylons from the nuclear station marched in place towards modernity, their long twilight shadows dragging night across the Romney.

Boone and Roper hunkered in the tumbledown looker's hut. A wily old dog, Roper had been running schemes for Mickey Box for years, specialising in rural jobs. The hut's brickwork was furred green, the corrugated roof intact. One side wall was buttressed and still complete, as was the chimney breast. The other wall had fallen away in a gash halfway up that stretched round the corner to the chimney. The bricks continued their drowsy collapse, red dust bleeding out into a talus at the foot of the wall.

'Can't see much from here,' Roper said, looking out the gap through binoculars.

A small brush of trees stood directly between the hut and the farmhouse almost exactly a mile away.

'That's why we're here,' Boone said. 'They can't see us either.'

Her walkie-talkie came alive with bursts of static, long and short.

'Fuck's that?' Roper said.

'Fine business. Come on.'

She picked up her rucksack and ducked out of the doorway, which sagged at the top where the timber frame had rotted.

'Fine business,' spat Roper. 'Anyone would think you were in the SAS, way you two fanny about.'

The hut sat tight between two sewers cutting through the marshes. They'd come on foot in the late afternoon, skirting round the wind farm to the north and crossing the ditches and dykes where they could. A few farmers' tracks ran out through the levels, but the nearest public road lay a mile away in one direction, well lined with trees and shrubs, and over twice that in the other.

A low mist gathered in the dark, and the pylons and turbines emerging from it were the only man-made objects they could see that way. It was an alien sight. In the sunken fields between the watercourses, hundreds of sheep nodded to graze, bleating in the dusky light.

'Most of them are in three distinct fields,' Boone said, pointing out the boundaries. 'They all bridge the ditches into the same field down the bottom there.'

'That leads to the farm?'

Boone nodded. 'There's a cottage just behind those trees. Two weeks, we've not seen anyone staying there.'

'Use it during lambing probably. Keep an eye on the flock every couple of hours through the night.'

'Farmhouse is further along that track.'

'How good's the road?'

'Can get anything along it as far as the cottage. There's a small barn there too. Beyond that, you'd need a tractor or four-by-four.'

'And why Friday night?'

'Every Friday they've gone to the cinema with the son and daughter-in-law. Have membership cards at the Kino. Eat there and catch a movie. Longest they're away from the farm on a regular basis in the dark. They go to the auctions at Hailsham, but that's daytime.'

Roper glanced about. 'No. Bit exposed for that. How long are they normally out?'

'Depends on the picture they see. They usually leave between quarter to and six. Eat beforehand, then the movie. Sometimes they're back before eleven. Other times, almost midnight.'

'Still be light when they go, then.'

'Can't avoid that. But we can get a truck up to the barn there by the cottage so it's out of sight. Set it up ready to go. Then it's about how fast the animals can be brought in.'

'Don't you worry about that.'

'What do you reckon then?'

'You can get the truck?'

'Mick can. No sweat.'

Roper gazed out across the wetlands, weighing something up. From a bottle in his pocket he shook out a purple pill and swallowed it dry. 'I know someone who'll be interested. Cuts and sells the meat himself, so we'll get a good price.'

Boone studied the older man's face. 'But?'

'But he's a little . . . temperamental. Hands on, too. He'll probably want in on the whole job. And he has rules.'

'Rules? What rules?'

'Frankly, they're whatever he decides they are at any given moment, but mostly it involves the way people talk to him. And you possess an awful quickness of the tongue.'

'I can be laconic if the job requires. Damn near monastic even.'

'It's that sort of thing would set him off.'

'Doesn't have a sense of humour, what you're saying.'

'He amuses himself.'

Roper ran his binoculars across the flat wetlands again.

'We going to need a man on the farmer when he's out?'

Boone shrugged. 'Maybe. The son lives in town, so he's not a worry. We've been toying with GPS for the farmer.'

'They always drive?'

'He doesn't drink. Wager he did once, a little too much.'

'That's good. Abstainers are usually reliable in habit.'

He looked back across the fields.

'Going to be about how many we can take in the time we have. Two at a time gives us a better haul. Thirty animals an hour per man?'

'At least, I would have thought.'

'Aye, in your mind it goes smooth and quick. Real life tends to be bumpier. We get sixty an hour all in, what will the van hold?'

'Big DAF 55. Weight won't be a problem. Body's over eight metres, two and a half across.'

'Good. All right, I'll bring it to my man. Tell him what we have and who's in. Conservative haul of a hundred and fifty. He'll easily double the deadweight price selling it cut on the black. Probably he'll put down ten grand if you're covering the op costs. It won't be a king's ransom, but not bad for a night's work.'

'Figure it as a dry run. If it goes well, we have a better idea.'

'What's that?'

'Cumbria. Roadside grazing. Animals are less spooked, and they're out in the middle of nowhere.'

Roper nodded. 'Let's see how the first dance goes before we get our fingers sticky.'

28

They met at an abandoned brickworks. Two huge sheds and a couple of Nissen huts all that stood, the kiln and chimney long gone. One of the huts was missing its corrugated skin, creepers twisting round the bare and rusted steel frame. The other, tar black with holes punched through it, was home to birds, their droppings like white paint splattered upon it. The sheds were empty. Cavernous brick structures, well lit by rows of great arched windows, mullioned and transomed, smashed or missing panes in each of them.

Evening, but the sun was still up. Boone had taken a couple of buses to within a few miles of the rendezvous. Half-hour walk across country, but she preferred being on foot, coming roundabout so she could have a good recce. A bag was slung over her shoulder, long and black like a soft guitar case.

A single-track lane ran off a spur from the B road, reclaimed by bushes in parts such that Boone doubted vehicles came down there often. Signs of traffic now, though – deep tracks in the mud and a few snapped branches up high, very recent from their sappy green breaks. The truck was already there.

She left the track and ducked through the trees, circling wide to approach the sheds from the side. One of them was without its huge sliding doors at both ends, the entranceways more than enough to accommodate the truck, hiding it fully from sight.

Monty stepped out from behind the almost intact Nissen.

'Saw you in the trees,' he said. 'Always like to come sideways.'

'Not sideways enough, obviously.'

'I remembered from before.'

He trotted off into the shed ahead of Boone. Fitz was leaning against the truck, a fifteen-tonne DAF.

'She's here,' Monty said.

'Who's she?' Boone said. 'Cat's mother?'

Monty lowered his eyes.

A walkie-talkie crunched, Fitz unsnapping it from his belt. He returned two bursts.

'Roper told the man about the radios and he liked the idea. No record of communications.'

'We all get them?' she said.

Fitz shrugged. 'Better deal with this. Stay here.'

He walked outside, ambled down the track a ways. Boone found a folding chair with a floral design leaning against the wall and shook it out, taking a seat. Monty took out a packet of fags.

'Not here,' she said.

'Right,' he said, putting them away.

He stole little glances at her, eyes on the scar across her cheek. She hadn't put any concealer on as she had a balaclava for later.

'You can ask.'

He shook his head. 'Sorry.'

'You always this bashful? Didn't say much the last time either. What did Fitz tell you?'

'Nothing.' He looked back towards the truck. 'Said don't start yapping as you wouldn't find me funny.'

'Does anyone?'

'You've got a thing, you two.'

'A thing?'

'You don't speak when you're working. Always nagging at each other rest of the time, but when it's on, it's all little signs or a look, and the other knows exactly what's going on. Must have known each other a long time.'

'Not really. Few years.'

'You're tight though. Simpatico.'

'*Simpatico?*' Boone laughed. 'I'm going to have to watch you.'

Fitz came back, pausing at the door.

'We have a thing, apparently, you and I,' Boone said.

'Thought you weren't going to tell anyone,' said Fitz.

'Monty figured it out all on his own. He's a very sensitive lad.'

'All right,' Monty said.

'Anyways,' Fitz said. 'Look what I found.'

Roper appeared in the doorway behind him, walkie-talkie clutched in his hand.

'Am I the only one doesn't have a radio then?' Boone said.

'Didn't give you one deliberately,' Roper said, 'knowing you're never happier than when you have something to whinge about.' He looked back down the lane. 'He always leaves it to the last minute.'

'What's the deal?' Boone said. 'With the girl's name?'

'There's this cracksman called Jere Hodder,' Roper said. 'Old pro, been at it donkey's. He once put it about that Sally was called such on account of him being cockless, having lost the whole shebang in some childhood surgery. Has to piss sitting down.'

'You believe that?' Boone said.

'No. But the point is, Hodder has difficulty with depth perception now since Sally extinguished a cigar in his eye, and he's doing a six after he broke his leg missing a wall jumping from a window whilst fleeing a beauty salon he had burglarised. So theorising on nomenclature isn't why we're here.'

'Still don't know why you're here at all,' Fitz said. 'It's summer. You're strictly a winter capers man. Aren't you supposed to be on the road?'

'Quit,' Roper said.

'Bullshit.'

'Quit.'

'Why?'

'Marilyn left. Germany somewhere, I think. Getting too difficult here. People up in arms about the quality of accommodation.'

Monty followed all this with a look of bemusement.

'Saw her in the paper. Marilyn,' Boone said.

'The thing in Wales?'

'Ran amok, they said.'

'There was a thing with—look, a car got damaged and a shopping trolley ended up in a tree. It was hardly bedlam.'

'Marilyn always was feisty,' said Fitz.

'Anyways,' Roper said. 'I'm not going to Germany. And it wasn't the same.'

'Sorry,' Boone said.

Monty raised a hand. 'Who's Marilyn?'

'His elephant,' Boone said.

Headlights swept across the window and a Land Rover came into view.

'Finally,' Roper said. 'They'll have dogs with them. It's him and his son. Boy's a bit of a knob.'

'Elephant?' Monty said. 'We just leaving that alone?'

Through a smashed window, Boone watched the protracted turning of the Land Rover. Eventually the passenger door opened. Sally was a bear of a man, well over six foot and with a waistline suggesting his prodigious appetites stretched well beyond his sexual perversions. Bald on top, thin, ratty grey hair falling about the sides to his shoulders, giving him the look of a seventies rocker put out to pasture.

Entering the brickworks, he looked them over one by one, walking up to Boone. Loomed over her as she remained seated.

'Christ, he weren't kidding. You are a mess.' His voice was deep and almost jolly. 'Every face like that comes with a story.'

'Picked a knife fight with somebody better.'

'Said you'd talk funny without saying much.'

Keeping his eyes on her, he pointed at Monty.

'This one belong to you?'

'Free-range like the rest of us.'

Sally turned to Monty.

'So there's no misunderstandings up front, you'll find me to be the sort who calls a spade a coon. But I don't mean nothing by it.'

He clapped Monty on the arm and moved on before the lad could answer. Boone's eyes found Monty's. She shook her head and he said nothing.

'Where'd you get this?' Sally said to Fitz, running his hand along the side of the truck.

'Fell off the back of a larger one.'

Sally looked back at Boone. 'You two could take the act on the road.'

Fitz opened the back of the truck, double doors swinging out either side. Icy vapour from its refrigeration unit curled up.

'Ramp?' Sally said.

'On runners inside,' Fitz said. 'Fitted it myself. Slides out clean, twelve foot. Lengths of two-by-one across it every foot.'

'Those?' Sally said, pointing at sandbags propped up against the sides of the body near the doors.

'For any unfortunate through-and-throughs.'

'Clever children,' Sally said, nodding. 'Think of everything. Is it clean, the numbers?'

'Plates on it now match a write-off whose paperwork went for a walk.

There's another set inside for after we get away. They match a delivery truck in Folkestone.'

'Two sets?'

Fitz unhooked one corner of the canvas siding on the body of the truck and pulled it away, revealing a different colour underneath.

'Painted up with supermarket markings. Off chance this goes south, it'll look like two different trucks if we show up on cameras. Bit of digging and they'll probably straighten it out, but it gives us time.'

'Roper said you weren't daft. Indulge me a stupid question, but we're not going to have trouble with it running?'

'Wouldn't be worth my salt,' Fitz said.

'Just like to hear you say it. So there's clarity if the worst comes about.'

'We good to go then?' Boone said.

'One thing,' Sally said. 'Mobiles. Hand them over if you have them.'

'We don't carry on jobs,' Fitz said, holding up the walkie-talkie. 'What these are for.'

'Aye, but I don't want none turned off and hiding in pockets. Don't like them, don't trust them, don't have them.'

Fingers in his mouth, he whistled loudly.

'Sure you won't mind my boy Ferg having a look-see.'

Sally's son was even taller and built like he lived to lift weights. Fitz held his arms out like the crucified Christ as Ferg ran his hands round his waist and patted down his jacket. He did the same with Monty before turning to Boone, gesturing with his fingers for her to get up. It was a perfunctory search, a demonstration of power rather than an actual attempt at finding anything. He unzipped Boone's bag and had a quick root about inside before closing it again, then nodded to his father.

'We haven't discussed contingencies,' Boone said. 'We know the routes to the rendezvous after, this place out near Benenden. We haven't discussed what happens if anything goes sideways. Is there a second location?'

'There is,' Sally said.

'Care to share?'

'I do not. Should the endeavour go tits up, which I trust it won't, then we'll let you know.'

'Handy for Monty here if he knows in advance. What roads, any issues for the truck, et cetera.'

'It comes to that, Ferg will take the wheel. He knows the routes.'

'Fair enough.'

'Good,' Sally said. 'Now that's all done, Fitz and Roper can go in the cab with midnight here, and you,' he said, pointing at Boone, 'can come with us.'

Monty pulled himself up behind the wheel and the truck rattled into life. Boone glanced at Fitz, something imperceptible passing between them, and followed Sally and Ferg out to their Land Rover. Two collies sat calmly in the back, as if being driven to appointments.

'You're in back with the ladies,' Sally said.

Boone got in and the ladies showed her their tongues. The truck turned out of the shed and passed them, swaying down the lane. As Ferg drove, Sally pulled out a small leather case and unfastened it. Inside was an old Astra .38 Special. He wiped it down and fitted a custom-vented and chamfered muzzle break.

'All things being equal, I prefer a captive bolt,' he said. 'Doesn't kill them, just drops them for the count. Blood's still pumping for when you hook them up and open the throat. Out in the field, though, things get a mite squirrelly. So I opt for a definitive solution.'

Popping open the cylinder, he began slotting round-nose bullets into the chambers.

'Poor little lambs don't know what they're in for,' he said.

29

A quarter-mile out, they stopped. Roper jumped down and disappeared through the hedges. GPS said the farmer's car had left, but eyes on would make sure. A few minutes later, three radio crunches gave them the go-ahead.

The gates were secured only with drop bars into the ground, and Roper had them open ready for their arrival. After closing them, he got up into the truck's cab. A tarmacked road led up past the farmhouse to the cottage near the barn. Beyond that, the tracks appeared on no maps, had no name or designation. Wildcat roads laid by farmers years ago and legitimised only by time and use.

Monty tucked the truck in tight behind the barn. The cottage hid it from the approach road and, more importantly, the barn kept it out of view of the fields where the flock would be coming from. Boone tried the handle on the rear door of the Defender, but it wouldn't open from the inside.

'Safety first,' Sally said. 'For the little ones.'

Ferg opened the other door to let the collies out, leaving Boone to scoot across the seats. Fitz was throwing down feed over near the ditches where the crossings from the other fields met. Sheep were already beginning to collect across the water. The sun was falling fast, and Ferg and

Roper headed out into the darkness, whistling and calling to the dogs as they corralled the rest of the herd.

'Where's this road lead?' Sally said, pointing at the muddy tracks branching out into the fields.

'Plan's to turn round, head back the way we came,' Boone said.

'Noah built the ark before the flood,' Sally said. 'Should things turn upside down, where does it go?'

Boone had scouted the land with a drone, which had been more fun than she cared to admit. 'Branches off all over the place. The fields are cut up with dykes and ditches, and most of the crossings might take the Land Rover but not the truck. The majority don't lead anywhere. Either dead-end at a wider sewer or loop back round. One of them goes out to the far boundary, but the firing range is out that way, so it's no kind of escape route.'

'Have to force our way out if they return then.'

'There's a tracker on their car. They move, we're out of here.'

'Always pays to assume something else is going to happen,' Sally said. 'Something you didn't foresee.'

Sheep cried out in the low light, their small shapes materialising after their bleats, leaping about the tufts of samphire. Ferg appeared among them, hands in his pockets, shepherd of a lost flock. Monty unlatched the rear doors of the truck and let them swing open. Six feet inside, thick plastic drapes hung down. He slid the ramp out and extended it as far as it would go, heeling it in the soft ground. The refrigeration unit hummed.

'Sheeting's in the cab,' Boone called to him.

Monty returned with two rolls of thick plastic. Inside the truck, he fastened one corner of each up on either side, spreading them out to form rough spinnakers. He placed the sandbags on top of them, keeping them down in the breeze that was building up.

Boone unzipped her long bag and pulled out a Browning .22 rifle, a pistol-grip affair with a hemispherical steel loop that the stock was anchored to. It had an integral moderator but she'd affixed an additional unit. She clunked in a magazine.

'Spry,' she said.

Sally had the Astra in his hand, a leather pouch on his belt filled with extra rounds. He walked the ramp with Boone up into the chilled body of the truck.

'You got gloves, midnight?'

Monty nodded.

'Get them on and get up here then.'

Monty stepped up onto the ramp halfway and got into the truck.

'You stand behind the drapes,' Sally said. 'They'll bring the daft beggars up one by one and we'll take turns putting them down. You grab them by the rear legs and drag them in back. Stack them high. This is going to be quick and messy and we're going to get out with as many as we can.'

And so it went. Ferg gathered the animals out in the fields and they came though the pen behind the barn, from where Fitz and Roper led them individually up the ramp to the back of the truck. Boone and Sally alternated the slaughtering, positioning the animals on the sheeting and sighting them through the forehead and down through their body toward the sandbags. Any splatter was caught by the plastic, the sandbags there to catch rogue rounds that went right through. They got a system working putting one down and hauling it off in less than a minute, Monty dragging the carcasses deeper into the truck as another was led up the ramp, Boone collecting her shells from the sheeting between each kill. Every six he put down, Sally emptied his cylinder into a bag and reloaded.

An hour in, they had shot almost eighty. Two hours, and over a hundred and fifty carcasses were piled up and the air was hung with tallow from the lube burning off Boone's brass.

Roper heard it first. He wheeled round, staring out into the now pitch darkness that had fallen over the fields.

'What d'you hear?' Fitz said.

'Another dog,' Roper said. 'Not the collies.'

Ferg came jogging in from the black, the collies at his heel.

'Think there's someone out there,' he said.

'Pack it up,' Sally ordered.

They climbed down out of the truck. Despite the chilled environment, Monty was sweating from his labour.

'Shit,' he said, having lifted the ramp up to slide it back into the truck.

'What?' Boone said.

'Didn't think this through. It won't slide back under the bodies.'

'Something always happens,' Sally said, almost happily.

'It comes out,' Fitz said. 'Jerk the end on the truck, and it comes off the rails.'

Boone did as he said, and the ramp lifted free from the runners. Angling it upwards, she and Monty shoved it into the truck, resting atop the carcasses. The barking was suddenly loud and clear, and a giant Kangal broke out of the night, jaws snapping.

Boone sighted the dog over her rifle, but it wasn't coming for her.

'The ladies,' Sally cried.

The two merle collies took one look at the thirteen-stone beast bounding towards them and were off, scampering around the Land Rover in a panic. The Kangal leapt for one of them but was taken clear out of the air by an explosion of shot that put one of the truck's headlights out with a *kish*.

Silence.

They all looked at Ferg, his shotgun still aimed at the downed dog, and then at each other, certain that the shot must have been heard for miles, probably as far as London or even Manchester. There was a scraping from the wounded Kangal as it pawed at the ground. Monty was already moving, pulling down the side canvases from the truck, revealing the name and logo of a popular supermarket. He stuffed the canvases in the back and set about removing the number plates and affixing the new ones.

Ferg pointed his shotgun at the stars and whistled for his ladies to heel. He let them into the Defender and closed the door. Boone broke down her rifle and bagged it, before rolling up the sheeting from the back of the truck.

Fitz was standing over the shot Kangal, which whined now and breathed irregularly. Boone joined him.

'Christ,' she said.

The dog was immense, as big as a man. The shot had hit it in the side behind the front legs. The wounds were fatal, but not immediately so.

'Fucker could have competed at middleweight,' Fitz said.

'Looks like it did,' said Boone.

The hound had cropped ears and old scarring on its shoulders and legs.

Fitz looked about. 'The rifle?'

Boone shook her head. 'Packed. And I'm neither leaving a ballistic match nor digging about in a mutt's skull to retrieve the shot.'

Sally walked over and drew a knife from his boot.

'Be quick,' Boone said, walking back to the truck. No further sound came from the dog.

They heard the voice as Boone was pulling closed the rear doors of the truck. Just a noise at first, then a cry. It was the shot that really got their attention, though, clattering against the side of the barn like a fistful of ball bearings.

'Get in the back of the truck,' Ferg said.

Boone stared at him, taken aback by this new twist.

'We need to get the fuck out of here,' she said.

'We don't know that this isn't you,' Ferg said, levelling the shotgun at her. 'Get in the back of the truck, now. All of you.'

There was more shouting and Ferg turned, discharging the shotgun out into the night. He swung the gun back.

'Gas-operated SPAS-12 with an eight-round tube,' he said. 'Still enough to go round.' He aimed it at Boone. 'Drop your bag and get in.'

Fitz jumped up easily into the truck and reached down to haul Boone and Roper in. Monty clambered up himself.

'We get where we're going, we'll sort this out,' Ferg said, shutting the door and latching them inside.

They heard him getting into the cab and the engine turned over, the truck lurching forward over the rough ground before finding the tarmac road again. They paused momentarily, the gates to the farm, and were then off in earnest.

'How fucked are we?' Monty said.

'Sally don't trust no one,' Roper said. 'His immediate assumption will be someone is fucking him.'

Monty was almost in tears. 'I don't want to die in no truck full of dead sheeps.'

Boone touched his arm. 'Take it easy, simpatico. We'll be fine. Let's just think this through.'

'What we need to do is bust these doors open and jump for it,' Monty said.

'He'll be following in the Land Rover,' Fitz said. 'He'll want sight of the doors the whole way. You jump, he'll turn you into corned beef under his wheels. And Ferg has a shotgun for the rest of us.'

'This is all wrong,' Boone said.

Fitz nodded. 'Way he reacted to the dog, and to the man.'

'He was quick with the shotty,' Boone said. 'And the second someone else appeared on the scene we should have been getting out any way we could. But he takes the time to get us in the truck. And what the fuck happened to whoever it was out there? They barely hit the barn with their shot, and then nothing.'

'Not making me feel any better,' Monty said.

'He's not a man to take chances,' Roper said. 'He'll drive us somewhere, and we'll have a chat. This'll get sorted out. I'm not denying he can be a headcase, but he's always done business straight with me.'

Monty slid down the side of the truck and sat on the floor. Boone crouched beside him.

'When they let us out, just keep your head down and say nothing,' she said. 'And if anything happens, if anyone makes a move, just run. We scatter and they won't be able to close us all down.'

Monty nodded.

Boone and Fitz exchanged a glance. It said what they were both thinking: this is bad and we need to do something as soon as those doors open.

'It'll be fine,' Roper was saying. 'It'll all be fine.'

The truck had been moving for about an hour when it came to a halt and they heard the driver's door open and bang shut. They got to their feet, galvanising themselves. The truck started off again, though, on a rocky road now, pitching and swaying. Boone steadied herself against the side. When it stopped a second time, it stopped for good, the engine turning off. Voices outside, too low to pick up their words.

Then nothing. Silence.

After fifteen minutes, they all sat back down.

'We here for the night?' Monty said.

Boone shrugged.

'He'll just be making sure we got out clean,' Roper said.

'You're kidding yourself,' said Fitz.

'If we're going to die here,' Monty said, 'I have a question.'

'Sure,' Boone said.

'Elephant?'

Boone laughed.

'Roper's a farm boy at heart,' Fitz said. 'Grew up on one in the West Country, didn't you? Very good with livestock. Makes them feel comfortable.'

'Fuck off,' Roper said. 'I work the season with a circus. On the road, through the country. Big cats and elephants. Did, anyway, until they sold Marilyn.'

'Okay,' Monty said, nodding as if that explained a lot.

The latch on the rear doors went and they all got to their feet, stepping away with their backs against the plastic drapes that separated them from the sheep who'd already met their fate. The doors opened and they guarded their eyes against bright beams of light. First thing they could make out was Ferg's shotgun aimed up into the truck, the black hole at the end of its barrel dark and enormous and distorting all human perception.

'Now then,' Sally said, heard but not seen. 'We have some things to clear up.'

The light was from the LEDs on the roof bar of the Land Rover. High-intensity beams aimed right at them.

'Get down,' Ferg said, directing them with his shotgun.

They followed instructions, dropping down out of the truck. The roof lights made it difficult to see exactly where they were, but it looked like some kind of farm. They were near a large brick structure, but there was open land on all other sides, dark trees in the distance.

'I apologise in advance for this,' Sally said. 'Most rude of me. But I'd rather beg forgiveness later for a lapse in manners than have civility cloud our present circumstances.'

'Sally, that weren't nothing to do with us,' Roper said. 'The dog and whoever that was. Swear to God. We'd scouted the place just fine and there was never anyone there. I mean, where did he come from? There's nothing out there but marshland.'

'My concerns exactly,' Sally said.

'Doesn't make sense, us double-crossing you,' Boone said. 'We could have gone in and got the sheep ourselves without you. You're our point of sale. We don't get paid without you. What was our plan going to be, taking you unawares out there like that?'

'Such keenness of perception, it's like you're clairvoyant,' Sally said. 'Asking the questions in my head before I could whet my tongue.'

Her eyes adjusting to the new light, Boone could see more of their surroundings. The large brick building included a barn, its doors open, revealing a mustard-coloured car, a seventies model. Beyond the building, perhaps forty yards or so, was a small white cottage. Both structures were in a wide clearing that rose around them on all sides in wooded bluffs. A digger stood to one side of the cottage, its two-part articulated arm folded neatly behind it.

There was a sound, so faint it was barely audible. She thought at first it was the wind, but it seemed to be coming from the building. Not a voice exactly, but moaning or soft crying perhaps, if it was a person at all.

'Dogs,' Sally said, pointing as if at the noise. 'Train them here. Little hobby of mine. Keep them locked up in the dark to make them mean. That one just got here and it's still a bit soft. Whines a lot.'

Boone cocked her ear to the night. Didn't sound like any dog she'd ever heard.

'Reconnoitring the rim was your task,' Sally said, moving things along. 'So who was this chap, wandered in with his dog?'

'We never saw anyone but the father and son on the land,' Boone said. 'The old man has dogs, but they shut them in when they go out in the evening. Like they shut them in tonight.'

'That dog wasn't one of theirs,' Fitz said.

'So just an ambler, out with his hound of a country eve?' Sally said.

'Just bad luck,' Roper said.

'Luck,' Sally mused. 'Resigning my lot to the designs and mischiefs of impish fates isn't sound business practice.'

'I just meant—'

Sally waved a hand to hush him. 'I understand what you're saying. We got away clean, and with a good haul.'

Roper nodded.

'No harm, no foul.'

'Exactly,' Roper said, nodding quicker now.

'Except for one thing,' Sally said. 'You've seen this place.'

'We don't know where we are,' Fitz said. 'You could drive us out somewhere in the back of the truck again. Leave us away from here, none the wiser.'

Monty was beginning to walk in place, heels going up and down.

'You think that's a good idea, midnight?' Sally said, noticing his fidgeting.

'Think I need to use the bathroom real bad,' Monty said, losing his battle with adrenaline.

'Free country,' Sally said.

Monty started to walk away round the side of the building.

'Nobody leaves my sight, though.'

Monty looked helplessly at him.

'Go up against the wheel there, like a good boy.'

Too desperate to do anything else, Monty turned his back on the rest of them and unzipped, letting great golden ropes hose down the wheel of the truck.

Sally moved up behind him. 'There's a lad has never had a second thought about his prostate,' he laughed. Then he drew the Astra and placed the chamfered end against the back of Monty's skull and pulled the trigger, mottling the side of the truck with his brains.

'No, you fuck,' Fitz cried out, charging at Sally.

Last thing Boone saw before something struck her from behind, turning out her lights, was the shotgun discharging and Fitz getting spun round in the air, falling in a heap, knees tucked up and hands clutching his middle. Monty lay face down, hands at his sides, steam still rising off his piss.

30

Boone woke up and immediately had a list of complaints.

For one thing, her head was not in a good way. Moving it hurt terribly, and opening her eyes only exacerbated the problem. For another, her hands were bound in some strange fashion. She was slumped on a stone floor, her wrists gaffer-taped with their insides together, and there was more tape down near the elbow so her arms were kept in an awkward position. There was tape everywhere. Some secured her arms to a length of pipe, part of a whole network that ranged down the centre of the large room like the frame of an unfinished wall. She tried testing it, but the way she was bound she couldn't get any leverage. She'd need to be standing. There was also tape between her fingers, fanning them out and preventing her making fists.

When she heard the breathing somewhere near her, the other side of the pipes, she was relieved. Someone else had made it. Roper probably, but hopefully Fitz. She twisted and tried to get a look, but the angle was against her and it was dark.

'Fitz? That you?'

Muffled laughter, almost choking.

Boone didn't speak again. Whoever it was moved around from behind her, coming round the pipes where they ended near large double doors at the end of the room. They played with a flashlight, flicking it on and off in her eyes, before turning on a series of lamps hanging in festoons along the system of pipes. When the coloured spots in her eyes stopped dancing, she saw the man, the full-bore horror of him.

His eyes were large and wandering, the rest of his face pinched and suffering. It ended below his upper lip, a wreck of hatchet wounds that had cut jawbone and tissue away so that what remained resembled a badly sewn-up sack. Speech was clearly beyond him. His head movements were careful, as if his ghost jaw hung still from his face and he feared it falling off. This was the goblin Lilly had spoken of. Some travesty of the darkest horrors imagined by Goya, but one even he would have shied from painting on his walls.

They looked at each other, and from his eyes Boone imagined his face would have been grinning if it had been capable. She turned her head at a fuss from another room, deeper inside the building.

Raised voices.

The scream that followed nearly made her weep.

She'd heard human sounds like it before, in other rooms she'd found herself in. Sometimes she could believe it was all one room.

The goblin made his noise again, that snuffling laughter, wet and whistling. The screaming continued elsewhere in the building and the goblin hopped from foot to foot, as if this was merely the prelude of things to come. Things Boone would be fully party to. Things she would not enjoy.

When the screaming stopped, there were footsteps and a door opened in a corner behind her somewhere. From the weight of them, she could tell who it was. A large man, Sally moved like he was up to his hips in water, wading rather than walking.

'That was even sorrier a sight than I'd imagined,' he said.

A polythene apron was wrapped round his bulk, broken lines of

blood dashed across it. Beside him stood a brindle bull mastiff, a little
white on its chest. He offered it a hand for a lick.

'Would have preferred to do this at the slaughterhouse, with all my
tools. But one makes do with what one has at hand. And Lorelei here
would have missed out.'

The dog stood tall and inscrutable, face blacker than wet coal. There
was a table against the wall, bearing some magazines and crushed
juice cartons. A couple of chairs were tucked underneath, and Sally
dragged one across, feet bumping along the floor. He sat wide-legged
in front of Boone, leaning in.

'It must have seemed like such a clever plan. With old Roper not
even in on it, I suspect. You must have been pleased with yourselves.
Thing is, I already knew you were going round asking questions about
me. Knew the whole time. And all I had to do was wait for you to
come to me.'

Boone followed the chain in her mind.

Caravan burning down.

Lilly fleeing town.

Sally knowing they were coming.

The simplest journey was always to follow your enemy to your own
destination, and they'd made it so very simple for him to follow them.
They'd walked right into it, and now he had Fitz and her.

'You're going to tell me what you know and what you came for,' he
said. 'Tell me who else is in on this plan of yours. The weed farmer
out on the estuary and his mad daughter? You'll tell me who the architects are.'

He stood up and moved away to the table, fiddling with something
he found there.

'The only thing you need to know before telling me these things is
that I am a serious man. And the surest way for you to know that is for
me to demonstrate it. Establish my credentials.'

Boone shifted on the hard floor and strained against her bindings. The pipes moved some, but the tape was fast. It was suddenly clear to her that she'd known for as long as she could remember that it would come to this, that a stop would be put to her. It was knowledge she had kept to herself, aware of the tragic fate that was due her through every conversation she'd had, through every meal, through every job, action or mission of consequence, through every pale shade of sleep. The one absolute end railing inexorably towards her. Harbouring that secret like a terminal disease.

The fat old man haunched down before her, smiling. Something in his eyes, a communion between them as if maybe he was privy to her secret, a diagnostician of desperate lots. He knew a mile off the look of the inevitable dead.

He fixed something round the ring finger of her left hand. Thread, she thought, until it pulled tight and cold against her skin like cheese wire.

'Your sort isn't going to have use for this particular one anyway,' he said. 'And Lorelei deserves a treat.'

'Wait,' Boone said.

She wanted longer, *needed* longer. Before she was to die, she needed to taste it, to really know its flavour. To be a savourer of death.

The dog barked and the old man yanked the wire taut and it cut right down to the bone. Boone stiffened and screamed, and when he wrenched hard and tore the flesh off, degloving the finger from the middle knuckle down, she saw her own bones like some ghoulish joke and passed out.

31

Boone came to again on the hard floor amid a warm bloom and re-alised she'd wet herself. The pain in her finger had annexed her hand and was drawing up invasion plans for the whole arm. It was a wave she couldn't quite get her head above for long enough to take a proper breath. Not really wanting to, she stole a peek at it.

Didn't seem real.

A gag from a movie.

She felt light-headed. Sally was gone but the goblin remained, sitting at the table reading a magazine. She saw the cover and probably he wasn't reading it exactly. Boone laughed, couldn't help herself.

'I'm trapped,' she said, when he looked over. 'And my finger's ruined.'

The goblin grinned as best he could and nodded his head in a man-ner suggesting there wasn't much to be done about either of those things. Momentarily, Boone was relieved. She didn't want to have to do anything about them. Didn't want to do anything at all. She understood it was easier to accept that circumstances had got out of hand and were now beyond her control.

Gradually, however, she began to think about things that had hap-pened in the past, in rooms not unlike the one she was in. She was in bad shape and no help was coming. It briefly crossed her mind that she had brought this all on herself, and to those gods that existed only to be pleaded with in such perilous situations, she promised a thorough review of her behaviour later, just as long as she made it that far.

The goblin leered at her over his years-old copy of *Knave*. She wondered what promises had been made to him. Like the dog, she would provide him with treats.

'Meet many nice girls here?' she said, smiling.

His eyes squinted into a grin again as he jounced up and down in his chair.

Staring down at her jeans, she said, 'Pissed meself.'

His moist laugh sounded like a death rattle. Boone twisted round and got on her knees. She'd read about techniques whereby pain could be boxed away in the mind and overcome, but her finger wasn't having any of it and she had to pause, her hands shaking badly. There was less blood than she would have expected, part of her having been turned inside out, but she felt cold sweats across her body.

'Made a right mess,' she said, battling to her feet, having to stoop to where her hands were bound to the pipework.

The goblin stood, wary of her movement.

'Does it show much?' she asked, turning her bum to him. 'The dark patch?'

A gout of drool hung from the corner of what used to be his mouth and he whinnied like a donkey. She'd got him laughing, his guard down.

'Dunno why you're laughing at me,' she said. 'Not like it's my fault you've got an arsehole for a mouth.'

He fell silent, staring at her.

'I mean, God. That's a face even a mother couldn't love.'

He recoiled at the sudden betrayal, any understanding between them gone off a cliff now. But the damage was done. On her feet, Boone stamped hard on a junction in the pipe. Two kicks and it gave way, Boone sliding her taped wrists off the loose end.

The goblin made for the double doors with his eyes alone, and Boone was upon him before his feet caught up, barrelling him into the table. They both went up and over it, the whole lot tipping on its side as they crashed to the floor. The tape loosened, Boone clawed it from her hands and unravelled it at her wrists. Grabbing a soiled copy of *Razzle* from the floor, she rolled it up tight, clutching it in her good fist with a couple of inches showing at the bottom.

As the goblin got up, she jabbed the long end at him, striking him in the eye. He wailed and covered his face, and using her fist as a hammer, she drove the stubby end of the stiff roll into his head, delivering more blows behind his ear as he bent over, then clubbed him with the long end until the paper folded under the force and lost its rigidity.

He was on the floor now, and she straddled his chest, going back to the short end protruding beneath her fist to pound away at his face. He whistled through his ruined jaw and she beat him for it.

Beat him to get away.

Beat him for everything that had happened and a few things that were yet to come.

Beat him because it felt good.

He lay motionless, snoring through the bloodied holes in his face. His cheekbone was relocated, forcing an eye shut, and thick strings of blood lay across his cheeks and the floor beneath. She let go of the magazine and it fell to the ground, unfurling slightly but remaining in a loose roll. What had been the stubby end was feathered and swollen red.

No telling how long she had, so she forced herself on. The tape they'd used to bind her was on the floor by the tipped table. Rolling him onto his belly, she secured the goblin's wrists behind his back and then wrapped his ankles up good and tight. Bending his knees, she fastened his ankles to his wrists behind him and left him on his side, his breathing loud and rasping. Then she used the tape to bind up her finger, wrapping it round three of them together.

Not debilitated, but merely drunk with pain, her mind tilted, sending her thoughts in a spiral. She almost went for the double doors leading outside, before remembering the screams she'd heard from further inside the building.

She pushed open the door in the far corner that Sally had come though, and from where the screams had emanated. Stone-lined hallways, rooms everywhere, and she with no weapon and no idea where she was going. Doors were locked either side, but she tried them all, before a sound reached her. A thin sound, a paper cut of a thing. A failing smoke alarm leading her to the fire.

The door was ajar, a lamp inside casting a severe wedge of light into the hall. She nudged it wider and surveyed the scene. It took a moment.

'Oh, Christ.'

32

Facing her, Roper was slumped in a chair tucked tightly to a small table. His hands were outstretched, palms down, and nailed to the table with black iron fencing pins. His fingers were missing and of them there was no sign. One eye was gone completely and the other dangled out on his cheek, and she could see from the ear-to-ear gash in his throat that he was quite dead.

The pitiful sound she'd heard was Fitz, who lay bunched up on the floor in the corner. Other than the shotgun wounds, from which he had lost a troubling amount of blood, he appeared just fine.

'Jesus, Fitz.'

She knelt beside him and touched his cheek.

'You still with me? Could do with you being your usual annoyingly stubborn self here.'

As white as his own ghost, but from the look in his eyes he was still there.

'Hold on,' she said.

She ran back to the milking parlour, the goblin still on the floor, and grabbed the gaffer tape. Back with Fitz, she helped him into a sitting position against the wall. She peeled his shirt away from his side, where it was thick with blood. He stifled a cry and turned his head away.

'All right. It's okay. Just need a look.'

It was bad. He was lousy with shot, his side peppered with black wounds. Shrugging off her jacket, she removed her top and pressed it tightly to the injured area. His howl broke above the pitch of his voice into a silent cry and he sobbed when it came back down.

'Need you to hold that there,' she said. 'Tight, Fitz. Need to do what we can here.'

He nodded, clamping a hand over the already sodden shirt. Boone held the tape on it and then had him lean forward as she wound it round his body, pulling it tight and going round until the tape was used up, firmly around him like a corset.

'Bit of podge you're working on there might have taken some of the impact,' she said.

He didn't laugh.

'Can you stand?'

He grunted.

'Turn onto your knees. Less strain that way.'

With Boone under his arm, he managed to fight his way upright, suppressing the urge to scream. Staggering against the wall, he steadied himself, taking a breather. He looked at Roper.

'Cut his tongue out,' he said.

Boone looked, and saw that they had.

'First thing he did,' Fitz said. 'Didn't have any interest in anything he might have to say. Rest was just for sport. Fed the bits they cut off to the fucking dog.'

Boone held up her hand.

'Me too.'

'Jesus fuck,' he said. 'We need to kill them.'

'We need to get out of here is what we need to do. We're unarmed, fucked up and don't know where we—'

A door banged shut.

'You hear that?'

He nodded.

'Someone's coming. We need to go.'

His arm slung round her neck, Boone dragged Fitz out the door and along the hall. It was a maze and she took whatever turns came up, getting distance and direction between her and their pursuers. They came to an open door. The room was strange, half of it tiled like a bathroom, tub and open shower in the corner, and the rest unfinished, save for a large wardrobe against the far wall. Its doors hung open and inside was another door, and from behind that came the sound Boone had heard outside.

The same crying, only louder now.

With absolute certainty, she knew it was no dog.

'Boone,' Fitz said.

'What the fuck is this place?'

Fitz spat a mouthful of blood down his front. Shouting behind them somewhere pushed them on, round a corner and past a row of small rooms, each no more than ten-by-six, with a bed and carpet. The corridors were lightless and debris littered the floor, Boone sweeping a foot out as she went to avoid falling over anything.

Eventually they came to a door leading out to a lean-to with a tiled floor. A lockless door opened out into the night air and they found themselves behind the dairy building, away from the truck.

Elbow pressed against his leaking guts, Fitz hobbled along, leaning on Boone. The cab to the truck was open, and with her shoulder pressed to his rump, she heaved him up into the passenger seat. Behind the wheel, she looked at the dash array and the gearstick.

'What the fuck, Fitz?'

'Split gears. Switch on the stick shifts from low to high range.'

'I don't know what that means.'

'Click it down. Pull off in second. Shift straight into fourth.

When we're rolling, switch up into high range and cycle through the rest.'

Boone caught sight of something in her side mirror. Ferg burst out through the double doors of the milking parlour brandishing his shotgun.

'You're going nowhere,' he yelled.

The shotgun cracked and the wing mirror exploded off the truck.

33

Boone fired the ignition. The truck spat into life and she crunched it into second, rolling forward.

'Facing the wrong way,' Fitz said. 'Need to turn.'

'Where the hell am I supposed to do that?'

Two more bursts of shot rattled into the body of the vehicle, and Boone shifted into the high gears and took the truck out onto the grass and around the dairy in a wide arc.

'Shift down,' Fitz said, the transmission roaring.

Boone wasn't listening. The truck tilted as it turned, the wheels sliding over the turf until they bit on gravel again, settling on the main track out of the clearing. A further shotgun report echoed out, but they were too far away. In the rushing dark beside them, Lorelei kept pace, her powerful shoulders rolling as she bounded along.

The track exited abruptly onto a narrow tarmacked lane, and Boone stood on the brakes. The truck stalled, and she panicked getting it going as Lorelei leapt up, gnashing at her window. The engine turned over and she followed Fitz's procedure again, pulling away in second as she turned onto the lane, then through fourth into the high gears, tearing away from the place as fast as she could.

Lorelei fell behind, snarling into the darkness.

'I'd keep them all in fucking zoos,' Fitz said.

'How you doing there?'

Slumped across the passenger seats, his hands pressed to his side. His colour wasn't good, his breathing worse.

'I appear to be bleeding.'

'We'll get you help.'

'Shotgun wounds raise questions.'

'Questions are better than the other thing.'

'No arguments.'

'Shit,' she said.

The road was narrow and high, cutting across the crown of a hill looking out over the Downs. In the distance, blue lights flashed.

'Police?' Fitz said.

'Bet Sally called them. He knows about Mick and Tess.'

'We talk, they die.'

'It's what he'll rely on.'

'You run,' Fitz said. 'I'll take the truck as far as I can.'

'No chance.'

'I'm not going inside.'

'You're not fucking dying either.'

'There's a phone,' Fitz said.

She slowed the truck to a halt. 'Where?'

'Door panelling.'

Searching the door with her fingers, she prised away a plastic panel. A pre-paid phone was taped behind it in a baggie, battery and SIM unplugged. She fitted it together and switched it on.

'You need to get out,' she said.

'*What?*'

She dialled a number. 'Mick? Fitzy's hurt. It's bad. I need you to come get him. We're north of Wye Downs, headed towards Canterbury.

You got a burner number I can text the exact location to? . . . Yeah, got it. Hurry.'

Fetching up the map application, she sent the phone's location to the new number.

'Come on,' she said.

She got out, running round to open Fitz's door.

'I've bled everywhere.'

'Let me worry about that. Come on.'

Taking his weight, she helped him down and walked him to the side of the road.

'Mick can be here in forty minutes with a heavy foot.' She looked up and down the hedged lane. 'In here,' she said, leading him through a gap at the edge of a gate and into the field beyond.

'Nobody'll see you in here behind the hedge. I'll lead them in the other direction. You stay still, wait for Mick.'

She eased him down to the ground. He caught her hand as she turned away.

'Boone, there's no way—'

'It's decided. I'm not shoving you back up into that cab.'

'Don't do anything stupid.'

'*Moi?*' she said, and was gone.

Back round the gate. Back into the truck. Back down the lane.

The valley beneath her lit up with swirling blue, sirens carrying on the night. She took the first turn away from them, rough-riding in the dark as the truck shook and swayed, no hope of stopping for oncoming traffic on the narrow lanes.

The headlights picked out a slash of white in the black. Side of a farmhouse. Boone slowed the truck, looking at the stick to shift down, and turned into the mouth of the driveway. She pulled up at the edge of a small field, twenty yards from the house.

Her gun bag was behind the seats, along with Roper's coat. Found

Monty's Silk Cut with a lighter tucked inside too. Putting the coat on, she retrieved her knife from her bag and assembled the rifle before getting out. A light came on in the house.

'What are you doing here?' someone yelled. 'This is private property.'

Boone let off three rounds into the sky.

'Stay inside,' she said.

'We've called the police.'

Boone fired twice more for punctuation. The only vehicle she saw was a BMW. Looked like the place was no longer a working farm, but the last thing she needed was a down-from-town country zealot with a never-used two-shot pest control piece. Hopefully they had called the police and gone to hide.

Quickly she strafed the side of the house, keeping her sights on the door and windows, and found what she was looking for – the outside tap. It was hooked up to an irrigation system for the immaculately kept front garden. Pulling the end of the hose from the tap, she dragged out as much of it as she could, yanking up the little stakes that kept it pinned to the earth. When she had enough, she cut it with her knife and then cut a shorter length from one end, carting both pieces over to the truck.

Behind the side guard rails, she unscrewed the fuel tank cap and fed the long hose in. Pushing the shorter section in beside it, she blew into it until diesel glugged out the other end of the long piece. She doused the inside of the cab, lifting the hose before gravity slowed it to a trickle. She blew again to get it moving and hosed down the outside of the truck. Unlatching the rear doors, she let diesel gush into the back before the elevation killed it.

Wheelie bins stood by the house. Tipping one over, she emptied out the bags and dragged it across, letting fuel siphon into it. When she had enough, she got into the back of the truck, pulling the bin up behind her, and sloshed the stuff over the pile of carcasses. The fumes were overwhelming. Working one-handed was hard graft, and she sweated heavily.

She tore strips from Monty's box of cigarettes for firelighters. The cab went up with a whoosh and she tossed another one in the rear. Removing the magazine, she threw the Browning into the flames, dropping the ammunition in a nearby bush.

Sitting down on the lawn, she watched the flames roll out of the truck like burning surf and wished she'd kept a cigarette. The pain in her hand was unusual, a faraway aching throb and yet up close unyieldingly sharp too. Searching Roper's pockets, she found a bottle of pills, thanking Christ for his habit that would sink a bull.

Oxy, and 120s at that.

'Beaut.'

Flicking the cap off, she tipped out a little purple number and popped it onto her tongue, swallowing to escape. It felt so good she wanted to kiss Roper on the mouth, but somewhere along the line he had been left behind and he was dead anyway and she was superstitious about such things.

She peeled the tape away from her hand. It was bad.

Sirens got awfully close awfully quickly. They'd done their arithmetic, the police, putting the home owner's call and Sally's tip-off and the blazing fire together, arriving on the scene in good time. The place was brighter than high noon, and they found Boone sitting on the lawn watching it like Bonfire Night.

Tasers were out, but at least she wasn't going to be mistakenly shot dead.

'Get on your belly, arms behind your head,' the officer said.

She did as she was told, and kneeling firmly in the small of her back he grabbed her wrist and saw her finger.

'Oh Jesus Christ.'

'I may need some help with that,' said Boone.

Cuffed in a front stack, she was led to a car and guided into the back seat. The pulse from her hand spread through her body like one all-encompassing heartbeat, and she sat back trying to calm it to a reasonable pace. Taking deep breaths, she examined the injury closely. Presumably they wouldn't just leave it like that, with her bones for all the world to see. No, there was nothing for it.

It'd have to go.

Snip snip.

She giggled.

The officers watched with interest, this strange woman holding up the denuded bone of her grievous finger as if taking afternoon tea.

PART FIVE

THE CERTAIN FATE OF ALL LIFE

34

Present day

Boone dreamed again of the sea.

A sheltered cove shimmering on a summer's last day, tide rilling across the sand. Swimming out beyond the calm and into the vast indifference, where it was deep and unchaste, for the sea was two things, probably many more. And so was she. Shoulders burning with the effort, land out of sight and the waters forging a black cauldron around her. The only way left to go was down, where voices were lost and she no longer knew which way was up and the future's true nature made itself known, eyes wide and unblinking.

The Transit stank.

Fingering crust from her eyes, she slid back the side door and planted bare feet on the cool concrete. She opened all the van's doors and pressed the button for the garage's scrolling door to wind itself up, exposing the shop floor to the new day. She bagged up the empty bottles, taking them upstairs to hide in one of the storerooms in case anyone popped by unexpectedly.

Under the shower, she waited for everything to come back to the surface, for life to return to her skin. She washed her hair, twice, and worked on her heels with a pumice. What teeth she had left she scrubbed, pondering whether to buy an electric brush, before cleaning her bridge and fixing it in place.

Two cups of coffee, another brush of the teeth, and she was in the Transit. It started first time and chuckled happily in idle. Mickey Box had looked after it. Four years since she'd been behind the wheel, she was heavy-footed and glad parking would simply be a matter of stopping. Plugging her phone into the stereo, she put on Baby Huey's only album, something she'd picked up in prison, and by the time she got to the headland had also gone through half of Betty Davis's *They Say I'm Different*.

The remains of the caravan still darkened the earth. A gull perched atop a crooked metal rod and laughed. Weeds and grass grew up among the wreck and a pair of eyes glistened in there, something else now calling it home. She got out. The gull tilted its head and watched intently. The field was empty, no sign of the Calvinist sheep – gone to spread his irrationalism across pastures new, or roasted for the Sunday table. She hopped the fence and walked to the cottage.

The Mercedes was a sorry sight, filthy and on blocks. A large Ford pickup sat beside it, child seat in the back of the double cab. Boone peered through the kitchen window. Nobody. She tried the door, finding it unlocked, and went inside.

'Hello?'

No answer. The living room was empty too, but the French doors were ajar and Mickey Box's head lolled over the back of a deckchair. She pushed the door open wide.

'Wondered how long you'd be,' he said.

'Mick, what's that godawful smell?'

He waved a hand towards where the scrapyard once was.

'Just the pile.' He got to his feet. 'Coffee?'

Covering mouth and nose, Boone nodded. In the kitchen, she shut the windows as he fixed the press.

'How long's that been going on?'

'A while. You get used to it.'

At the table, she ran her fingers through its familiar grooves. 'Where's everyone?'

'Just me. Tess is working a shift. Back soon. The boy's at school.'

'School. Jesus.'

On the fridge door she noticed a menu for upcoming school meals. Different world.

'Time kills us all. You just beginning to notice?' He put a mug in front of her and sat down. 'You look tired.'

'I'm fine, Mick.'

'Just did a four. Nobody's fine after that. Not talking to a civilian here, remember.'

Noise from the past life she couldn't recall, echoing in the present. Sending Mickey Box down for GBH many moons ago, the beginning of her kinship with him and Tess.

'Fancy starting a group?' she said. 'Talk about our feelings?'

'I don't want to hear anything about your feelings. Inner workings of the creatures of this planet remain a fucking mystery to me, and one I have no inclination to unravel.'

'How is she, Tess?'

'Mostly right as rain.'

'Mostly?'

'Bit of a moment a while back, about a year after you went in. Remember that one she worked with, Donal?'

'The comedian.'

'Aye, right funny cunt. Turned out he liked to party, liked a good time. Pills, bit of salt. She went off for a few days and I had to fetch her back.'

'Shit.'

'Been golden since. The boy helps, keeps her on an even keel.'

'Does she know?'

'That you're out? Not exactly. Knows it was due, but not that they pushed it up. That copper friend of yours came by here the other day, mind.'

'Barb?'

He nodded. 'Testing the waters, my guess. Whether Tess had seen you, what sort of mood she might find you in. I could have told her it didn't take divination to know you'd present as a mardy cow.'

Boone raised her cup in acknowledgement. They sipped their coffee in silence until she couldn't take it any longer.

'I'm helping them. The police.'

'I know.'

'You know?'

'Young girl found near the dairy. Visit from a DI. Your release moved. *Administrative reasons*, as if I'd swallow that. All adds up.'

'It's about Sally.'

'Aye.'

'He ever show himself to you in any way? Warnings or the like?'

'Man does his homework, as far as I can tell. That would have told him, he shows his arse to me, one or the other of us would have to be put in the ground. You pleading guilty and keeping your mouth shut meant he could keep his distance.'

'Me coming out seems to have stirred him up.'

'Activity inside?'

'Couple of fights.'

He half smiled. 'Deep swell of pity for whoever drew that job.'

'Yeah, well. I'm coming for him now.'

'Can't help with that. Haven't heard anything about him. Don't particularly want to.'

'Just wanted to let you know. Something else – they found bodies at the dairy. Roper and Monty.'

'They identify them?'

'No.'

'They want you to tell them.'

'Said they want the families to know.'

'Mighty white of them. Their people were told, and were looked after, far as that goes. Roper had form. How come they didn't find his name?'

'No teeth. Fingers had been taken even if he had been more than old bones.'

Mickey Box thought about that. 'Forty odd years ago, probably before all that DNA malarkey. Anyways, you can help them out there. Kenneth Harcroft Roper. Wife's dead. He has a daughter with a different woman, but nothing connects them on paper. They won't find her.'

'And Monty?'

'His sister was seen to, well as anyone can be after that type of shit. Monty was what he answered to in the streets, not what his people called him. Leave them wondering on him.'

'Okay.'

A car pulled into the drive, turning round beside the cottage. Tess was laughing with another girl before getting out and waving her off. Boone stood when she came in the kitchen and Tess did a double take.

'Fucking hell.'

'It's not that bad,' Boone said.

Beaming, Tess ran over and threw her arms round her. When Boone was slow to join in with the hug, Tess grabbed her arms and pulled them around herself.

'Okay,' Boone said eventually. 'You can let go now.'

'Never.'

Finally relenting, Tess clutched Boone and shook her gently. 'Why didn't you say anything?'

'Didn't want a big fuss.'

'It would have been a little fuss.'

'Any fuss.'

'Right. Sit down. I want to hear all about everything.'

'Well, the accommodation was fab and the people there were so nice. There was lots to do in the evenings and the weather was just super.'

Tess turned to her father. 'Didn't lose the lip in there, then.'

'Take twenty-five to life for that.' He finished his coffee and got up. 'This is going to get girlie, so I'll see myself to the stables for a few hours.'

'Still in business, then?' Boone said.

'He's not growing,' said Tess. 'Goes to the old stables and potters about. Watches telly, or he has his tools there and he tinkers with stuff.'

'Fixed that toaster,' he said.

Tess scoffed. 'A new fuse?'

'What the hell happened?' Boone said.

'Respectable businessman now,' Tess said. 'Arcade on Sheppey actually turns a profit, and the rent from his properties is a tidy sum.'

'Jesus.'

'I know,' Tess said. 'He'll be voting for the bosses next.'

'Don't vote,' Mickey Box said.

'He's a traditional socialist, you see,' Tess said.

'Don't like encouraging any of the bastards.'

Tess patted him on the shoulder. 'The inevitable outcome of enough bootstrapping is voting for the biggest knobhead on the ballot. It's the dream of the self-made man.'

'I don't have to listen to this. I have fuses to change.'

When he had gone, Boone said, 'What the hell? The mountain of shit in the scrapyard? No more weed?'

'Didn't have the taste for it without Fitz. Didn't want to deal with the distribution himself, and didn't trust anyone else to do it. The pile is what's left of a refuse collection firm he ran for about three months.'

Tess made more coffee and busied herself. She opened a shopping bag she'd brought in, pulling out and holding up clothes for Jim. School trousers and some polos. She cleared cups and dishes on the side, picked up toys from the floor. All the while, she watched Boone quietly.

'What?' said Boone.

'What what?'

'I feel as if I'm being scrutinised.'

'Where are you staying?'

'Got a sort of flat. In Lark.'

'Sort of flat?'

'Mick sorted it. It's—spacious.'

'When did you get out?'

'Couple of days ago. It's been mad. There's a thing I'm helping Barb with. She got me out early.'

'She was here last week. That girl on the news, the one they found wandering the countryside. Dad said that wasn't a million miles from where he went that night. Night you were arrested. Night he went to get Fitz.'

'Yeah.'

'How are you, Boone? You seem—I don't know.'

'Getting used to the pace of life outside again. Liberty is exhausting. Listen, there's something I have to ask you. A favour.'

'Okay. But only if you agree to something first.'

'Hmm. What?'

'Well, you getting out early is good because it's Jim's birthday.'

'Oh God.'

'You have to come.'

'Don't like parties.'

'No party. An intimate gathering of a few important folk.'

'Don't like folk.'

'You've already missed so much. He's going to be six.'

'Are you emotionally blackmailing me with your only child?'

'Yes. Yes, I am.'

'And you promise it's not a party?'

'Gathering. Very small. Low key.'

Boone sighed. 'What does one buy for a person that small?'

Tess clapped in delight. 'Excellent. So, what was this favour?'

'I need to find a mutual friend of ours.'

35

Forty minutes later, Boone was in Gravesend.

The Transit nosed through the gates of a scrapyard on the shore of the Thames, just upriver from the old fort. Cars were stacked in tin hills, from freshly delivered wrecks to doorless shells to heaps of parts. A stubby finger of river water cut into the shore, a kind of graving dock where a floating house-pier was moored, a steel gangway connecting her to dry land.

Boone spun the Transit round and parked. A Portakabin functioned as the yard's office, but it was locked up and dark. There were lights on aboard the pier, though. Knowing she was being watched, she stopped at the edge of the dock, toes on the gangway, and waited.

The pier had two structures, with an open space between them where the gangway led aboard. The entire length was covered by a roof with multiple peaks, like a wedding marquee held up by poles. The sides of each structure had been fitted with four sets of sliding double doors, most of them curtained off from within.

The end one slid aside and he rolled himself out in a wheelchair, moving easily along the smooth decking, shotgun across his lap.

'All right, Fitzy?' she said. 'Permission to come aboard?'

36

With effort, Fitz pushed himself to his feet, shotgun aimed at Boone.
He looked behind her into the dark yard.

'Just me,' she said.

'What do you want?'

'That's nice. Old friend comes to visit, one who pulled you dying
from a torture chamber and then took the fall for the whole racket.'

'What do you want?'

'I want you to help me find Sally.'

Directed by the shotgun, Boone made her way along the deck to
the doors Fitz had emerged from. A large living room spanned the
pier, floor-to-ceiling windows in the opposite wall. A table and four
chairs sat to the left, and the end wall on the right was covered with
bookcases, hundreds of volumes in several languages.

Two chesterfield sofas in aged soft brown leather filled the middle
of the room, two art-deco club chairs angled near their ends. Boone
loved a club chair.

'Uh uh,' Fitz said, when she went to sit. 'Jacket off.'

Shrugging off her jacket, she draped it on the table.

'Lift your top.'

'Christ.'

Fitz raised the barrel of the gun.

'Fine,' she said, rolling her top up to under her bra and turning round. 'I don't think they tape mics onto people any more, Fitz. They just use phones or tiny devices it'd take you a lifetime to find.'

He stared at her.

'Can jump in the canal if it'll make you feel better?'

'Will you promise not to come back up?'

He looked smaller, and his hair had begun an erratic retreat from his forehead, which hadn't improved his flinty attitude.

'I'm sensing hostility here.'

'Sit. Not there,' he said, as she went for the club chair. 'Sofa, in the middle where I can see your hands.'

He sank slowly into the sofa opposite, still gripping the shotgun.

'Fitz, honestly. Why would I come to hurt you? And what makes you think you would have known about it if I had?'

'Saw you coming a mile off.'

'Of course you did. I came in the front fucking door. Cameras out in the road, and on the gateposts, and all over the yard. I was hardly avoiding them. On the other hand, there are half a dozen old tubs moored to the floating dock not a quarter of a mile away. If I'd come across the river by night from Tilbury, spent a day hidden aboard one of them, then swum up unseen in the muddy waters by your old boat ramps and caught you rolling along, up and clonking you on your head before you knew it – if it'd gone that way, Fitzgerald, all anyone would have found was you and your chair in the water beside this pier of yours, and they'd have figured you accidentally wheeled your gimpy arse to a damp grave.'

'Only reason I'm even mildly concerned at this fantasy is my suspicion it's some kind of foreplay for you. A thought that turns my stomach.'

Boone smiled. 'How are you, Fitz?'

'Wondering what you're doing here, going on four years of radio silence.'

'I was a tad busy. You see about the little girl in the news?'

'Keeping their cards close to their chest, details-wise.'

'Found her about two hundred yards from the gate to Sally's dairy. I'm not sure what they were doing with her, as nobody has been in the building for years, but I don't have any doubt she was behind that hidden door the night we were there.'

Fitz frowned. 'They've been holding her since then?'

'Doctors say they had her from birth. Ten or eleven years now.'

'How the fuck is that possible?'

Boone shrugged. 'She can't talk. Or think. Or do anything other people can do, except redefine our capacity for horror. And here's the kicker – she's Sarah Still's daughter.'

'Bloody hell. That girl really did fuck your life up.'

'Police got me out early so I could help them.'

'Oh aye? Turned back the other way, have we?'

'I was jumped a couple of times recently. Sally looking to tie up loose ends.'

'Number of people who've tried to rip your face off over the years, how do you know it's not just a natural reaction to your charm?'

'As upsetting as it is for me to admit, I've missed you, Fitz.'

'Course you have.' Fitz made the shotgun safe and stood it against the sofa.

'I never really got the full story. Mick wouldn't talk about it.'

'No, I don't suppose he would. He found me where you told him, there in the field. Lost a lot of blood by that time. He'd brought his man with him, the old army doc who had that bother over there. Worked on me in the back of the car, pulling out bits of shot. I'm type O, and Mick gave all he had when we got to the doc's place. Battlefield surgery, he called it. Didn't really take, though. There was infection, and the damage was deep and in my guts.

'I didn't want him to, but the doc took me to casualty at the Maritime with some cockamamie story about my gun going off when I was preparing for a spot of hunting. Said he'd found me. Mick staged the scene at the scrapyard, used my blood. Police never saw Mick, never connected me to the job. Didn't believe a word I told them, but what could they do? Scene looked legit, and I'm licensed, so the piece was legal.'

'The wheelchair?'

'Don't use it much. Long day, is all. Sometimes it's just easier. Was in it for almost a year, though. Stoma bag for months. Half a dozen surgeries. Few talks with your lot about gun safety. There's damage to the hip, too, starting to scrape where the joint was clipped. Thought it would be all right, but it's looking like it needs replacing.'

'I'm sorry, Fitz. I really am.'

'Don't be daft. Still alive. Looking at the state of you, reckon I got off easy. Besides, I knew the cost of doing business.'

'Wasn't business, though, was it? It was my stuff.'

'Mick was keen on taking Sally out. Thought there'd be profit in it, finding out the scope of his operations from the inside. Plus, he never would have let you walk into the shit alone.'

'Did Mick check the dairy back then?'

Fitz nodded. 'They were gone the next day. Nothing there. He went back again a few weeks later and they'd done some thorough housekeeping. Stripped the place. New walls covering things over.'

'Yeah, I've been there. Police are taking it apart.

'Roper and Monty?'

'Boot of a car buried in the field. Police don't know who they are yet. Mick says I should give them Roper, keep shtum on Monty.'

'Sounds about right.'

'You've no idea what happened to Sally afterwards?'

Fitz pointed up to a bookshelf behind her.

She looked. 'What?'

'The GTO.'

The shelves were deep, and in front of one row of green-spined Penguins were arranged several model cars.

'Didn't know that was your sort of thing.'

'It isn't. Get the GTO down.'

'I don't—GTO?'

'Red one with the curvy front like a snake.'

She handed Fitz the model. From a drawer in the coffee table he found a set of tiny screwdrivers and removed the base of the car, allowing the engine block to be taken out from beneath the bonnet. It pulled apart, revealing a USB plug.

'Made that myself,' he said proudly.

'I was worried about the state of my life, but yours makes me long for death.'

He slid a laptop out from under the sofa and plugged in the memory stick. Scooting along the sofa, he patted the seat beside him.

'If this is some of your Japanese porn.'

'Took me a while to get right after what happened. Surgeries, the bag, the wheelchair, what have you. Time operates differently. All you think about is what's wrong with you. How much you hurt. How hard it's going to be to recover. Plus, me and Mick sort of came to a bit of an end.'

'Yeah. Nobody's talking about that. He found out about Jim, I assume?'

'I told him.'

'That was clever.'

'After the first operation, I had an open wound. I was in intensive care with a hole in me, fucked up on morphine and thought I was going to die. Telling him seemed like the thing to do.'

'Surprised he didn't reach inside you and finish the job.'

'He paid to have me transferred to a private clinic and have specialists see me. Paid for the consultants and nursing fees. Paid for everything. Then told me if he ever saw me again he'd put a bullet in each eye.'

'Sorry.'

'That was the last I saw of any of them.'

'Even Tess? She told me where you were.'

'I let her know. I send money, but she says she can't spend it without Mick knowing, so I put it in an account for the lad. Every now and then I get an email with pictures. I told her not to bring him here, or come herself. Never seen Mick like that. He wasn't angry, he was—I don't know. Something. I didn't want her getting on the wrong side of it. Better this way. He's so good with the lad anyway.'

'So were you.'

'Not the same. He didn't know I was his blood. I was just some odd bloke who was always around.'

'Fitz—'

'I was all fucked up for so long after the shooting, I wouldn't have been any use to him. When I started returning to some kind of normality, walking again, getting around fine, I got to thinking about Sally. Went out to the dairy, and it was just like Mick said. All cleared out. We didn't know where any of his other places were, and Roper was the only connection we had. The dairy was owned by a woman called Constance Bobb.'

'Police are trying to find her, without much luck.'

'She's in a care home in Gloucestershire. Tracked her down a couple of years ago. She's gaga, though, hasn't a clue. I don't think it's her real name. I found her birth certificate, and it says 1907 on it. This old dear was getting on, but she wasn't Methuselah. Wouldn't surprise me if the real Constance Bobb died in infancy. Loads of lonely old ducks around these days, nobody left to give a shit about them. Sally finds some elderly girl gone in the upstairs and switches her into the identity, puts her in a home. Puts property in her name and he's insulated. Probably he's done it several times.'

'You visited her?'

'Pretended to be an old neighbour. They said her nephew was paying but he was overseas working. She didn't know anything, though, didn't know one day from the next. You can give her to the police, there won't be anything she can tell them.'

'They could track the payments, perhaps.'

'Gone to all this trouble, they won't have overlooked that. It'll be in a cover name or a shell company. Always a way to hide stuff. Me and Mick did it for years.'

'So she was a dead-end?'

'Not exactly. She's the director of a couple of companies, including a building firm that picked up some council contracts back in the eighties. Renovating properties for them. Residential homes for children.'

'Christ, they were well and truly embedded.'

'I went to the local paper, said I was writing a book about buildings in the area. Remembered what you said about the boy you'd been looking for . . .'

'Noah.'

'. . . and that place he was at, Eastry. Found this.'

This was an old photo from an event at the kids' home, all kinds of dignitaries in attendance. The main subjects were Hanley Moss, MP for Lark at the time, and a local constable. In the background, over Moss's shoulder, at least twenty-five years younger than Boone remembered but unmistakably him, was Sally. The copper was a familiar face too.

'Christ, I know him,' she said.

'The plod?'

'Came round after the caravan fire. Fuck did he say his name was? Reckoned there'd been a complaint, and maybe it was best if I moved on. I thought it was just a Kent Police thing. Not too popular with them since the whole Blackborne business. Made them look foolish as they didn't break it.'

'Maybe he was there for Sally instead.'

'Yeah. There's another policeman there too, but his face is turned away.'

Fitz flicked through several more pictures. 'They had these in their paper archive. Took me ages. That second copper doesn't appear in any of the others, though. Police could have been there legitimately that day.'

'Yeah, but not the fella who came by after the fire. That's too much to swallow. Him there with Sally and Moss, and then years later coming to see me when I'm looking for Sally? Thought at the time it was strange, because he was a sergeant. Why involve himself? But if he'd been giving cover to men like Sally and Hanley Moss for all those years—'

She stopped dead.

'What?'

Boone pointed out a face in another photograph, a man standing beside Hanley Moss.

'Yeah, he's one of them too,' Fitz said.

'That's Jerry Killock.'

'You know him?'

'He worked in children's services. He was under investigation when he died, and then everything was brushed under the carpet. It was before Savile, and nobody wanted to know.'

'Under investigation for what? Nonce stuff?'

Boone nodded. 'He worked on Noah's case. And he was Sarah Still's social worker too.'

'This is all tied up with the men who abducted you.'

'It's everywhere. I thought it was just a group of men who used their power to do what they want, but it's deeper than that. They had people in social services, people in the police. It's institutional. How did you mean, he's one of them?'

'You have to see this. Apologies in advance.' He clicked about the folders on the USB stick. 'Mick said Roper told him, long while ago, that Sally made films. Thought he shared them online with other animals. In my convalescence, I brushed up on my Tor, did a bit of deep-sea diving in the murkier reaches of the internet. Ended up finding these dark nets you access through this old Japanese software. Shit you've never seen the likes of. I had no idea where I was looking. Spent months staring at it. Pure fluke, I found myself looking at . . .'

'Killock?'

'Watch this.'

Fitz played the video file.

'Recognise it?'

'Yeah.'

It was one of the small bedrooms at the dairy, still carpeted and furnished. The camera was high up in a corner. A young boy lying straight as a pencil on the bed. Killock came in. He spoke with the boy, but there was no sound.

Boone watched as the video played. 'Fuck.'

'I don't think he knew he was being filmed.'

'There's no way he would have allowed himself to be identified.'

'Strange that it was put online at all. You said he was dead, though?'

'Years ago. Still a risk, given the police knew about him.'

'That fuck Sally loves his power games. I have other videos shot there, but the cameras are in the rooms. Like, close to what's going on, not up at a high angle. You can't see faces, though. Out of shot or they're wearing masks. Having people on video like that, it's a way of controlling them, isn't it? Showing them he might have other footage where they're identifiable, and proving he's serious by putting Killock out there.'

'If we're going to get anything from this, I have to take it to Barb.'

'I'm not a grass.'

'This isn't grassing. Fucking hell, Fitz. Grassing. The bollocks that gets put about. This is how they get away with this stuff, some bullshit code. Same reason coppers get away with corruption and outright criminality, on account of other coppers thinking police investigating police is a worse crime than anything else an officer could do.'

'Still working with the other side.'

'Only side I'm on is the victims of these men. I hunt and catch animals, Fitz. It's all I know. And I don't much care who helps me do that, so long as they get caught.'

'Here's where I am,' Fitz said. 'I've been sat here for four years waiting for an opportunity to find the man that did this to me. And here you are, presenting me with a chance. But if I help you find this piece of shit, then there's something you have to help me with.'

'Sure. What?'

'You have to help me kill him.'

'No.'

'No?'

'*You* have to help *me* kill him.'

37

'I thought you'd just plug it in your computer and have a gander,' Boone said.

'You handed me a mystery memory stick from fuck knows where and just expected me to open its contents on a networked police computer?' Barb said.

'Yeah?'

Barb shook her head. They stood huddled with Barry and Storm behind Barb's desk, where, on an un-networked laptop, Jane Scheune, a bod from Cyber Crime, was examining the contents of the fresh USB stick Boone and Fitz had transferred the material to.

Barb tried to follow what Jane was saying, but really she was thinking only about her hair. A curly-haired girl, she looked as if she'd never even thought about straightening. She wore it up, casually bunched as if she was getting in the bath, but it had remained perfect all day. Electric coils here and there, a dark helix hanging over one eye. Barb's hair had never dried the same twice; she'd end up looking like a malevolent dandelion if she attempted such a thing.

'It's clean,' Jane was saying. 'Almost as if someone didn't want us to know where it came from.'

Barb eyed Boone. 'Almost.'

Opening a folder, Jane brought up the pictures from the event at Eastry.

'Where's this from?' Barb said.

'Local paper,' said Boone.

'I'm saying, where did *you* get it from?'

'A friend.'

'At least try to make your bullshit sound plausible,' Barry said.

'You know, you're old enough now to be half the prick you are,' Boone said.

'Shut up, both of you.'

'That's Roy Fuller,' Barry said, pointing at the police officer.

'Jane, could you give us a moment?' Barb said.

'Sure.'

'And we're okay to flick through the rest of this?'

'Yep,' Jane said. 'I have to drop in to CSE. Give me a bell when you're done and I'll grab the laptop back.'

'Great. Thanks.'

'I don't like this,' Barb said, after Jane had left her office. 'I've known Roy Fuller a long time. There have been stories about him. Graft. But he's well thought of by coppers who work with him. We have to be absolutely certain before we wade into this, because we won't be popular.'

'Look who he's with,' Boone said. 'Hanley Moss, a serial paedophile who evaded detection for decades; Jerry Killock, who groomed vulnerable children from inside social services; and there's Sally in the background, a violent predator and murderer. All together at Eastry, which proved a fertile hunting ground for them. And then thirty years later he shows up when my caravan burns down right after I start digging into all of this.'

Barb shook her head.

Boone said, 'I know you get hung up on the distinction between what we know and what we can prove—'

'Hung up?' Barb spat. 'It's sort of a fundamental pillar of juris-fucking-prudence.'

'But how many times have you had an instinct about something that you followed through on? What we know steers us towards what we can prove.'

'I think that among the litany of things you've forgotten is every single modern investigative technique. Instincts, for fuck's sake. We work with evidence, Boone.' She turned to Barry. 'What do you think?'

'I think if he wasn't a copper we'd be all over him. Turns up at key moments, decades apart, in the same investigation. Having police protection explains a lot about how these people carried on with impunity for so long.'

That surprised Barb. She had expected Barry to toe a company line.

'Sally knew Abigail liked women,' Storm said.

The other three stared at her.

'O-kay . . .' Barb said.

'You said he told you that *your sort* wouldn't be needing that particular finger,' Storm said to Boone. 'Right before he . . . did what he did.'

'Yeah,' said Boone.

'Your sort. Your ring finger. Leaving aside that he's still living in the 1970s, he was making a point that he knew about you. But how did he know? Did you introduce yourself, hello, I'm Boone and I like women?'

'I did not.'

'Right, so he knew. Fuller saw me when he came to look at the caravan that day.'

'Saw you where?' Barb said.

'In the back of Abigail's van.'

'I was living in the van after—'

'Yeah, I get the picture,' Barb said. 'You think Fuller filled Sally in?'

'I think it makes sense, if he'd been sent there to gather intelligence.

Sally knew what was coming. He was getting solid information from somewhere.'

'There's another copper there,' Boone said.

'Can't make him out,' Barry said, squinting.

'We need to be careful about dragging any old person into some vast conspiracy,' Barb said.

'We need to see Fuller's financials,' Barry said.

'We can't,' said Barb. 'There are ways of doing things, channels to go through. And we have next to nothing other than a hunch. We couldn't go to Professional Standards with this. We'd be laughed out.'

'They'd have to open an investigation,' Barry said.

'And Fuller would find out. Those cases take years to come to fruition. Everything would get cleaned up before we got near it.

'What, then?' Barry said.

'Go at him sideways,' Boone said. 'Ask him for his help, make it look official, like you're asking him what he remembers about the photo, but leave him in no doubt that you like him for it. Rattle his cage.'

'How?' Barb said.

'Bring me with you.'

'No way.'

'He knows I was looking into it,' Boone said. 'Four years ago, that's why he came to the caravan. If I'm there, he'll know that you know. Hopefully he'll panic.'

Barb sat back in her chair, looked to Barry. He raised his eyebrows.

'Shitsicles,' Barb said, resigning herself to the plan.

'There's video too,' Boone said. 'Confirms Barry's theory about hidden cameras.'

'Video of what exactly?' Barb said.

'Killock. And a boy.'

'Well. Isn't that brilliant.'

They watched the video in stony silence.

'It's hard evidence on Killock,' Barry said when it had finished. 'Provides cause for Social to open his files to us. Perhaps we can identify the boy.'

'This is your territory, Storm,' Barb said. 'Liaise with Social, gather all the material you can. Also, I want you to check out this Constance Bobb, go see her at this home in Gloucestershire. Get a statement if you can, but if she's not up to it then talk to the staff. Find out about visitors. Who pays the bills. Anything. Rest of us will go see what Roy Fuller has to say.'

Storm drew Boone aside. 'I'm going to see Molly. Talk to Ravi about what he thinks can be done for her. Will you come?'

'Yeah, I'll come.'

Solange played in the SUV. Neither of them spoke, but it was comfortable, and Boone remembered that fleeting feeling of what it was like to be with someone without wondering what they were thinking. When they pulled into the car park at the Redfearn Institute, something occurred to her.

'You might want to talk to Harry Eustace. He worked with Killock and told me that if the police ever got interested he would do all he could to help.'

'Don't know him. Local?'

'Four years ago he had an office in Lark. Give me a sec.'

Boone called Kent social services asking for Eustace and was put through to his voicemail, which gave a mobile number. She called it.

'Hello?'

'Harry? It's Abigail Boone.'

'Good Lord.'

'Been a while.'

'Yes. I heard about—that's to say, I read in the papers what happened.'

'Yeah, there's no way to explain that in a way that'll make sense.

Listen, I've been talking with Kent Police, and they're actively investigating Jerry Killock now.'

'I heard.'

'Things have escalated. There's compelling evidence against him and they're preparing warrants. I wondered if I could put a detective in contact with you, maybe get things moving a little quicker.'

'Sure thing.'

'Great. I'll give her this number and she'll call you. Thanks, Harry.'

Storm stepped out of the SUV. 'Reckon he'll be much use?'

'Can't hurt to have someone there we sort of know.'

Storm had called ahead, and Ravi John met them at the door and showed them to the observation room. Molly was next door with a female doctor, playing with plastic shapes.

'Much progress?' Storm asked.

Ravi shrugged his chin. 'It's so early. With the shapes, she's still taking some of them, adding to her pile of stuff in the corner. No comprehension of what we want her to do, identify the shapes, put them in the holes. I can't even see a pattern in the ones she keeps.'

The girl stood up, holding a red triangle, and walked in lurching little bunny-hops to the corner, adding it to the rest of her hoard.

'She's moving more,' Boone said.

'We take her out every day, encourage her to move around,' Ravi said. 'She's probably walked more in the last week than she has in the rest of her life. That's why she struggles, why she hops more than walks. She has hip and back problems, but it'll be a while before I can get her to cooperate with a physio.'

Boone thought of how tired she herself got just walking when she first came out of prison, and what it must be like to have spent your entire existence in a cell but not to understand what either a cell or existence were.

'What about communication?' she said.

'I still have hopes for some form of sign language,' Ravi said. 'Getting her to express basic wants, and maybe understand some in return. If we get that far, we can see how much we can build on it. Did you find the people who did this?'

'Working on it,' Storm said.

He took his glasses off and cleaned them. 'She's incredibly wary of people, especially men. We've found it better for her to work with female doctors.'

'Is she eating?' Storm said.

'Soft food. We're trying to get her off the baby stuff, but she loves it. All she has ever known, I suspect. We're trying mashed fruit, try to work her up to solid bits at some point. She likes bananas.'

Ravi saw them back to the front door.

'It's okay, us coming here?' Storm said.

'I'm glad someone is maintaining an interest.'

'Good. We'll come back soon, then.'

They sat quietly in the SUV. Boone watched the birds murmur over the lake, which caught the sun like a field of broken glass.

'The sign language idea sounds promising,' Storm said.

'Mmm.'

'Developing some way for her to externalise would be life-changing.'

'Ravi seems to know his stuff.'

'Abigail.'

'Yeah?'

'Look, I know that in your experience what the police do can seem insufficient in many ways—'

'Oh, I think they've been sufficiently involved in this mess so far, wouldn't you say?'

'We don't know what happened. And we should wait and see what the investigation turns up before—'

'Taken from her mother at birth and raised without love or nurturing or any kind of gentleness. The worst conditions animals are made to suffer are better than what she got. And it was all done for one end – the sexual gratification of beasts.' Boone was shaking, rage coursing through her. She wanted Sally and Ferg and Fuller and anyone else who was involved. She wanted to tear their lungs out.

Storm touched her arm. 'Look—'

'She served that purpose from so young an age it doesn't bear thinking about. The cost of it, the cost to her, was total. They took everything she had, everything she would ever have been, and replaced it with horror. She was never allowed to be a child, never allowed to become a person. She can't speak, I don't even know if she can think. Can she think, Storm? Can she understand any of this? Is there any kind of thought process going on? She represents a truth so terrifying, so colossally fucking sickening, that it can't even be looked at straight. It's like staring at the sun, it'll send you blind.

'Absolutely nobody connected to the making of that truth can afford for their involvement to come to light. Ever. That's why people are dead. That's why I lost a finger, why they tried to kill me, why they came for me again in prison. And that's why I have to find them. I don't care who they are – criminals, predators, social services, the police. It's all the same to me. It all leads to the same end.'

38

The next morning, Barb and Boone sat outside a three-bed semi on a suburban estate, post-war sprawl that had once been orchards. The road was narrow, cars parked to the kerb one side and on the grass verges the other. It wasn't clear if this was a methodical system or had taken hold by chance.

'I can see three skips just from here,' Boone said. 'Scaffolding over the back there, so that'll be another one.'

'Surrendering to destiny and settling for loft extensions in lieu of the dream move to Tunbridge Wells,' Barb said.

'Want to play I Spy?' Boone said.

'Ten,' Barb said.

'You've never played this game before, have you?'

'I'd have at least ten bodies on this place in a kosher operation. Two-man teams. One at each end of the bullshit alley behind the house. Another sat out here watching the door. And two more parked at either end of the estate to pick him up when he runs.'

'Sounds thorough.'

'And what do I have? Me, Barry, and a sociopathic convicted sheep rustler.'

'That last one counts for probably three or four of Kent's finest, though.'

'Come on,' Barb said, getting out.

Knocking on the door, she slipped on her politest smile. Roy Fuller was in his fifties, a career uniform man. His face had an ageless, bovine look, and sunlight coursed in rivulets through his brilliantined hair.

'Inspector,' Fuller said. Noticing Boone, his eyes flicked between them.

'Sorry to bother you on your day off, Sarge,' Barb said.

'Nothing on but a bit of kip. Back on nights later.'

'I'll keep it as short as I can, then. Could we come in? I need your help.'

Fuller held the door open and gestured to the front room. Floral wallpaper and an old Baxi Bermuda with back boiler in the chimney breast. Other than the flat-screen TV, the place looked untouched since the seventies. Barb wondered if he'd inherited it.

'I'll make tea,' he said, disappearing into the back somewhere.

Boone crept through after him. When she returned, she made a gesture with her hands like using a phone. Barb edged into the hall-way, spying into the kitchen through the hinge-crack in the door. Fuller was typing on his mobile as the kettle boiled.

'Use the lav, Sarge?' Barb said.

'Uh, yeah, just through there.'

He fumbled the phone into his pocket.

'Cheers.'

She stood in the small WC, giving it a minute before flushing and running the tap.

'Should have gone before I left,' she said, breezing back to the living room.

The carpet had a shine from decades of shuffling feet, sun-bleaching and changes in pile where furniture had been moved. Children in mantelpiece picture frames were young, but there were no signs they lived there. Barb recalled a wife, but if the kids were Fuller's, they'd be older now. He brought through a tray sporting a rather delicate china set. Nothing in the house looked like it belonged to him.

'Sugar? Milk?' he said.

'Just milk,' Boone said.

'Me too, thanks,' Barb said.

Fuller added a splash of milk to one cup, left Boone to fend for herself.

'Now, I know they didn't let you back on the force,' he said. 'In fact, last I heard, you were locked up in Brabazon.'

'Apparently Kent Police hadn't been catching any villains in my absence, so I got a mulligan,' Boone said.

Barb dodged the tea, which looked like he'd boiled kidney stones. 'She's out on special,' she said. 'Helping us with our inquiries.'

'Oh aye?' Fuller said.

'I'm hoping you might be able to help too, Sarge.'

'Try my best, ma'am.'

'There's not many coppers been working the area as long as you. What we're looking into has a historical element to it. It's a long shot, but I want to put that memory of yours to work.'

'Right you are, ma'am.'

'We're looking for a face, seems to have cleared off the scene now, but would have been busy round these parts probably from the late seventies onward. Went by the name of Sally.'

Fuller smirked. 'Sally, ma'am?'

'Yes. It's actually a chap we're looking for. Odd name, I know.'

'No, I know who you mean, ma'am. But it's just an urban legend. Or a rural one, I suppose. There was all sorts of activity put down to this Sally, but it was just the usual suspects using the name as a cover.'

'Yes, that's what we heard. But witnesses have told us there was an actual individual. Lived in plain sight, might even have been a pillar of the community. I think people probably knew him without knowing he was Sally.'

'Not sure I can help you, ma'am. Far as I knew it was a fairy tale.'

'Of course. But we've had someone identify the man in a photograph, you see. And that's where you might be able to help.'

'Ma'am?'

Barb produced a printout of the photograph from the local paper.

'This would have been about thirty years ago,' she said. 'Some kind of community event at Eastry House, when it was still a children's home. That's Hanley Moss, and that would be you beside him.'

'Sure,' Fuller said. 'He was the local MP back then. Used to see him at events like that all the time. Very active in the community was Hanley.'

'Especially among the young people,' Boone said.

Fuller flashed her a look.

'Absolutely,' Barb said. 'And like I said, this Sally chap probably attended these events without anyone knowing who he was. You see, that's him there.' She pointed out the man in the background behind Hanley Moss. 'That's Sally.'

Fuller shook his head.

'This was decades ago, ma'am. I didn't even know everyone there then, let alone recall them now. I'd helped the people at the home with a couple of runaways and they used to invite me to these things. I don't even remember the picture being taken. It was probably more for old Hanley, getting the boys in blue on his side, nice shot for the local rag. But I have no idea who that bloke is.'

'Like I said, long shot,' said Barb. 'Oh, you wouldn't happen to know who the other copper there that day was, would you?'

'Other copper, ma'am?'

Barb produced another photo, with the back of the second policeman visible.

'His face isn't in the shot, but I'd like to ask him whether he knew the gentleman in question. We're desperate to speak to anyone who was there, to be honest.'

Fuller made a pretence of studying the picture.

'Couldn't say, ma'am. It was that long ago. I don't remember the day itself. I suppose it must have been one of the local bobbies.'

'Yeah, we thought that, but couldn't narrow it down.'

'Sorry, ma'am.'

'Ah well. No harm in asking. I appreciate your time, Sarge.'

'Of course. Only sorry I couldn't be of more use. Tricky things, cold cases.'

'They are,' Barb said. 'But this isn't cold. It's playing out now. Scorching. We're identifying new as well as historical crimes. Possible institutional sexual abuse covering decades. It's going to be massive, Sarge. Growing legs by the day. We're getting fresh bodies, and the Chief Super is signing off on GSM interceptors, ISMI catchers. All the toys.'

'I see.'

'Anyways, I don't want to take up any more of your day off.'

'No worries. Let me know if you need any help on the case. Always around to lend a hand.'

'Take you up on that, Sarge.'

They stood up and he showed them to the door.

'Nice seeing you again, Royston,' Boone said, smiling sweetly.

'Uh huh,' he said.

Couldn't close the door behind them quick enough.

'ISMI catchers?' Boone said as they got back in the car.

'Make him think twice about getting on his little prepaid handset. Nearly dropped it in the tea when I asked to use his lavvy.'

'Now what?' Boone said.

'Now we wait.'

39

Barb slumped down in Barry's SUV, a few doors along from Fuller's. It had darkened rear windows and she faced the other way, keeping a close eye in the mirrors. This was the inconspicuous part of the plan. Barry was parked up in her Audi at one end of the alley running behind the houses to the garages, while at the other end sat Boone in a Ford Escort, the provenance of which she had been somewhat vague about.

The wrapping of a chicken and avocado sandwich and two empty crisp bags tied into neat bows lay on the passenger seat. A small water bottle remained half full; Barb worried she'd need the loo at a crucial moment.

Fuller was on nights as custody officer, getting back at half seven. Hadn't stirred until the curtains pulled back at about two, package from Amazon an hour later. At four, his battered Peugeot estate rolled out of the alley.

'He's moving.' Boone's voice, crackling over the walkie-talkie.

Barry had picked up a set for a small fortune from Argos. Seventeen hundred channels, voice scrambling, privacy codes, and they'd had to let Boone set them up because they hadn't got a clue. She'd enjoyed that a little too much.

'He's headed east,' she added.

'Probably going to skirt round the park and get on the A20,' Barry said. 'Maybe the motorway. I'll get out ahead of him.'

Barb pulled away and sped down a parallel road, turning in time to see Fuller cross in front of her.

'I've got him,' she said, falling in behind.

'If he was headed for Maidstone, he'd have gone the other way,' Boone said. 'I'll cut through the estate here and intercept him on the A20.'

'Roger,' Barb said, immediately regretting it. 'Wilco,' she added. 'Fuck it and out.'

She popped a fruit pastille in her mouth. The bag had split, sugar granules filling the plastic tray by the gearstick. Barry wasn't going to be amused by that. There was still a little school traffic around, and a car pulled out of a side street between her and Fuller. A red light stopped Fuller at the junction with the A20, Barb rolling to a halt behind the other car.

'Waiting for the lights at the A20,' she said into the radio.

On the green, Fuller pulled away, heading east. The car in between didn't move, its lights going dead as the driver stalled.

'Cock swabs,' Barb said, hitting her horn.

The driver held his hands up, like this was all beyond his influence. Pulling the wheel hard to the side, Barb angled to go round him, but oncoming traffic and cars piling up behind made it impossible. Eventually the car in front lurched forward, but didn't get far as the lights went red again.

'Oh you grape-dicked twat.' She got on the radio again. 'Fucking car stalled and trapped me at the lights. Fuller is away down the A20, out of sight.'

The driver ahead held his hand up in apology. He wore a black beanie and Barb really wanted to throw it in a puddle, maybe not even take it off first.

'Anyone got anything?' she asked.

'Coming up to the A20,' Boone said. 'Only room for one car on these streets and some idiot was parking. Be there in a sec.'

'I don't see him,' Barry said.

'Bollocking bollocky bollocks,' Barb said, not across the air.

'I'm going to follow the A20 out to the motorway and hit the M20 going for Ashford,' Barry said. 'See if I can't catch him if he's gone that way. Boone, you stay on the A20.'

'Aye aye, Captain,' Boone said.

'Boss, you good to stay at the house?'

Barb grunted. Holding down the button on her two-way, she grunted again. When the lights went green, the man in the beanie pottered off on the rest of his day. Barb pulled a questionable uey and drove back whence she came, parking in the exact same spot near Fuller's house. She didn't have eyes on either end of the alley. Absolute fiasco. She waited twenty minutes anyway, until Barry came back on the radio.

'I didn't see him.'

'Good job we're not trained fucking operatives or anything. This would have been an embarrassment otherwise. What about Boone?'

'Haven't heard from her.'

'I'm not sitting outside Fuller's house all day. We've missed him. Knowing when he comes back doesn't do us any favours. Meet me back at the Shed.'

Barb stropped into the Shed hoping to find someone to blame. Instead, she saw Storm sitting at her desk in the bullpen, returned from Gloucestershire already.

'Wasn't expecting you back today.'

'Left at five this morning to beat the traffic, so I was all done there by midday. I got you a coffee.'

'How did you—'

'Barry called a few minutes ago.'

'Did he reach Boone?'

'Nope.'

'Can you call her?'

'Already have. Phone's unavailable.'

'Of course it is. Come on.'

Barb unlocked her office, tossing her bag onto the low filing cabinet. Pulling the lid off the coffee, she inhaled deeply. She kicked her shoes off and sat behind her desk.

'Well, we had a shit day. How about you?'

'So the care home is paid for by a company that lists Constance Bobb as director. It's registered at the cottage beside the dairy.'

'A great big infinity loop of shite. Where do the funds come from?'

'There's a substantial amount of money in their accounts. Enough to cover the care home costs for years. Most of it stems from several historical payments. Two were from people named as minority partners, look like investment capital. But when we tried to trace them, they're fraudulent accounts. Looks like false identities were set up years ago and left to mature. There's no telling how many similar setups there might be.'

'Great.' Barb took a loud slurp of coffee. 'And she could tell you nothing useful, good old Connie Bobb?'

Storm shook her head. 'Staff said she has good days and bad days, but good days just mean she's not screaming the walls down and throwing food everywhere. On the rare occasions she is coherent, she has no recollection of much. Doesn't know where she is or why she's there.'

'Is she actually Constance Bobb?'

'I don't know. Boone was right about the birth certificate showing her to be over a hundred, which seems unlikely. The home only had a copy on file, though. Most of the documents they had seen related to the cottage and her company. All of that looks legit on the surface, so they didn't question it.'

'And they're getting paid each month, so why would they? She couldn't have checked herself into this place, though. What about visitors?'

'Woman I spoke to didn't work there when Constance arrived. Their records have her grand-nephew moving her in. Apparently lives and works abroad, a contractor of some kind. Name he used looks false, and the number is dead. There's an email address I have Jane looking at. There's only been one visitor since then, a man who said that – wait for it – he used to live on the farm next to hers near Canterbury. That was a couple of years ago.'

'What was his name?'

'She didn't recall.'

'He didn't have to sign in?'

'He did, but it's illegible. Deliberately so.'

'Fuck. Did anyone remember what he looked like?'

'Yeah. I spoke with a Jacqui Trudell. She's the team leader of the care assistants. She remembered the man, said it stuck in her mind because he was the only visitor Constance ever had. She was vague, though. Said he was tall and dark-haired, maybe some stubble. She did say he walked with a pronounced limp. An injury, she thought, as he was in his mid-forties or thereabouts.'

'Who do we suppose that is?'

'Anyone's guess.'

'That's good work, though, Storm. It's the details that break cases, always is. Methodical work and analysis.'

'I haven't got to the best stuff.'

'Well go on then. But don't be expecting two pats on the back in the same day.'

'We got the full file from the original Jerry Killock investigation, and collected the materials from social services. There's loads of it and

I didn't know where to start, so I just started flicking through it over lunch when I got back. His personnel file was in there. There was a note that the original detectives had requested a list of his authorised time off, presumably to see if the dates matched up with anything. Children going missing, whatever. None of it panned out, but something else caught my eye.'

She showed Barb a handwritten list of dates with reasons for absence beside them.

Barry rapped on the glass door and poked his head inside. 'Okay to join?'

Barb waved him in. 'While we were out not finding our arse with either hand, Storm here has been solving the case single-handedly.' She took the sheet. 'What am I looking at?'

'This one, April 1999,' Storm said. 'Funeral. Sister-in-law.'

'Right . . .'

'There's no mention anywhere of Killock having been married. So his sister-in-law must have been his brother's wife. But we didn't know about any brother either. We looked, because if he had this other house near the sea where he took his victims, maybe it was in the name of a relative.'

'He was probably making it up. Which of us hasn't had three grandmas die?'

'Except I dug up his birth certificate and it turns out Killock is his mother's name. She died years ago. Left him a flat in Maidstone, but we checked that out. She'd lived there alone for years and he sold it off immediately. The father is listed as a Robert Oster. He's dead too, but he has another son, also Robert Oster. Killock's half-brother.'

'It's amazing really,' Barb said. 'Most people, when they're right all the time, I find hating them comes pretty easily. But you I just like more and more.'

'Get ready to fall in love,' Storm said. 'I called him, and he tells me he had nothing to do with Killock, despises him. Had to move house on account of people spreading rumours about him and it blowing back on Oster. Says they shared a father, but never lived together or hung about growing up. Killock's mother was Oster Senior's bit on the side; always promised to leave his wife for her but never did. So Killock's mother eventually shacked up with some other bloke, an artist. Oster said his name was Clem, but couldn't remember his surname. Get this, though – he says this Clem inherited a big house by the sea when his parents died in a car accident.'

'Where's this house?'

'That's the thing. He didn't know. Said he never went there, but Killock mentioned it at their father's funeral. Last time they saw each other. Apparently Killock stayed in touch with this Clem after his mother died. Gives us something to go on, though.'

'Don't see many Clems these days,' Barb said.

40

The Escort idled by the air pump on the forecourt of a petrol station as Boone waited for Fuller's Peugeot to go past, dropping in behind him on the Ashford road.

Barb's dulcet tones floated over the air. 'Fucking car stalled and trapped me at the lights. Fuller is away down the A20, out of sight. Anyone got anything?'

'Coming up to the A20,' Boone lied. 'Only room for one car on these streets and some idiot was parking. Be there in a sec.'

'I don't see him,' Barry said. 'I'm going to follow the A20 out to the motorway and hit the M20 going for Ashford, see if I can't catch him if he's gone that way. Boone, you stay on the A20.'

'Aye aye, Captain,' Boone said.

'Boss, you good to stay at the house?'

There was a pause and then a grunt over the radio. Boone removed the SIM from her mobile and made a call on a prepaid handset Fitz had given her.

'Where are you?' she said.

'I headed west in case she continued to follow and I got caught between them,' Fitz said.

'Barb was not happy with you.'

'Nothing I could do. Have no feel for the clutch at all, me. Bricks for feet. Stall the bastard all the time. I'm looping round. You still got him?'

'Uh huh. He's turned off. Backtracking, I think. Headed west in the residential streets north of the A20.'

'I'll cut in back here and come out in front then.'

They followed Fuller for forty minutes, handing him off between them as he circled the town, taking a meandering route through quiet neighbourhoods, crossing his own path several times, before heading through the city centre.

'Thinks he's losing Russians or something, this one,' Fitz said. 'Be making chalk markings on fence posts before we know it.'

Fuller crossed the river and the railway into the quieter streets of Fant and drove in behind a block of flats, to a long line of garages. Fitz followed on foot and watched him swap cars, leaving the first one in the garage where the second had been.

Less concerned about having a tail now, he drove in such a way to avoid traffic cameras. Trailing him at a comfortable distance, they followed him southwards out of Maidstone and in a wide loop through sleepy villages, eventually heading north and ducking under the motorway.

He stopped in a village a couple of miles from Ashford. Thin roads overhung by mature trees, winding between stone-walled gardens. A coach house pub suggested it had once been on the way between two more important places, but was now a destination only for visiting relatives and Sunday-lunchers.

Fitz parked in the pub car park, Boone pulling up alongside. They wound down their windows.

'See the place there, opposite the church?' Fitz said.

'Nice pad.'

'He parked the other side. Went in a few minutes ago. Didn't see who lives there.'

'Stay here and get on him if he leaves.'

'What are you doing?'

'Paying respects to my dead nan.'

With her camera, Boone went to the church – St Mildrith's, mostly early English with a spire added later. She liked it, as it was exactly the kind of place the English cloistered their gods in, rather than letting them be at large in the world.

A small graveyard shaded by several large oaks ran along the side of the church that faced the house Fuller had visited. Boone moved between the graves, their markers so old that the countless passing seasons had either filled them with moss and grime or worn them smooth completely. Stone palimpsests beneath which everybody or nobody might be interred. Graves were for the living, but anyone alive when these ones were planted, along with at least half a dozen generations after them, had long since joined the dead in the earth.

She sat with her back to one of the larger gravestones, shielding her from the view of the church, and peered over the ancient boundary wall at the house. An hour later, the front door opened, Fuller stepping out. Boone scoped him through her camera and fired off dozens of shots. Fuller turned back and another man appeared from the shadows behind the door.

'Holy shit,' Boone whispered.

John Bardin.

Retired Assistant Chief Constable John Bardin.

If she knew about this, Barb would drop an ovary.

41

Boone left Fitz watching Bardin and followed Fuller long enough to see he was obviously headed back to Maidstone before letting him off the leash. She turned her radio back on and called in.

'Where the hell have you been?' Barry said.

'Folkestone. Think I might have dropped out of range.'

'Hell did you go to Folkestone for?'

'Thought maybe he was making a dash for the port, so I followed the A20 to the coast.'

'And?'

'Didn't see hide nor hair of him. What about you?'

'Nothing.'

'Where's Barb?'

'I'm here,' Barb said.

'Hello.'

'Don't fucking hello me. I've been calling you.'

'Calling me? Oh shit. Phone's dead. I'll charge it.'

'Our agreement was you'd be in touch at all times.'

'Yeah, my mistake. I don't have a charger thing in this car. Fuller's a bust then?'

'Yeah, but Storm came up trumps. She's been talking with a

half-brother we didn't know Killock had. Might have a lead on the house by the sea. The name Clem mean anything to you?'

'No,' said Boone truthfully.

'Someone Killock's mother used to knock about with. An artist, apparently. Had a large house on the coast. We're trying to track him down.'

'Do you need me back there?'

'Don't know. Why?'

'Well, I could run this Clem by my source. See if they know anything.'

Radio silence for twenty seconds.

'Barry's telling me he reckons this source of yours is made up and you're stringing us along.'

'Have you considered that the source is real *and* I'm stringing you along?'

'Get your phone charged. I will call you at random and inconvenient times.'

'And bring my fucking walkie-talkie back,' Barry added.

Boone clicked the two-way off. She also left the mobile Barb knew about turned off, certain as she was that they were up on her and monitoring its movements. She called Fitz on the other phone.

'You still on him?'

'He hasn't moved.'

'I'm going to grab the Transit and head back your way.'

'Accounted for yourself to the fuzz?'

She hung up.

By the time she'd picked up the Transit from Lark, Fitz had told her Bardin was on the move.

'He left on foot in fancy dress. Baseball cap and Aviators. Man his age, looks ridiculous. Walked to a campsite outside the village and came out in a battered old Astra van. We're stopping for gas.'

'Better top up too,' she said. 'Don't know where he's going to lead us.'

The next seven hours were torture.

Keeping away from motorways and towns of any size, Bardin slouched west and threaded a line between Crawley and London, arcing back south of Guildford and Farnborough and heading inexorably across the Wessex Downs. Boone caught up soon enough, and they followed him front and back, switching occasionally. Through the Cotswolds, they crossed the Severn and passed Hereford on the way to the last outposts of Englishness. There, nestled among the hills of the empty borderlands, they tracked Bardin to a remote farm at the end of a lonely road.

With no way to follow without being spotted, they found the mouth of a field to pull up in and prepared to look suitably lost if anyone chanced upon them. The moon was full and hung like a giant wafer above the grey horizon, picking out the eyes of sheep standing aslant on the hillside. Studying aerial pictures online, they identified several private roads that skirted round behind the farm, but none that they could drive without attracting attention.

'I'll have a recce on foot,' Boone said.

Fitz didn't object. Aching everywhere after the drive, walking wasn't on his agenda.

Camera round her neck, Boone followed a treeline that marked the enclosure of a large field as well as the border between England and Wales. Couple of miles and she came to a larch grove that that looked to have been planted for timber but never felled. Standing in ordered rows almost fifty feet high, the trees provided good cover to watch the farm.

Clunking the night module onto the camera, she added a catadioptric lens and studied the farm's layout through the greenish veil. A large barn stood near the main house, and in the background was a dump site with several shipping containers. Bardin's van was still there, but there was no visible activity. It didn't matter. Minute she saw it, she knew this was the place. Predators had favoured habitats. Remote, extended outbuildings, only one access road. She knew he was there even before she saw Ferg walking Bardin to his car.

Sally never emerged. Boone remained a while longer after Bardin left. There were two vehicles: a tarped-over Land Rover, and a little Suzuki jeep. Neither moved.

Boone hiked back to where Fitz was waiting and showed him the pictures.

He jabbed a finger at Ferg. 'Prick pulled Roper's eyes out. I owe him.'

'We do this, we're in and out and leave nothing that links us to it. You're not taking anyone's eyes, Fitz. We're here to end them because they need to be ended, but five years from now there won't be two people sneaking about in the night waiting to do for us because we did something stupid here.'

'Only thing I want with his eyes is to look in them when they go out.'

'We need to do this right, but I don't know how much time we have. Barb is working the case from another angle. We need to find the routines and habits that will get us close.'

'You're the expert.'

Boone let that go. She'd never been certain whether Fitz knew the truth about the deaths of Hanley Moss and Teddy Blackborne. Seemed Mickey Box had told him, though. Of course he had.

'The Landie is under covers,' she said. 'Suzuki looks used, though. Got me thinking. They wouldn't risk anyone coming here, deliveries or what have you. I bet Ferg goes out for food at least a couple of times a week. Didn't see the old man.'

'He'll be there. They've never been apart.'

'Listen, I need to go back home.'

'I know.'

'There's something tomorrow—'

'Wish him a happy birthday.'

'Fitz.'

'It's fine. Really. It's good.'

'Do you want—I thought I could get a photo maybe?'

Fitz nodded.

'All right then. You'll have to keep eyes on the house here, see the comings and goings. You want the Transit? There's a bed in back. Khazi.'

Fitz regarded her like that was a gambit to some trick.

'Thought it'd be comfier is all,' Boone said. 'There's going to be more walking than you'll like.'

'Sure.'

'Right then. Couple of days?'

'No rush. I'll get the lie of the land and call you.'

'Good. Well then. Try not to get yourself killed.'

Boone took the motorways back, hitting the M25 just after the morning rush hour and noodling her way back through Kent to the south coast. She turned her phone on near Lark and found a dozen missed calls from Barb and some salty texts.

'Hello, Barb?'

'Fuck have you been?'

'Here and there.'

'Do I have to put an ankle tag on you?'

'I had a bit of a drink last night.'

'Boone—'

'I know. I know. But you don't do a four without picking up habits. And you certainly don't fit back into the world without succumbing to a few more.'

Barb sighed. 'Did you talk to this mysterious source?'

'Didn't pan out. What about you?'

'Still looking for this Clem.'

'Barb, tomorrow – it's Jim's birthday. Tess's boy. I was wondering . . .'

'Yeah. Of course. But – and I want to be absolutely clear here – if your phone is not on, I'm having you picked up.'

'Right. Thanks, Barb. And sorry.'

'Uh huh.'

Boone locked Fitz's car in the garage and headed up to the flat above. After a quick shower, she skipped the nightcap and fell into the virgin sheets of her bed, asleep as soon as she closed her eyes, dreaming cheerily of doing battle with her enemy.

42

She awoke in a panic, taking a minute to recognise where she was. Light outside; she'd slept through to the next day. She showered and dressed and sat on the bed. Mooned out, no thoughts at all, not even registering what she was looking at. Another habit she'd picked up inside. At other times, her thoughts slipped beyond language. Obscure, unspeakable things.

The vibration of the phone brought her round, a text from Tess. Boone hoped it was a rain check on going round to the cottage. She didn't know much, but she knew the last-minute cancelling of plans was the sweetest feeling there was. The ecstatic relief of being let off the hook, of getting time back to yourself, or not having to make an effort to go somewhere. That was a gift.

But it was a sternly worded reminder. Jim's birthday, already missed too many of them, blah blah. A few people, Tess had said. There was nothing as terrifying as the platitudes of folk. Some people could sound sincere talking to strangers, idly shooting the breeze and chatting in a manner that relaxed people, made them instantly liked by all. Then there was Boone.

A word or two put anyone at ease, but she never had words. She possessed the worst kind of wit, the in-the-shower or dead-of-night kind where she could sound clever and brilliant and talk her own ears off when she was alone, but her brain reliably failed her in the company of living things. The art of conversation was as alien to her as playing the violin, and four years inside had only sharpened her anxiety on the issue.

Before all the pleasures of company, she had another obligation to tick off. Taking Fitz's Astra, she drove to the edge of town, turning into a private lane. Before she reached the set of mechanical iron gates that spanned the road, she pulled over. Reversing, she eased the car off the road and between some trees, parking it where it wouldn't easily be seen from either direction. The property at the end of the private road was surrounded by a wall that in places turned to a chain-link fence where the terrain made a wall impractical. At one of these spots, she climbed the fence and hauled herself over. The woodland both sides was identical in every respect other than ownership.

As she walked, the Victorian pumping house came into view. A towering great place, it sported huge arched windows that rose over thirty feet, and was crowned by a castellated rooftop terrace offering picturesque views of the coast. Boone maintained her distance, keeping to the woods until she found the wandering gardens behind the house. There, tucked away in a quiet little corner on a leather kneeler with trowel in hand, was who she was looking for.

'Knew you'd be out here with your hydrangeas.'

Kate Porter looked up, not startled but a little confused. Hilting the trowel in the earth, she removed her gloves and stood up.

'That's a snowball bush, but it's an easy mistake. Berries should come through soon, and its colour lasts through the autumn.'

'Out of touch with my horticulture.'

'What are you doing here? I don't mean—your last letter, you had a release date. But that's not for—'

'They let me out early.'

'Good behaviour?'

'What do you think?'

'It's good to see you, Boone.'

She was sincere, Boone could hear in her voice that she meant it, but there was something else too. A sadness. Thoughts that she'd put away, buried, that Boone's return had now excavated like a dog digging up old bones.

Boone smiled. 'You look good.'

And she did. Boone had thought twice about coming, but Kate had her original release date and sooner or later something was going to end up on the news that she'd put together.

'Thank you for the things you sent to Brabazon. The books especially. You have no idea how much they helped in there.'

'Of course. Truth is, I felt slightly responsible. I got you involved in the whole business and then you got arrested because of it.'

'Got arrested because I was an idiot.'

Kate glanced around as if it had suddenly dawned on her that Boone had snuck onto the land somehow.

'Wasn't sure if Mr Porter would be in,' Boone explained.

'Yes. Yes, he is.'

'Figured it best not to involve him.'

'No. That is for the best.'

'The reason I'm out, I can't say much, but it has to do with what happened that night. The police have opened an investigation.'

'The girl. The one on the television.'

'Yes.'

'She's a victim of Sally.'

'I wanted to tell you that things were happening, but it's best you don't contact me. Don't get involved. I haven't forgotten about Noah, though. I wanted to tell you that.'

Kate sighed. 'I have.' She looked back at the house and across her gardens. 'No, that's not true. Forgotten is the wrong word. I've become accustomed to not knowing what happened to him, the details of it. He's dead, and it was Sally or Jerry Killock or someone connected to them. I don't think I need to know more than that. The rest of it is a weight I've become used to carrying. You said when we first met that we don't always get the answers we were looking for. I think I got enough.'

'That's good. I'm glad.'

Kate took Boone's hand. She glanced down at the nubbin before closing her fingers tightly around Boone's.

'Boone, if you're still involved with this on account of me, because you think you have to find out what happened to Noah, then please stop. I've already cost you so much. Take your freedom and run.'

'Too late. There are other matters that need settling now.'

'I don't think I can be any part of it. I just can't wait around for someone to tell me – what exactly? It won't be good news.'

'No, you're right. This should be behind you. I almost didn't come for that very reason, but you might have seen something on the news.'

'I'm glad you came. I am. Maybe when it's over, when you've done whatever needs doing, we can get together. Coffee and a natter.'

'Pretend we're playing humans.'

'Boone, have you got someone with you in all of this? Someone watching your back?'

'I think so. Yes.'

'Good. It's good there's someone taking care of you. You don't always do a good job of it yourself.'

They hugged, and Boone left Kate to her garden, retracing her steps through the woods, bunking over the fence and returning to the Astra. Lacking any plausible excuse not to go, she struck out for the cottage and Jim's birthday gathering. Spot of Eugene McDaniels on the drive, whizzing along to *Outlaw*. Turning onto the narrow lanes of the headland an hour later, she parked up so she could see out *Headless Heroes* too.

When she finally drove up the tree-lined track to the cottage, what she found was pure horror – a dozen cars parked on the grass, the place festooned with birthday bunting and balloons. The piercing wails of kids, something like the damned. She thought about turning back before she was sucked in, but someone else was coming up the drive. Spinning the car around in the field allocated for parking, she left it facing the road, primed for a getaway.

Children ran amok. A bouncy castle strained against its staked tethers and everywhere was perfumed by smoking charcoal from Mickey Box's barbecue. Parents congregated in groups along a natural perimeter, the mums all sunglasses and flowery skirts, the dads in shorts and polos. Sandals abounded. It was too large a herd for Boone to edge into from the outside, so she ducked into the kitchen.

On the counter, upturned glasses stood in neat rows on trays. Bottles of red, a few empties, and some white in the fridge. Boone could happily have drunk from the bottle, but she'd need to drive home and was guarded about drinking in company. She found a cafetière and a canister of beans and made coffee, mostly just so she'd look busy if discovered by a stray parent.

'Didn't see the van.'

She turned and found Tess watching her from the back door.

'Driving something else today.'

'Wasn't sure if you'd come.'

'Nearly turned round when I saw all the cars, but then I spotted the bouncy castle. Mad for them, me.'

'You look like shit, old man.'

'It's like people think I was at a spa for four years. Coffee?'

Tess nodded and Boone fetched another mug.

'A gathering, you said. Few people. Low key.'

'Uh huh.'

'Looks like a lot of people. Looks like a party.'

'Does, doesn't it?'

'Don't like people. Don't like parties.'

'But you do like me. And you do like Jim. So suck it up. And think of it this way – when they've all gone, you'll have the bouncy castle to yourself.'

Jim came bounding in from outside, full of the joy of youthful birthdays, stopping dead when he saw Boone and clamping himself to his grandfather's leg when he came in behind.

'Good grief,' Mickey Box said. 'Look what the cat dragged in.'

Jim laughed. 'Look what the cat dragged in.'

'Cheers, Mick,' Boone said.

'Was thinking of putting the meat on,' he said to Tess.

'Okay,' said Tess. 'There's some salmon in a marinade in the fridge, and stuffed peppers we can put on too.'

He looked at her.

'Some people don't eat meat,' she said.

Mickey Box looked at the boy. 'What do we call people like that?'

'Scurvy knaves,' Jim said.

'Exactly. And we run them off our island.'

'This is my life now,' Tess said to Boone.

'I got him a thing,' Boone said, pointing at a plastic bag she'd left on the table. 'It's not wrapped because—well, because it's not. But there it is.'

Jim looked to Tess. 'Can I open it?'

'Don't look at me,' Tess said.

Jim looked at Boone.

'Go on then,' Boone said. 'It'll look awful silly sitting on the table all day.'

The boy tore the plastic bag off, and unwound a second bag Boone had wrapped the book in.

'Bears!' he cried.

'However did Boone know you would like that?' Tess said.

It wasn't really a children's book, but it had a lot of photographs, including one of a grizzly about to introduce itself to a caribou that Jim seemed to particularly appreciate.

'I'm going outside to cook and frown at people,' Mickey Box said.

'Oh, and I need to count how many are for the fish,' Tess said. 'Keep an eye on him for a sec, will you?'

'Huh?' Boone said, but she was alone with Jim.

He flicked through the book. 'Polar bears are my favourite.'

'That so? And why's that?'

'Yeah, they're basically invisible and, and you can't see them in the snow. And the men look for them with, uh, infrared, but they can't see them either.'

'They sound like ninjas.'

'Yeah, and they eat seals. And sometimes whales. They wait for days and hours at holes because the whales have to come up and they blow water out through their blowholes.' He blew his lips, spittle flying everywhere. 'And then the polar bear gets them.'

'They're very ferocious.'

'And their hair isn't white.'

'It isn't?'

'It looks white but it isn't white.'

All little boys needed was someone they could explain stuff to. It wasn't a need that ever left them.

'Five for the fish,' Tess said, hurrying back in. 'Which I'll have to serve because Dad will take great glee in explaining the nature of fishing in forensic detail to them.'

A little girl joined them in the kitchen and sat with Jim under the table, where they whispered and laughed and then chased each other back outside as part of some game grown-ups could only wish to be a part of.

'Polar bears aren't white, apparently,' Boone said.

'Imagine learning new things every day that blow your mind,' said Tess.

'He's doing well.'

'Jim? Yeah, he's great. Easy-going little fellow. And Dad's brilliant with him.'

'Always helpful when your grandad is an actual pirate.'

'Listen, there's something I need to talk to you about.'

'Okay,' Boone said. 'Want me to hang around after this is done?'

'It's going to have to be sooner, I'm afraid.'

'Why's that?'

'Because it's rather time-sensitive.'

'I don't understand.'

'A while ago, must be almost a year now, I met someone online.'

'Internet dating?'

'No, nothing like that.'

'I hear good things.'

'It's not dating.'

'Although I read somewhere that they're all owned by the same company. They just market them at different groups.'

'Boone, will you shut up a minute?'

'Yep.'

'I met someone and we became . . . friends, I suppose. Anyway, he's someone you know. And he's here now.'

Boone stared at her. Tess looked out the window towards the bouncy castle. Boone followed her gaze, saw a young man chasing around with Jim. A young man with the face of her son.

'Quin,' she said.

43

'He wanted to tell you,' Tess said. 'It was my idea not to. Figured you'd make an excuse at the last minute.'

'It's fair,' Boone said.

'We talked about going to see you inside, but it didn't seem right. He said a couple of police officers dropped round to say you were out and had been making friends and influencing people again, that he should be vigilant. He called to talk about it, and we cooked this up. It's better than seeing you in prison, isn't it?'

'Yeah. Better.'

'Please don't be mad. At least not at Quin. Be mad at me.'

'I'm not mad. I don't know what I am. How did—I don't quite get any of this.'

'He friended me on Facebook and we got to talking.'

'Quin friended you.'

'Yes.'

'You're internet-dating my son?'

'We're not—it's not dating. Jesus.'

'I still don't understand.'

'He found me on Facebook and we got talking and sometimes we meet up.'

'You meet up? I don't even—what on earth do you talk about?'

'International currency markets, the Middle East, the lamentable state of musical theatre. What the fuck do you think we talk about? What on earth could we two people in particular possibly have in common?'

'All right, all right. It's just thrown me a bit, is all.'

Quin had seen them. He waved, and Boone raised a hand.

'Go speak to him,' Tess said.

'Yeah. Will it be okay if I come back and murder you later?'

'I'll be here.'

'Good.'

Boone shoved her hands in her pockets and headed out. Quin said something to Jim and watched him run off to the bouncy castle with the girl he'd been under the table with. Boone nodded towards the path that led out to the water and along to the tip of the headland, and they met halfway.

'I remember how much you like surprises,' he said.

'It's okay. I'll get over it. I'll kill Tess, and then I'll get over it.'

They walked quietly along the creek. She felt him stealing glances at her, and realised it wasn't just that time had passed – he hadn't seen her face before, her scars. She looked as different to him as he did to her. She went to say something and so did he and they both apologised.

'You go,' Boone said.

'I was going to ask how it was. Inside. Not how it was, I know it wasn't a holiday. How you were. How you've been.'

She smiled.

'Seems a stupid question now I've asked it,' he said.

'No. I've been okay. I don't recommend it, though.'

'No. I don't suppose you would.'

It was painful and Boone found herself wishing something would happen they could talk about. A comet landing or a tidal wave, something like that. The pile came to her rescue.

'Oh Christ,' she said, covering her nose. 'That thing is awful.'

'The pile.'

'What was Mick thinking? And how is it even legal?'

'Everyone says that,' said Quin. 'My understanding, it's probably the least suspect thing Mick's ever done, but everyone is amazed by it.'

'We should turn back,' Boone said.

'Actually, it's better when you go past it. The wind usually comes off the estuary, and if you're around the other side of the trees you don't really notice it so much.'

'Explains the barbecue,' Boone said.

'Yeah, I bet he lit it up hours ago. Probably replaced the charcoal three times.'

They found the fallen tree at the tip of the headland where many a time Boone had sat with Tess. Online activity in the prison was strictly monitored, and social media was *verboten*, but Boone had quickly worked out the best people to know in order to get access to mobile phones. She'd never admit it, but she had occasionally watched people from afar: Twitter and Instagram accounts, little windows into some version of the outside world.

'So, uni then,' she said.

'Second year coming up.'

'Doing?'

'Criminology. I couldn't do joint honours with English lit, but they've let me take some electives.'

Boone laughed. 'You're certainly your parents' child.'

'I get to do the third year abroad. America, hopefully. There's a great criminology department in Maryland I want to go to.'

'That sounds fine, Quin. Just fine. You in digs or at home?'

'At home. Dad got me a car. It's only forty minutes to Canterbury.'

'You drive?'

Quin as a young teenager was one thing, but she felt she would never accustom herself to the strangeness of him as a man.

'I'm nineteen,' he said.

'Well, that's no excuse.'

He smiled. 'You're funnier than you used to be, I think.'

'Prison hones the wit.'

'I meant before—you know. You were funny when you came back from the clinic after you were hurt.'

'Everyone was funny there.'

'Did you get any tatts when you were away?'

Away. She smiled. He said it so seamlessly, she could imagine him practising the best words to use. She started to roll up her sleeve.

'You are kidding,' he said.

'Yes. Yes, I am.'

'Jesus,' he said. He was quiet a moment before he added, 'Tess told me.'

'What did she tell you?'

'About what happened. I mean, she didn't tell me exactly, but she said it wasn't what it looked like. That it was a means to an end.'

'That sort of thing doesn't make a difference when you go up before the courts.'

'Makes a difference back here, though. She said you did time to protect people. Protect us.'

'She probably should have stressed that there was only a threat because of me in the first place.'

'The police came to see me and Dad.'

'Yeah, sorry about that.'

'They told us to be careful. This is the same threat?'

'Nobody will come after you. They're too busy trying to hide from me.'

Quin smiled. 'Still hunting.'

'Only thing I know.'

'It's good,' he said. 'What you do, the things you've done, they're part of why I went to university to do what I do. When I was younger, it was hard for me to remember that you were the victim in all of this. The first victim.'

'It happened to all of us.'

Quin nodded.

'You know, maybe we could all do with a little forgetfulness,' Boone said. 'If you could forget some of the things I did, some of what I became. Maybe then we could start over, and you could tell me about yourself. I'd like to know who you are, if you want to tell me.'

'I do.'

'Good. I want to hear everything. School. This car of yours. Girls.'

'Girls?' he said.

'Or boys.'

'No, it's girls.'

'Well, that's something we have in common now.'

'Oh, Christ,' he said, face in his hands.

'Too much?'

Still hidden, he nodded.

'Since we're not on the subject, how's your father?'

'Yeah, he's good. He's—there's someone.'

'Ooh, he has a girlfriend?'

'Yeah. Is it okay talking about that?'

'Are you kidding? Tell me everything. Is she a doctor?'

'Yeah. I—how did you know?'

'I don't remember anything about how we met, your father and I, but my strong belief is that he always wanted another doctor, and probably thought he did have when we first got together. Do they talk shop at the dinner table?'

Quin made a face and nodded.

'Yeah, he'll be happy as a pig in muck with that,' Boone said. 'Good. I'm glad for him. He didn't deserve any of what happened with us. Neither of you did.'

Quin stood up suddenly. 'Shit, I almost forgot.'

'What?'

'I have something.'

He took out his wallet and slid a photograph from one of the pockets. Small, black and white, it was of a young girl sitting on the knee of a man perhaps in his mid-twenties.

'Good God,' Boone said.

'That's your mum,' Quin said. 'And her dad.'

'Yeah.'

'Crazy, isn't it?'

It certainly was. She remembered the picture from when Jack had got them all out when she first came home, telling her the story of her own family as best as he could remember from what he'd picked up over the years. Being the only child of two dead parents, her uncle also gone, there was nobody else about to help them fill in the details. The craziest thing – Quin was now the spitting image of Boone's grandfather.

'It's uncanny,' he said. 'Freaked me out. Dad said he died young.'

'Yeah. Leukaemia.'

'There are a couple of other pictures of him when he's slightly older, though. So it's like looking into the future.'

'He was a handsome man.'

'Indubitably.'

Sounds like his father, Boone thought, and smiled.

'There's loads more stuff,' Quin said. 'Me and Dad found these boxes when we were sorting out the attic. Pictures and slides, and I found a medal.'

'Golf?'

'Yeah.'

'That was my dad's. Something to do with his work. I don't remember it, but there's an inscription on the back. I'd forgotten all about that.'

'I can bring it to you.'

Boone thought of all the stuff she'd lost when the caravan burned down. All the pictures of her past life turned to ash.

'It's your family too,' she said. 'I don't want to take stuff from you.'

'That's daft. Tess told me about the fire.'

Mind-reader too.

'I had a thought,' he said. 'Me and Tess, we meet up sometimes. She brings Jim. We go to the pier or the beach. Daft stuff. We should all go somewhere for the day. I can bring some things with me. There are other pictures. Some of your mum and dad.'

This had Tess's fingerprints all over it. A nice public day out in a group so there was no pressure. She really would have to hug that girl.

'Yeah, that sounds great.'

'I'll let Tess sort it out. She's large and in charge.'

'She is at that. You and her—'

'It's nothing like that.'

'No, I know. She said. I think I owe her an apology. When she told me you two were in touch, I reacted strangely. It took me by surprise. I'm glad you reached out to her. I think you'll do each other a lot of good.'

'It's weird. We're nothing alike really, and the way we grew up is so different.'

'That's what I mean.'

'She told me you tried looking for your mum. Before you were away.'

'Didn't get very far.'

'She went to Canada, right?'

'That was the story. I'm not sure it was true. I had a friend in the police look into a few things and it turns out my mother never had a passport, so I dunno. Maybe she changed her name. Identity fraud wasn't exactly a sophisticated endeavour back then.'

He was quiet. Losing mothers possibly a subject too close to the bone. She noticed an earbud hanging out of his jacket pocket and thought of the way he used to listen to records from her teenage years, giving them to her on an iPod in an attempt at drawing her memory out, or maybe just to share something with her.

'I used to have these mixtapes she made,' Boone said. 'Literally, cassettes that were older than me. I spent ages working out all the songs, because she hadn't listed them, and then hunting down the albums. Remind you of anyone?'

He lifted his iPod from his pocket. 'Still got all of your music on here. Tastes might have widened a bit through school and uni, mind.'

'Oh aye?'

'I'm a student. I like fuzzy psyche stuff.'

'Here,' she said, getting out her phone. 'Check this.'

She whipped his earphones out of his iPod and plugged them into her phone. Pressing the buds into his ears, he listened to what she played. He looked almost surprised.

'This is great.'

'Uh huh.'

'What is it?'

She showed him the screen: 'My Bleeding Wound' by The New Year.

'Never even heard of it.'

'There was only this single, but the dude released an album later as Sexual Harassment. Scuzzy eighties synths.'

'That sounds amazing. Where'd you find him?'

'A friend. When I was *away*. She got me into soul and funk stuff.'

'She still . . . away?'

Boone shook her head.

'Do you see people outside? People you met in there, I mean?'

'Not her.'

He pulled the buds slowly from his ears. 'Dead?'

Boone said nothing. She caught him looking at her scar again and he glanced away quickly.

'We should talk about it,' she said.

'I didn't mean to—'

'It's okay. You didn't see me after I got out of hospital back then.'

'Does it hurt?'

'Not any more. Not really. Some tightness occasionally. I forget about it, and then catch sight of myself in a window or the blackness of my phone. It's a funny thing. But I've got a better one now.'

'A better one?'

She held up her hand, waggling the nubbin.

'Fucking hell.'

'Yeah, that one's a doozy.'

'How did it happen?'

'We'd need more time and a lot more alcohol.'

'We can do that,' he said.

They ambled back to the cottage past the stinking pile, eventually catching the whiff of barbecued meat. Tess brought them plates with burgers and lamb and mountains of potato salad and cauliflower couscous. Boone ate like it might be the last time for a while, and the other two laughed.

'What?'

'Julie Christie,' Tess said. *McCabe and Mrs Miller.*

'Daryl Hannah with the lobster in *Splash*,' said Quin.

'I hate people who eat like sparrows,' Boone said.

Tess went to tend to a collision on the bouncy castle, kids lying in havoc, tears everywhere.

'I should be going,' Quin said.

Boone shook her head. 'It's me who should leave.'

'Are you joking? And get out of all this? Besides, Tess would have my guts for garters. Said it'd take an alignment of celestial bodies to get you here. I'm not one to second-guess the cosmos.'

'I can give you a lift? Drop you somewhere.'

'Car, remember?'

'Won't believe that until I see it.'

She walked with him round the front to where the cars were parked up.

'Hey!' she said, as Quin opened the door of a convertible Saab 900 that was older than he was. Black with tan leather seats. The roof was down and it looked great.

'Hey,' she said again, running her hand along the top of the door.

'It's the new shape,' he said apologetically. 'Tried getting an older SE but they were expensive and all had some miles on them. Dad wouldn't go for it. This had one owner and less than fifty K on the clock. It was cat C after the bumper came off in a prang and the bonnet had to be replaced. But it runs like aces.'

'I miss my Goose.'

'What are you driving now?'

Boone glanced round at the Astra. 'Borrowing that, but I have a Transit.'

'Really?' He laughed. 'A van?'

'All beaten to shit, but she'll fool you. There's a new block under the hood. V6. Machined out from a single cam to duplex chains driving dual overhead cams. Lowering springs and rear shocks.'

Quin was still laughing. 'I don't—'

'It can shift and maintain it round bends. Plus, there's a bed and a bog in the back.'

'You're one of a kind,' he said, starting up his engine.

Watching him drive off, she decided she'd take that as a compliment.

Several years earlier, after Boone returned home from the clinic and it had become clear to everyone that the memory loss wasn't a passing problem, she finally worked up to asking Jack about her family. She felt like an evacuee in her new home, sent to live with strangers – kind strangers, but strangers nonetheless – and she generally tried to keep conversation to the basics: 'What about that wind last night?' 'Good day at work?' 'Tea?'

She had found Jack in his study looking at old photo albums and figured it was as good an opportunity as any.

'What's that?'

'When I picked Quin up from his drama group, I was telling him about his earliest forays into thespianism. He played a mushroom in a school play when he was five. He didn't believe me, but I know there's a photo somewhere.'

An antique barrister's bookcase stood in the corner behind the desk, home to all the albums and boxes of photos the family had. The bottom up-and-over door was open and Boone got down on her knees and had a look through.

'Looking for something specific?'

She shook her head. 'No. Maybe. My parents.'

Jack got down beside her, sitting cross-legged. 'That box there.'

She pulled out a shoebox and lifted the lid.

'Afraid they're not really sorted. We found them when we were clearing out your uncle's house.'

'You never met them, my parents? My dad, I mean.'

Jack shook his head. 'You mum was gone when you were a baby, and your father died in a car accident when you were nine. Your dad's brother took you in after that, moved you down to Kent.'

'What was he like?'

'Your uncle? I only met him once. We were at university in London and the two of us were getting serious. We were making plans for me to visit in the summer, spend the weekend. Get to know him. Then he was diagnosed, and everything happened very quickly. I didn't tell you, but I got the train down to Canterbury to see him, to ask for your hand. He thought that was funny. Old-fashioned. I think he appreciated it.'

'Did I ever talk about Dad?'

'He took you to the football. And the movies. And gîte holidays in France. You were that young when he died, I'm not sure you ever had more than a child's impression of him. You spoke about your uncle a lot. How strange it was when you first went to live with him as you barely knew him, but how great he was over the years and how much you loved him.'

'I barely knew him?'

'He and your father were estranged. I don't know the details. I don't think you ever did. They hadn't spoken in a long time, though, and when you saw him after your father's death, it was the first time in years. You were aware of him, but I'm not sure you remembered him.'

'Huh. It must have been equally strange for him.'

'He never married. You said there were a few women, but he never got deeply involved. I know you encouraged him to as you felt he was keeping people at arm's length to protect you. I got the impression he enjoyed bachelorhood. Children had never been part of his plan, but when you came along, he ran with it. You were dreadfully fond of him.'

Reaching for a taupe-coloured album, Jack hesitated and pulled his hand back.

'What's that?' Boone said.

'Our wedding day.'

She opened it, drawing an interleaved tissue page away from a picture of her and Jack standing on the steps of a church.

'Check you out with your snazzy double-breasted three-piece.'

'That was all your doing. I had some morning-jacket-type affair lined up, but you made an executive decision. Good job, too.'

They fell quiet and Boone realised he was smiling. For the first time she saw nothing but joy in his face, thinking about the woman he had fallen in love with, the people they used to be together. Shorn from his wife, his partner, his best friend, she knew he was no longer the man he had been.

Something about the pang of guilt that caused her felt thrilling.

Quin's Saab disappeared out onto the headland lanes. Boone thought about Jack, about the amount of pain she had caused him, and wondered how it would be if she tried to contact him. Reconnecting with Quin was one thing, but Jack was the only conduit she knew of to the nitty-gritty of her past life. To her mother. She was afraid he would think she was an absolute piss-taker if she showed up one day asking for favours, though.

The party petered out, parents removing stuffed and tired children and leaving behind paper plates and cups, chewed chicken bones, and enough potato salad to last a week. A man in a van came to collect the bouncy castle. As its insides escaped and it slowly sank to the ground like something going bad, he kept glancing towards the pile, trying to make sense of what he could smell.

Boone helped Tess clear up, trailing round the garden, filling a bin bag with party dregs. Later, as Tess bathed Jim and put him to bed, Boone made coffee and sat outside with Mickey Box. She tried to bring up the subject of the pile and the apparent shuttering of his other enterprises, both criminal and almost legal, but he was vague and distant so she dropped it. When Jim was around, he was alight with the boy, but otherwise he appeared battle-fatigued. Boone got the idea he believed the child to be some form of requital for the winding-down of his outlaw ways.

He swapped his coffee for single malt, and it was more effort than she would care to admit for Boone to turn down the offer.

He savoured a few sips and said eventually, 'You seen him, then.'

'Yeah.'

'Thought you'd come to offer observations and advice on the matter.'

'No.'

'No, bollocks.'

'What's done is done. Who's better off the way things are now?'

'Better's nothing to do with it. Like you said, what's done can't be changed. Any of it. Let's agree on all that and leave it there.'

'Okay, Mick.'

She made her excuses and went inside, looking for Tess. She had read to Jim and now watched him sleep, pulling the door closed and coming down the hall when she saw Boone.

'Think he enjoyed the day,' Tess said.

'Castle, presents, getting chased all over by pretty girls. What's not to like?'

'And you?'

'Yeah, I'd like those things too.'

'You know what I mean. Quin.'

'It was—something. Something new.'

'It's something old, Boone. It's what life is. Not all that other stuff, running around after bad men. That's the opposite. This is home. This is family. This is love.'

'Uh huh.'

'Don't do that.'

'What?'

'React to the word like it's a bad smell. You know, it wouldn't hurt you to tell people you love them sometimes.'

'Tess?'

'Yeah.'

'I love you. Sometimes.'

Tess sighed and went to walk past her, but Boone caught her arm and pulled her in close, holding her.

'Thank you,' she said.

'You're very welcome.'

44

Boone couldn't sleep for thinking of the farmhouse and of Sally and of the things she was going to do. She packed up Fitz's car with fresh clothing and some food. He had given her an address, a flat in Gravesend. The key was in a plastic magnetic box behind an old iron downpipe, and floorboards in the bedroom came up to reveal two shoulder bags wedged between the joists. She didn't open them.

Driving through the night, B roads and byways, she kept one step ahead of the rising sun. Fitz had found himself a spot up on the dyke behind the farmhouse. A small cutaway in the earth, supported by centuries-old brickwork showing through like old bones. The grass was long and offered ample cover, the earthwork rising behind so he wasn't exposed against the horizon.

Verge of day, Boone walked the woodland, picking her way along the ancient rise to Fitz's side. Wordlessly he handed her the field glasses and she scanned the house.

'Seen him?'

Fitz shook his head.

'Not at all?'

'Only Ferg.'

'What do you think?'

'I think they're both in there. Ferg stays in most of the day. Goes out for a spell at night. They're complacent. Security is for shit. I went down there and had a nose about. The Suzuki has a canvas back and I slipped a mobile inside. First night, Ferg went out and I tracked him on its GPS. Data was patchy, but he popped up in Hay-on-Wye, came back with takeout food. Did the same last night, and then he went out again for two, three hours later on.'

'Where to?'

'Hereford. Parked up on a main road, from what I could tell. Stayed an hour or so. Getting his end away, if I had to guess.'

'How long is he gone for food?'

'Forty-five minutes all told. Maybe less. Battery on the handset has gone now.'

'You want to get some shuteye in the van?'

'Yes please.'

'Left a bucket of chicken in there.'

'You're something like a fairy. We moving on this tonight?'

She nodded. 'Brought everything we need. I'll come back down and get you later.'

'Fine. Until dusk, then.'

Fitz hobbled off, stretching the night out of his leg and side as he went. Boone settled into the earth and waited. She'd long ago learned the skill of patience in the hunt, different to the endurance demanded by incarceration. Prison was vigils and voices and occasional violence. Outside, among the bird stir and distant animal calls, she waited like the woods wait for the night, for the predators to come alive, for the world to show its teeth. It felt like nothing, like time's unblinking eye. The house held its breath with her, no movement or signs of life. How long would they remain holed up in this place? How long would they trust they were safe? Already too long, and with luck a little longer.

The sun fell behind the dyke and a milky gloomth descended on the farm. Boone moved unseen in front of the bluff, back into the trees to the north, watching for lights, listening for engines. The van was parked outside a holiday cottage in the middle of refurbishment that had halted some time ago. She rapped on the side door and Fitz slid it open almost immediately.

'Made coffee,' he said.

She got in, hauling the door shut behind her. The two of them in there, it was warm and muggy. She took the coffee and bunked over into the front seat, feeling beads of sweat rise on her brow as she drank.

'So?' he said.

'Nothing.'

'Same as the other days. What do you reckon?'

'I'm surprised they stayed after Bardin's visit. Must have a contingency somewhere. They'll be ready to leave.'

'Getting sloppy. Too many years roaming free and untroubled.'

'When Ferg goes for food tonight, we'll go in. Secure the old man and wait for Ferg to come back. If they still have videos, I want them. I want what evidence there is, anything that can implicate others. If it was more than just Sally and Killock, I want them all.'

'Could get messy.'

'Anything happens, we put them down and clear out.'

'You think the old man will be prepared? Tooled up?'

'Lived his whole life prepared. Bet he has a small arsenal in there. You see a weapon, drop him first and we'll sort the rest out later. Taking the place quick and fast is the only way this is going to work.'

Fitz thumped his thigh. 'Not as sprightly as I once was.'

'Long as you have my back, it'll go smooth.'

Heat had steamed the windows, and Boone fingered a rough plan of the farm on the glass, the lines running like fresh paint.

'When we have Sally wrapped up, I'll stay in the house, you wait outside somewhere. Follow Ferg in so we have him both ways.'

'You know the route out?'

'I've got fresh plates. How does the car tie to you?'

'It doesn't.'

Boone thought about that. 'Could use that. Maybe come at the house directly. Burn it at the scene after and take the van out. North round Hereford and Worcester. South of Birmingham and Coventry. Stay to B roads and country lanes. Take our time, all night if we have to. Work our way across as far as Suffolk, come down through Essex.'

Fitz nodded. His life had been plans based on the assumption that the worst thing that could happen was right around the corner, because for all you knew it was. That was how you survived.

'Everything's clean and ready to go,' he said, glancing at the table. The two bags Boone had picked up in Gravesend had been emptied onto it. Four pistols, a bag of ammunition, a hunting knife, two walkie-talkies. To that he'd added two rolls of gaffer tape. Boone always had that in the van.

'No reception for shit round here,' he said, handing her a two-way.

'I'll go in on foot,' she said. 'Walk the treeline to the north and come in through those larches from the west. I'll crunch the radio three times when I'm in place. Then another three times when I see Ferg go. You drive in, right up the drive, beams on full. The land is flat and open from the road to the farm, so if he's watching, he'll see you coming. Turn into that waste ground a few hundred yards from the house. I could see a few wrecks in there, and some container units. Hide the car behind them so Ferg won't see it when he comes back. There are fields out there, trees marking the boundary. Head out into them and come around as far west as you can. Any fireworks start, find cover and stay there. I'll get into the house.'

'And if Sally doesn't see me arrive?'

'Keep coming round and I'll hit you on the radio.'

He slid a plastic bag across the table. She opened it and pulled out a tactical vest.

'Level 3A,' Fitz said. 'Stop a .44 slug. A Tokorev. Any blade you like. Take most of the bite out of a shotgun blast. Wear it or I'm not going in.'

'No argument from me,' Boone said. She'd have taken grenades if he had them. Taking off her jacket, she strapped on the vest over her shirt. She selected two of the pistols, both MAC 1950s.

'Fucking hell, Fitz. Where'd these come from? The Algerian War?'

'They're clean and reliable and don't jam. Hammer might nibble, though.'

'I'll be right.' She loaded them, nine rounds in each, and filled her pockets with loose ammo. 'Last chance to back out and go home.'

'Look at you,' said Fitz. 'All wet of nose and shiny of coat. I'll see you in the trenches.'

Boone kept the trees between her and the farm, remaining in the open so she could see the ground before her in the low light. She found herself breaking into a gentle run. Her bones hummed. Inside her something was building, coiling up into a tense mass waiting to be unleashed. Anger, excitement, fear, revenge: words did it no justice; they were paltry things beside what she felt. She understood why people spoke nonsense about destiny. The feeling was larger than herself.

Through the darkness of the larch grove she took a more methodical path. She saw the house. There was a light on in a back room downstairs, and another upstairs. The Suzuki was parked out front. She sent three bursts down the radio and received three back.

She checked her weapons again. She ran scenarios through her mind. This was a story she had drafted four years ago, honed it in whatever cells she had occupied since. She'd been over it countless times, imagining every outcome so none would be surprising. Having walked into one ambush laid by Sally, she'd sworn never to let it happen again. This would be a tale as old as the dyke behind the farm. She wasn't there just because Sally was a paedophile and a murderer. *Just because.*

He had mutilated her. Put Monty down like a lame dog. Tortured and killed Roper for sport. Maimed Fitz. She owed him a reckoning. How many had said that before? Had harboured revenge in their hearts? Held it so tight it became part of them, like a tree that grew round iron railings, swallowing them, making a foreign body part of itself? Despite the script she followed being tattered and torn, the ending came upon her now like something new. A brightness and thrill that made it feel unexpected, and yet natural. Branches snapped off and became sticks.

The upstairs light flicked off. Three minutes later, Ferg appeared outside and climbed into the Suzuki. As it headed off down the track, she crunched the radio three times and heard back in kind.

Curtains were drawn in the lit room downstairs. Boone ran low and hard for the house, reaching the side wall without any indication she had been seen. Back pressed to the stone, she edged round the corner to the window. There was no angle of sight inside.

Moving beneath it, she made her way around to the front. She heard the engine and then saw the headlights of Fitz's car, dipping and rising and eventually turning off the drive and disappearing. No activity from the house.

Keeping low, she traced her way round again. The back door was locked, but peering through the glass she could see the key in the other side. Brass-handled Victorian lock that looked as old as the house. She radioed Fitz, headphones plugged into her handset.

'You near?'

'I can see you,' he said.

'Good. Come here then. We're going in the back door.'

Fitz appeared out of the dark, low and fast and grimacing.

'Key's in the other side of the door, but there are twelve glass lights in it,' Boone said. 'We'll keep it simple. Smash the light, turn the key, go in fast and hard.'

Fitz nodded.

They braced themselves against the wall either side of the door. Boone counted three and put the glass in with the handle of the hunting knife, clearing the frame. Reaching through, she unlocked the door and pushed it open, Fitz moving through with his gun raised. She followed closely and moved past him to cover the hallway. The glass shattering had sounded like a chandelier dropping onto a ballroom floor, but just seconds later it was dark and silent.

Boone indicated a door rimmed with light. Fitz took up an angle and Boone pushed the door open, dropping to her knees and taking aim. She frowned. Most of the room was dominated by a large hospital bed, a drip stand beside it. The top end was raised slightly. Boone stood, pistol trained on the bed's occupant, then edged closer.

She let out a laugh.

His skin was grey, like a cut of beef left out too long. A hand, tubes taped into it, lay still on his chest. Electrical monitoring equipment beside the bed was switched off, but had it been on it would have shown no signs of life.

Here was Sally.

The man. The myth.

Her scourge. Her salvation.

Served up to her now like the punchline to a joke only she didn't know was being told. Lowering her weapon, she looked at Fitz like he was a sommelier and the cork had a bit of a whiff. He shrugged. Edging forward, he prodded the old man in the ribs with the dark end of his pistol.

'Dead,' he said.

45

Boone studied the face. Bluish discoloration around the lips and nostrils. Petechial haemorrhages bloomed across his cheeks and in his flat eyes. His tongue had been bitten.

'I don't think we can bring him back for you to kill again,' Fitz said. 'Looks a bit past that.'

She wanted to laugh.

She wanted to scream.

She wanted to set fire to the whole fucking world.

'What are we doing?' Fitz said.

The room was filled with junk. Cardboard boxes, books, pill bottles, ornaments, papers. No furniture had been removed to accommodate the bed, just pushed to the edges. Chairs stacked against one wall, folding table shoved beneath a window. There was barely room to move around the bed. A walking stick and crutches leaned against the wall, vestiges of Sally's last days of movement.

Boone pointed to an AC adaptor on the floor.

'Computer. You search here. Go through all of this thoroughly.' She indicated a cupboard and a sideboard against one wall. 'Any computers, or devices of any kind. Hard drives or storage. Anything. I'll check the other rooms.'

She moved silently through the rest of the house. The living room had a sofa and a telly and not a lot else. She had noticed a satellite dish on the rear wall of the house. The kitchen was large but dated. The only food in the cupboards was breakfast cereal and various sauces and condiments. A bowl sat on the side with dried porridge glued to it. Peering inside the bin, she found a cornucopia of takeaway cartons and foil trays. Ferg wouldn't or couldn't cook for himself, and like a dying spider, Sally had existed on heat and darkness alone.

Upstairs, only one of the three bedrooms looked used. Even then the wardrobe and drawers had been emptied and most of the clothes were packed into two bags sitting at the foot of the bed. A few used garments hung on the back of a chair. Ferg was ready to go but wouldn't leave his father.

Downstairs, Fitz had been doing some renovating. A plasterboard wall had been torn away where it had disguised an alcove between window and chimney breast.

'What have you got?' she said.

Fitz held up an external hard drive.

'How'd you sniff that out?'

'Girls can always lock their diaries. Boys have to be more creative with weed and porn. And there was a USB cable going through a hole in the wall.'

'No computer?'

Fitz shook his head.

'It's encrypted,' a voice said.

They spun round, guns pointed at Ferg.

He raised his hands slowly. 'I'm unarmed.'

Fitz beckoned him further into the room with his pistol. 'Four feet from the wall. Hands out flat and fall against it so you're holding your own weight.'

Ferg closed the door and did as he was instructed. Fitz patted him down and nodded to Boone.

'Didn't go for food?' Boone said.

'Been waiting for you two. Running about in the woods and up there on the dyke.' He looked round at Fitz. 'She's better than you, but ain't neither of you special forces.'

'I'll just shoot him and we'll be off,' Fitz said.

'Hard drive's passworded,' Ferg said. 'Thirty characters. You won't guess it.'

'Won't be a problem,' Boone said, unsure if it would be or not.

'He said you'd come,' Ferg said. 'Said this wasn't new to you. Said you were a hunter.'

It was one of those things that everyone there knew was true, so that the words were like a current in the air between them. Boone looked at him for a long time. She didn't want to speak, afraid that it would snap off his line of thought.

'He never believed what they said about Hanley. That he shot the Blackborne woman and then shot himself. Some cunts are too full of themselves to consider it, he said. I said maybe he had cancer of the arse or something. Bardin got us the paperwork. Investigation reports, autopsy. Strong as a bull, old Hanley. When Dad read about the ammo, though, how it was home-made, that was when he knew. Hanley didn't know guns like that. He could shoot. All his kind can. But he didn't *know* guns. Dad knew someone had done for them. Knew the work of a hunter when he saw it. First time he met you, he knew exactly what had happened. Said that deep down, inside where it matters, you was just like him really.'

'I'm nothing like him.'

'You enjoyed it. Killing them. Look at you, here now with your guns and your vests and your plans for more killing. It's who you are. You should do it. I'm not giving you that password.'

'Fair enough,' Boone said.

'Let me say goodbye.'

'To him?'

'He said I should put a quick end to him. When Bardin came here, that's what he told me after. Said it was coming anyway, and if I did it I could get away clean. Burn the place down, destroy everything and just vanish. It's always been just me and him, though. Dunno where I would have gone.'

Boone flicked her head towards the body. Ferg muddled around the bed, his big boots scraping and scuffing the junk on the floor, the wheeled stand the IV hung from. He pressed his forehead to his father's, whispering something. He kissed him on the lips.

'He's torched the place,' Fitz said.

Boone looked back at the door, thin rolls of smoke wheeling up from beneath it. Fitz tried the handle, and when he opened the door they heard the live cracking of the fire, black smoke pushing its way in. He shut it again.

'Too late,' Ferg said.

He had a sawn-off from somewhere, hidden in the bed perhaps, and brought it up beneath his chin and fired.

'Christ,' Boone said.

Fitz stared at the mess on the ceiling. The body on the floor. The gun beside it.

'Home-made shells,' he said.

'What?'

'I bet he filled them himself. Murder-suicide. He's got you here and he's made it look like Blackborne and Moss.'

'Shit.'

'Boone, we can't go through the house, see if he's left more ammo. We need to get out of here.'

'Window,' she said.

Fitz tried it. 'Fucking screwed shut.'

'Break it.'

Fitz grabbed the walking stick from against the wall, mahogany with a brass collar, and swung it by the ferrule end, shattering the glass with the handle. He swept the edges of the frame to clear the hanging fragments. They climbed through and stepped back from the building. Ferg had done a thorough job. Flames illuminated every window and caught hold of the house with zeal, already curling over the roof.

Boone felt herself emptying, things she had held as certainties running out of her and leaving behind them a drought of whatever it was that made up people.

This wasn't what she had thought it would feel like.

She had thought she would feel triumphant, standing there warming her hands against the fire in her enemy's house.

She had thought a lot of things.

What she thought now was that Ferg had been right.

She did have murder in her heart, for she was only human.

46

'Got him,' Storm said, standing at the door to Barb's office, possibly awaiting applause.

'Yeah?' Barb said, well-chewed end of a pen in her mouth. 'Who's he?'

'Clem. The artist. Clement Stevens, born the eighth of June 1929.'

'Who'd you get that from?' Barry said.

'I've been calling all the galleries in Lark. There's one just off the promenade that's been there for a while. The owner said he maybe remembered a Clem, couldn't be sure. But he gave me the name of a couple of local writers. Art historians. One of them was familiar with Stevens' work. Said he exhibited a few times in town in the late seventies, early eighties. Then moved to a big house up the coast and withdrew into seclusion. Hasn't heard anything about him since. If he continued painting, he didn't show anyone in the art community round here. In fact, my contact assumed he had died.'

'What is he, ninety?' Barb said. 'Let's hope there's life left in him yet. You get an address, then?'

'Oh yeah. Right off the Queen's Road.'

They crowded round Storm's desk to see the online map on her screen.

'Looks like it has this whole plot between the road and the beach,'

Storm said. 'Private woodland to the north and south. Beach is a public right of way, but there look to be hedges there, and the house is set back.'

'Sea breeze there, you wouldn't be able to hear a drowning toddler anyway,' said Barb.

'Warrant?' Barry said.

'With what?' said Barb. 'We can't connect the place to any crime. He's definitely still there?'

'It's the address on record for the pension,' Storm said. 'And he's still registered to vote there.'

'Let's pay him a visit,' Barb said. 'See what we can see.'

Barry's mobile hummed softly in his pocket.

'Hello?' he said. 'Yeah. Hold on a sec.'

He held his fingers up to Barb – five minutes – and nipped out into the corridor.

'You know where this place is?' Barb asked Storm.

'Less than ten minutes. Right up the coast.'

'If we don't get an answer, or it's obviously empty, then we'll knock around at the nearest neighbours. See if anyone knows Clem, or has seen anything at the house recently. We'll probably have to cobble together something for a warrant. Trying to pass Boone off as a snout isn't going to do us any favours, though.'

'I'll check with the utilities. Prepare Section 29 requests and see whose name is on the bills, where the payments come from.'

'Yeah, good. Anything that can tie it to Killock.'

Barry opened the door and poked his head in.

'Word, Barb?'

'By all means,' Barb said, following him out.

They walked down the corridor to a small nook that housed vending machines.

'Am I going to need a Crunchie bar, Barry?'

'Let me start by saying this,' he said.

'August fucking beginning to proceedings,' she said. 'To be followed by some pain-in-the-fanny development as words like those usually are.'

'It's about Boone.'

'Of course it is.'

'I started looking at the Moss/Blackborne deaths again.'

'That was murder-suicide, Barry. We looked at it hard.'

'Did we?'

'There was no sign of coercion. Moss's gun was there, the shells matched. Equipment back at the lodge. Look, we all know they were up to their pits in that evil shit. We just couldn't prove it. It wasn't exactly a surprise that he chose another way out of it, though, the attention there had been.'

'One thing always bothered me.'

'What?'

'His pipe.'

'What about his pipe?'

'There was old burnt tobacco on the ground near where we found him. His pipe was in his pocket, freshly packed. Why would he tap his pipe out and then refill it, right there, and then moments later murder his friend and kill himself?'

'He murdered someone and then topped himself, Barry. I'd say they were the big stumpers, rather than his smoking habits. Clearly not in his right mind.'

'I sent a request out to other forces, asking about similar deaths in the time before Boone was locked up. Murder-suicides or shotgun suicides where there were . . . anomalies. Home-made ammo. Weird settings. Victims having been under investigation. Stuff like that.'

'And?'

'Nothing.'

'There you go. Overactive imagination.'

'But there might have been one the night before last.'

'How's that?'

'West Mercia just gave me a bell. They had a strange one. House fire at a farm out in the middle of nowhere, on the Welsh border. They found two bodies inside. Both dead before the fire. One was an old man. He was in a hospital bed, they're not sure what killed him yet. No smoke in the lungs, though. Tests are being run, they figure he was terminally ill. The other body was a man in his forties. What looks like a self-inflicted shotgun wound. They found other stuff in the house. Two pistols. Couple of other shotguns. Capping and turnover equipment. Just like Moss and Blackborne.'

'You think Boone killed two randoms out in the hills?'

'I don't think they were randoms. I think it was Sally and his son.'

'Join the dots for me.'

'The care home that Constance Bobb is in? The woman who owned Sally's dairy? It's near Tewkesbury. About fifty miles from this farm in Herefordshire where all this mayhem went down. West Mercia say they can't find anything to identify these men. The property was owned by a shell company, similar set-up to the dairy here in Kent. Offshore, though. They haven't been able to trace any directors. We've seen this sort of thing before, and not just with Sally. It matches all the things Boone alleged in the Blackborne investigation. She was right. They were all in on it, Sally was involved in it from the off, and now she's hunted them down and killed them.'

'We don't have any evidence of that.'

'Oh come on—'

Barb put a hand up. 'I'm not saying it isn't true. I'm saying we can't prove it.'

'There's what we can prove and there's what we know,' Barry said.

'Well, now you sound like Boone.'

'What are we going to do?'

'I really wish you'd just left this mess well alone, Barry.'

'Yeah, I know. But I didn't. Do you know where she was the night before last?'

'She's been out of contact. I traced her phone to Gravesend, but then it went off. I think I know who she was with, though.'

'She'd have known you were tracking her. Like when she went out of range with the two-ways on the Fuller tail. Who knows what she was up to there.'

'What do you mean?'

'I mean, if these bodies are Sally and his son, how did Boone find them? And is it coincidence that she finds them a couple of days after we rattle Fuller's cage? You believe he was involved, right?'

'Yeah. Yeah, I do.'

'He rabbits, obviously going to meet someone given the effort he put into losing any tail. We lose sight of him. Days later, Sally turns up dead.'

'Boone never lost him.'

'Boone never lost him.'

'Fuck, Barry. Just kill me now. I'm serious. I don't think I could do it myself, but if I go out and lie down in the car park right now, you could back over me a few times in that tractor of yours. The shitshow this is going to become is going to drown me anyway.'

'Should have slapped an ankle tag on her.'

'We didn't have time.'

'We didn't have time because she said we didn't have time.'

'All right, all right. Spilt milk.'

'What does it mean for us now? I mean, if Sally's dead . . .'

'Request everything West Mercia have. Tell them you think you might know who the deceased are, or that we have aliases for them anyway. Christ knows if we'll ever find out who they actually were.'

'And Boone?'

'We tell her nothing. Don't let on that we know. Don't tell Storm, either. Just keep it between you and me for now. Until we get a better handle on it.'

'She's a fucking serial killer, Barbara.'

'Jesus, Barry. She's not Sutcliffe, going round with a hammer.'

'Four murders. They follow a pattern. She's got it into her head that she can decide the fate of these people herself. She's not going to stop now. What if we identify more suspects in this case? What if she decides this Clem Stevens deserves knocking off? We need to arrest her.'

Barb almost laughed. 'With what? We have literally no evidence.'

'Two days out from a double murder? We nick her, search that place of hers and that bullshit van she drives about in. I mean, what's that about? You know who has vans like that? Predators. There'll be something.'

'And what if there isn't? Then we have to release her and we'll never find anything because she'll know we know and she'll make sure we won't get a sniff.'

'We can put her back inside. She's out on Special. Say she's of no further use. Must be something we can use to show her in breach of her licence. Send her down for the rest of her sentence.'

'Again with the sounding like her.'

'So what then?'

'We work it, and keep it low profile. We don't even know for sure who these two bodies in the fire are. Let West Mercia do their thing, get them to keep us in the loop. I'll keep Boone on a tighter leash.'

'We still going to knock on this Stevens?'

'Killock is worth investigating even if both he and Sally are dead. Kids went missing, Barry. Were probably murdered. Their families are owed our best efforts to find out what happened.'

'Yeah.' He reached out for her hand. 'You okay?'

'No, I'm not fucking okay. I knew she was a bit off, and prison made things a lot worse, but I never thought she'd go this far. She's my friend, even with everything. And now I have to prove she's a killer. I don't have many friends, Barry.'

'Sorry.'

'We're all going to be sorry by the time this is done.'

47

Storm drove the force Skoda, Barry beside her and Barb in the back. Barb was quiet, trying to keep a lid on any thoughts or feelings, because they were forming all wrong. She'd suppressed a simmering anger at Barry, which was mad because he hadn't done anything other than good coppering. Boone was the one she should be furious with, but she kept coming back to her first thoughts when she saw the girl Molly in her hospital bed, impossibly small; that whoever was responsible deserved worse than the law could mete out. Wasn't her call to make that kind of judgement, though.

She wanted a long drive, the Scottish Highlands and back, long enough to get her head right. She'd barely begun comfortably staring at the passing landscape, snatches of the sea every now and then between the littoral grass and the coastal houses, before they had arrived. A head-high hedge ran the length of the estate on the road, a plantation of majestic mature elms behind that. High wrought-iron gates with curved tops stood between stone pillars at the mouth of the drive, but were secured only by drop bolts and a simple latch. Barry swung them open and they drove in. The elms extended the length of the estate in either direction, and lined the private drive.

The house itself, though large by any normal standard, felt oddly small in comparison to its grand surroundings. Its ground-floor rooms featured double bays, front and side, and four windows were evenly spaced across the first floor. A pair of great gabled dormers projected from the steeply sloped roof. Though a view of the beach was obscured by hedging from the road, the house itself, sitting on a rise, undoubtedly offered a vista of the Channel.

'Jesus, this has to be worth a fortune,' Barb said, looking about at the land.

'Thirty-five acres,' Storm said.

'He inherited it, you said?'

'His father was big brass in the army. Major General Stevens. Bought it decades ago, early sixties.'

'No vehicles,' Barry said.

'Garages round the far side,' Storm said.

They parked out front, land side of the house. Four stone steps cut into the earth led up to a narrow gravelled area by the door. Thick old nets hung in the windows, ceding no view inside. Storm banged the knocker, a large knot of brass rope. She banged it again.

'Letter box,' Barb said. 'Have at it.'

On her knees, Storm pressed open the metal plate.

'Mr Stevens? Are you there, Mr Stevens? It's Kent Police. Can you come to the door?'

'There's someone in,' Barry said. He was standing back, looking at the upstairs windows. 'Something just moved the curtain.'

'Mr Stevens,' Storm yelled again. 'It's the police, Mr Stevens.'

'Might be incapacitated,' Barry said. 'Might need us to go in.'

'We're not bollocksing up a case on an illegal entry, Barry, because you want to play Frank Burnside.'

'I'm telling you, there's someone in there,' Barry said.

'If only occupancy was grounds to put doors in,' Barb said. 'Would make policing a lot simpler.'

She wandered round to the side of the house. A wooden gate leading out to the beach had almost been swallowed up by the thick hedge.

'You two stay here,' Barb said. 'Keep trying at the door. Ninety,
might be deaf as a post. I'm going to take a look down at the beach.'

The gate put up stiff resistance, obviously unused in years. Eventually
it scraped open and Barb pushed through the encroaching hedge and
out to a scrubby area above the sand. Down near the water, a woman
was running with a dog, a golden retriever, the incoming tide splashing
around her ankles. When she looked up and saw Barb, she waved.

'Another escaped patient,' Barb muttered, waving back.

The woman was headed up the beach towards her, jogging almost.

'Christ, here we go.'

'Hallo!' the woman cried from a distance.

'Yes, hello there.'

'Have you bought the place?'

'Sorry?'

'The old Stevens place, are you the new owner?'

'I . . . uh, no. I was looking for Mr Stevens, in fact. Clem Stevens.'

'Oh, he's been gone for years now.'

'Really?'

'Yes. I assumed he died, but there was nothing in the local papers.
He kept himself to himself, so I'm not sure what happened. Possible he
just moved away.'

Barb looked back through the gate to the house.

'You're sure he's not still here?'

'Haven't seen him in yonks. Probably fifteen years.'

'Shit,' Barb said.

'He was a painter, you know. Not a bad one either. I used to see him
all the time, couple of mornings a week at least. He'd sit just outside
his gate, sketching this or that on the beach. Getting ideas, he'd say.
Then he just stopped coming out.'

'You live round here?'

'Oh, yes. Sorry.' The woman offered a hand. 'I'm Camilla.'

Of course you are, thought Barb.

'Barb,' she said.

'I thought it would be lovely if someone new had moved in there. The current ones are so awful.'

'You know them?'

'No, not exactly. For years there was seldom anyone around. Occasionally a man. My husband thought he'd seen him driving in when old Clem still lived there, but I'd never noticed him. I shouted hello on the beach to him once or twice and he completely ignored me.'

'The nerve,' Barb said.

'I should say. Didn't see him much after that. I thought maybe he was a nephew or something. Inherited the house from Clem. Then he disappeared and there was a younger man, though he wasn't here very often at all. But about three or four years ago, someone else seemed to move in. Keeps himself to himself, but I think he's ill.'

'What makes you say that?'

'His face, you see. It was like some of it was removed.'

'Around the jaw?' Barb said.

'Yes! You must know him then.'

'I've heard stories,' Barb said.

'I don't understand,' Camilla said. 'So you know the present owners?'

Barb took out her warrant card. 'Camilla, I'm going to need you to repeat everything you've just said to a colleague of mine.'

Camilla sat in the car and gave a statement to Storm as Barry knocked absently on the door.

'What's the plan?' he said.

'Wait here. Make sure nobody leaves. Storm takes what we have to a magistrate and begs for a warrant. The description Camilla gave matches the disfigured man Boone saw at the dairy. I think we have enough to reasonably suspect Clem Stevens is no longer alive and the people at the house are involved in activities that are germane to an ongoing investigation.'

Barry knelt down and peered through the letter box.

'Can't see shit. Flight of stairs maybe. Hello? Hello, it's the police.'

A cry from inside maybe. Barb and Barry looked at one another.

'You hear that?' he said.

'Was that inside?' said Barb.

'This is the police,' Barry shouted. 'Can you hear us?'

They heard a strangled call, barely human.

'Jesus,' Barry said.

He stood up, taking a few steps back from the door.

'Barb?' he said.

'I don't know,' Barb said.

'Life and limb, Barb. Life and fucking limb.'

There was another sound, louder this time. A shriek that pierced the walls of the house. Barb ran back to the car.

'Camilla, you need to leave here right away,' she said. 'Take the driveway, and hurry, please. Go back to your house immediately and lock the doors. An officer will be round to you later when we have the house secure. Storm, we need backup.'

Barb ushered Camilla out of the car and off down the drive, watching the woman trot along with her dog snaking around her legs. Storm radioed for immediate assistance. Then she opened the boot, dragging out stab vests.

'Barb?' Barry said, taking his.

Barb nodded.

'I'll go round the back,' Storm said, already running as she strapped the armour on.

Barry sized up the door. It was heavy but old, and the frame around it had seen better days. One big boot didn't open it, but they heard the frame cracking like kindling. His second kick sent it flying in.

'Kent Police,' he announced, slipping into the shadows within.

Barb felt that familiar chill, her hands turning to ice.

48

This was a mistake.

Barb could already see herself having to explain later how it all went to shit. She pushed that stuff from her mind, concentrated on what was in front of her. She didn't have eyes on Storm, who'd gone round the back to find a way in, or hopefully just to watch for people trying to leave.

The house was double-fronted, two large rooms at the front, two at the back. The geography in the middle was a little hazier, but there was a wide staircase and a couple of doors beneath it. Barry checked the room on the left. Barb slid through the opposite door into a dining room.

Dusty. Unused.

There were double doors through to a kitchen at the rear. She kept tight to the walls and ducked her head in.

Uneven lino floor.

Forty-watt bulb.

Dead clock on the wall.

Another door led back into the hall. She edged past the stairs, pressing herself into the wall. It was cool and dry and she laid her cheek against it, flattened her palms to it. When a figure walked out into the hall behind her, she instinctively dropped to bent knees.

It was Storm.

Barb wanted to loosen her vest. It was like someone sitting on her chest.

Storm pointed upstairs. Doors were closed and curtains pulled up there, impossible to see anything in the dim. Barb nodded. Storm took the flight quickly, feet to the edge of the steps, eyes on the roving darkness above.

Barb was on the first step, following, when Barry appeared in the hall. She indicated that she was backing up Storm, and he nodded. He tried one door beneath the stairs, a WC. The door next to it led down to a cellar. Barb motioned for him to follow her, but he pointed down and disappeared through.

Upstairs, the landing led off in both directions. Storm went one way and Barb the other. It was fusty, the light dull and yellow through stained nets. The rooms were bedrooms, decorated in a different time for a different people. Brass-framed beds, dark-wood furniture, woollen blankets. It was like a museum of how things used to be. Lights didn't turn on; some windows were sealed up.

The house conspired against them. Boards groaned under every step; doors whined as they opened. Barb felt her breathing hasten, her vest constricting further. Just the noises of living would give her away. She thought she heard someone on the stairs and went back out to the hallway. Storm came out from another room.

Barb pointed to her ear. Storm nodded.

They could see nobody.

A door led to stairs up to the attic. Barb slowly took hold of the handle, her grip around it wet. Turning it gently like the dial on a safe and—

A yell from downstairs.

A cry that in any other circumstance could have been anyone's but that she now instantly knew to be Barry's.

Her feet were moving before she even thought, carrying her down the stairs and through the door to the flight down to the pitch of the cellar. She could hear Storm behind her, boots on the wooden steps, surprised she could make out anything over her own breathing.

There were multiple rooms in the cellar, and they came down in the middle. Barb pointed one way and sent Storm the other. Recklessly she barrelled through doorways, caroming off low furniture unseen in the darkness, until someone shoulder-checked her, sending her backwards over a wooden sawhorse, feet coming up above her head as she slammed down on the back of her shoulders, all the air gone from her.

On her hands and knees, she tried to inhale, managing great whoops of nothing, like the inside of her lungs were knitted together.

'Barb?'

It was Barry. She'd run headlong into Barry. She reached up, touching his arm, trying to tell him she'd be all right, but sounding like a drowning victim.

'Did you see them?' Storm said, from the next room.

'Who?' Barry said.

'There was someone here, I thought.'

'No. But through there . . .' Barry pointed to a blackened doorway, 'there's someone. He's dead.'

He helped Barb up and sat her on the sawhorse. The room was stuffed with junk. Rusty tools. An old twin-bar Coronet lathe stood against one wall.

'You okay, Barb?'

'Yeah.'

'Sorry, I was coming to get you to show you the body, and you just appeared.'

'The body,' Barb said.

She followed him through a door into a smaller room, maybe eight feet by eight. The ground was sunken and felt like fresh earth, as if the hard stuff had been dug away.

There he was. Propped in a corner, head tilted back at an ugly angle where his throat had been sliced down to the spine. Blood was soaking into the soil beneath him.

'Jesus,' Barb said.

She went closer, to get a view of his face. The jaw was scarred and misshapen – the goblin Boone had seen at the dairy, and Camilla had seen here.

'It's one of Sally's people,' Barb said. 'We need SOCOs in this place, top to bottom.'

'Yeah, I'll get on—'

Upstairs, a floorboard creaked. They both looked.

Then footsteps clacking on the stairs as Storm raced up. 'Stop!' she yelled, in pursuit.

'Christ, get after her,' Barb said.

Barry was off, as fast as he could. Still collecting herself from the fall, Barb was slower. When she got to the top of the stairs, she couldn't see either of them, didn't know which way to go. She chose the back of the house and found an open door leading out, squinting against the sun.

'Barry? Storm?'

She ran on towards the outbuildings behind the house. The stable-style doors were open and Storm stood in the middle of a totally empty garage.

'Storm?'

Storm looked back at her. 'It's fresh,' she said.

Barb frowned, not understanding.

Storm ran her foot across the ground. 'It dips in the middle. Con-crete. Wasn't laid that long ago.'

'All right,' Barb said. 'We'll get the SOCOs to have a look. You see anyone?'

Storm shook her head.

'Barry?'

'No,' Storm said.

'Come on.'

They walked back to the house and down the hallway. The front door was open and Barb could see Barry sitting on the steps outside.

'Get away from you then?' she said.

He ignored that.

'Thought we'd have to chase after you in the car.'

She touched his shoulder and he slumped sideways, a low whine escaping his mouth.

'Jesus fucking Christ, Barry.'

Eyes wide like plates, hands clamped to his side where someone had gone in behind the stab vest.

Blood like a faucet leaking everywhere.

Storm pushed Barb aside. She unfastened her vest and pulled off her sweater, holding it tightly to Barry's side, directly to the wounds.

'Barb, call it,' she said. 'Barry, were you cut anywhere else? Barry, can you hear me?'

Barb was on her knees, hands slick with his blood.

'Barb, we need an air ambulance,' Storm said.

Barb looked at her. Wiping her hands on her legs, she found her radio and pressed the emergency button. She could already hear sirens from the response to their initial call. She spoke calmly and quietly.

'Kilo Whisky, this is Bravo Two-Two. Code Zero at same address as backup request. Queen's Road between Cinque Ports golf course and sailing club. I say again, Code Zero. Officer in need of emergency assistance.'

Storm was leaning over Barry, her ear to his mouth. The sirens got louder and police cars roared up the drive, uniforms spilling out. Barb directed them to surround the house and secure it from the outside, but not to go in until a firearms team arrived. She spread other constables out to the garages and into the surrounding trees to see if they could find this ghost that had fled the house.

An ambulance arrived quickly; they'd been eating their lunch near the sea. The paramedics eased Storm out of the way and took over with Barry. He was unconscious. There was a pool of his blood running down the steps into the gravel.

His black face was ashen, almost unrecognisable.

A second ambulance arrived, a whole team working on him as he lay motionless. One of the paramedics explained that air support was landing imminently and he was being taken to London.

Barb nodded.

This was all happening elsewhere and elsewhen, like watching home movies.

'Barb, can you help me with something?'

Storm needing her. Barb followed to the Skoda and sat in the back, Storm climbing in beside her. Barb accepted a bottle of water from her and drank.

'Thought you'd be more comfortable here,' Storm said.

The helicopter was landing, flattening a pool of grass around it.

'We should see to that,' Barb said.

'Let them do their work. I'll find out where they're taking him and we'll follow.'

Barb took another sip of water. 'He said something to you.'

'I don't know what he meant. I'm not sure he knew what he meant.'

'What was it?'

'You stay, I think he said. What it sounded like. You stay.'

'You think he meant the house?'

'I don't know.'

'Jesus, I don't know how this happened,' Barb said.

But she did.

It had that feeling of inevitability about it, like the unexpected often did in hindsight. Fate was just another name for what you found in place of what you were looking for.

PART SIX

WHO WAS CHANGED AND WHO WAS DEAD

49

The hospital was an exercise in the abstract.

Barry had been whisked there by air ambulance and had been in theatre ever since. Nobody had seen him, and little information was forthcoming. It felt unreal. Without witnessing him in a bed with tubes and wires and tape over his eyes, Barb couldn't accept it. It was an ongoing trauma, something that wasn't yet done with her.

Storm had tried to drive her, but she wouldn't hear it. When it became clear the localised search for the suspect wouldn't yield anything, she left Storm in charge and took the Audi. An ACC showed up with an entourage and they were given a room to wait in, but he could get no more information than Barb. Barry was in theatre; surgeons were fighting to save his life. He had lost a significant amount of blood and suffered catastrophic organ damage.

Detectives from another firm were already there, run by a DCI who Barb knew a bit. He asked her to stop by in the morning, if possible. Give a statement. For the first time, the language struck her as odd. Statements weren't gifts. They weren't given, they were taken. She'd said he could take it immediately if he liked, and sat with him and his sergeant.

Gifts all round. She gave her statement, and they gave their sympathies and assurances they'd catch the bastard.

Barb said she was going for some air and walked the corridors on her own. She spotted a constable taking away Barry's bloody clothes in a bag. He had nothing to wear now. She supposed they'd have him in a gown of some sort when he was out of surgery. He'd be in bed for a while, but he'd want his own clothes. She made a note to pick some up.

As she walked around, nurses approached her twice, in between doling out furious care to patients. 'Can I help you?' they said, meaning she should explain herself. She showed her card and they left her to it.

Barry's parents arrived, brought by uniforms. She'd met them before, but they didn't know about the two of them. Nobody knew. Rather, they'd never told anyone. It had been a wonderful secret for so long, but now, suddenly, it was crushing. She shook hands with Barry's father, laid a hand on his mother's shoulder. Mr Tayleforth mentioned he'd had his appendix out, trying to make some connection with the building he found himself in. They had a family liaison officer, though, and didn't need Barb.

She'd have liked them to need her. She longed to be needed, but the only one who might need her had far greater needs now. She wondered what the hell she was doing there. Her phone buzzed. Storm.

'Yep?'

'Barb, you all right?'

'He's in surgery. Nothing new. We won't know anything until morning, I don't think. His parents are here, so that's good. And the ACC is staying, which he didn't have to.'

'Yeah, but are you okay?'

'I'm coming back. Nothing I can do here anyway.'

'We got something.'

'From the house?'

'No. I mean, yes, there's loads there too, but this is different. Boone is here.'

'I'll be there in an hour.'

She told the ACC she was headed back to the Shed, and for some-one to keep her in the loop. He told her she should get some rest. She said she would. She caught the lift before the doors closed and was followed in by a dewy-eyed family who'd obviously had one of those trips to the hospital you'd rather were reserved for other people.

So many things to lose in hospitals. Clothes and appendixes. Friends and lovers.

50

Boone could feel her drinks failing her, the miserable prospect of a clammy soberness in that tiny bright room in the offing. Her mouth was dry, the back of her neck damp. She thought about getting up and leaving, calling later to say something had come up. Then she wondered if the door was locked. She didn't want to check.

The television had carried the story about Barry. That was when she knew she had to bring the drive in sooner rather than later. She and Fitz had tried to open it, buying a brand-new air-gapped laptop from a local independent supplier. Fitz spoke a bit of computer after his trawl through dark nets looking for Sally, but encrypted hard drives were beyond him. So Boone had downed a couple of gaolhouse gimlets and come in, asking for Storm, presenting her with the drive.

The door opened. Storm, with no papers or folders or accompanying officers. Probably left to call Barb, tell her their recently sprung informant had resurfaced. She sat across the table.

'Thought you'd forgotten about me,' Boone said.

'No, you didn't.'

'No, I didn't.'

'Barry was stabbed fourteen times. He is still in the operating theatre, where he has been for over twelve hours. Catastrophic damage to his liver, a kidney, a lung and his stomach. Nobody wants to say it, but the odds of any kind of recovery are long, in the same way life is.'

'How's Barb?'

'You knew about them?'

'Only a hunch. She never said anything. She told you?'

Storm shook her head. 'The way she fell apart, though.'

'She's at the hospital?'

'Heading back now.'

'What was the house? How did you get there?'

'You mean how on earth did we make any headway in your absence?'

'That's not what—'

'Where have you been?'

'I told Barb that—'

'She had no real idea where you were. She was trusting you, trusting that your usual myopic endeavour would bear fruit, even if the methods were questionable.'

'Look, I knew nothing about this house or you going there or any of it. None of this can be laid at my door.'

'I hope not.'

'Who was there?'

Storm sighed, brushed imaginary lint from the thigh of her trousers. 'We found the man you said was at the dairy. The scarred man. Your goblin. He was killed when we were standing outside, in order to cause a distraction, we think. We heard him, kicked the door in; the suspect used that to get around us and outside. We had split up, and Barry must have found him out there.'

'I don't get it. Who is the suspect?'

'I was hoping you could tell us.'

'How would I know? I don't even know how you found the house.'

'I told you about Killock's half-brother. This man he told us about, this Clem. Knocked around with Killock's mother, way back.'

'Honestly, Storm, I don't know who he is. Neither does—'

'Your source. Yeah, you said. Well, we do know who he is. Or was. Clement Stevens. He was an artist, and the house was his. Found bones under concrete in a garage that I expect will turn out to be him. We also found the remains of a woman. No identification yet. We think the bodies had been moved from beneath the cellar, and fairly recently.'

'Trying for a permanent arrangement.'

'Looks like.'

Boone leaned back. She cast her eyes around the bare walls.

'Why are we in here?' she said.

'The investigation has been widened to include the attempted murder of a detective constable of Kent Police. Access to and control of all relevant information and material is now a paramount concern.'

'Okay.'

'The hard drive, whose is it?'

'It's connected to Sally.'

'And where did it come from?'

Boone shrugged. 'We both know I'd be lying.'

Storm sighed. 'Stay here,' she said, as she left again.

When she returned, she had a clutch of folders held against her chest.

'We're going to need to get one of your lies on record. Tosh will lead the interview. Would you like to arrange for a solicitor to be here?'

Boone shook her head, almost smiled. Storm was the kind of clever that could be relied upon. She'd sized up the situation and now wanted only to get from it whatever would best help the case.

'I suggest you keep it simple, then. It'll be recorded, and it'll be under caution.'

This time, Boone did smile.

'None of this is funny, Abigail.'

'No. No it certainly is not. It was admiration, not amusement.'

'Don't fuck with me or I'll pull you and all of your fantasies apart and have you explain the whole sorry mess in front of a court.'

Boone held her palms up. 'Yes, ma'am.'

'You really should have legal representation.'

'It's like porn with condoms.'

'Abigail—'

'Let's go.'

Storm left for a few minutes, returning with Detective Constable Mackintosh. She turned on the cameras and tape recorder and Mackintosh read Boone her rights.

'You produced and gave to my colleague a hard drive,' he said.

'That's right.'

'Where did you get it from?'

'It was given to me.'

'By whom?'

'I don't know.'

'Care to elaborate on that?'

'It was left at my home.'

'How?'

'How? No idea. A stork left it for all I know.'

'Where exactly was it? What was it in? A bag, a box?'

'It was on the ground outside my front door. There's a yard, it's mostly protected from the street. It was in an unmarked Jiffy bag.'

'When was this?'

'Day before yesterday.'

'Do you still have that Jiffy bag?'

'No. Yesterday was recycling day.'

Mackintosh gave her an even gaze. 'Why do you think it was left outside your door?'

'I'd been asking around. Trying to help with the investigation into the girl who was found.'

'Molly.'

'Yes, Molly. If I had to guess, I'd say it was something to do with that.'

'What's on the drive?'

'I don't know. It's encrypted.'

'Would you have brought it to the police if it hadn't been?'

'I suppose that depends on what's on it.'

'Meaning?'

'Meaning if it was just a load of illegally downloaded Pink Floyd MP3s, then no, probably not. If it was material relevant to the investigation, then yes.'

'Yes? Because you share with the police everything you know that is relevant to the investigation?'

Boone felt the ground shift slightly beneath her. 'That a question or a statement?'

'Let's move on.'

Storm was sitting beside Mackintosh, back from the table slightly. She opened one of her folders and pulled out a photograph on glossy A4 paper. It was a small piece of jewellery, a seahorse possibly. Although tarnished by dirt and time, Boone thought it familiar somehow.

'Do you recognise this?' Mackintosh asked.

'I don't know. Maybe.'

'Maybe?'

'I think I've seen it, or something like it, before. I'm not sure where.'

'It was found with the remains of a woman at the house on the coast. We believe it is a nose piercing.'

'Oh shit.'

Storm leaned forward. 'Abigail?'

'How long had she been dead?'

'Hard to say,' Mackintosh said. 'Years, anyway.'

'It's Lilly Bancroft.'

Mackintosh referred to his notes. Storm didn't have to. 'The woman who was at Eastry House as a girl?' she said.

'She had a seahorse piercing when I went to speak to her about Noah Maxwell.'

'And nobody has seen her since that day. Any ideas on how she ended up buried in the garage of Clement Stevens's house?'

'Probably because she was mixed up with the same people you're looking for.'

'Which people?' Mackintosh said.

'Sally. His son.'

'We know where they are.'

Boone swallowed thickly.

'West Mercia Police were called to the scene of a fire at a house on the Welsh border,' Mackintosh said. 'Two bodies were found there. Both were dead before the fire started, or at least very soon after it began. An elderly man, who had late-stage cancer, had been suffocated, probably by a pillow. A younger man, who DNA tests show to be his son, died from an apparently self-inflicted gunshot. I say apparently, because there's some evidence of the presence of a party or parties unknown. A window shows signs of having been broken from the inside out.'

'And you think the dead men are Sally and Ferg?'

'You don't?'

'Unless I'm missing something, it seems a bit of a leap.'

Mackintosh sighed. 'We have a number of circumstantial connections. We're confident these are the men we have been looking for.'

Mackintosh had other questions about the house and about the provenance of the hard drive, and then variations on the same questions in a cursory attempt at testing Boone's story. When they were done, Storm pulled her aside in the corridor.

'What are we going to find on the drive, Abigail?'

'My guess? Some deeply unpleasant films.'

'If this came from that house in Herefordshire, then we're not even nearly done with the questions, and you should really get yourself a lawyer.'

'Yeah.'

'Barb wants you readily available at all times.'

'Here?'

'Just available.'

'I'm meeting Quin.'

'Really?' Storm's faced changed. 'That's great, Abigail.'

'Yeah. We saw each other briefly the other day, and he suggested this. Tess is bringing Jim, we're all meeting at the pier in Lark.'

'See? Not everything is emptiness and despair. And you didn't even have to join a book club.'

Boone allowed that was true. But emptiness and despair were well known to her now. They were things she had feared, things she had armed herself against and gone to war with. Life was larger and even more terrifying when the enemy was dead.

51

Tables were laid with partial and complete skeletons, the bones brushed clean. Some were smaller than others. Many weren't human. For Barb, bones were the nitty-gritty. Bones were impersonal. Stripped of skin and tissue, they were artefacts, clues that yielded facts about the investigation. It always seemed different when they had faces and eyes and fingernails and belly buttons.

'At what point is it acceptable to dig up the dead?' she said.

'Hmm?' said Middlewitch, examining a pelvic bone.

'Is there a line of indecency that one mustn't cross? More in terms of archaeology than criminal affairs, I mean.'

'An expiration date of sanctity?'

'I suppose so.'

'Hard to say. I expect if you started shovelling up Edwardian bones from cemeteries, you'd meet with some resistance. Historical digs rarely encounter problems in this country, though, probably because the Sky Bastard holds little sway. Cultural agents tend to be stronger.'

'These could be any age, for all I know,' Barb said, looking across the laid-out remains. 'Tudors or Normans or druids.'

Middlewitch measured a small femur. 'If only. Aside from the two found in the car, we've identified remains from five skeletons. None of them are adult, and none of them are complete.'

Storm appeared behind the observation window and did a double take at Barb. She asked with her fingers whether she should come into the laboratory. Barb nodded.

'Didn't think you'd be here,' Storm said.

'Investigation has only become more crucial, not less.'

'How is Barry?'

Barb shrugged and shook her head at the same time. Storm didn't pursue it.

'Dr Middlewitch,' Storm said.

'Dr Mathijsen. Or Detective Constable. Doctor Constable? We really should settle on an adequate title.'

'I can think of a few,' Barb said.

Storm waved at the remains. 'Where are we with all this?'

'Well, I had just about sorted out what we found at the dairy when Barb brought me another site with multiple bodies,' Middlewitch said. 'The gentleman killed at the scene is on ice. We have the bones of a male, probably seventy-five or eighty years old. I don't have a cause of death for you there. No obvious signs of violence.'

'So he might have died of old age and someone buried him rather than reporting it?' Storm said.

'It's possible.'

'Tallies with what the neighbour told me,' Barb said. 'They used to see the old boy out on the beach painting quite a lot, and then he was gone. Pension is still going into an account, and bills are being paid out of it. Like they used him as a front for the house.'

'The other body?' asked Storm.

'A female, thirty-five to fifty,' said Middlewitch. 'Death by strangulation. Hyoid bone was broken. There was also a spiral fracture of the ulna.'

'From someone twisting it?' Storm said.

'Impossible to tell, but in conjunction with the other injury it is certainly a possibility.'

'The teams are still out there digging,' Barb said, 'so God knows what else they'll bring you. We think most of the activity there was limited to the last four years, after they were forced to abandon the dairy. So hopefully it won't be a full-on horror show like that place.'

'Boone recognised the piercing,' Storm said. 'The seahorse. Said it belonged to Lilly Bancroft.'

'She was the first person who told Boone about Sally,' Barb said.

'Are we thinking Sally killed her?'

'Sally, or whoever this other maniac on the loose is. We had four identified players. Jerry Killock, who died years ago. Sally and Ferg, who we're pretty sure are crispy corpses. And the man with the scarred face, who's in Dr Middlewitch's freezer. Now we have another, unidentified suspect, who was at the house we can connect to Killock, who probably killed the goblin, and who tried to murder Barry.'

'Boone has never mentioned anyone else she thought was involved.'

'No. But I'm beginning to suspect that the sheer tonnage of what Boone hasn't mentioned to us could knock the moon out of its orbit. How did she react to the news about Sally?'

'It threw her,' Storm said. 'I'm not sure. She's always been hard to read. Easy on the surface; she's permanently angry. But I've never been sure of the whys and wherefores.'

'The hard drive?' Barb said.

'With Jane in Cyber Crime. She said if the password is thirty random digits it could have an entropy of two hundred and fifty-six bits. But if it's a pass phrase, then she should be able to get into it quite quickly with a dictionary-based program.'

'I'm sure that'll be full to the brim with delightful surprises.' Barb took a deep breath and looked about the lab. 'Any more for any more?'

'The stuffed toy you gave me,' Middlewitch said. 'The one found with the girl?'

'I'm not sure I want to know what samples you found on that,' Barb said.

'There was a beetle inside it.'

'A beetle.'

'A wood-boring beetle. This species is particularly fond of wood from wine caskets.'

'Sounds like a sensible species,' Barb said.

'There were wine caskets in the cellar of the Stevens house,' Storm said.

'Indeed.' Middlewitch nodded. 'And we found the same type of beetle there too.'

'So the girl was definitely kept there?' Barb said.

'Soil found on the toy also matches samples from the basement, so I'm very confident it was there at some point.'

Barb turned to Storm. 'I can't figure it out. They kept her at the dairy. Could have been there her whole life up until that point as far as we know, which would be—'

'Six or seven years, probably,' said Storm.

'Six years. Then Boone blunders in there with all her bullshit, and they decide the prudent thing is to clear out. Killock is dead. Clement Stevens is dead. Someone has taken over the seaside house; either Sally or someone connected to him.'

'This mystery fifth suspect.'

'Yeah. And they move Molly and keep her there. But then what happened? Why did they move her again, and why back to the dairy of all places? And how did she get away?'

'I might be able to help with the last question,' Middlewitch said.

'The man with the scarred face, he had a bite mark on his hand. A deep one. Maybe a week or ten days old. Nothing to do with the assault that killed him. From the size, I'd say it was a child.'

'Molly?' Storm said.

'I can have my odontologist do a comparison if we had an impression of the girl's teeth.'

'I wish you good luck with that,' Barb said.

'She bites him and runs,' Storm said. 'She couldn't have got far, though. Didn't get far, in fact.'

'Probably he panicked,' Barb said. 'Boone said she thought he was a bit . . . touched. Quite aside from whatever happened to his face—'

'Ablative jaw and throat surgery for a tumour,' Middlewitch said. 'Crudely done. Abroad, perhaps.'

'Yeah, well,' Barb said, 'it's the cancer I feel sorry for. But if he wasn't the sharpest of tools, then he's out in the middle of nowhere, bleeding from the bite, the girl's hobbling off as best she can, and he goes to pieces and flees the scene.'

'I don't understand why he was taking her back there, though,' Storm said. 'If they removed her from there in the first place, fearing Boone would spill the beans about the dairy, then why return her?'

'Boone thinks this all started because she was due to be released,' Barb said. 'Sally, or whoever, was worried that she would come looking for them again. Not an unreasonable concern, as anyone who knows the mad cow will attest. Maybe they were taking Molly back there to kill her? Put her with the other bodies?'

'Still seems a risk,' Storm said. 'If you're worried someone is going to tell the police about a specific place, a place containing multiple grave sites, adding to them doesn't do you any favours. If anything, it would only leave better trace evidence. These men have successfully hidden themselves away for decades. The one thing we're sure of is that they're not idiots.'

'Sally was ill, though,' Barb said. 'Another one who got the cancers he deserved. We don't know how smartly they were operating if he wasn't capable of calling the shots any longer.'

Storm's phone beeped, and she read something.

'Hard drive,' she said.

'That was quick,' Barb said. 'See? Maybe not as clever as we thought they were.'

52

'We have programs that run endless combinations of words from various dictionaries. A lot of them we compile ourselves from different sources. They include things like song lyrics, film and book titles, nursery rhymes, proverbs and well-known phrases. I mean, given enough time and CPU cycles, I can hack any password, no matter how random. But most people do the heavy lifting themselves by making things memorable. They think they're being smart coming up with a long phrase instead of a password, but they're doing my job for me at that point.'

Jane Scheune was disgustingly young. Barb found it a worrying tendency of hers to fear youth the older she got. They'd spent their entire lives in a digital world and moved through it with an ease and fluency she would never have, having grown up analogue and learned the new order. Push notifications she could deal with. Encryption and password entropy could get stuffed.

'So what do we have?' she said.

The young woman blanched.

'I checked to make sure the individual files weren't encrypted too. They weren't.'

'And?'

'Videos. And pictures. I didn't—it's not stuff I wanted to see.'

'That's all right, Jane,' Barb said. 'I don't want to see it either. Anything else on there?'

'Yeah. There are spreadsheets and other documents relating to crypto payments.'

'Bitcoin?' Barb said, finally feeling down with the kids.

'No. Bitcoin's increase in value has made it unwieldy. Transaction costs went up and it can take too long to get the actual payments. Criminals and people on dark webs have found alternatives. The payments we've tracked were made in almost a dozen different cryptocurrencies. They've tended to follow the prevailing criminal trends. Whatever the drug traffickers are using, that's the currency of choice.'

'They know what they're doing, then,' Barb said.

'That's the weird thing. They seem quite capable at this sort of thing, but the password was so easy to break.'

'What was it?'

'It was thirty-one characters, not thirty like we thought. You know the nursery rhyme with the cat and the fiddle? The last line of that. "And the dish ran away with the spoon." No spaces, first letters of all words capitalised, and the numbers seven and three at the end. Got it in less than half an hour.'

'Whoever dealt with the payments probably made the password easy for someone else to memorise, in case they couldn't access the drive,' Storm said.

'Someone who was terminally ill, say,' said Barb. 'Making it easy for their idiot son.'

Jane handed Barb a different hard drive, along with a folder.

'Clone,' she said. 'And a map of the drive on paper. Most of it appears to be organised by date. From what I saw, the file names might refer to locations, but I didn't check enough of them to be sure. A few folders are out of chronological sequence, though. There are fewer files in those ones, but the faces of the men in them are clearly visible.'

'They're not in the others?' Storm said.

'Not in most of them, no. There was no digital mosaicking or anything. They wore masks in the ones I saw, or simply kept their heads out of shot.'

'This is going to be the shittest job ever,' Barb said.

'There's just over three terabytes,' Jane said. 'There is some duplication, though. You've got the AVCHD files from the cameras, and then they've converted some of them into a container format, presumably to distribute. Matroska, in this case. The file names are the same but with different extensions for the conversions.'

'Can we watch them through that crazy CCTV viewing thing?' Barb said.

Jane crinkled her nose. 'That's good for simultaneous multiple cameras and stuff, but it's not necessary for these files.'

'We've got VLC on computers in a viewing suite at CSE,' Storm said.

'That'll do it,' Jane said.

They let Jane go and went to the main building, to the Child Sexual Exploitation digs. Storm booked out the suite for the rest of the day and they settled in.

'You've had experience with this stuff before?' Barb said.

Storm nodded. 'You?'

'Briefly. Never sat down to watch hours of it.'

'You don't have to. We have officers who, for lack of a better word, are trained to cope with it.'

'The idea of delegating this filth is even worse. Besides, it'll tell you all you need to know about the rest of my life right now that I'd almost rather be here.'

'This isn't a casual thing, Barb. Especially when you're dealing with other stuff. There's nothing wrong in requesting specialised officers for the task.'

'Right now, we don't have to watch them to determine whether CP cases can be brought. We need to see if we can identify any of the men, work towards finding this fifth suspect from that angle.'

Storm plugged in the hard drive and found the folder Jane had told them about where the faces of the men were clearly visible.

'That's Killock,' Barb said, when the first one opened. 'Is it the same video Boone had?'

'No,' Storm said. 'Similar, though. Shot from a high angle. Hidden camera in those small rooms in the dairy.'

'How the fuck did none of this ever come to light about the man? He was in social services for thirty years, for Christ's sake.'

Storm opened a file from a different folder, one that had been converted for online distribution. 'Look at this one. The guy clearly knows the camera is there. It's low and close up, focusing on the girl. He keeps his head out of shot, like maybe there's a monitor there, or he can see the screen on the camera itself. He bobs into a view a couple of times, but he has something over his face.'

'Tights,' Barb said.

'Yeah. But he was prepared, is my point. He knows it's happening, knows what the video is going to be used for. The other one, I don't think Killock knew the camera was there. Boone had about a dozen files, and the one with Killock was the only one where a man was identifiable. I think these videos are about something else. Sally filmed men and then used the fact that they were visible against them.'

'Blackmail?'

'Or just control, probably. Keep people in line. The perpetual threat of being unmasked. Killock died, though, and they decided to use the files.'

'Bit of a risk, given he was connected to them.'

'I bet they knew he couldn't be tied to them in any real way. I mean, we still don't even know Sally's real name. Releasing the video could have been part of the same threat. Letting the other men know that their faces could appear on the dark web at any time.'

'Particularly effective if some of them were more connected to Killock than they were to Sally.'

They played the other videos from the hidden cameras, filmed from high up in the corner of the small bedroom cubicles in the dairy, boys and girls led in. Most of them were still and docile, through drugs or dissociation.

It was Storm who spotted him.

She sat bolt upright. 'Shit.'

'You know him?'

He was probably in his early thirties, with a full beard. Tall and rangy.

'That's Harry Eustace. Maybe ten years younger, but definitely him. Jesus, I only spoke to him the other day. Still works at social services now.'

Barb squinted at the screen. 'Eustace? Boone mentioned him before.'

'Christ, she met him. Four years ago, when she was looking for Noah. Asked him for help. She called him the other day to facilitate us getting the files from social. Dammit. He would have known exactly what we were looking at. He used to work with Killock, too.'

Barb was frowning. 'Eustace, Eustace, Eustace. Fucking Eustace. That's what he was saying.'

'Who?'

'Barry. It wasn't "You stay". He was telling us who stabbed him. He'd been through the Killock files, he knew who Eustace was.'

Storm was already on the phone.

'We need to do this right,' Barb was saying. 'Don't let him know we're coming. I want everything we know about him. I want warrants for everything.'

53

Late afternoon and the road turned quiet, the kind of focused calm only found in the antecedence or aftermath of pure mayhem. No cars. No passers-by. Tactical police, all in black, emerged slowly as if seeping from the pores of the street. Thin lines of ants scurrying along the low brick walls of front gardens, closing in on the target house from both sides.

A neighbouring door opened and an officer broke rank, silently ushering a mother with a buggy back inside, his H&K G36 downwards and out of sight at his side.

Barb watched through binoculars from an upper window down the way. Downstairs, the woman who owned the place frantically made tea for everyone, mortified by the prospect of unwatered guests.

A nod from the tactical commander.

The AFOs were in place, front and rear, to breach. By the front door she could see them huddled behind the shield officer, as the entry specialist came up from the rear with a big red key. There would be a Remington down there too, should the door prove to be barricaded.

The order was given and the door flew inwards on the first smash, armed officers swarming the place. Then the transition period, the bridge between two states. Before and after. Either Eustace was in the house, or he was not. If he was, he would leave either in cuffs or on a stretcher. Schrödinger's suspect.

She heard the commander's radio squelch. He looked up at her. A single shake of his head.

'Come on,' Barb told Storm.

A period cottage, two-up-two-down with a cellar, sporting a spacious rear extension and a converted attic with original dormer. Decorated like it was about to be sold: beige walls and tan carpets, bright and antiseptic kitchen and bathroom. One neatly arranged bookcase in the sitting room. Kitchen cupboards well stocked. Bed neatly made, pillowcases pristine. The basement was stonewashed and used for storage, rows of uniform cardboard boxes containing old clothes or files from his work.

'There's not a single photograph,' Storm said.

Barb looked around. 'He doesn't have family. Orphan. We don't really have much on his background, though.'

'Neat and tidy,' Storm said. 'To the point of being meticulous.'

In the kitchen, Barb opened a cupboard. 'Seen worse. Herbs and spices aren't even arranged alphabetically.' She turned to a SOCO. 'Computers?'

'Two,' the man said. 'Laptop, open on the dining room table. Another down in the basement. Looked like it hadn't been used in a while, probably an old one.'

'Get them back to Jane Scheune as soon as, please.'

Storm was on her phone and cupped the mic. 'Uniforms at Eustace's work say he hasn't been seen since he left the office yesterday morning. And from the mail by the door, he didn't come back here either.'

'He has ground to run to,' Barb said. 'Somewhere he had prepared.'

Storm made another call, hushed tones in the corner.

'The videos on the hard drive,' she said when she got off. 'I had someone in CSE look at them more thoroughly. It's hard to tell, because he keeps his face out of the frame, but they've tentatively identified Eustace in several other films. We're sending them to Dundee. There's a woman at the university, a doctor, who specialises in hands. Pigmentation, markings, fingernails, vein patterns. Some of the videos are of a good enough quality that we hope she can positively match the suspects' hands to other videos where we have their faces.'

'That's good for when we arrest him,' Barb said.

'The officer who looked at the videos identified three distinct locations. The cells at the dairy; four separate rooms at Clement Stevens's house; and a third room somewhere else that we haven't identified. One of the videos that he believes features Eustace was shot there. It's a small room with a bunk bed in the background.'

'Where he's hiding, you're thinking.'

'If it's secure enough for him to film at, he'll probably feel safe there now.'

'Could be anywhere.'

'I asked Mackintosh to look at the financial stuff on the hard drive. There were some company names. Might be properties owned by them or their directors. He's also checking for any holdings under any name linked with Killock.'

'All right, good.' Barb nodded. 'We'll not find anything here. Place is like a dressed set. It's arranged to show to normal people. There'll be nothing of his other life here.'

They were alone in the kitchen. Barb trailed a fingernail along the counter top, making a gravelly sound against its rough finish.

'Let me ask you something,' she said.

'Okay.'

'Boone. Do you think she's dangerous?'

'She who is short of memory and long of fang does a great job hurting herself.'

'Thanks, Confucius. To others, I mean. To the general public.'

'The general public? No, I don't think so. She's reckless. I used to think of her as an accident waiting for a victim. Dangerous in the same way train wrecks or ferry disasters are.'

'Those things are a threat to the general public.'

'What are you really asking me?'

'Whether she could hurt people, I suppose.'

'You know she could.'

'And kill?'

'Look, Barb, Abigail and Barry didn't see eye to eye, but—'

'No. God, no. Not that. I think it's clear Eustace is our man. I meant in a broader sense. The things she investigates, the way she hones in on the people she believes responsible. It's like her world is narrowed by anger. I wonder where that might lead.'

'The fire in Herefordshire?'

Barb shrugged.

'She can become obsessed,' Storm said. 'Look, all of us believe that the things that mean the most to us are universal. Love. Family. Friends. Work. Money. These are the things that fill our days. They're what most people recognise as the building blocks of life, because they're what we've always seen from when we were born. They are the things our parents did. All Abigail knows is a world of peril. She was born in a little room of death and survived to live a life that was never meant to be. Her building blocks are different.'

'So you don't think the old Abigail Boone remains at all?'

'It's difficult to talk in those terms. I never met Abigail before what happened. Trauma like that can profoundly change people. Inheritance takes many forms. We get some things through our blood, we get some things from a wider reservoir we all share. And other parts of us are given to us in different ways.'

'Jesus. I was looking for reassurance.'

'She's been out of prison five minutes. It's early. She's in contact with her son again. That's a good sign. She lost everything she has, so regaining some of it can only help.'

Barb got her phone out, fiddled about.

'She's down in Lark. Out at the cliffs, near the lighthouse. Go fetch her.'

'Now?'

'I want to see her. I want to know everything she knows about Eustace. Everything she ever told him. And everything she knows that she hasn't told us.'

'Barb, I think she's—'

'I know what she's doing. I don't give a shit. Go get her, and bring her to me.'

'Back at the nick?'

'She won't talk on record. No, I have a better idea.'

54

It was unseasonably warm, heat unsteadying the air even first thing. Boone regretted arriving early as there was so little shelter. She pulled the hood of her jacket up and sat on a bench with her back to the sea. At nine, the small coffee shop opened, the owner setting out chairs on the pavement, unfurling a tatty Union Jack awning. She went inside and made do with an Americano. The sun was already on the shop window, so she sat near the back, finding an angle where she could keep an eye on the pier.

She mothered her drink, deciding she'd had more than enough caffeine already, and nearly jumped out of her seat when she saw Quin's Saab go by. Lurking by the window, she watched him park in the small car park on the front and fetch himself a display ticket. Let him wander over to the pier before heading out after him.

'Hey.'

He turned, his smile promising the beginning of laughter, and approached her eagerly.

'Hi,' he said, opening his arms and embracing her. 'Glad you're here. Tess is always late.' Looking about, he cupped her elbow. 'Come on. Let's go over here.'

They walked onto the shingle beach. It was low tide and they crunched down under the pier, standing in the cool strip of shadow beneath it. Quin sent a text.

'Let her know where we are when she eventually gets here.'

He stooped to pick up a handful of pebbles, selected a likely candidate and tried to skim it out over the surf. It sank first splosh.

'Probably doesn't work in the sea,' he grinned. 'You used to be good at it.'

'I did?'

'Sure. We went to Ireland once. To . . .'

He paused, unsure of himself now he was stepping back into memory.

'I want to hear,' she said.

'We were in the mountains. Where all the flint is.'

'Wicklow.'

'Yeah. I was little. We drove up on a road that had huge drops either side. Probably wasn't anywhere near as bad as I remember. There was a lake up there. We had lunch and skimmed stones for ages. You could get them miles out.'

'Oi,' Tess shouted from up on the promenade.

They waved and climbed back up to her, leaving their reminiscing for the ebbing tide.

The day ripened apace, the three of them led round by Jim, who seemed to hold the secret of turning fuel into limitless energy. He played stall games, rode donkeys, flew on the zip cord, and was most delighted when Boone won him a four-foot stuffed giraffe at the shooting range, compensating for what felt like a deliberately calibrated pull to the left.

They lunched at The Ballroom at the head of the renovated pier, floor-to-ceiling windows upstairs offering a panorama of the sea. When they'd finished their meal, Quin took Jim out to the end of the pier to shout at seagulls and look through the penny telescopes.

'You almost look happy,' Tess said.

'Funny, isn't it?' said Boone. 'Week ago I was in prison and had no idea any of this was going to happen.'

'And the other stuff?'

'I thought that was done until what happened with Barry. I don't know who did that or how they fit into things.'

'But Sally is gone?'

'The police certainly think so. I don't think there's any way for them to confirm it for sure, but everyone seems satisfied that the bodies found in the fire were Sally and his son.'

'And what about you and Fitz? Are you certain?'

'Happy to take the police's word for it, trusting they know what they're doing.'

Tess looked far from convinced, but Boone didn't want to get into a discussion with her about what had gone down on the farm in Herefordshire.

'How is he?' Tess said. 'Fitzy?'

'About the same as Mick. I can't believe the two of them are living, what, ten or twelve miles apart in exactly the same foul mood as one another. Frankly, I don't know how you let that happen.'

'Me? How is this my fault?'

'You need to talk to Mick.'

'He won't listen to me.'

'He will only and always listen to you.'

'You didn't see him. He was so mad he was almost Zen.'

'I've seen him now. He looks like an old man. And that pile needs fixing. And that boy used to love mucking about with Fitz, whether he knew they were blood or not.'

'I've tried to ask him before and—'

'Do you want Fitz back in your lives?'

'Of course.'

'Then don't ask. Tell him. Tell him what you want and why. Get them in the same room. You had no problem being decisive when it was getting me and Quin together.'

'Happiness certainly makes you feisty, doesn't it?'

Later, they drove down the coast to the cliffs, with Jim insisting Boone ride in the back of the SUV with him so they could discuss her marksmanship and he could tell her that Tess had told him several times that he wasn't to ask about her scar. Which he didn't. Boone had her camera, and from atop the cliffs she showed Jim the chalky grin of the French coast.

Tess had brought drinks and snacks. Behind the lighthouse, they sat out on the grassy shelf in the breeze and watched Jim scamper around, until he decided that weeds and flowers looked tastier than carrot sticks and Tess had to chase after him, scooping greenery out of his mouth.

'Vile creatures, kids,' Boone said.

'You can't say that.' Quin laughed.

'Why not? I used to be one. Well, I assume I did.'

'I used to collect morning fluff,' he said.

'Morning fluff? Do I want to hear this?'

'Almost certainly not. I'd get into bed with you and Dad and pick the lint out of his belly button.'

'Oh, Jesus.'

'And you'd make a face pretty much like the one you're making right now.'

Tess wandered back carrying one tuckered-out and slightly tearful Jim, still spitting bits of flora.

'He's tired and grumpy,' she said. 'I better get him back.'

'I'll drop this one off,' Quin said.

They drummed on the window and made faces as Tess strapped Jim into his seat, and waved profusely when she left. Jim was already falling asleep.

'I used to love that,' Quin said.

'Eating weeds?'

'Falling asleep. It was a kind of magic of childhood. I'd fall asleep in a car or in someone's house, but wake up somewhere else. In my own bed, or once I remember coming round on top of a pile of coats in someone's spare room.'

Boone laughed, mostly to cover a pang she felt. Her memory had been whipped out as easily as tonsils, and since then pleasant events had been few and far between so she hadn't fostered her memory as a harbour for sentiment. Listening to Quin, though, the things she couldn't remember broke her heart, because they'd happened in the past and the past was gone.

'I have something for you,' he said, opening the boot of the Saab. 'That stuff we talked about before. Old pictures and what have you. Your father's golf medal. I've scanned all the photos, so I've got them backed up. You should have the originals.'

They sat in the car and flicked through the pictures. Some colour, some monochrome, some somewhere in between. All different shapes and sizes. The wayward fragments of a life forgotten.

'You look like her,' he said, holding a picture of Boone's mother.

'I know. That freaked me out when your father first showed me all of these. Like the universe was mocking me. Telling me it had all happened before, whether I knew it or not.'

'Look in there, inside that envelope,' Quin said. 'The big folded one. There are letters and stuff in there.'

'Uh huh.'

'The postcard?'

Boone found the card. It was a photographic image of a view from Signal Hill across the harbour to the town of St John's on Newfoundland. On the back was written, *Dearest John, I'm sorry. Be happy. Your Sandra.*

Boone stared at it, her mind blank.

'Found it by chance,' Quin said. 'Do you remember those Victorian-style postcards?'

Years ago, just after the whole memory debacle, she'd found a thick packet of old-fashioned resort cards in amongst her father's things. They were blank on the back, part of someone's collection, though she couldn't imagine whose.

'I dropped them, and they went everywhere,' Quin went on. 'Putting them back in their packet, I found that among them and remembered what you'd said. Your father must have slipped it in there.'

'I probably never looked though them,' Boone said. 'Just pulled a couple out to see what they were and ignored them.'

'Abigail Boone the detective,' Quin said.

'Oi.'

He grinned. 'What do you think it means?'

Boone couldn't get over it. How could there be a postcard if her mother had never held a passport. How did she leave the country?

Quin said, 'Mum, you think it's real?'

She looked at him. Mum. She hid how much she enjoyed that.

'It looks like her handwriting,' she said. 'There are letters she sent Dad years before.' She rooted about in the large envelope. 'Here. The way she embellished the S in her name? Looks the same.'

'So she did go to Canada?'

'Maybe,' she said.

Maybe she was a woman who knew how to make herself disappear, she thought. Maybe, forty years apart, they had more in common than Boone had realised. The truth was, she hadn't thought much about her mother in prison, and even less since reuniting with Quin. For as long as she could remember, it had felt as though the reservoir of loneliness and fear would only continue to swell and rise around her, but now it seemed that so too did the consolations of love, if she would only allow them to.

During that brief twilight between her accident and her imprisonment, her relationship with Quin consisted largely of them both wondering if it actually existed. Now more familiar with herself, she could see more of her in him, a tangible connection. An expression or a gesture, the way he sighed. How much of ourselves did we inherit and how much were we given along the way? He was funny, made her laugh. In his company, she found herself wondering what that unusual sensation was, and would realise she was smiling. He made her feel. He made her want to feel more.

For the first time, she was realising that the future could be within her, something to converge with rather than an external force whose propeller blades she charged headlong into. She had reconciled herself to her life's work, the hunting of people who did harm to the vulnerable. Resisting it had been to resist gravity, which was hopeless, as gravity came from the heft of the world. She could see now that the work didn't have to mean removing herself from the world, though.

'I was thinking,' she said tentatively. 'Maybe one evening, if I cooked dinner—'

'Yes.'

'Yes?'

'Of course.'

'I have this stuff with the police to sort out. I thought it was done, but . . .'

'Tess told me about the policeman who was hurt. I'd seen it on the news but didn't realise you knew him. How bad is it?'

'Bad. Barb's not really talking about it, but she didn't sound hopeful.'

There was a quiet moment, the sharper edges of their shared history passing close by.

'This thing I do,' Boone said. 'Finding these men, these monsters. I thought that in order to do that, it would be better to insulate myself. Cut off all ties. Because of things that happened to me, like the thing that has happened to Barry. More I think about it, though, more I believe I got that wrong. You have to have connections with people, for the exact same reasons. Because of what happened to me. Because of what has happened to Barry.'

'Those things could happen to you again.'

'I've been reckless. I sought confrontations because I believed they would give me something.' She pointed to her heart. 'In here. But they didn't. They took things instead. More things. There are other ways of doing what I do. Ways that won't put me and people I care about in hazard.'

'You're not getting sensible, are you?'

'There's a distinct danger of it, yeah.'

'So you help Barb catch whoever hurt Barry, and afterwards we'll get together. Break bread.'

'Definitely.'

'And I can see this new place of yours.'

'I'm suddenly having second thoughts.'

Somewhere along the line she'd found his hand and held it now. Big, much bigger than hers.

'I was thinking,' he said. 'About you and Dad.'

'Go on.'

'I know things ended—weirdly. And I don't know how you both feel about this, I haven't spoken to him, but I was wondering about the two of you being in the same place together at some point.'

'You have something specific in mind?'

'It's not for a couple of years yet, but my graduation. I'd really like for you both to be there.'

'There's no blame at your father's door with what happened between us, Quin. That was all me, and I'd love to be at your graduation, as long as it's not a problem for him. I don't imagine it would be. Even if he couldn't stand the sight of me, he'd do whatever you wanted.'

'I've never got the impression of any animosity from him. Just sadness, the first few years. I think he's past it now.'

'Good. I was half thinking about reaching out to him, actually. This stuff with my mum, and my history in general. He's the only link I have.'

'Mum.'

'Hmm?'

'Mum.'

She looked up at him and saw his gaze was elsewhere. She followed it and found a Kent Police Skoda.

Storm approached the Saab. 'I'm sorry,' was all she said.

The thing with gravity, it wasn't just too strong to resist; it was strong enough to bend time and space.

55

Barb stood with her back to them at the foot of the four stone steps that led up to Clem Stevens's house by the sea. Boone got out, but Storm remained in the car. She said nothing when Boone looked back at her.

'I used to think it was metaphorical,' Barb said. 'Getting blood from a stone. Like, how could you wound stone? How could you make it bleed? It's more literal than that, though, isn't it?'

She stood back so Boone could see the dark stain on the bottom and second steps.

'It's that cleaning blood from stone is fucking impossible.'

'Look, Barb—'

Barb slapped her sharply across the mouth, and then again.

Boone stood in stunned silence, like a scolded child overwhelmed by the confrontation. She wanted to cry.

'Barry died twenty minutes ago,' Barb said. 'You're going to tell me everything I want to know, and there'll be none of your bullshit.'

Storm stepped out of the car. 'Barbara.'

Barb held up a finger.

'She'll talk. Here and now. No recorders. No witnesses. Only us. Barry is dead, and I know who killed him, and I mean to find him and see him punished. And she will help with that.'

'You know who killed him?' Boone said, confused.

'Eustace,' said Barb.

'Eustace? *Harry* Eustace? I don't understand.'

'We got into the hard drive,' Storm said. 'There were videos on there, like you said. In some of them, the men are identifiable. One of them is Eustace.'

Barb said, 'We thought Barry's final words were "You stay". But he was telling us who stuck a knife into him. Who stabbed him fourteen times. Who murdered him.'

All of this was breaking over Boone's head quicker than she could come up for air. 'I don't—'

'You don't have to. All you need to do right now is answer my questions to my satisfaction. Firstly, the hard drive. It came from that house in Herefordshire. The house where Sally and Ferg died. Explain.'

'I don't know,' Boone said. 'I found it outside my door. Perhaps my source—'

'Oh shut the fuck up,' Barb snapped. 'For Christ's sake. Your source? Your fucking source? It's Fitzgerald. That's obvious to everyone. The pair of you, out at the Welsh border to confront Sally and Ferg. You end up with the hard drive and they end up dead and burnt to a crisp.'

'We didn't kill them,' Boone said.

'No? Like you didn't kill Hanley Moss and Lady Blackborne? I don't believe you.'

Boone sucked her bottom lip. Her face smarted. It had begun to swell immediately. She wondered if the gathered dead of her life trailed behind her for all to see like baby ducklings.

'Barb, I swear to you that I did not kill Sally or his son,' she said quietly. 'And those other deaths, you investigated them yourself.'

'West Mercia found a cache of weapons and ammunition in Herefordshire,' Barb said. 'Shotgun cartridges, hand-loaded. Same as the Moss murder-suicide. Did you think nobody would notice the pattern?'

'Sally was sick,' Boone said. 'He was in a bed with drips and moni-
tors and when we got there, he was already dead. Someone had
smothered him. Ferg turned up and told us he had done it, that his
father had told him to. And then he pulled out a shotgun he'd hidden
in the bed and blew his brains out in front of us. If the ammunition's
the same, then maybe they killed Moss and Blackborne. I mean, why
would I leave my own weapons and shells there to be found?'

Boone amazed even herself with her facility for bullshit.

Barb just laughed. 'You were right, you know? You were right all
along.'

Boone frowned.

'My friend Abigail Boone, she's gone. She's been gone for years. She
died in that flat in east London and you're what was left in her place.
Having you here is like being haunted by some dreadful spectre. It's
obscene. You're an abomination.'

'Barb—'

'Don't you fucking Barb me. All these things that have happened.
How many of them were avoidable if you had just been frank with us?
What would have happened if you had just let the police handle police
business?'

'I'm sorry about Barry, I really am,' Boone said. 'But I didn't kill
him. I didn't even know Eustace was involved, and that's the truth. I
gave you the hard drive, for God's sake. Did I hide things? Yeah. Fine.
But don't you lecture me on what should be left to the police. How
much help were the police to Sarah Still? Missing for years and found
buried in a fruit farm with her hands hacked off. How much help were
you when I was abducted? I don't remember anyone kicking in the
door to rescue me. How much help were you when Roo was taken?
None. Had to find her myself. How much help were you to Noah
Maxwell? Still missing, three decades later. And what about Sarah
Still's daughter, Molly? Taken at birth by powerful people. Prominent

people. And abandoned into an existence of horror and misery. How did the police help her?

'How much help were you to the fuck-knows-how-many children raped or killed by Sally, and Jerry Killock, and now Harry Eustace, apparently? In fact, not only were you of absolutely no help, but it was your lot who actively hindered investigations and facilitated the crimes those men perpetrated. At this point, I can't even be sure they didn't participate.'

'This going to be about Roy Fuller again?'

'How do you think these men got away with it for so long, Barb? You think they're geniuses, or fucking invisible? This shit is institutional. Killock and Eustace in social services, finding vulnerable kids. And men inside the police drawing investigations away, helping cover it up.'

'Bullshit. Bloody hell, Boone, you'll say anything at this point. Roy Fuller is filth, but I'll not listen to you blame this on the force when—'

'I didn't lose Fuller,' Boone cut in.

'What?'

'The day we were tailing him, I didn't lose him like I said. And I didn't drive out of radio range to Folkestone.'

'No shit. Tell me something I don't know.'

'Okay. I followed Fuller to a house in the country, where he met with John Bardin.'

'John Bardin? You mean—'

'Yeah, that John Bardin. Retired ACC John Bardin of Kent Police. And then we, Fitzy and I, followed him across the country to a farmhouse a few hundred yards from the Welsh border, where he met Sally and Ferg and told them that we were coming. The same police you want me to leave matters to are the very people allowing it to happen.'

'You can prove this?'

'Photographs of Fuller and Bardin. And then Bardin and Ferg.

Sally was bedridden, presumably. I don't know if it's enough for the courts.'

'So you decided to take matters into your hands and save us the time and expense of a complicated trial. How very altruistic of you, ta very much.'

'I told you. We didn't kill them. Sally was already dead and Ferg used the shotgun to make it . . .'

'Make it what?'

'Nothing.'

'No. Please do go on. Make it what? Make it look like you did it? Make it look like your previous handiwork?'

'His shotgun. His ammunition. I was nothing to do with it.'

'Barry was convinced, you know. Absolutely, cast-iron, one hundred per cent certain that you murdered Hanley Moss and Lady Blackborne in the woods that day, and then made it look like a murder-suicide. He was almost impressed by it. The pipe was what bothered him. He couldn't work out why Moss would empty and repack his pipe if he was going to kill himself. Small thing. Tiny thing, really. But it was enough to work a little worry line into the case for him. And the more he looked at it, the surer he became that someone else's hand was at work. Your hand. He was right, wasn't he? Sally and Ferg, I don't know. Maybe you're telling the truth about that. But Moss. Blackborne. That was you.'

'Listen, Barb—'

'I want to hear you say it. I want to hear you say you did it.'

'I want to hear you say it's a bad thing that they're dead.'

'I'm a fucking police officer, Boone. So were you, once.'

'And what good did that do? They've operated for decades with impunity. Aided and protected by the same people who were supposed to stop them. My life got blown up exposing them, and still nothing happened.'

'How do I not arrest you right now? How am I not supposed to bring four murder charges against you?'

'I didn't kill Sally or—'

'Je–sus Christ.'

'I'm not in cuffs because you don't have anything on me, and you never will.'

'Oh, if I start digging into this, believe you me, I'll find something.'

'Then do it. I'd love to have my day in court. What would your case sound like? How would it begin? Motive? Ladies and gentlemen of the jury, Boone killed these two peers of old Blighty because they did interfere with and murder young children of a number we cannot specify. You name the day, I'll get in the dock and tell everything I know to anyone who'll listen.'

Barb sat on the bonnet of her Audi. Her shoulders sank.

'You'd never get out of remand alive,' she said.

'Probably not, no.'

'I don't know what to do with you. I don't know what to do with any of this.'

'Yes you do. You're Detective Inspector Barbara Bowen and someone has killed one of your officers. You're going to find him and you're going to bring him to account.'

'And you?'

'I'll help.'

'How do I let you run around, knowing what I know?'

'I'm not going on safari. When Storm found me earlier, I was with Quin. I was with my son. His childhood was stolen from me, Barb. My first memories of him are as a teenager. Then I got myself jailed and missed him becoming a man. I don't want to miss any more. I don't want to become something that shames him.'

'Bit fucking late.'

'I'm not looking to hunt. I'm looking to capture.'

'Well, if you pinky promise not to kill anyone else . . .'

An unstill silence followed, a frisson between them, the air crackling with things unsaid but agreed upon, not confessed but conceded.

Barb looked to Storm. 'What do we have?'

'Mackintosh sent me a list of properties that we've tied to either Killock or Eustace, via various aliases and company names. Looks like they had quite the housing portfolio. Most of them are rentals, handled by a management firm. Killock had been buying them up since the eighties. We've got uniforms knocking on them.'

'Land rent was always the toffs' big earner,' Barb said. 'Maggie made it the national industry.'

'And the Chief Super has been after you,' Storm said.

'Yeah,' said Barb. 'They'll be concerned about crossover. The Killock thing and Barry's murder. I reckon they'll take everything Eustace-related away from us. Maybe remove me completely.'

'They wouldn't do that,' Storm said.

'Who knows how long they can trust me to remain emotionally stable, eh? We don't have long. Chief Super won't allow days of property searches as part of the broader investigation. When he finds out we think Sally and Ferg are dead, so there's no chance for any prosecutions, he'll want us to start wrapping things up.'

'If Boone's right about all this, then who can we trust?' Storm said.

Barb shook her head. 'Nobody. But we can't hide the investigation that exists on paper. What isn't official, we keep between the three of us until we know what's going on.'

She looked at her phone.

'Nine missed calls. He'll have the raging bossman shits by now. I better go back to the Shed and see him.'

'Where do you want me?' Storm said.

'You said we're knocking on doors, the rentals?'

'Yep.'

'Any other properties of interest?'

'South of Lark, there's a plot of land. Had a look online and it appears to be a field. Nothing built on it.'

'Check it out anyway. Take this one with you,' she said, jerking her head at Boone. 'And it'd be nice if she didn't kill anyone.'

56

It was Storm who broke the silence.

'You okay?'

'I'm not sure. An hour ago I was talking to my son and allowing my-self to imagine new and pleasant futures. A lot has happened since then.'

'You know Barbara better than I, but I think if she was seriously going to move on you, you'd be in custody right now.'

'And if she doesn't, it could ruin her. She does nothing and some-one else tries to lay Sally at my door, it'd end her career.'

'If you didn't kill him, how could anyone do that?'

'The sniff of it would be enough.'

'You said you found him dead. You had gone there with the inten-tion of ending his life, though.'

'That a question?'

'No.'

'Anything you do want to ask?'

'No.'

'You think Barb's making a mistake, though.'

'I think murder is murder, Abigail.'

'Bullshit. Everything's a situation. There are different kinds of fac-tors. Different kinds of people.'

'And what kind were Hanley Moss and Theodora Blackborne?'

'The kind that needed killing.'

'Maybe we just talk about something else.'

'Fine weather we're having. Going anywhere nice this year? That top really suits you.'

'This is it,' Storm said, pulling the car over to the side of the road, two wheels on a thin grass verge.

Boone looked about. They were only separated from the sea by a couple of hundred yards, but the view was completely obscured by houses, their rear gardens backing onto the road. Opposite, the ground rose steeply in a thickly bushed bank.

'Where?' she said.

'Other side of that bank,' Storm said.

'Don't see a way through to it.'

'There.' Storm pointed. 'Public footpath sign.'

The green sign and its post had been almost completely swallowed by a tree. Boone could just see the red circle of a no-cycling sign above it. Storm eased the car over as far to the side as she could and they got out. Behind the sign was a wooden stile, and beyond that a pathway leading up the bank in timber-faced steps cut into the earth. The pathway carried on the other side of the bank along the edge of the fields before turning inland fifty yards further down.

'It's that one,' Storm said, looking at her phone and pointing to a field in the other direction.

A low wire fence bordered the path. Boone shrugged and vaulted over it into the field. She heard Storm land behind her.

'You used to hate getting your boots dirty,' Boone said. 'Faces you'd pull if we took a stroll by the caravan.'

'Things change in four years. You think you know a person.'

'I'm nothing now that I wasn't the day I met you.'

'You're a killer.'

'Day I woke up in that flat, I'd have killed the men who abducted me if I could have.'

'You're a thief too.'

'The sheep? That wasn't—that was because of the other thing. It was to get to Sally.'

'So you'd never done jobs for Mick before that? All those trips you went on and never talked about?'

First time she'd met him, even Storm had known Mickey Box wasn't a Michael. Boone made a face and grumbled beneath her breath.

'Stop being childish,' Storm said.

'You liked all that stuff.'

'I did not. What stuff?'

'Mick and Fitz, being close to all that outlaw caper.'

'Don't be absurd.'

'I don't know a lot, but I know what I know,' Boone said.

She looked about the field. The earth had been ploughed years ago but had been left to grow over and hadn't been tended to in some time. Nearly waist-high grass swayed gently in the breeze, the ground uneven below it.

'How do you even get into this place?' Boone said. 'Bunking over a fence from a public path can't be the only way.'

Probably four hundred yards long as it ran parallel to the road, the field was half that wide, going further inland. At the far reaches in that direction was an earthen rise, up to head height in places and perhaps twenty yards in length, artificially made as if soil had been bulldozed into a pile. Picking her way carefully across the treacherous terrain, Boone made for it in hope of a better view.

Scrambling up the slope, she found another country lane the other side. Not far along there was a gated entrance to the field that had been obscured by the ridge. The embankment itself was wild with bushes and thick blackberry brambles, limiting where she could walk atop it.

'Gate round here off another road,' she said.

Storm walked around to the other side of the rise, where the gap between it and the fence was wide enough for a vehicle to park.

'Tyre tracks maybe,' she said, crouching down.

'Recent?'

Storm shrugged.

'The buffalo are safe with you on their trail.'

'Shut up.'

'Why on earth would anyone come here?' Boone said. Shielding her eyes with her hand, she looked up and down the field. There was nothing she could see, but the grass was long and it was heavily hedged along two sides. Something could be hidden amid the growth.

'There's nothing here,' Storm said.

'Just this mote, or whatever it is,' Boone said, kicking the heads off dandelions on the ridge around her.

The dense briars rolled off the edge into a patch of lower ground that extended to the hedge with the adjoining field. Boone edged along the slope of the finger-shaped rise, the brambles catching on her and tugging her clothes, until she got to the end. Where the ground fell back down to field level, there was a patch of brown, dead growth, so tightly packed together it looked as if it might have been arranged by hand.

She jumped down from the embankment and came at the bushes from another angle, nearer the hedge. She was almost invisible there, hidden from the road by the overgrown pile and sheltered by the hedge and long grass from almost any other view. She tugged at the brown branches and they lifted away as one, a rude gate thatched together from dead shoots. Beneath it, painted green, was some kind of concrete protuberance, with a metal hatch on top.

'Storm, over here.'

By the time Storm had worked her way round, Boone had the hatch open and was staring down a square shaft with an iron ladder bolted into one wall.

'What the hell is this?'

'Bunker, looks like,' Boone said.

She found the flashlight on her phone and shone it into the blackness. The walls were a grubby white, streaked with mossy lines. The floor, fifteen feet below, looked wet.

'Fuck it,' she said, stepping in and finding the top rung with her foot.

'We can't go in, Abigail. We need a warrant.'

'You said we had warrants for all the properties.'

'Yeah, but we didn't know there was . . . whatever this is. I'm not sure it's covered. We should probably apply for a new one.'

'Must be joking. It's literally an underground lair. I'm going in.'

'We can't.'

'*You* can't. Do you see jackboots on me? I don't mind a bit of trespass.'

She lowered herself into the shaft and was gone, phone in her mouth, flashing broken shards of light around the murk beneath her. At the final step, her foot went through the rung, which had come away on one side, and she stumbled backwards, falling against two large water barrels.

'Abigail?'

'I'm fine. Bottom step is broken.'

The floor under the ladder was a grille, covering a soakaway. A small nook behind the ladder housed a chemical toilet. An open doorway led from the small chamber at the bottom of the shaft to the only proper room in the structure. Fifteen feet long and half that wide, a metal-framed bunk bed standing against the far end, with a counter built against the left wall housing a rudimentary kitchen: washbasin, small fridge, portable stove with butane bottles. Cupboards underneath stored dried foodstuff. A kettle had water in it, and a cup in the basin looked recently used.

When Boone started yelling, Storm only touched about three steps on the way down, bursting into the room not knowing what to expect. She found Boone sitting on the bottom bunk, smiling sweetly.

'Abigail, what the hell?'

'Warrant, schmarrant,' Boone said.

'I thought you were—unbelievable.' She forgot her anger as she took in the room. 'Christ, this is the place. This is where the other videos were shot.'

'Someone's been here,' Boone said, jerking her head towards the sink. 'Underground bunker. Hidden entrance in a wholly unremarkable field. Perfect, really. He has water. Twelve-volt battery for a bit of power. Weird place.'

'Old observation bunker,' Storm said. She looked at her phone. 'I have to call this in. No signal. Come on, let's go back up.'

'Hmm,' Boone said, peering inside the cupboards.

'Don't touch anything,' Storm said. 'Forensics will have kittens.'

She clambered back up the ladder and Boone dawdled about, looking in the nook where the toilet was, trying to see behind the water barrels. There was a disappointing lack of evidence of anything other than someone's very recent presence.

Stepping up onto the ladder, she heard voices. Storm on the phone, she thought, but then there was another voice, a male voice. Storm was trying to placate him, but her tone was familiar, as if she knew him.

Eustace.

He'd returned, and having killed one cop, he wouldn't be pleased about finding another at his hiding place.

Boone dropped lightly back down to the floor. Grabbing the end of the rung that had come away from the rest of the ladder, she quickly worked it this way and that until the other end snapped loose, providing her with a weapon of sorts. Quickly but quietly, she climbed up the ladder, keeping below the mouth of the shaft.

'There's no need for the knife,' Storm said. 'I'm unarmed and alone. You're in control here, Harry.'

'Harry. As if you've any idea who I am.'

'This doesn't have to go badly, Harry. You've already got the whole force out looking for you. They know I'm here.'

She was talking to Boone as much as Eustace, letting her know the lie of the land. Her voice was moving away from the entrance to the bunker, trying to get Eustace focusing in another direction.

Boone chanced a peek.

Storm had backed away further into the field and was looking at the mound. Boone couldn't see Eustace because of the bushes. He was either on top of the mound or just in front of it.

Keeping low, she lifted herself out of the shaft and crouched down beside the concrete entrance. Seeing his head, up above the mound, she sank down lower. If she was going to do something, she'd have to do it fast.

Getting a firm grip on one end of the iron rod, she sprang out and charged him, roaring at the top of her voice. Eustace's head swung round when he saw her. Maybe surprised that anyone would come at him when he had a seven-inch KA-BAR knife, or maybe bewildered by the sight of a wild Boone brandishing a metal bar, he remained rooted to the spot.

Pulling her arm back, as she reached the foot of the mound, Boone let fly, throwing the rod like an axe. End over end it tumbled through the air and clonked Eustace above his eye, sending him reeling backwards.

He didn't hang about. Sliding down the far side of the mound, he got into a blue Astra and floored it, wheels spinning and throwing up clods of mud until the tyres caught on the tarmac lane and he was off, Boone standing atop the mound, watching him go.

'You okay?' she said.

'Yeah,' said Storm. 'You?'

'Sort of glad he scarpered. Not sure what I was going to do when I didn't have the metal rod any longer. You get the plate?'

Storm nodded. 'Calling it in.'

'He'll dump it, but he won't have anywhere to hide now.'

57

A patrol car arrived and uniforms secured the scene and awaited Forensics. Storm drove Boone back to the Shed to take her statement, but Barb met them at the door.

'She'll be speaking to detectives from Braintree,' she said.

'Essex are taking over?' said Storm.

'Anything to do with Eustace is theirs now. Barry's murder, and any and all offences committed prior. ACC is putting a team together from across Serious Crimes. They want officers who weren't connected with the case or its historical antecedents. We thought it best if they came from our sister force. Extend them every courtesy.'

'We're not just going to—' Storm started.

'And then meet me afterwards,' Barb said.

Boone told the detectives what had happened at the bunker, and gave them a rundown of her previous with Eustace. Barb watched the feed with great interest.

'Melee weapons now, is it?' was all she said when Boone came into her office afterwards.

Storm and Mackintosh were there, and Jane appeared, having pulled apart Eustace's hard drives and gone through his online histories.

'Nothing,' she said. 'Mostly work stuff. We're liaising with social services on what we should and shouldn't see from that. Rest of the stuff is benign. He has some magazine subscriptions, downloads from them. Film and music titles, nothing salacious. There are some MP3s, but he also has a Spotify account.'

'Browser history?' said Barb.

'Work stuff. Some news sites. Apparently he liked fishing. But there's no dirty stuff.'

'None at all?'

'Not even the Mail Online.'

'Maybe he has a porn phone,' said Mackintosh. 'You know, a spare handset to—'

'Probably divulging too much information there, Tosh,' Barb said. 'But you have a point. We know he's filmed his abuse. And he must be familiar with Sally's dark web sites. No camera was recovered, so missing devices are a possibility. We got a warrant in with his ISP?'

Storm nodded. 'And his mobile provider. They're both falling over themselves to get us full histories.'

'Remind them it would be unfortunate if the press discovered they were hindering an investigation into a cop-murdering child rapist. That would be tricky for them to explain.' Barb looked at Boone. 'What do you know about Sally's online behaviour? The dark sites and what not.'

'Nothing,' Boone said.

'You had the video of Killock, and a bunch of others.'

'Fitzy got them a couple of years back. Some Japanese software? That stuff all changes so quickly.'

'Let me know the details and I'll get into it,' Jane said.

'I can give him a bell. No way in hell he comes in here, but I'll ask him what he knows.'

'I can arrest him, if need be,' said Barb.

'That's not how you get Fitz to talk. You cuff him, you'll get nothing.

He'd do a stretch just to spite you. If you think I try your patience, I've nothing on him. Let me deal with him.'

'Thanks for letting me know how to get people talking. A wonder I ever got along in this job without you.'

'Where do we stand with the original investigation?' Storm said, stepping in before things got off colour.

'Still ours. Upstairs want the investigations run separately. We're to liaise with West Mercia over these bodies, whether they're Sally and Ferg, see if we can get anything on them. Jerry Killock and how he tied into this remains our concern, but anything that leads back to Harry Eustace we're to hand over to the murder inquiry team. Okay?'

They all nodded.

'Okay. See you tomorrow then. Not you, Boone. I'll call you if and when. I recommend you stay at home until you hear from me.'

Outside, Storm offered Boone a lift back to Lark.

'She's dealing with what happened to Barry,' she said. 'Just let her get on with it and try not to antagonise her.'

'It's more than that and you know it. It's the other stuff, and the fact that Barry was the one who told her.'

'Well what do you want, Abigail? A medal pinning on for shooting two people?'

'Be four people if Barb has her way.'

'She doesn't believe you killed Sally. She just—we're police, Abigail. Even if you didn't kill Sally, we need to know this sort of thing isn't going to happen again.' She glanced at Boone.

'Man's dead. Can't argue it would be better some other way.'

'Abigail . . .'

'Kept the girl in a box, Storm. In a fucking box, from birth, every day of her miserable life, to be brought out only to be abused in unspeakable ways. Happened so often that it became her everyday, became the only language or process she ever understood. It was the sole truth of her existence. My killing that fat piece of shit would have been a gift to the world.'

'Killing isn't justice, Abigail.'

'No, it isn't. It's vengeance. Bollocks to justice. What has she done for any of us? Daft cow standing there in a blindfold. You think she unsighted herself? Did she fuck. Promise you, as sure as I am of anything, it was a man who slipped that over her head. What a joke. Don't need the scales, don't want the blindfold. Fine with just the sword and seeing where I'm sticking it. You show me a justice who's watching what she's doing, and we'll talk again.'

Storm kept her eyes on the road, said nothing.

Killing wasn't the problem for Boone. She'd done it before and had lost no sleep. It wasn't the ones she'd killed that came back, lurking between the trees at the back of her mind, beckoning her into the dark. It was all the others who'd been lost.

Sarah Still.

Barry.

Roo.

Always Roo.

To dull the edge of the silence in the car, she called Fitz.

'It's me,' she said.

'People always say that, even though their name comes up.'

'Conversations have to start some way. How would it be if I just launched into whatever it was I called for?'

'Suits me.'

'No witty gambit? No introductory preamble? What are we, barbarians?'

'Boone.'

'The videos you got off the net. The one with Killock and the others.'

'Aye?'

'Police want telling how exactly you got them.'

'I used an old Japanese program to access a dark net. Sally cleared off that soon after, though. Listen, I'll give you the details later. I've got something on right now.'

'Ooh. A lady friend?'

'I have to go.'

The line went dead.

'Hmm. That was perfunctory even for him.'

She looked around, realising they weren't heading for Lark. 'Where we going?'

'To see how Molly is doing.'

'Yeah,' Boone said. 'Yeah, okay.'

Late afternoon, clouds glowed like hot coals above the lowering sun. A Kent Police Skoda was angled up on the grass beside the automated gate on the private road into the Redfearn Institute, one door open and a constable sitting with his legs outside, talking on the radio. Another constable sat in the small booth and leaned out when Storm pulled up and lowered her window, showing her card.

'What's this?'

'Press found her,' the constable said. 'All ins and outs to be checked.'

'Shit. How many?'

'Just the one been here so far.'

'Local or national?'

'National. Redtop shitrag. He caused a bit of a fuss. No doubt there will be more once they print it.'

'How the hell did they track her down?'

Boone snorted. 'Yeah, I can't imagine who told them when only about a hundred coppers know.'

The long boom of the barrier lurched upright and the constable waved them through. The grounds of the clinic were mostly deserted, just a few staff cars remaining. Storm grabbed a shopping bag from the back of her SUV. Ravi John, looking rather gnawed on, was sitting on a bench with a cigarette burning down between his fingers. Storm sat beside him.

'Going that well?'

'Bad day. Long, bad day.'

'Heard about the reporter.'

'That wasn't a reporter. Didn't want a statement, didn't ask after the girl's well-being, didn't even come to reception. He was found trying to get into a utility door round back.'

'You don't think someone from here tipped him off?'

'If they did, they didn't do a very good job. The door leads to the storage rooms for the gardening staff. They don't give access to the building proper. But I don't think so, no.'

'How's Molly?'

Ravi scrunched his eyes shut. 'Ask me another one.'

'We can come back if it's not a good time.'

He shook his head. 'No, you should come up. She's been calmer the last few hours. This morning was . . . difficult. It's pointless drawing together any firm thoughts on her condition at this early a stage, but she's so deeply traumatised, and so utterly unequipped to handle . . . anything, really.'

They walked with him into the clinic and up the stairs to the suite where Molly was cared for. From the observation room, they saw the girl pressing herself into a corner with her knees drawn up. A nurse sat quietly on a chair across the room.

'We have someone with her twenty-four hours,' Ravi said. 'Finding the balance of when to interact and when to leave her be is the challenge at the moment.'

'Last time, you talked about sign language,' said Storm.

Ravi shook his head. 'I really don't know. It's what I'd like to do, but we're probably talking about months, if not years away.'

'And speaking?'

'I'd be amazed if she learned a language to any level of competency now. What these people did to her, it's probably the worst case I've ever seen.'

'Well, most of them have been . . . accounted for,' Storm said.

'What does her future look like?' Boone said. 'What's the endgame here?'

'There is no end,' Ravi said. 'Not for someone like her. There's going to be a slog and we'll do what we can to make it incrementally better. Better being a relative term. It's not going to be a long process – it's going to be an endless one. It's going to be the rest of her life. Short term, it'll take us a couple of months to draw up a real plan, something that will see us working towards establishing communication. That's the main step now. It's as if she has just been born and we have to help her put everything that has happened previously behind her and start again.'

Of course there would be no end, Boone thought. Endings needed stories to come before them, and Molly had no story. Had no life. If there was any fortune to the events at all, it was that she would be cared for now, that things were as good as they would get. She tried to imagine a future for the girl, but coming back from a beginning that bad would be a miracle. She'd never know the world, or make herself known to it.

'We have this,' Storm said, taking the stuffed dog out of the carrier bag.

'This was hers?' Ravi said.

'She had it when we found her.'

'Okay. I'll see how it goes. I'm not sure how she'll react to it, so I might leave it a while. Hopefully she'll get used to her new environment, start to find faces familiar. Then maybe I'll give it to her.'

Molly burst from her corner suddenly, scuttling along the wall towards the nurse, whom she spat and hissed at. The nurse remained calm, but Boone was startled at the display of ferality, the unhumanness of it.

'You'll have to excuse me,' Ravi said.

'We'll see ourselves out,' Storm said.

'Give her a few weeks to settle in, see where we are, and then we might try visitors. If you're up for it?'

'I'd like that,' Storm said. 'Let me know.'

Boone nodded and murmured something. She felt the tug of some nearly insurmountable obligation to the girl, knowing now as she did that she had been in the dairy at the same time. That perhaps she could have spared her four more years of unimaginable misery. Boone also knew a few things that nobody else around the girl would. Knew about not having a past, about becoming reborn. She knew there were some broken parts of yourself that you could never repair, never get over, no matter the good intentions of others.

The drive to Lark was quiet. There was an unspeakable weight to the things they were doing, a weight that manifested in the stolen life of that mindless girl and in the meaningless death of Detective Constable Barry Tayleforth. Things that didn't need to be talked about, not yet.

A modest sunset was burning out behind the empty lot across from Boone's garage.

'You want a coffee or something?' said Boone.

'I would, but Barb is still going to be at the Shed. I don't want her there alone all night.'

'No, quite right.'

Boone got out and swung the gate open.

'Abigail.'

Storm was standing with her car door open.

'Yeah?'

'You were wrong.'

'About what?'

'I'm not married. Not really. We separated months ago. Turns out architects and charity galas are exactly as boring as you made them sound.'

'Sorry.'

'I'm not. We had some fun and along the way learned we weren't right for one another. Not full time. I still speak with her occasionally. We both knew pretty quickly that it wasn't going to work.'

'Good job you're a police officer now. Loads of time and opportunity to find someone new.'

'Yeah. Good job.'

Boone waved her off and went inside. The big, empty flat wasn't bearable, so she started up the Transit and went for a drive. She wanted to be around someone who would make her smile, so she headed for the cottage and Tess. Four years in prison, asking for something as simple as company, as basic as human comfort, she might as well have to learn Spanish to do it. Just rolling up in the van seemed the easiest option.

When she got there, the place was dark. No lights, no vehicles apart from the wheel-less Mercedes. The back door was locked. Cupping her hands to the glass, Boone looked through the window, but found no signs of life.

She texted Tess and waited in the van half an hour without a reply before pulling out and driving back towards Lark. She couldn't do it, though. The thought of the flat was punishing, its bare walls bristling and cold. Like the future, it was a chamber where emptiness gathered and became trapped. That afternoon, just a few hours earlier, she had been with Quin and seen light before her. Now there was a crevice through which light barely made it.

She drove towards Maidstone, to the quiet street where Roy Fuller lived. The lights were on in the living room, curtains open. In the early dark, it was still baking, the dry heat oppressive when she turned off the air in the van and stepped outside.

Back to the window, Fuller was watching a war documentary. She knocked on the glass. He looked round and frowned, before getting up and coming to the door.

'You alone?'

'Uh huh.'

'What do you want?'

'You haven't heard? Sally's dead.'

Fuller paled, eyes flitting about as he took that in.

'Thought Bardin would have filled you in,' Boone said. 'Probably he's too busy worrying about himself now you're both balls-deep in it.'

'Bardin? I don't—'

'Knock it off, Roy. You can't shit a shitter. And I lie like the winter snow. Did you really think you weren't followed? All that car-swapping nonsense?'

Fuller looked up and down the street. 'I don't know what you're talking about.'

'That's good. It's good to be cautious. Too little, too late, but never mind.'

'Visiting an old pal isn't a crime. Sometimes I have a spot of fun, making out there might be a tail. Bit embarrassing, but it's just a game. Anything John's involved in is strictly—'

Boone held a hand up. 'I really don't give a toss, Roy. I'm not interested in helping anyone build a case. You were a means to an end that saw Sally and that boy of his burning in a fire on a farm in Herefordshire. There are photos of you and Bardin, photos of Bardin at the farm. And Jerry Killock's dirty little secrets are coming to light. Eustace is all over the national news. Child raper. Cop killer. The stink of it will be on you for ever.'

'I'm nothing to do—'

'Like I said, couldn't give a toss. I just wanted you to know that we know. And soon, everyone will know. If it was up to me, I wouldn't have followed you in the first place. I'd have put you in the trunk of a car and driven you to some quiet, desperate place and got what information I needed. Left you hanging from a tree with a note begging forgiveness from your children, who hate you anyway. I saw the pictures in your living room. All from when they were young, years back. When was the last time you saw them, Roy? Imagine their shame when this breaks.'

'You can't be stupid enough to threaten a police.'

'Who's threatening? And who's police? You won't be for long. Best case you get your papers in before they can shaft you. And the worst . . . how do you reckon you'd do inside, Roy? I don't recommend it as a lifestyle choice, and I was only in Brabazon. You'll be Cat A with the beasts and the maniacs and the ones who talk too much.

'CPS wouldn't even need that great a case against you. They'd only need a whiff, just put the barest trace of it on you and you're in a cell the rest of your days because any jury would want someone to fucking die for what happened to that little girl. An ex-cop involved in a paedophile ring? That's bacon multiplied by bacon. Bacon squared. I don't see you making that, Roy. Do you?'

She turned to leave.

'Listen,' he hissed. 'I was never anything to do with their filth. It was just coin, same old protection money. I didn't know what they were into.'

'Bullshit. You knew. And even if you didn't back then, that girl they found has been all over the news.'

'I didn't know back then.'

'Still ran to Bardin and squealed, though. You're done, Fuller. Your life is shit now. I'm going to watch them send you down. I'm going to enjoy thinking about you in Belmarsh.'

She felt sweat running down her back and legs as she walked. Could smell it off herself. Someone had tossed black bin bags into the skip across the street and she heard flies buzzing against their insides. In the van, she put the air on full.

Driving into coal country, she found a field of wild red grasses, with sheep's sorrel and harebells. An earthy track turned off the black-top lane and she reversed the van into it, parking it out of any human sight, the grass brushing halfway up its side panels. She folded the bed down and killed all the lights, leaving the curtain behind the cab undrawn so she could see the pinprick stars through the windscreen. She hoped sleep would find her quickly.

She wanted to think of nothing. Plans were too large a concept for her, her heart and mind lived by piecemeal alone. She found staying the course difficult, even just within the narrowness of her own life.

58

Her awakenings brought with them a smorgasbord of memories, some fleeting, some static, and some opaque and mutated, reconditioned ringers for reality. They were without perspective; drab days in Brabazon caroming off the flickering horrors of finding Roo mutilated and near death, leading into awkward dinners with her son and ex-husband. She wondered if she didn't have enough memories yet to lend them perspective, or if that was simply how the mind arranged things. Eventually, the order in which these things coalesced became what we called the self.

Years ago, immediately after her *accident*, she would fight sleep as waking up felt like losing her memory all over again. The first consciousness of each morning was a void. Not light or dark but purely empty, an absence of thought or recollection so yawningly vast that the coming of any new day terrified her.

Since leaving prison, those first moments when she was coming to were her favourite. She felt young and lithe, free from the burdens she had saddled herself with. She suspected that as life went on this would not be the case; that she would, as all people did, accumulate memories – too many, more than any one person needed – and would awaken in a glut of reminiscence, wearying her bones as soon as she stirred.

There was a mild panic whilst she tried to remember what she'd done with her dental bridge, scrambling round the van with a sour, toothless mien until finally finding it in a plastic beaker in the cup holder on the dash. Hunger rose up within her like a new discovery, and she realised she hadn't eaten since lunch the previous day. Her clothes were crumpled and she smelled like she lived in a van, so she stopped at a drive-thru rather than going to a café, and picked up two breakfast muffins, bolting them like a dog snaffling leftovers at the table.

Back at the flat, she ran a scalding-hot bath and sat in it for an age, holding her breath and spending long periods beneath the water. The sound of submergence was the sound of her blood. Pruned and shivering, she eventually climbed out and lay on her bed to let herself dry. She tried to read, but couldn't keep at it. Since her release she hadn't read at all, when inside she had devoured books to pass the time.

She called Tess but got no answer. She called Storm and was told there had been no sightings of Eustace, but the blue Astra had been found abandoned, tipped over in a roadside ditch. She called Fitz and it went straight to voicemail. She called Tess and again got no answer.

Then a number she didn't know called her.

'Hello, Tess?'

'Afraid not,' said Eustace.

'How did you get—'

'You gave it to me. Busy little bee, helping the police with their inquiries. Helpfully telling me exactly what they were looking for.'

'They're going to catch you. You're all over the television, the news. Matter of time.'

'Yes, I suppose you're right. You know, Sally said you'd be a problem. I didn't really see it, but he knew. You showed him up close and personal at the end there, killer.'

'Ferg killed him, not me.'

'Yes, a little birdie told me as much. Also said their deaths look an awful lot like those of Hanley Moss and dear old Teddy Blackborne.'

'How is Bardin? Does he know we have pictures of him with Fuller and with Ferg? He's another one whose time is up.'

'He claimed he hadn't been followed, but he was never much for the out-in-the-field coppering, was Bardin. He was strictly a political animal.'

'Was? What have you done?'

'Thought you'd be glad to see that one go. You cut a swath through the others with such relish. I wasn't going to tell you. Was just going to wait until they found him. But then I thought, maybe they won't. It isn't as if he has any family, or even any friends. I believe he may sit on the parish council, as his type are wont to. Maybe they'd have given him a little knock when he didn't turn up to discuss planning applications or playing fields or water sluices and the like.'

'This what you called to tell me?'

'I called to see how you were.'

'I'm just lovely. Why don't we meet up for a coffee and you can see?'

He laughed. 'I hope we will talk later. I just have one more thing to tick off the list, and then I'll be done. But I'd enjoy a chat. I believe there are many things I could tell you. All about Noah Maxwell, for one.'

'Bullshit. You couldn't know. You'd have been a child yourself when he was killed.'

'They tell many stories, my fellow travellers. Keep their own histories.'

'We're excavating the dairy. And the house at the sea, Clement Stevens's place.'

'You won't find him at either of those.'

'His mother just wants to bury him, Eustace. For all you've taken, give her that. Give her that one thing.'

'I can't help her.'

'But you said—'

'You have more pressing matters to concern yourself with than the decades-old grief of a woman who, let's be honest here, was hardly the model of a loving parent.'

'What are you talking about?'

'I've never had children of my own, but I've observed parents over the years. Countless parents. Countless children. It's a remarkable bond. They say you only really learn about love when you have a child, but I don't think that's true. I think you remember what you already knew. A child's love for its parents is unconditional. Becoming a parent, you're rediscovering that love you once felt, channelling it in a different way. More a refresher than a lesson. The real lesson lies in what happens when you take away either the parent or the child. That's when you can really learn something new.'

'What the fuck are you up to? Eustace?'

The line was dead. Boone thought of the empty cottage the previous evening. Of her calls to Tess not being picked up. She rang her mobile again, but there was no reply.

'No, no, no, no, no.'

She pulled on the clothes she had earlier discarded on the floor and ran down to the van. Connecting the phone to the radio, she kept trying to call Tess as she drove. A2 through Canterbury, onto the motorway and out to the headland. An hour's drive in barely forty minutes, speed limits a thing for other people.

She wished she had a shotgun. Pulling up down the drive, she grabbed the wheel lock and clutched it like a weapon. There was a car there she didn't know. She ran up to the wall of the cottage and kept low, hurrying round the corner in a crouch to the kitchen door.

Peered through the window.

Nobody there.

She tried the door and found it unlocked.

Eased the handle and let it swing open silently.

She moved quietly through the kitchen and down the stone-floored hall. Tess's room was empty. So was Jim's. Nobody in the lounge.

Laughter. She could hear laughter, outside somewhere. Opening the rarely used front door, she crept round the cottage and came out at the back.

There they were.

Tess and Jim and Mickey Box and Fitz. Blankets laid out, a good spread of food, full-on picnic-type affair.

'Boone?' Tess said.

'What's with the wheel lock?' Fitz said.

Boone looked back behind her at the cottage. She scanned the field. It all felt like some kind of prank.

Tess stood up and came over.

'Boone, what's wrong?'

'I called you. I've been calling you for the last couple of hours.'

'Phone's inside on charge.'

'I texted you last night. I came round and you were gone.'

'Sorry. I was at Fitz's. We all were. Dad drove me and Jim there. We had a nice evening, and Fitzy came over for a picnic. Kick a ball around with Jim. What on earth is going on with you?'

'I called you too,' Boone said to Fitz.

'Yeah, I was ignoring you. Couldn't be bothered getting into all that dark web stuff. It can wait.'

'But he said he was going to take one of you away.'

'Who did?' Tess said. 'Take who away?'

'Eustace. Harry Eustace.'

'The man on the news?' Mickey Box said, standing now. 'He's coming here? Fitz.'

'On it,' Fitz said. He struggled to his feet and headed for the cottage.

'It's 4472,' Mickey Box said. 'Gun safe. I changed it.'

Fitz nodded and went inside.

Tess took Boone's hand.

'Boone, I don't understand.'

'Neither do I. He called me. He said he had one thing left to do. He was talking about the love between a parent and a child, and how one of them losing the other was the real lesson in life. You weren't picking up. I thought he'd come here.'

'Why would he come here? If he's trying to mess with you, why would he come here?'

'To hurt you.'

'Boone, you're a parent. Jack's a parent. Where's Quin?'

The wheel lock fell from Boone's hand.

'Oh, God.'

59

Fear, like a phenomenon of speed, affected time as well as the mind.

Boone was on the phone as soon as they were moving, pleading with it to be answered as it rang out again and again.

'Fitz.'

'I'm moving faster than anyone should, but I can only move as fast as I can,' Fitz said, weaving through mercifully light traffic.

He hadn't let Boone get behind the wheel. Bypassing the gun safe where the registered weapons were kept, he'd gone for the hidden cellar room and fetched Mickey Box's very favourite and very illegal Benelli. 'Seven point three pounds of bloody-mindedness at forty yards,' as Mickey Box would say.

He was going to handily beat Boone's recklessly short trip over to the cottage, but the minutes stretched out like fingers in the back of a spoon. She called Storm.

'Abigail?'

'I need you to send people to Jack and Quin's, right now.'

'What's going on?'

'Eustace called me. He made threats. I think he's going for my family.'

'Where are you?'

'I'm on my way, but I'm not going to get there quickly enough. I need armed officers there. I need everyone there.'

'Abigail, what exactly did he say?'

'Storm, please. I'm going to be late. Please go there.'

Storm agreed, sensing panic in her voice and not recognising that as something she'd heard before. Boone hung up and called her back almost immediately.

'You better send some uniforms to John Bardin's house too.'

'Bardin? The old ACC?'

'I think Eustace killed him.'

'Jesus.'

'He knows he's short on time. He's tearing everything down before he's caught.'

There was no good road for speeding coming into Lark. Fitz kept to the A2 as far as Dover to give himself a dual carriageway, before playing chicken with oncoming traffic on the Lark Road up the coast.

When they got to the house, the place she had for a brief time called home, they saw everyone had beaten them to it. The place was cordoned off and police lights painted its white walls blue. An ambulance was parked up on the grass out front. Boone saw gloved paramedics exiting the front door and her face crumpled.

'No,' she said, tears starting in her eyes.

Acid tears that bit into even Fitz, who was shaken.

'Maybe they're for Eustace,' he said.

Boone got out of the car and ran. Fitz called after her, but she was gone. Cutting through a public right of way between two neighbouring houses, she got out onto the coast road that ran between the properties and the beach.

Sprinting as hard as she could.

The boundary fence.

The tall gate.

There were no police outside the rear yet, though she could hear them behind the fence, the back doors of the house open.

The gate was locked. Gripping the top, she pulled herself up, feet scrambling for purchase, and hauled herself over. Storm was standing at the door, her back to her. She heard Boone's feet on the decking and grabbed her before she could charge into the house.

'Abigail, no.'

'Let me in, let me see him,' Boone spat.

Storm had her beneath the arms, her hands clamped together behind her back. Over Storm's shoulder, Boone could see a man face down on the floor, hands cuffed behind his back. His head was clean-shaven and slick with blood, his face too when he looked up at her and smiled. It took Boone a moment to realise it was Eustace, hair and beard shorn to avoid detection.

Officers pulled him to his feet. Even in all the horrors of her life, Boone had never seen so much blood. His shirt was sopping with the stuff, head and face covered as if a bucket had been upturned over him.

'What happens to the child makes the man,' he told Boone, grinning as they dragged him off down the hall and out the front door.

'What does he mean?' Boone said. 'Storm, what's he saying? What's he done? Fucking let go of me.'

Storm released her, stepping back.

'You know I can't let you in the house, Abigail. It's a crime scene.'

'Fuck that. I want to see Quin. Where's Quin? Where is he, Storm?'

There was that much blood on the floor that one of the armed officers slipped and almost went over. Another detective started moving them out of the house now that it was cleared and contained and they'd stomped great bloody boot prints everywhere.

It spread out across the tiles slowly from behind the breakfast bar, quicker through the grouting before the thicker flow followed. It looked black on the floor. Boone edged sideways, more of it coming into view, before she saw a hand.

'No,' she whispered.

Storm spun her round.

'Quin's safe. Just calm down. He's upstairs. We'll be bringing him down. Eustace didn't hurt him.'

'Then who?'

She turned back and got a better angle round the breakfast bar.

His sandy hair.

His eyes, dead as buttons.

His throat sliced, yawning open right through to the spine.

'Oh Christ, Jack. Oh no.'

Storm took her by the arms and led her back towards the door, out of sight.

'Quin can't see that,' Boone said. 'You can't let him see his father like that. Cover him, or get a screen to put across the doorway. You can't let him see that.'

Storm looked away.

'What? What's that look? You said he wasn't hurt.'

'He isn't. But he's already seen his father. Eustace made him watch when he killed him.'

Boone closed her eyes.

'He let him run upstairs when he was done. Quin locked himself in the bathroom in his room.'

'His room doesn't have a bathroom.'

'It—he has the rear room, the large one. There's an en suite.'

'Moved rooms,' Boone said.

'We were on the way when he activated the alarm button. At almost exactly the same moment, a 999 call came in from a mobile. Eustace. He gave the address and said he'd killed a man. Told us to come pick him up. The front door was open and he was sitting on the sofa there when we arrived. Knife was on the kitchen counter.'

Boone saw the blood on the upholstery of the sofa in the sitting room that seamlessly shared the large extension with the kitchen-diner.

'He surrendered without fuss,' Storm said.

'I need to see my son,' Boone said.

Storm showed her out the back door.

'Come on, let's walk round so we don't contaminate the scene any further.'

The rear gate was open now, armed officers outside along the street. The coast road had been taped off too, people starting to gather at an almost respectful distance. They walked round to the front of the house and Boone saw Quin coming out the door.

'Quin,' she called.

She jogged up to him, pulling up a few paces off, unsure of what to do next. He said something to the detective with him and approached her.

'Quin, I—'

'You said it would be different.' His face was small and furious. 'You said it wouldn't be like it was before. That there wouldn't be any danger. People you cared about wouldn't be in hazard was what you told me.'

'Quin, I'm so sorry.'

'Now look at me. You've made me an orphan.'

He turned away from her and allowed himself to be led by the detective to a waiting police car. Boone didn't go after him. There was a pain only a child hurt by its mother knew. A pain that Boone herself had once known, before she lost her past. Childhood was a myth for other people. She couldn't remember those perilous and frisky days, back before she feared the unspooling of time.

Before she had learned that the surest way to live with things was to no longer be able to remember them. To resist trawling through the murk that dilated in the place of her past for shards of memory, some vatic glimmer.

Before she knew the only meaning would come with the stopping of the heart.

60

Fitz waited all night. He followed the police car that carried Boone back to the Shed, parking up in a space reserved for the public. Refusing all offers of hospitality, he sat outside on a bench dedicated to a sergeant who had passed following a heart attack in the new custody suite.

Boone gave her statement about Eustace's call. Constables had put John Bardin's door in and found him hanging from his heels above his plugged bathtub, throat slit and nine pints of blood collected beneath him. She was questioned about that too. She left out that she had photographed Roy Fuller meeting with Bardin, and then followed Bardin to Herefordshire and photographed him with the soon-to-be-dead Ferg, deciding discretion to be the better part of valour when faced with doing more prison time.

Quin must have been there at the Shed too, but Boone never saw him and nobody answered her questions about him until she received a curt response from Barb.

'He's nineteen, he can do whatever he wants.'

Storm brought her a coffee. 'It's shit,' she said, handing it over.

'Eustace?'

'Chatting away merrily.'

'Really?'

'Incredibly cooperative. Confessed to murdering Bardin right out of the gate. Says he did it because, and I quote, "He was a worm, he never admitted to himself what he really was." He's dumped Fuller in it too. Officers went round to arrest him.'

'Good. He deserves it.'

'They found him dead. Hanging from the balustrade.'

'Huh,' Boone said.

'Eustace told us about Molly. He's blaming Craddock for her escaping.'

'Who the hell's Craddock?'

'Your goblin. Or "that half-faced simpleton", as Eustace calls him. Thomas Craddock, we think. His parents died when he was ten and he was taken into care. Ran away from his foster family and was disappeared.'

'Don't tell me.'

'Killock was his case worker. Eustace said Sally had to move Molly after you were at the dairy. Eustace had taken over the Stevens house after Killock's death, and Sally reached out to him. They kept her in the cellar there. You know, they never named her. Not even among themselves. Anyway, when it became clear you were coming out, Sally got a bit nervous. He was on his last legs, and Eustace suspects he was paranoid. Didn't trust anyone else to keep things under control, so was trying too hard to clean up. He told Eustace to kill the girl, leave no trace. This upset Craddock. They gave her to him occasionally, like a reward. He didn't want to let her go, so he drugged her and took her from the house and headed back to the only other place he knew.'

'The dairy.'

'She woke up as he was getting there and made a bit of a fuss. Bit him when he tried to calm her down, and got away. He panicked and left her out there. Eustace found him back at the Stevens house and locked him in the cellar. Said he was waiting to hear from Sally. Bardin read about the fire in Herefordshire and told Eustace.'

'Bardin. Was he . . . ?'

'Eustace says he liked young girls. I don't know if he'd lie at this point. He's been forthright about everything else. Bardin isn't in any of the videos on Sally's hard drive, though. Eustace says the two of them, Bardin and Sally, went back years, to when they were young men. So who knows what the nature of their relationship was.'

'And Lilly Bancroft?'

'Eustace killed her right after she spoke to you, four years ago.'

'Fuck. I told him I'd spoken with her.'

'This isn't on you, Boone. No more than car crashes are the fault of the men who laid the road. Eustace is a killer. A psychopath. He's talking about it as though discussing what's for lunch. Fact that he'll never see the outside world again doesn't faze him in the slightest.'

'I thought he was helping.'

'So did I, so that makes me as guilty as you. He buried Lilly in a shallow grave in the cellar at the Stevens house, and then he concreted her beneath the garage when Sally started getting worried about you. Eustace also said he torched your caravan himself. Said the doors were unlocked so he just waltzed in. Doused the place in petrol. Watched you sleeping for a bit. Then lit a match.'

'Well. That won't keep me awake at night, at all. Thanks, Storm.'

'I told you about locking those bloody doors. Look, I have to get back in there. We're going to be days talking to this bastard.'

'Sure.'

'I'll call you.'

It was light outside when she found Fitz on the bench, his breath smoking on the cold air.

'You okay?' he said.

'Feels nostalgic, you waiting for me at police stations.'

'Fucking freezing, and this bench will have given me the piles.'

'Why didn't you come inside? They're not contagious, they're just dicks.'

'Because the Benelli is racked in the ceiling compartment of your van and I figured if I kept it in view the whole time, I could, by clairvoyance and fucking mind control, deter anyone from finding it.'

'Okay.'

'Now, we're going back to the cottage, because Tess said she'd kill me if I let you go anywhere else.'

'Okay.'

She dozed in the van as he drove, head against the window until she was jolted awake turning onto the drive to the cottage. She said she couldn't sleep and then dropped off instantly on the sofa, Tess tucking a blanket around her. She couldn't recall her dreams, but she awoke with a profound sense of dread.

61

The next day, she drove herself back to the Shed, reasoning that she was still on Special Purpose Leave and therefore expected to help out the investigation until explicitly told otherwise. But Barb knew the score.

'He's not here.'

'Who?'

'Fucking who. Quin. And he's not at the house either. That's still sealed off, so don't go poking around.'

'Is he okay?'

'No, he's not okay. He watched a madman cut his father's throat.'

Boone recoiled slightly, and Barb softened her tone.

'He's angry and sad and upset and confused. But he's dealing with it as well as I've seen anyone deal with this sort of thing.'

This sort of thing. Boone suspected she too once had a scale by which to compare the very worst days of other people's lives.

'What about the practicalities? Anything that I can do so Quin doesn't have to. The formal identification?'

'He did that.'

'Jesus. Look, if I can't see him—Barb, there's so much stuff people will be looking for someone to take care of with Jack gone. A person is swallowed up by byzantine bureaucracy when they die. Quin shouldn't be doing all of that.'

'I know. But I can't do anything. The one matter he was clear on was not seeing you.'

Boone was struggling with the sense of death's finality. Life took things, as it doled them out, by degrees. At some point in her past life, the three of them – the Boones: Jack, Abigail and Quin – had got together as a family for the last time without any of them knowing it. Perhaps the day before Boone disappeared, all of them sitting around the table sharing a meal, talking about their day or about what was on the telly or about the unseasonable warmth/cold/rain. Now the three of them would never be together again, no matter what turns life took. Boone thought back to the last time they were in each other's company in any capacity. She had been brandishing a shotgun at an old man who had been no threat, frightening Quin in his own home, and Jack rightfully asked her to leave. No taking that back.

She wondered how close Quin was to his friends. How close he was to Tess. Would he get the help he needed to see him through this? Though she couldn't remember feeling part of a family, couldn't speak to how that felt at all, she knew a thing or two about being alone. She knew what it was to feel lost and afraid and not have anyone to hold onto when all you wanted was someone to wrap your arms around, to feel their arms around you. She hoped desperately that her son had someone to hold onto.

'I take it you don't want me here then,' she said.

'Actually, there is something you might help with. You know Kate Porter a bit, don't you?'

Boone blew out her cheeks. Knowing Kate Porter was what had started all of this, how many lifetimes ago now?

'Yeah, I know her. Why? Has something happened to her?'

'No, she's fine. It's just—'

'Has Eustace talked about Noah? He claimed on the phone he knew something.'

'Have you spoken to her at all recently?'

'We wrote occasionally when I was inside. I dropped by and saw her when I got out, mostly to tell her to keep clear. Didn't want her in Sally's line of fire.'

'Look, she's coming in. It might be helpful if there's someone here she knows.'

'Okay.'

'You can wait in here,' Barb said, showing Boone to a family room with comfy chairs and a table littered with magazines. 'I'll have coffee brought. Don't complain about it.'

Boone sat there for almost an hour, pointedly ignoring both the coffee and the magazines in case someone was watching her through a camera. When the door finally opened, a young female constable showed in Kate Porter but said nothing to Boone.

'Hello, Kate.'

'Boone. They called you in too then? You know why we're here?'

'What I told you about when we spoke, as far as looking into things? I've been working with the police on that.'

'Looking for Sally?'

'They've found him, Kate. He's dead.'

Kate considered that quietly. 'Good. That's good. It must be that man Eustace, why they called me. Perhaps he knows what happened to Noah. I read that he was a social worker.'

'Listen, Kate. Eustace told me he had information about Noah, but he cannot be trusted. Anything he says is half-true at best, and probably a trick of some kind. He's psychotic, but sly. Cunning. And he does things to amuse himself.'

'Was he involved with taking Noah?'

Boone shook her head. 'He would have been only a boy himself. He's someone who got involved with Killock later on. From what we can tell, Killock recommended him for the post in social services. We're not sure how they met.'

There was a knock on the door and Barb's face appeared.

'Mrs Porter? Hi, I'm DI Bowen.'

'You can call me Kate.'

'Kate. I'm Barb.'

'Do you know where he is? Where my boy is?' Her eyes bulged with tears and Boone took her arm.

'Shall we sit down?' Barb said.

Boone eased Kate down onto a sofa and sat beside her. Barb perched on the edge of the chair across from them, elbows on her knees.

'You found out what happened to him,' Kate said. 'Just tell me.'

'Kate, I asked Boone to be here because you know her. But I have some difficult things to tell you, so if you'd like—'

'Boone can stay. She was the only one who tried to help me find my son.'

'Okay,' Barb said. She placed a small clear plastic bag on the table. It contained a dirt-encrusted Lego figure, a medieval soldier in blue and black livery wearing a flared helmet with a nasal guard. 'Can you tell me if you recognise this?'

Kate covered her mouth.

'Take your time,' Barb said.

'Noah had one like it. It came from a box of half a dozen or so little men. I stole it from Woolworths because I couldn't afford a birthday present for him. He carried that one everywhere. Where did you find it?'

'It was in the cellar of a house that belonged to a man called Clement Stevens. He was an artist.'

'I don't know him.'

'No. Well, he knew Jerry Killock. It's a big house on the seafront, north of Lark.'

Kate turned to Boone. 'The house that girl Lilly spoke about?'

'We think so,' Boone said.

'That's where Noah is buried?' Kate said. 'That's what this man Eustace told you?'

'No. That's not what he told us.'

'So you called me in to identify the Lego?' Kate said, confused.

'We've conducted various forensic tests, including DNA comparisons,' Barb said. 'And we got a match. Kate, have you ever had any other children?'

'What? No. After Noah I had a—well, I couldn't have any more. And my husband didn't want children anyway. Why? I don't understand.'

'We don't have a sample of Noah's DNA on record. We didn't keep databases like that for missing people back then. But a private investigator you hired supplied us with a sample of your DNA for the national database several years ago.'

'I remember.'

'One of the samples we've taken as part of this investigation matched with your own. It's a mitochondrial match with a living person.'

'What does that mean?' Kate said.

'It means you're this person's mother.'

'Noah's alive?' Boone said.

'He can't possibly be,' Kate said. 'Where is he?'

Barb gave a little cough. 'The match is with Harry Eustace.'

'What?' said Kate.

'Oh, Christ,' said Boone.

'We'd like to take further samples from you, to make sure nothing was contaminated, but . . .' Barb trailed off.

'The scar,' Boone said. 'Noah had a scar on his chin. It's how I recognised him when Kate first approached me.'

Barb nodded. 'Eustace has the scar. He wore a full beard to cover it, but now he's shaved, you can see it.'

Boone thought back to Eustace getting arrested. He was so blood-soused she couldn't make out the scar.

'Wait,' Kate said. 'This is—I don't understand. Boone, you said this man is a psychopath. He killed a police officer. He was a social worker for years. I don't get what you're telling me. How can he be my Noah? It doesn't make any sense.'

'We don't know a lot at this stage. Eustace won't talk about it. Can't get him to shut up on almost any other subject, but not his own history. I can tell you that we believe Jerry Killock removed Noah from Eastry House and made it look like he ran away. His name was changed. We've found a grave for a Harold Eustace, who died in infancy and has the same date of birth as Eustace's official records. From what little paperwork we can find, it looks like Killock home-schooled him for years, massaged any local authority interest.'

'But you need qualifications and stuff, don't you?' Kate said. 'To be a social worker.'

'He has NVQs from college that got him onto a degree course. By that point, we're theorising he was completely assimilated into his new identity.'

Kate was shaking. 'Is he—I mean, has he done the same things? Was he like Killock?'

Barb looked at Boone.

'Tell me,' Kate said quietly.

'At this point, he has confessed to five murders. We'll be charging him with the deaths of one of my detective constables, with Lillian Bancroft, with a man called Craddock, with a retired assistant chief constable and with Boone's ex-husband.'

'What?' Kate said, looking at Boone. 'I didn't—'

'It's okay, Kate,' Boone said, taking her hand.

'How can it be?' said Kate.

'We will also be bringing multiple charges of child sexual exploitation,' Barb said.

'No,' Kate said weakly.

Slowly she slid off the edge of the sofa and collapsed into a tiny heap on the floor, like a trap closing around her own anguish. Boone knelt down and held her, but it was as if she had vacated her body temporarily.

'I'll get someone,' Barb said, leaving them.

Kate had longed to know about her son's fate. She had believed him dead and told herself that whatever death revealed would be beautiful. Death commanded respect and bestowed grace. Life was horrid and ruinous. But life was truth, and that was what she had wanted too. What she had always said. *I just want to know the truth.*

She had believed truth would give her something, satiate her in some way. But truth was no nourisher. Truth didn't quench. Truth was an empty vessel, and emptiness spread like disease.

62

Life became twilight. A waiting place between different existences, where Boone carried a weight of expectancy, although for quite what she was uncertain. Kate Porter withdrew completely, and when Boone visited her she was told by her husband she had checked into a clinic for treatment. Some things there were no cures for.

Boone took up cycling again. Riding down the coast road south of Lark one day, she saw wreckers had moved in on Eastry House. With its roof removed, the long arm of a high-reach excavator had pulled down one side of the place and the rest of it had begun to tilt. Men were fixing wooden boards to the iron palisades on the wall around the estate. Soon, even the ruins would no longer be visible.

The messages she left on Quin's phone went unanswered. She told him she was still going to cook a meal for him, telling him when and that he could just show up if he wanted. And if he didn't, that was fine too. She told him she loved him, and for the first time in her new life she knew she meant it.

She decided on paella, because she knew how to cook it and because it was one of those things stuck in her mind from before, so she assumed she had cooked it for Quin when he was a boy. She liked that it could be served in the pan on the table for them to help themselves, some degree of interaction.

That afternoon, she went down to the dockside market for fresh ingredients. She liked to chuck a bit of everything in, picking up mixed seafood as well as chicken and chorizo. She wondered what she was doing. For weeks she had tried her best not to think about what had happened to Jack, because the sight of him dead on the kitchen floor had horrified her. Because she knew she was culpable. Because reconstructing in her mind the way her son had looked at her made her cry every time.

Cooking dinner wasn't going to cut it. Quin's father was murdered and he was forced to watch, and there was nothing that could be done about either of those things, and there was nothing that could be done to bring him back to her.

She walked the walls of the old harbour to the Round Tower, a squat stone fortification on the seafront that once housed a fourteen-gun battery in defence of the nation. Now dark and empty, its embrasures stared dolefully out over the Channel. The weather had taken a turn, a gloriously British autumnal turn that erased skies and left in their place a drab smear stretching beyond any horizon in sight. Beneath it, the tide flowed back out, the sea lapping at the medieval walls, leaving them furred with things green and brown. She looked down into the colourless waters, as inviting as the loop of a noose.

People had been hurt.

People had died.

Roper and Monty, on the killing grounds of the farm, butchered by a man they were unwittingly abetting Boone's attempts to capture. Lilly Bancroft, murdered by Eustace because Boone had told him her name. And now Jack, slaughtered by the same psychopath as a message to Boone.

A message that lay not in his senseless murder, but in the manner in which she had allowed it to happen. How things might have been different had Boone thought first of her own child and his father, rather than of Tess and Jim. How she might have reached the house before Eustace could cut Jack's throat with Quin watching on helplessly. How she might have saved him, and saved herself too through the promise of new life and new love with Quin.

How how how.

Existences had been extinguished because of her. Lives decimated by grief because of her. The sorriest part of it all was she wasn't sure whether what she felt now was sadness or the overwhelming vacuum of emptiness. She imagined she could look inside herself and find nothing, as if her spigot had been pulled and her last reserves drained. Gutted. Hollowed out. The only feeling that remained a desperate longing for the love of her son, and even that felt like an act of selfishness she should be ashamed of.

The water slopped up the wall. Boone took a deep breath, scouring her lungs with whips of salty air. What was the sea but the most ancient and powerful force on the planet? Its origins were older than life itself, and if there was any sacredness in the world at all, perhaps it was to be found in the departed being given over to its depths.

'Abigail?'

'Hmm.'

'What are you doing?'

Without looking round at Storm, Boone raised an arm, carrier bag swinging in the hand. 'Mussels. Prawns. Squid. Your general mollusc and crustacean selection. Bit of chicken. Good chorizo. Surprising variety of veg and fresh herbs. Garnished with vinegar and ennui.'

Storm took the bag from her. With a thumb, she wiped the wet from Boone's cheeks. 'Shall we walk back?'

'Sure.'

The retreating waters had exposed the old stone rim of the tidal pool, velvet with algae and kelp. The nose of a shopping trolley protruded from the sands that had filled it long ago.

'Saw Eustace is on remand,' Boone said. 'Undisclosed location.'

'He's on close supervision in Belmarsh. Broadmoor specialists are assessing him.'

'And there'll be no trial?'

'He pleaded guilty at the PTPH to all five counts of murder.'

'Good. If he'd made Quin go through court hearings and give witness testimony, I'd have got myself locked up again and killed the bastard myself. Broadmoor, though.'

'They have to. What happened to him as a child, the way he was brought up. He'll be sentenced to a whole-life tariff by the judge, but he'll be kept in a psychiatric facility. His case is as unique as Molly's in its own dreadful way.'

'Has he filled in the blanks?'

'No. Won't answer any questions about his childhood, or how he became Eustace. He said he'll only talk to Kate Porter about it. He calls her Mrs Porter.'

'He can never be allowed in a room with Kate.'

'I agree. In any case, her husband won't let us speak to her. She's under supervision herself.'

'Yeah, I know.'

'We've put together a plausible theory from what we do know about Eustace. You'd already worked out that Killock groomed him, starting when he was living with Kate and intensifying once he was taken into care at Eastry House. Got the boy thinking that coming to live with him was his best option, then staged his runaway together.

'It's not clear exactly where he lived, but there is evidence he spent time at Clement Stevens's house on the coast. There has been quite a response to the investigation, other people who were at Eastry as kids coming forward and talking about the abuse they suffered. Several of them were taken to the Stevens place and remember a boy being there. Not being held against his will.

'This fits with the way a predator like Killock would operate. While the boy still thought of himself as Noah Maxwell, he made him complicit in the abuse of other children. Then it wasn't as simple as him being able to just walk away. He was too deeply embroiled in the horror of the place. Perhaps the new identity, using the Eustace name, was a way for him to deal with that. Disguised himself until he no longer thought of it as a disguise. Eventually, being Harry Eustace was all he knew.'

'Jesus.'

'It's guesswork, but educated guesswork. I'm sure as the investigation goes on we'll shore up our thinking on it. Eustace also mentioned that he might talk to you.'

When Boone said nothing, Storm added, 'I said I reckoned you'd be willing to spend five or ten minutes in a locked room with him.'

Boone didn't laugh.

'Seriously, though. I said it was a terrible idea, but he mentioned it several times in interviews, so I had to raise it with you.'

'I never want to hear about Harry Eustace again until someone comes to tell me he's dead.'

Back at the garage, Boone quietly busied herself with the readying of ingredients. She chopped all the vegetables and put them in separate bowls, and Storm joked it was like she had her own cooking show. It didn't elicit much of a response, so she put bottles of white and rosé in the fridge to chill and went to make a phone call. Boone briefly poached the chicken before roasting it, putting the rest of the ingredients to simmer in a wide pan.

She barely noticed Storm had left the room.

*

Early evening. Barb stared at the screen in her office. It had taken almost a minute to stutter into life and the first thing it did was load up the email and blink at her as it presented one hundred and forty-seven unread messages. She didn't even shut it down, just pressed the button and held it until the damned thing turned off.

She hadn't been in since the previous day. No, the day before that, lunchtime, so more than two days. Court that afternoon, burying Barry yesterday, and meetings with the firm investigating his death this morning, followed by seeing Quin. Stopped notifications on her phone too. Everyone could fuck off.

Her desk phone rang, and on instinct she picked it up.

'Bowen.'

'Didn't think you'd be there,' Storm said.

'You called me where you didn't think I'd be?'

'I was going to leave a message.'

'Just popped in to check my mail, but then thought better.'

'Anything I can do?'

'Pretend to be me and do all the stuff I'm supposed to have done for the last couple of days.'

'How's Quin?'

'He's staying with—'

'Don't,' Storm said. 'I'm not allowed to tell her, and I couldn't not tell her.'

'Yeah, fair enough. He's how you'd expect.'

'He had the funeral?'

'They had a private ceremony. Jack was in a relationship, she was there. Few of his friends, and a couple of Quin's. That was it. He didn't want an announcement in case the press turned up. Or Boone.'

'She wouldn't have. Not without his permission.'

'You've seen her?'

'I'm at hers now. She's been making herself crazy preparing for a dinner she asked Quin to.'

'Storm, the boy's not going to—'

'*I* know that. She does too, but it's a distraction. You should come, though.'

'What? No.'

'Why?'

'Me and her, I don't know. I haven't spoken to her in weeks.'

'You still blame her for Barry.'

'No. I never did. I was just . . . angry. Furious. Boone had nothing to do with what Eustace did. It's just all the other stuff. I don't really know where we stand.'

'So come round and find out. She worries me. I don't think she's been coping since she came out of prison, but now she's . . . I don't know. I can see despair.'

'I will speak to her. Just not now. It's been a shit week and I want to sleep for a year or so before I tackle a problem like Boone.'

'Well don't just sit at home alone.'

'I like sitting at home alone.'

'It's different now, though.'

'I'm fine, Storm. Really. I'm going to head off, have an early night. Have fun with dinner at nutbar's.'

'I'll tell her you said hi.'

'Yep.'

Driving home, she listened to Fiona Apple's *The Idler Wheel*. It cut off mid-song when she pulled up outside. She threw her bag and coat down on the sofa and walked through the apartment turning on all the lights, even upstairs. She'd developed an intolerance to darkness, couldn't abide it. Loneliness leaked from the shadows and light beat it back into dark corners.

She opened the fridge. Half a pepper, with its seeds still so it'd keep, and a cling-filmed onion piece. Chicken breasts, a two-pack but she could freeze one. She'd have to get used to cooking half as much now. Did packets of sauce come in single portions?

'All right, fuck it.'

It was no real surprise to Boone when she opened the door to Barb. She looked out into the forecourt behind her.

'You alone, or does this end with handcuffs?'

'I suspect if I leave you two alone, anything could end in handcuffs,' Barb said, easing past Boone and clumping up the stairs. 'I've got wine,' she said over her shoulder.

'Barb, you made it,' Storm said. She glanced at Boone. 'I told her to come, but I thought—'

'I told her I wasn't coming, but then I thought fuck it and came without telling anyone.'

'She does have wine,' Storm said.

Boone nodded.

Barb sat on one of the sofas and opened the wine. 'I don't mind swigging from the bottle, but some folk prefer glasses.'

Boone fetched three glasses and Barb poured, each of them right to the brim. One of Barb's finer qualities, Boone felt, was how she filled glasses so you had to lean in and sip from them like a small bird.

'There are cushions on the floor,' Barb said, pointing.

'I don't have a table and chairs,' Boone said.

'I'm not sitting on the floor.'

'It was going to be fun. I've made paella. Pan on the table, everyone helps themselves.'

'Sure. But not from the floor.'

'Help me get plates?' Boone said to Storm.

Storm nodded and followed her to the kitchen area. She put on some music, Dinah Washington.

'Just . . . be nice,' Storm said. 'Yesterday was—'

'I know.'

'She's here. That's something. I thought you wouldn't want to be alone.'

'Indeed I do not,' Boone said. She'd obsessed over the meal for weeks, fully aware that Quin wouldn't come, and when the day came she found herself just wanting to be alone. She'd been miserable company for Storm, who was trying so hard.

She considered the columns of unopened wine bottles on the kitchen counter. 'How many bottles did you bring? You driving?'

'Thought maybe I'd just stay until I was sober enough to,' Storm said in a low voice.

Boone imagined Storm's arms wrapped around her. Imagined not being alone.

'That works.'

'I'll be fine with the couch,' Barb called out. 'Or maybe the back seat of the Audi. Too old to be listening to you two shagging, and it's over a ton for an Uber home from here.'

To mitigate any abject mortification, Boone grabbed the pan and carried it over to the low table, also laying out mixed olives and airy Galician breads. She and Storm sat on cushions on the floor with their backs to the sofa, plates on the table, and after making a face, Barb slid down and joined them.

'You've done work,' Barb said, casting her eye round the place.

Mirrored tiles lined the brick walls, reflecting the flickering candles Boone had placed everywhere. She hated the harshness of the overhead lights and seldom used them. Throws and cushions covered the sofas, and rugs had been laid on the bare floor. The place almost felt warm.

They picked at the food in silence, but there was too much unsaid for them to simply enjoy a meal together. Eventually Boone put down her fork and cleared her throat as if she had things to say.

Barb got there first.

'How about this? We don't talk about Barry, because I really just fucking can't. And we don't talk about old shit, because right now I really just don't fucking care. And you top up my glass so I can get head-in-the-bowl cry-myself-to-sleep rat-arsed.'

'I can do that,' Boone said, lifting the bottle.

Barb finished off what was in her glass before positioning it for a refill. 'To get it out the way, I spoke with Quin earlier.'

'How is he?' Boone said, taking a mouthful of paella so she had something else to concentrate on.

'He's safe. He's coping as well as can be expected. I can't tell you where he is, and this one asked not to be told so she can't say. But he's not alone. And Tess has visited him.'

'She told me. Said he wouldn't speak about me.'

'A bomb detonated in his life,' Barb said. 'Not the first one, either. It'll take time.'

Boone shook her head. 'He's never going to forgive me now. He was just starting to be okay with the last time.'

'Abigail, none of this is your fault,' Storm said. 'Especially not what happened to you when you lost your memory.'

Boone snorted. Like that mattered when it came to the arbitration of guilt and forgiveness. 'I'm not even sure I believe I deserve forgiving this time. Jack would still be alive if I hadn't got into any of this.'

'Deserve's got nothing to do with it. Forgiveness isn't earned. You don't deserve it any more than you deserve love. It's a gift. Quin will know when he wants to give it.'

Boone put down her fork and shut her eyes.

'I'd just started to see him for who he was. Started to see my son. Thought it was a beginning of sorts.'

Now it felt like the tail end of someone's life. The remnants. There had been a time, alone in the various cells of her own construction, when she had cherished only the most formless of longings for some better life. Her future had only one shape – the beast that preyed upon the vulnerable, and the hunting of it.

Then the real thing had crept up on her unseen and unbidden, got back inside her again after years and taken hold once more.

A son.

A life.

Love.

Like anyone for whom love was an undiscovered land, she could barely say it aloud, felt uncomfortable in its presence when others said it. But with Quin it had all seemed so easy, the future laid out before her with crystalline clarity.

Eustace had snatched that away from her. Jack was dead. The man she had once loved. The father of her only child. And her son now hated her for it.

Yet she knew other beasts were out there, and she knew she would again hunt them, no matter what it had cost her already. Knew it deep down inside herself in the way she knew any of life's immeasurables. Knew it how she knew she loved her son. The glimmer of that love, of that better life, mocked her now, like joy's spoor fading in the rain.

'What he's feeling now isn't what he'll feel for ever,' Barb said. 'You're his mother. You'll always be his mother.'

The candles guttered, their light no longer quite reaching the hems of the room. Boone couldn't smell the food. The walls were brick and the room almost empty. Unseen, like a coal seam blaze, the past was on fire again, burning burning always.

'It's a nice thought,' she said.

Acknowledgements

Writing is the product of myopic madness, but publishing is a collaboration. Thanks are due:

To Nicola Barr and Toby Jones who – and exactly how will never be adequately explained to me – made all this happen.

To everyone at The Bent Agency.

To everyone at Headline.

To all booksellers.

To Patrick for what I see in my mind when I think of my books; to Hunter for championing; to Jane Selley for providing sorely lacking elegance.

To friends.

To family.

To you.